BEDLAM MOON

BEDLAM MOON TRILOGY

KATHY HAAN

Copyright © 2022 by Kathy Haan

All rights reserved.

Registered with the U.S. Copyright Office: Registration No. TX0009093518.

No part of this book may be reproduced in any form or by any electronic or mechanical means, including information storage and retrieval systems, without written permission from the author, except for the use of brief quotations in a book review. For more information, email kathy@idyllicpursuit.com.

ISBN 979-8-9855077-0-6 (eBook)

ISBN 979-8-9855077-1-3 (Paperback)

ISBN 978-1-960256-08-9 (Hardback)

First edition August 2022

Book cover design and map by Leo Burk and Kathy Haan

Edited by Fervent Ink

Published by Thousand Lives Press, LLC

To my dad, who is beyond the veil. Stories are a kind of magic that allows me to relive our precious moments together.

And to my mom, who never complained when I'd spend all my days locked in a room with my nose in a book, and who told me I was smart so much, I eventually believed it. I wouldn't be half the woman I am today without your tenacious positivity.

(Please skip the sex scenes)

IMPORTANT NOTE

The Bedlam Moon series gets progressively darker with each subsequent book. Please take caution and check out the TW/CW at kathyhaan.com/triggers. Do not read if it will negatively impact your mental health.

CHAPTER ONE

ime is a funny thing. The worst moment of my life is so fresh in my memory, but twenty-six years is an entire lifetime to be away from her. I was eight years old when she vanished. Long enough to remember her, but not long enough to hang on to the details.

There's a sign outside the entrance to the long, overgrown driveway that leads to the cabin. It reads, *NO TRE3PA33ING* with inverted S's. Below the sign is a little alien ship attacking Earth, although I'm not sure how ominous any would-be trespassers think it is.

I turn my Jeep off of the main logging road and drive down the gravel entrance, which snakes around giant pine trees and wildflowers. Weeds grow amongst the rocks, cracking them apart and taking their place. After the last set of evergreens, the vegetation grows thin and the driveway opens up into a clearing in front of the cabin. The old place sits on a hill overlooking a small pond that ripples in the early summer breeze.

My hands shake involuntarily as I pull the Jeep next to the cedar log cabin. The old beams of sunlight stream through the branches of the pines and oaks, creating an oasis of light in a patchwork of darkness. I place the vehicle in park and shut off the engine. *So many years.* I slide my trembling hands under my thighs in an attempt to steady them and lean against the headrest before closing my eyes.

I thought I'd never come back here again, let alone find the place, but somehow my heart knew the way. The police tape around the weather-warped porch has faded to a warm, soft yellow color reminiscent of a baby chick.

This is where I last saw Mom.

She went out to catch breakfast at the little bluegill-stocked pond on our property. She hadn't returned by the time I woke up, so I went to look for her. The fish was good that time of year, and she wanted to fry up a batch of fresh fish cakes for dinner that night. Her fishing pole and tackle box sat next to her chair, but she wasn't there. They never found my mom, and with no dad around, they sent me to foster care.

Now I'm back at the place where my entire world fell apart.

But there's a bud of hope blooming in my chest when I open my eyes and turn my gaze to the small brown package, still untouched, sitting on my front passenger seat.

Whenever I'm traveling the world, my best friend Hannah receives mail for me and lets me know what bills I have. When she got this package, she forwarded it to the concierge at the Minneapolis airport so I could fly back from the Amazon and see if this leads me to more clues at the cabin.

When I relax my hands and slow my breathing, I reach for the box and place the parcel on my lap. After taking a few deep breaths—like my former therapist taught me—I use the Jeep key to pierce the packing tape Hannah placed around it. I pull out the white slip of paper and worry my lip while reading the scrawling print.

Lana,

I'm sorry I didn't send this to you sooner. This was in your mother's things, and Annabelle would want you to have it now.

Love,

D

The handwriting is unfamiliar. I set the mysterious letter on my seat and unfold the cream-colored tissue paper at the bottom of the box. Nestled within it is the key that Hannah told me about. The new key in my hand is strange; its handle a deep, dark metal with a pattern of blue and red gemstones embedded in the surface, too many to count. It almost seems to vibrate with energy, ricocheting through my limbs.

Not an ordinary key, indeed.

I turn it over in my hand and trace the intricate details with my finger. Tilting my head back against the headrest, I vaguely remember my mom having a similar key, but this isn't hers.

I remember little about hers, other than its weight and the pearly sheen that glimmered in the light. When I had friends over, we'd spark our imaginations, dreaming up stories of how her key could open any door in any house. Mom wasn't too keen on my fascination with it and would insist I be gentle with it.

Now, I have a similar key of my own, but who sent it? An array of small, vibrant blue and red gems adorns the entire handle. There are far too many to count, and I have a strange suspicion these might not be ordinary gems.

Palming the key in my hand, I grab my backpack from the floor of the passenger seat and toss the letter, box, and tissue paper inside. Stepping out of the Jeep, my gaze lands on the aged humble abode I spent every summer in during my youth. After twenty-six years of neglect, the wood is weathering, and a pang of guilt hits my stomach that I haven't been back to look after the place.

I grip the police tape and ball it up before shoving it into my jacket pocket, cursing as thunder cracks in the distance. I look up. The sky is blue, but along the horizon, storm clouds threaten to drop a lot of rain.

I cup my hand over my eyes as I peer into the glass on the wooden door. Inside the cabin everything is just as it was when I left it; in the kitchen is an oak table where my mom and I would roll out dough for biscuits. One of the legs is a little shorter than the others and makes a wobbling sound when you rest your elbows on it. Part of me thought Mom did that on purpose so I wouldn't.

Standing back from the door again, I eye the keyhole, slightly larger than a dime. The door is a dark green, with a large brass knob in the center. I've come too far not to try it.

I position the key against the hole, not sure if it will fit. The key feels warm and tingles in my hand. What is happening?

A black barrel sprouts from the bottom of the keyhole and darts around like an insect. It starts to spin faster and faster, like a drill bit, the sound of metal sliding against metal. Just as quickly as it began, it stops, exhaling a puff of smoke and leaving a hole large enough for me to fit my pinky finger through. I glance around the property in disbelief, wondering how someone pulled such an elaborate prank on me. And *why?*

At first, the key doesn't look like it will fit. I push on it anyway, and the bit shrinks and slides into the keyhole perfectly. I turn the key, and it rotates smoothly in my hand as the door unlocks. I push the door open, and it creaks with almost thirty years of disuse.

No ordinary key, indeed, I think again before placing it in my jacket pocket.

With my hand on the doorknob, I step over the threshold and close the rustic, wooden door behind me as I take in my familiar surroundings. It's like stepping into a time capsule: the worn pine floorboards, the fieldstone fireplace with lopsided cinder blocks for hearthstones, and the red and purple oval rug made from old t-shirts draped in front of it. On particularly chilly nights, I'd fall asleep on the rug while playing with my dolls. By morning, my mom had scooped me up and placed me in bed.

I glance over at the kitchen. The old oak table that had been covered in so much spilled food and craft projects as a child is still here, and the cabinet with glass doors is still above it. Inside there are all my old school photos, ribbons, and medals.

I step over to my rocking chair and stare at the ashes in the hearth, long cold, as a melancholic ache crushes my chest. In front of the fireplace is my white stuffed gorilla I named Kongo after watching it in theaters. Thinking back on it, I was far too young to see it, but Mom let me anyway. She'd given this to me when I got my tonsils and adenoids taken out. It kept me company through many late-night bedtime stories, where she'd read me R.L. Stine books until I was old enough to read them myself. All of my Barbie dolls are still stacked next to it in an unceremonious heap.

The cabin isn't huge but it's big enough for two people; a tiny kitchen, a Queen-sized bed, a twin-sized bed, and a couple of rocking chairs placed in front of the fireplace along the opposite wall.

The entire property is off-grid, and there are still a few logs in the holder next to the fireplace, but I will need to gather some more firewood if I plan on being comfortable tonight. This far North, thunderstorms can often welcome evenings just on this side of cold. After bringing in the rest of my bags and the supplies, I look for the ax we kept here for chopping wood and I find it in our tall cabinet in the kitchen.

Walking outside, a dark gray rain jacket on, and new hiking boots squeaking on the soggy overgrown path that wraps around the cabin, I make a mental note to clean the leaves off it in the morning.

In the shed I find protective glasses and a splitting wedge, which will make my job a lot easier. With the storm headed this way, I don't have much time to get the job done. I'm happy to find a felled black walnut tree nearby. Mom always hated them, and not because they dropped huge green husks that fell from them and clogged up our push mower.

I spend forty-five minutes chopping wood, resting on my knees every thirty seconds. It's the same thing I do when I travel so people don't see me huffing and puffing while climbing the hills of Riomaggiore. Only then, I turn around and snap pictures so it looks like I'm meaning to stop, and not just out of breath.

So, I might be a little more than out of shape.

The sky darkens until it's difficult to tell when one log splits into two, and that's when I give myself permission to stop. The first of the raindrops hit my cheeks, helping cool my overheated skin. Exhaustion takes over me after the back-breaking labor and carrying the split logs into the cabin to nestle in the wood holder next to the fireplace. I contemplate heading straight to bed, but a rumble in my stomach warns me otherwise.

I didn't know how hungry I was until I smell the smoky, spiced scent that now tickles my nostrils. I follow the odor around the side of the cabin, straining to find the source of the smell. And then I whip my head up when I hear the crunch of gravel out front.

As I approach the front of the cabin, I spy a tall, shadowy figure stalking up the driveway, and I freeze mid-stride. Ice bubbling to the surface of my blood, I stand still, like a deer caught in the sights of a predator, more afraid than I've ever been. I'm in the middle of nowhere, and the fading light of day, coupled with the storm right near us, gives the area an ominous feel.

Who on Earth is here?

"I'm sorry for frightening you, *Sahira*." He has an accent that I can't quite place, and his voice is like liquid honey.

"Who ... who are you?" I fumble to turn on the flashlight on my phone.

I point the beam of light at the figure, slowly closing the gap between us. In front of me is a man built like a granite mountain, and I glance around for any sign of another person.

The second I determine he's alone, my eyes lock onto him, drinking in every detail as if my life depended on it—and it might— his jet-black hair resting across his forehead, terra cotta skin, and dark eyelashes that frame striking blue eyes, like gemstones caught in the light of the setting sun.

He appears to be in his early thirties, his complexion flawless enough to pass for a professional model on any magazine cover. Paired with his tailored suit, so at odds with the Northern woods, he appears as though someone plucked him from the pages and deposited him in my path.

My heart thrashes in my chest at the intensity radiating from his gaze. Raw emotion flashes across his face, as though I were the answer to every question, prayer, and hope he's ever had. I feel undressed in front of him, like my soul is laid bare before him and he cradles it carefully in his hands. I'm overpowered by a flood of emotions so powerful I can barely breathe.

I should be afraid and curse myself for leaving my ax by the chopping block. Instead, I continue to freeze where I'm at, staring far longer than is acceptable for a first encounter.

The man standing before me is more than just beautiful. He's exquisite. My mouth hangs open slightly as I take in his well-defined arms hidden underneath his tight two-piece suit, his lean waist, and the way his strong legs take root in the ground below him. He must be well over six feet, and his broad shoulders hold a confidence I don't feel right now.

My eyes travel to his face. He has a dark, sun-drenched look to him that makes me think he's from the Middle East, although his blue eyes suggest I might not understand what the hell I'm talking about.

Is he an investigator? Did Hannah let them know about the box I received?

The corners of his mouth curl up, revealing a brilliant straight set of teeth, radiating kindness. Like a warm embrace, I'm overcome with a feeling of peace, one I don't fully understand. How could his smile be so captivating and comforting? Was it the soft twinkle in his eye or the slight curve of his lips? I'm aware I should be afraid, but instead, I feel a strange sense of safety, especially as the intensity in his eyes fades.

I angle my body toward the man on the driveway, giving a little wave as I push my long, tangled hair behind my ears. My rain jacket hangs open, and that's when I notice my oversized t-shirt and black leggings are covered in dust and small bits of wood. I desperately need a shower and my muscles ache from chopping wood. I should run for the ax, not get lost in this stranger's eyes.

"I'm Osgood Finlandian, but you can call me Oz. I own a cabin down the road and thought I'd check out the place after I drove by and saw tire tracks leading here. No one's been here in a good twenty-five years, so I wanted to make sure people weren't breaking in."

Twenty-five years? While true, the man in front of me can't be over thirty-five or forty. I don't recall any other kids living nearby when I was little. Unless you count the occasional family staying at the campgrounds between here and the entrance to the forest.

"Thanks for looking in on the place. I'm Lana Chapman-Sawyer. This is my cabin, but I haven't been here since I was a kid." I'm still wary of the stranger in front of me.

"Ah, okay." He runs a hand through his thick, jaw-length hair. "You're the woman whose mom disappeared here ... I'm sorry."

And there it is—the inevitable moment when people remember the scared little girl whose mom vanished. My stomach flip-flops at the idea that this beautiful stranger knows about the absolute worst event of my entire life. It broke me, and I've spent the rest of my life trying to find the pieces again.

"Yeah," I absentmindedly toe gravel at my feet. "I was eight when she disappeared. I'm back to piece together what might have happened to her." No sense in hiding the story; he already knows it.

Everyone did.

"Would you like some help? My family has owned a lot of this forest for several centuries, and I don't think there's another person alive who can navigate these woods better than I do."

I think about that for a moment, digesting Oz's offer, and consider the odds. Investigators spent years trying to figure out what happened to Mom, to no avail, so I could use the help. Besides, despite being startled when Oz first arrived, I believe I can trust this man. My intuition has never steered me wrong before.

"Actually, that would be great. Thank you. Uh ... I'd invite you in, but I haven't settled in yet, and I'm still trying to find my bearings." Glancing at the storm, I wince. The nice thing would be to invite him in, especially as the rain picks up, but I'm still hesitant.

While I don't have a lot of belongings, my stuff litters the table and both of the beds. I'm also very certain that the bra I'd taken off and flung across the room as soon as I got in the cabin is on full display somewhere on the floor. With that realization, I throw my arms over my chest and zip my jacket.

Oz averts his eyes. "Not a problem, Lana. Would you like to come over to my place, and we can map out a game plan? I've got a hot shower. You can freshen up while I make us something to eat. You've had a long day from the looks of it."

Ouch. Was he admitting I look like shit? Despite my embarrassment over my disheveled state, the idea of being close to him stirs up something inside me.

"I'd kill for a hot shower, thank you. Let me grab a few things really quick." I start walking away but hesitate, turning back to meet his gaze. "Just wait here, okay?"

He inclines his head, and I pivot on one leg before bolting up the creaking porch steps to the cabin, taking them two at a time. Adrenaline courses through me as I slip on the top step, and in a horrifying second, I stumble. My arms stretch outward, desperate for something to grab onto, but instead of the unforgiving ground, my hands meet those of a stranger. He catches me as I trip, his muscled arms holding me steady. His skin is cold, but his touch sears through me like fire, blazing a path through my chest before pooling low in my belly.

Oz helps right me, and I dust myself off. He saves my dignity and doesn't say a word. Mortified, I run into the cabin to grab my stuff, and after shutting the door, I shrink down against it.

Well, that was freaking embarrassing.

I collect myself against the door, but then I remember Oz is still waiting outside for me, so I dart across the room, grabbing clean clothes and some toiletries. I pause my hand over my makeup bag and consider whether I should bother putting on makeup after I shower. He's seen me at my worst, and it is late in the evening. I don't want him thinking that I'm trying to impress him.

I mean, I *am* trying to impress him, but I don't want him actually *knowing* that.

Who am I kidding? Of course I'm going to put makeup on. Sure, he's probably not interested, but I can always bring my best self, right?

Maybe this man likes thick chicks, and we'll spend the evening rutting in the woods.

A wicked grin crosses my face, and I grab the makeup bag and toss it in my backpack. *Careful, Oz; I'm a man-eater when I have my hair and makeup done.* With that thought still on my mind, I exit the cabin, locking the door behind me.

A grin spreads across Oz's face, and his two eyebrows rise in unison. "All set?"

The air between us is perfumed sweet with a hint of spice and vanilla, so I take a deep breath through my nose before I respond. Perhaps it's the wildflowers at the side of the house.

I give him a nod, and we start down the long driveway. Now that I'm side-by-side with Oz, a breeze sends another aroma up my nose of Earth and elemental, which is likely the storm that seems to be holding out on us. I can't help but take a deep breath to inhale more.

As the leaves and gravel crunch beneath our feet, I gaze down at Oz's leather shoes. Why is he dressed so nicely out here? They're huge and had to have cost more than my entire outfit combined.

"Size fifteen." Oz quirks an eyebrow at me.

I glance down at my boots. "I thought I had big feet."

He smirks. "Where were you before you came back to the cabin?"

Do I explain that after my adoptive parents died, I had an early mid-life crisis and sold everything I owned so I could escape and travel the world? That, since then, I've traveled through much of Europe, Central, and South America, hitching rides on boats and buses and clinging to the sides of trucks? I'm not sure if he's ready for that level of crazy yet. Instead, I tell him about South America.

"I was traveling in Colombia for a bit, and I stayed near Leticia in the Amazon Rainforest, right off the Amazon River."

"I spent a lot of time in that area, so I'm familiar with the Amazon. ¿Habla Español?"

"No. I took Spanish, but I remember little. Are you fluent?"

"I speak a few languages, and I've done a lot of traveling. I have business dealings all over the world."

As a free-spirited person, I feel even more inadequate learning those things about Oz, and I can only imagine what he thinks of me now. The gal who got an MBA only to give up a lucrative corporate job in pursuit of adventure.

The rain starts, and I pull my hood up. Oz plucks a black umbrella out of the inside pocket of his coat. We continue small talk and walk another half mile, wedged together under his umbrella until we reach the entrance to his cabin's driveway. He starts up the pavement, and I follow suit, but there's no cabin in view at all, although I spy light through the trees. My nerves stir a little.

"It's about a quarter-mile walk. Are you going to be alright?" He eyes my obviously brand-new, never-been-scuffed-before hiking boots.

I tell him to press on, although my heels are chafing.

Eventually, the "cabin" comes into view. The only word that comes close to describing this place is "compound." His definition of cabin and my definition of cabin differ wildly. His definition is grand, mine simple; he focuses on what you can see, I on what you cannot but feel.

The jack pine trees standing between me and the lodge-like building are so tall that I can't see their canopy in the dark. Each window of the place is at least twenty feet high, and a single door— just as big—sits at the front.

It's beautiful, and it fits him. Though, the idea of Oz living here, alone, in this seclusion doesn't make sense to me. Where are his friends? His family? If anything, it stirs a deep sadness in my chest.

Is he alone, too?

Embarrassed, Oz admits he got a little carried away when designing the place.

His cabin is resplendent in forest green with warm wooden beams. I step back and crane my neck to take it all in. The wood is stained a deep oak color, and the roof is made of cedar, which softens the security lights that filter through the trees. Scents of dirt and moss tickle my nose.

I can't breathe, can't think of anything but the big, lonely home in front of me. Yes, it's warm and inviting, but are the halls hollow and free of the pitter patter of little feet? Do the walls hold a lifetime of memories, or secrets of sorrow, too?

The wooden front door and the window frames, even the roof beams look as if they've been whittled by hand. Understanding dawns on me now. Each and every square inch of this place is meticulously crafted, with a heart and an artisan's soul. Details I'd been too naïve to notice now come alive. From the driveway, this place is foreboding and a little cold. But up close? At the heart of it?

This is Oz.

My feet carry me up the stairs, and my heart places me somewhere I never thought I'd be again—home.

Wait, *home?* I shake my head. What the hell is wrong with me? I don't know this man, nor have I ever been inside his home. And I definitely didn't know this place sat right next door until today.

He holds the door open. "After you."

As I step inside, a cool gust of wind rushes through the side of my hair, billowing it back. Oz steps around me and takes my jacket from me, and places it in a closet near the front door. A glow of firelight warms the cold moisture off the marble floor as I step in.

I am at his *house*. This is a *big* house, but I can feel the warmth from the decor, which echoes sentiments of an old world gone by. A vintage chandelier, its beaded chain dripping with crystals, hangs from the vaulted ceiling and casts light upon the entry. All around the walls hang artwork, its curator one with a unique eye for the past and how it could inform the present.

My eye catches a painting across the foyer, and I step closer to capture a better look at the artwork. The painting is of a curvy woman, dressed in nothing but a sheer blanket draped around her ample bosom and tiny waist. My face heats at the signature in the bottom right corner of the canvas—*O. Finlandian,* painted in big loopy swoops.

He painted this woman, stroke by stroke, with such passion she seems to come alive under his brush.

Lucky girl. I pull at my filthy shirt, feeling like an intruder in my dirty clothes, and ask Oz to show me to the bathroom so I can shower.

He walks me past the expansive kitchen, where I inhale the smells of baking bread, up the wooden stairs, and down to the bathroom at the end of the hallway. It has a standalone, deep jetted tub along one wall and a marble-tiled walk-in shower along the other.

Oz flicks on the towel warmer and sets a very fluffy bath sheet along the top bar. "Do you want a towel for your hair, too?"

He must spend a lot of time around long-haired women, but probably not enough time around curly-haired ones. "No thanks. Because I have curly hair, I usually wrap it in a t-shirt to dry."

At that, he inclines his head, leaves the room, and returns with one of his t-shirts.

"Oh, you don't have to … "

"I insist." He extends his arm towards me, the t-shirt clutched in his hand.

I reluctantly take his shirt from him and set it on top of the towel, giving my thanks. He leaves the room, and I lock the door.

Foolish to be here, in a stranger's house using their shower, but let's not push it by leaving the door unlocked. I won't make it easier for him to murder me.

After undressing, I pick up his shirt, hold it up to my face, and inhale deeply. *It was him earlier;* that intoxicating aroma of earth, vanilla, spice, and an elemental sort of scent reminding me of thunderstorms.

My mind races with a million questions. What kind of crazy am I, drawn to a stranger like this? I want to trust him, but at the same time, he has that irresistible charm that all the women in true crime documentaries fall for. Still, he has a lovely Burberry-scented body and a face that could make even an angel cry.

Or sin.

Those pants of his hug his sculpted thighs so tightly, and I'd be a fool to not be attracted to him. I wonder if he's as into me as I am him?

Gods help me.

CHAPTER TWO

I emerge from the bathroom fresh-faced and much better than when I first entered it. I don't want to seem too desperate, so instead of my usual matte red lipstick, I opt for a pink gloss. My hair is still a little damp, but I don't want to spend an hour in the bathroom when Oz is downstairs making us dinner.

No matter what he's making, I'm sure I will love it. I'm a foodie and will eat pretty much anything—like when I had beetle larva on a stick in Peru. I even ate durian frequently and kind of liked it.

As I make my way down the hallway, the incredible aroma of Italian spices, herbs, and vegetables teases my nose. Oregano, garlic, rosemary, basil, tomato, and perhaps pasta or fresh-baked bread. I practically fly down the stairs, eager to eat since I'd had nothing since Duluth earlier that day.

"I thought I smelled pasta!" I nearly swoon, eyeing the giant bowl of handmade, oiled Mafalda noodles in a caprice white melamine bowl on the table. Next to it, a pan of focaccia bread studded with black and green olives—the way to my heart.

Oz carries over a giant bowl of pasta sauce and sets it down on the live-edge wooden table. He asks to take my backpack off my hands, and he puts it away while I gaze at the painting of the naked beauty in the foyer. Absently, I notice he's pulled out the chair for me and waits for me to sit.

"Oh, thanks." I take my seat, hoping he didn't think I was waiting for him to pull out a chair for me so I could sit.

Clad in a burgundy fitted merino wool sweater and black skinny suit pants, he must've changed from his business suit while I was showering. He's rarely the type I go for. His style is a level of class that's out-of-reach for me. But I'm thinking that no matter what this man wears, his clothes are expensive, and he looks like he walked off a GQ ad.

Meanwhile, I have on a pair of black leggings and a red oversized off-the-shoulder sweater. Comfort over style, always. Being in his presence doesn't make me uncomfortable, though.

"Thank you, but you didn't have to go through all this trouble for me."

"Was no trouble at all. I was planning on making this tonight, anyway. I started the focaccia this morning and now I have company to enjoy it with. Sweet wine, right?"

"How did you know I like my alcohol to resemble Kool-Aid?"

"I have just the thing." He grabs a dark bottle from the fridge and pours me a glass.

I sniff the contents—knowing this is what cultured people do before drinking wine—and take a sip. Sweet raspberry notes coat my tongue, and I close my eyes as my thoughts drift to a time when I was picking raspberries with my mom as a kid in these very woods.

A shimmer of ice dances across my lips. I gasp and open my eyes.

"Are you alright?"

"Yes, sorry. This is delicious. Who makes this, so I know what to ask for the next time I'm out at a restaurant?"

"I do. I'm afraid you won't find this in a restaurant, but I'm happy to give you some any time."

"You cook, you make wine, you speak many languages, you can navigate your way around these woods, and you obviously clean." I dart my eyes around his pristine house, admiring the wood beams and trim. "What else are you good at?" I grab a slice of focaccia and add pasta and its sauce to my plate.

"I suppose you'll have to find out."

That was a bedroom purr if I ever heard one. I nearly spit out my fork-full of food. He's flirting with me. This perfect specimen of a man is *flirting with me*! A surge of heat spreads between my thighs, and I clear my throat.

I like a man who is direct. His directness is far sexier than men I encountered in Italy, who on *three* separate occasions, catcalled and called me Shakira all over that country. I'm twice her size in both width and height, but I suppose my curly hair and tan are what did it.

Oz changes the subject after I can't think of a clever response to his open flirtation. I hope he doesn't think I'm not interested; he's left me speechless, which is a first.

He asks me about my travels, and I tell him about selling everything in an early life crisis after my adoptive parents died. After a few more bites of food, Oz asks me who bound my magic.

"Magic?"

He gestures to my hands. "It is cruel to put a bind on a witches' magic. Who did it?"

Nervous laughter bubbles out of me and I glance around. "A witch?" I shake my head dismissively and take a bite of bread.

His mouth forms a thin, tight line. "How do you explain your ability to discern people's emotions, determine what ingredients someone is using by aroma alone, the way ice bubbles in your veins when a vampire looks at you, you dream of the fae, and have a buzzing sensation any time you're close to enchanted artifacts?" His voice is booming now. "And you think people call you *Shakira*. They aren't saying *Shakira*, they're saying *Sahira*, which means *witch* in Arabic."

I stare at him blankly. "How the *hell* do you know that?" My pulse quickens and I recoil. Is this man stalking me? I scoot my chair back and move away from the table. My breathing shallows, and I dart my eyes to the closet my backpack is in. Do I need anything in there before I run for it?

Oz follows my gaze and puts his hands up. "If I wanted to hurt you, I would've done so by now. Think about it, Lana. Don't listen to your head. What is your *intuition* telling you?"

I whip my head back to him, and a chill wracks its way through my body. My entire life I've had incredible intuition, and I can sniff people out better than others can. Although, I only recently started getting this buzzing sensation. The first time had been at the airport when I picked up the package Hannah mailed me from her place in Montana.

Then, there was the incident where the key shrank to fit the keyhole at my cabin … and wait. Did he say, *vampire?* Vampires aren't real. This man is insane, or I've lost my damn mind.

"Look, Lana. You probably think I'm crazy. I'm sorry, but I thought you knew—surely your birth mom told you?" He strides towards me and holds his hands up in a placating gesture.

My breathing quickens when he reaches towards my hands. My body acts before my brain can catch up. I place my hands in his and he turns my palms facing up, though I don't dare move. Weaving his hand over and over several times, energy springs to life inside of me. It races up my arms, blasting through every cell and nerve ending, blanketing me in a warm hug. I startle and nearly fall as I yank my hands back.

There is a tingle in my fingertips where I have them curled close to me and out of his reach. My heart thrashes in my chest, and I hyperventilate, shaking my head as though I can deny what my eyes witnessed, what my body felt.

"No," I breathe. "This isn't happening."

In preternatural speed, he cups my cheek. I'm about to recoil from his touch when a strange sense of calm washes over me, like a gentle caress easing my panic, and instead of pulling away, I lean into him.

His words rumble against my ear, sending a chill through me. "From across the room, knock the glass over."

Moving without a thought, I stalk to the kitchen and stare at the glass of wine on the table and raise my hand towards it. *Tip over,* I urge it and instead of tipping the glass over, the bottle of wine shatters and its contents spill on the tabletop. My eyes widen and my knees threaten to buckle.

Oz ushers me to my chair, but I can't take my gaze away from the wine pooling on top of the wood table. He settles next to me, hand still in mine.

My shoulders slump. "N-no ... it can't be. I can't do magic. I'm not a witch. There is no way." I whisper to myself, as though telling myself *no* will change the evidence. Who am I trying to convince? Him or me?

He scoots his chair back and stands with a determined look on his face. Oz commands me to stand and face him, and I do as I'm told, though my logical brain screams at me to hesitate. His hands cup my face and the sensation of ice bubbling to the surface in my blood is difficult to ignore.

"Do you trust me?"

Shaking my head, I yell, "I don't even know you!"

"I asked, do you trust me?" His voice is stern.

Before I can tell him I do, I'm silenced by the shock of his cool lips pressing into mine. I close my eyes and lean into his kiss. My arms wrap around his broad back, and intense warmth spreads between my thighs. The aroma of spicy earth and elemental is a welcome assault on my nose.

Only one thought runs through my mind now, and that is what I want to do to this man. My head no longer stands a chance—my body isn't listening to reason. This wouldn't be my first romp with a stranger. I could do a one-night stand. Right?

Oz pulls back as I come up for air, my heart racing.

"Open your eyes, *Sahira.*" He has a hint of carnivorous satisfaction in his voice.

My eyes open slowly, and I meet his intense gaze, but this time his eyes are a pale blue. I can make out the little yellow sunflower around his irises. A shiver runs through my body, shaking me out of my lustful trance.

I dart my vision around the unfamiliar surroundings. Thick drapes adorn tall windows, and incredible paintings brighten the walls. The moon casts light on globs of cobalt and crimson staining canvases so stunning, they belong in an art gallery.

"Where are we?"

"Lana, you envisioned what your mind wanted at that very moment. This is my bedroom." He has an amused expression, pointing to the four-poster cherry wood bed against the far wall. Piled atop a thick comforter are at least a dozen pillows of various sizes.

Mortified, I throw my hand up to my mouth, and I shake my head. This is impossible. I'm dreaming; it's the only way to explain what's happening. I may as well give into it.

"Do you believe me now?" He's hesitant; unsure.

"Maybe." With my hand still covering my mouth, I begin to feel a little woozy. He helps me to the chaise lounge at the foot of his bed and I sit.

"You must have a lot of questions."

I signal my agreement, feeling so conflicted internally. One half of me thinks this is a dream, and the other realizes how real everything seems.

"Alright, shoot." He kneels in front of me so he's at eye level.

"If I'm a witch, that makes you ... a vampire?" I blurt out and cover my mouth again. I hold my arms and rock in the lounge to soothe myself.

Vampires *can't be real*. I have lost my damn mind. Or, maybe instead of dreaming, I am *dead*; he killed me, and my twisted brain is playing out this messed up fantasy in my head as the last stand before I sink into my eternal dirt nap.

But, if I *am* a witch, maybe vampires are real? That would explain how he was so fast to catch me, and why he looks at me like he wants to eat me. He has this god-like way about him.

He answers my question with a dip of his head, and it takes me a moment to recall what I asked him. Oh, yeah. I remember now.

"Do you want to bite me?" I'm surprised by my body's reaction to my question; a warm, tingling sensation erupts at my core at the prospect of him sinking his teeth into my flesh.

"More than anything, but I'm not going to, Lana. I've been a vampire for a very long time. I have far more control than any vampire you'll ever meet."

I'm not sure this is the answer I want, and not because the thought of him biting me terrifies me. In fact, it is the exact opposite—it excites me. "What other things can you do as a vampire, besides bite people?"

"Well, a lot of things I suppose. I'm fast, and I have excellent hearing and vision. I'm far stronger than most people, and I am immortal, although they can kill me." Oz rattles off his list as though he were telling me what groceries to pick up at the store. "Eating garlic isn't an issue, and I go outside during the daytime. Sleep is unnecessary. And ... I can read minds." That last bit was but a whisper, but I still heard it.

"Can you read mine?"

"Yes, man-eater." He looks like the cat that caught the canary.

I want to throw myself off a cliff out of sheer mortification. How on earth can I be around someone who can read my mind? I bury my head in my hands and grip the hair on my scalp.

And ... oh gods. This means he heard every salacious thought I've had all night.

"I try not to intrude, but sometimes your thoughts are so loud I can't stay out. You're like a siren, inviting me closer to the dangerous shore, and I'm a lost sailor about to meet my doom. I can teach you to keep me out, though. If you want to, of course. What gets me is the fact that you're more concerned with my hearing the titillating thoughts in your head and not the fact that you're in a room, in the middle of the woods, with a vampire."

He has a point, although my intuition has never steered me wrong. Osgood Finlandian won't hurt me. *Can't* hurt me.

Oz grabs me by the wrists with one hand and uses the weight of his body against mine to hold me down on the chaise lounge in one swift movement. His heavy thighs press against mine as he turns my head away from his face, exposing my neck. My chest heaves when his lips brush my skin; they are like ice. It doesn't hurt, but it sends a message that he's in control of this situation, not me.

I hold my breath, half of me terrified, and the other more delicate parts of me ache for him to bite, but it never comes.

"Lana, never for a moment believe any vampire can't hurt you, myself included." His eyes are a soulless black, and sharp fangs protrude from his mouth. As fast as he sprung on me, he lets me go and kneels in front of me.

I lay there, momentarily stunned. In the time I take to blink, Oz's eyes are back to their normal, piercing blue. My heart still races at the predicament I find myself in. If this is real, then I'm grateful to have unlocked a piece of the puzzle that is me; if I'm a witch, this might make solving the mystery of my mom's disappearance so much easier.

I simply have to learn magic.

CHAPTER THREE

I'm so shaken up, I thank Oz for his time and hurry back to my own cabin. In the comfort of familiar surroundings, I take a week to practice magic indoors, but fail miserably. Without instruction, I managed to break three ceramic bowls, a wooden chair, and a vase I made my mom in art class in Kindergarten. We used to pick wildflowers, and she'd place the yellow, misshapen glass on the window sill in front of the sink in our kitchen, proudly displaying my elementary pottery skills.

After moving my practice outside, I stopped breaking things. Sure, I made divots all over the yard with errant magic, but those are easily repaired. Several weeks of it, though, has made my lawn look like a war zone.

Oz stops by occasionally to check on me, to see if I have any questions for him, but I turn him away because I don't trust him—or myself—yet.

Until now. He ambles up the driveway, looking all sorts of handsome with his easy smile, mussed hair, henley, and denim jeans. He carries a box of papers with him. In it, I find article after article about *the woman who vanished.*

"You did this for me?" Something thaws in my chest.

He worries his lip. "I want to help you find answers."

Each evening, on the floor of my kitchen, we pour over the articles one-by-one, looking for any scrap of hint or clue. We spend the entire summer searching for some semblance of my mother's disappearance. We find none.

~

It's fall when we get to the last article, and I hold it in my hand, crestfallen, as I drop it back into the box. It's late evening, and Oz offers to answer my questions again, and this time, I agree. Before this, we'd kept our conversations to my mom's case and anything other than magic and supernatural creatures.

Oz and I make our way back to his 'cabin,' and I'm very careful to guard my thoughts. I haven't quite figured out how best to keep them to myself, so for now I'm singing the same song in my head, repeatedly.

99 bottles of beer on the wall, 99 bottles of beer ...

Take one down, pass it around, 98 bottles of beer on the wall ...

"Sahira, if you sing that song one more time, I might bite you yet."

Then stay out of my head, I think while grinning at him as I help clear the table where we'd just devoured tacos.

"You're impossible."

I've grown to like Oz calling me Sahira. He says it like a term of endearment, and our developing friendship feels good. At this point, it's more than budding, really; I spend most my time with him.

Together, we load the dishwasher and I thank him for supper. We're in for a long night, so I wonder if he has any wine left. I have so many questions.

"Want to sit on the back porch?" Oz grabs a bottle of his wine from the fridge. "I have some couches and blankets out there and an outdoor fireplace to keep you warm."

Yes, please, I think. Although I should start talking out loud if I want Oz to stop listening to what's in my head. It's useful when there are difficult to articulate thoughts. Sometimes, it's more intimate, too.

There are two white couches on each side of the coffee table on the back porch. On one end is an enormous fireplace, and opposite that is an overstuffed love seat. I opt to sit on one of the white couches, and Oz sits opposite me on the other.

The vampire uncorks the bottle of wine and pours each of us a glass. He proposes a toast to "answers," and I clink my glass against his and take a big gulp. I might need a little courage for some questions I have coming his way.

At this, he covers me with a dark gray Sherpa blanket.

"So, you eat … How can you do this if you're dead? Do you go to the bathroom?" He's never excused himself to go, and I haven't asked until now.

He chuckles, amused this is the first thing I ask.

"Not dead, per se. More like—undead. I can eat regular human food, but I must eat blood to survive. I eat food because, like you, I *like* the taste of it. However, I never fill up. It absorbs into my stomach … I think." Oz looks off to the side, as though absorbed in thought. "And I don't have to go to the bathroom. I enjoy taking showers and baths though; it's relaxing, although I don't sweat."

Interesting. I suppose that comes in handy. Briefly, I wonder if female vampires menstruate. Before Oz can respond, though, I answer my question, *probably not*. I don't think they can reproduce. He nods at my thought process.

"Do you need sleep?" Thinking about the gigantic bed upstairs my newfound witch abilities teleported us near, a blush creeps up my cheeks.

"No. I use the bed for other things, Sahira."

I breathe in deeply as the pleasant spicy aroma of earth and elemental fills my nostrils. Heat unfurls low in my stomach.

"What is that wonderful fragrance?"

His eyes have gone pale blue with the almost iridescent yellow sunflowers around his irises.

I take a swig of the wine in my hand, and for the first time, I notice how strong his arms and hands look. The sleeves of his sweater scrunch up around his forearms, accentuating their strength. My breath hitches in my throat at a brief vision of those arms tangled around me, hands exploring my depths.

"My arousal. And I sense yours, too, Sahira. Every change in your emotion brings a transformation of your scent, long before your thoughts give you away."

A shiver runs through my body. I'm wide open and exposed, yet equally aware my friend and I share the same yearning.

"Careful, Vampire. You don't want to do something you'll live to regret."

Without skipping a beat, he responds. "Good thing I'm already dead-ish."

My thoughts threaten him with a dangerously good time, but I reel them in because I still have a lot of questions, and I'm not one to roll in the hay casually, despite my earlier thoughts. Maybe five or ten years ago I was, but now I look for companionship before my more carnal desires.

Usually.

I switch gears. "How old are you?"

"I'm not sure. Back then we didn't celebrate birthdays."

My eyes grow wide and I cock my head to the side. I rack my brain, thinking of which civilization started birthday celebrations. I contemplate this while tracing the stitching on the couch with my finger.

"The Ancient Egyptians. They're the ones who first started acknowledging birthdays. It started with a pharaoh; I think?" I whip my head up and meet his eyes. "There is *no fucking way* you're over five thousand years old!" I take the last swallow of my wine and Oz empties the rest of the bottle into my glass.

"My best estimate is I'm somewhere around five and a half thousand years old."

I ponder this for a moment, trying to connect the dots in my mind. *Five and a half thousand years old?* He has striking masculine features and looks Iraqi. Or Sardinian? Georgian? Despite his darker complexion and jet-black hair, he has these beautiful blue eyes that I find myself lost in often. Where have I seen blue eyes with this skin tone?

An enormous piece of the puzzle reveals itself to me, like fitting the last cog in a wheel, and I blurt out, *"You're Sumerian?"*

"Bingo."

He's from the first complex civilization known to man. "Oh. my. god." I punctuate each word. "You speak way more than a few languages, don't you? And how are you so big? I thought the Sumerians were super short?"

"Yeah, I do. Although, I don't remember any of the ancient ones. No one speaks them, so I have no one to practice with. When you become a vampire, you're an apex predator. That means bigger, taller, faster, stronger; made to kill."

There are a hundred million questions I want to ask you, I think. Where to begin? *You're so ... old. But you look a little older than me?* The next logical question is: "As a vampire, you're immortal. Does this mean I am, too?"

Holy smokes, that would be cool. I don't know a thing about witches, other than what I saw on Bewitched reruns on Nick at Night. A pit of sadness gnaws at my stomach. Was my mother a witch, too?

"Witches *can* be immortal, but to live forever, they first have to go to a place called Bedlam. There, witches can learn from the fae how to become immortal. Most witches stay there, safe with others like them. But some witches come back once they learn more magic. Witches that aren't settled down with a human family often end up staying. To gain access, you need a grimoire, a Bedlam Moon, and an Ebbswick key. Your mother was a witch. You couldn't be one if she wasn't."

"I understand none of what you said." My shoulders slump in defeat at not knowing who I am.

Oz leans forward and pins me with his stare. "I can teach you, Sahira—if you let me."

I'm comforted by these words.

"For starters, a grimoire is a book of spells handed down through a witches' family. Bedlam Moon is what human astronomers call a Blood Moon. It happens twice a year."

"Fae forge Ebbswick keys at the beginning of time. It rarely reveals itself to a witch until he or she's ready to receive it. Sometimes it falls in a witches' lap, or it passes on through the family. Without this key, a witch can never enter Bedlam, and thus can never learn how to be immortal. If a witch doesn't want to go to Bedlam, she can still find the Ebbswick key useful. It will open any lock."

A rush of excitement runs through my body as I realize I might own one of these. I tell Oz all about the magical key that unlocked the cabin. Maybe he *is* telling me the truth.

"How did it arrive?"

"Someone mailed it to my best friend's house in Shelby, Montana with a note saying my mom would want me to have it. They only signed it with a first initial: 'D' and gave no return address. The package did route through Iowa, though."

He ponders my words for a moment. "Whoever sent the package might know what happened to your mom, or maybe they can point us in the right direction. I have a friend in Salem who has a lab specializing in forensic science of the magical kind. I bet she can figure out who sent this to you."

"That would be amazing!"

"We can fly out in the morning." Oz glances at the clock right as it gongs two bells.

Two o'clock in the morning already?

"Fly?" I wonder if the legends that vampires can turn into bats are true. I imagine myself clinging to the back of a gigantic bat, with its wings flapping through the cool air.

"No." He tries to stifle his laughter and clears his throat after taking a sip of wine. "No, I can't turn into a bat; I have a plane. We'll have to leave early. Maeve gets kind of ornery if she can't have the lab to herself in the afternoon. You're welcome to stay the night."

Oh, but of course he has a plane. The idea of staying the night makes my heart race. I respond with our usual cat-and-mouse. "Are you sure I should trust sleeping under the same roof as a vampire?"

I catch a trace of the spicy aroma, begging me to allow his sweet release.

"Well, I won't be sleeping. And besides, I'm the one who should be afraid: there *is* a man-eater in my house." He cocks an eyebrow at me.

There it is again; I want to throw myself off the nearest bluff at the reminder of the mortifying statement I made the night I first met him so many months ago.

"No need to blush. I love the way your mind works."

Though I've spent every day this summer with him, my soul thinks I've known him for a century. Still, I have so much to learn about him *and* my newfound magic.

"Would you like me to walk you up to my bedroom, or would *you* rather do the honors?"

I swat him in the arm with a throw pillow. "You're welcome to show me to the bedroom the *proper* way, thank you very much." Although, the idea of getting there my way stirs the depths of me to life. At that moment, I knew Oz could detect the desire radiating off me like a beacon, promising him safe passage if only he comes to port.

Oz takes my hand and pulls me up from the couch. I follow him into the cabin and shut the French doors behind me. He traces a finger down my forearm and interlaces his fingers with mine. An electric current sizzles between us, matching the aroma of spice and a late fall thunderstorm flooding my nostrils. He pivots towards the stairs and leads me up them, our fingers still entwined.

When we reach the landing, I glimpse his much paler blue eyes with hints of yellow. If he's in the mood, I can sense it and see the change in his eyes.

The vampire continues leading me down the hallway and into his bedroom, passing artwork with his moniker in the corner of each.

I'd better shut the door, just in case. With a thought, the door slams shut behind me. I startle at the unexpected noise.

"You're getting better at telekinesis."

"Would you look at that?" Testing my telekinetic abilities, I think Oz should kiss me right about now.

No telekinesis required.

I'm surprised by the sudden unfamiliar voice in my head when he wraps his chilly hands around my waist and then up my back, drawing me in for a kiss. He pulls back, searching my eyes to ensure that yes, this is what I want, even though my mind is begging for it.

With my confirmation, he pulls his shirt up from the back, and I help him peel it off over his head. My breath becomes shallow and my heartbeat speeds up as I draw my gaze over the hard curves of his muscles. Once I've had my fill, he scoops me up and carries me over to his bed.

I pull my sweater over my head and toss it, not worrying about where it lands. All I care about is here and now and satisfying the urge I've felt since the moment I laid eyes on this painfully beautiful, other-worldly creature.

His powerful hands carefully explore my body, and one reaches under the cup of my bra and kneads my breast while kissing the curve of my hips. Unsatisfied with this, he reaches one hand behind my back and unclasps my bra, freeing my ample bosom from its lace prison. He bites his lip as he eyes the bright red lace and tosses it behind him.

Oz traces his tongue along the slope of my breast and then across my nipples, which perk up in response.

I shudder in pleasure. Aching to have him right here and now, I pull his face up to mine and kiss him as I shuffle out of my leggings.

He plants kisses on my neck and continues down my collarbone, over my nipples, and pauses when he reaches my underwear. A feral grin adorns his face when he spots the matching lace panties.

With a firm grip on my hips, he moves me so my butt rests on the edge of the bed, and he kneels in front of me. The sight of him on his knees causes my heart to flutter. Oz grabs my ankles with each hand and props my feet on either side of his head. With one hand, he pulls my panties to one side, revealing my wanton need.

The aroma of my sex invites him in, and he takes his index finger and traces the opening before easing the tip into me. I let out a soft moan, and Oz gives a low growl in response. His feral reply has me tightening the hold I have on his sheets; reaching, searching for more.

Oz's icy mouth meets my warm sex and his tongue parts my folds. I arch my pelvis towards him. Once I'm wet, he eases a second finger into me and the pressure of his wide fingers against the walls of my channel riles me up.

His fingers work in unison with his tongue, and I never want this to stop. I want Oz to have me, right here and now, and I wrap my heels around his bare back and anchor his head to my source of pleasure. I beg him to enter me so I can claim the most intimate parts of him.

He continues hooking his fingers in a 'come hither' motion, hitting right where I need him to. I don't want to climax yet because I want to enjoy our release together, but this thought only causes Oz to quicken his pace as the pressure builds at my core.

Let go, he commands inside my head, now ravenously devouring me. He pulls my clit between his lips and I pulse and tighten around his fingers at the onslaught of pleasure erupting inside of me.

I am left trembling, fully at his mercy as he plants sweet kisses on my mound, as though thanking her instead of me thanking him. He rests his head on my inner thigh and gives it a small nibble.

"You, Sahira, are positively intoxicating." He grins at me with his head still between my thighs. With the back of his hand, he wipes his glistening chin and mouth.

Scooping me up again, he places me under the heavy black duvet cover on his bed. I study the way he slides off his black pants, and admire the way his butt looks in his silk boxers and the smooth way his abs move before he joins me in bed.

"Oz?"

"Yes?" He nestles in closer to my body and cups my right breast in his hand, teasing it with light strokes of his finger.

"Describe my scent for me?" Earlier tonight he explained supernatural creatures all have their own scents.

"Like this." He brings his mouth to mine, and my tongue explores his plump mouth. I suck lightly on his tongue.

Vanilla and peaches, I muse, while feasting on the faintest remnant of my pleasure in his mouth.

"Oz?"

"Yes?"

"Why don't you want to have sex with me?" I am quiet, trying not to sound hurt. "Have you ever slept with a witch before?"

"I've never been with a witch before, and I want to have sex with you, Lana. Badly. I want to take you, and it took all my strength not to do it when you begged for me to." He tucks a stray curl behind my ear. "I've been around for a long time, and one thing I've learned is humans, with their finite life, rush into sex. I want to savor every part of you, and I hope you'll let me when the time comes."

Hearing those words cheers me up. I rearrange myself so I drape my arm and leg over Oz as though he is my personal body pillow. My leg brushes against his firm erection, and I smile—quite satisfied—as I drift off to sleep.

CHAPTER FOUR

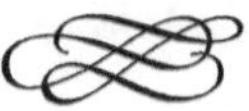

$\mathcal{I}$ stir awake at the faintest butterfly touches, tracing the curves of my breast. Each icy touch of Oz's finger leaves a trail of heat, as though he is stoking a fire within me. Although my eyes are still closed, I can sense it's daylight now, and a wave of wonder washes over me as I realize last night wasn't a dream.

"You smell wonderful, Sahira." His voice is but a purr in my ear. "You dreamed of me."

I groan and open my eyes, meeting his sultry gaze next to me. "So do you." I can't contain the smirk on my face. "What will you do about it?"

He growls in frustration. "We don't have time for what I *want*. Our driver will be here in forty-five minutes to take us to the airfield. We'll eat breakfast on the plane."

I shift so I'm sitting up on my elbows. "About that ... can we push the flight back a bit? I have things to take care of at the cabin."

"Of course. I'll drop you off at your place, and you just let me know when you're ready."

I grunt as I flop over and swing my legs out of bed. Oz takes my hand so I can sit up. Today, he wears smart, casual denim jeans, a white shirt, and a dark blazer.

I think I might need to elevate my choice of clothing.

He eyes my generous figure. "I'd prefer it if you weren't wearing any."

I suddenly feel very exposed by the natural light pouring in through the windows, so I cross my arms over my chest and bite the inside of my cheek while I look for the rest of my clothing.

Oz moves in and wraps his arm around my waist. "Sahira, you forget I'm a creature of the night; I can feast my eyes on every inch of you, no matter if the lights are on or off. I take great pleasure in the perfection before me." He emphasizes his point by pulling me tight against his erection. Spice consumes the space between us, and I nuzzle my nose into his chest to have it closer to me.

He pulls back. "You should dress now. I will leave you to it, other-wise we'll never leave my bedroom." Mischief dances in his eyes before motioning over my shoulder. "Your backpack is on the chaise lounge."

I take a quick shower and change into a pair of skinny jeans and a white blouse. With no time to style my damp hair, I throw it up into a messy bun. I dig at the bottom of my makeup bag and find my mascara and no-smudge red lipstick. I'm done in sixty seconds and I race downstairs.

Oz drives me back and we ride in silence the entire way. When we arrive, I give him a quick peck on the cheek and hurry to unlock the front door.

I toss my backpack on the kitchen table and cross to one bed and flop onto my back. Everything I know—or thought I did—has changed. I take a deep breath and my chest constricts like I have an elephant sitting on me. Why would my mom hide that we're witches?

Then there's Oz. Why would he spend so much time helping me? Hours, days, weeks, and months he's spent helping me find evidence. Sure, maybe he's attracted to me, but the way he behaves towards me is like I hung the moon and stars. I trust him, but how does that saying go? *Trust but verify?*

With that thought, I do what I should've done the night I met him: I pull out my laptop I shoved under the bed and fire up Google. I type in "Osgood Finlandian," and click on the "news" tab. Articles from major networks like BBC, Time, and Forbes fill the results page:

"312 Iraqis Fleeing Al Qaida Arrive in USA With Help of Philanthropist."

"Meet the winemaker who donates 100% of proceeds to charities."

"Philanthropist Osgood Finlandian works to support mental health initiatives in war-torn countries."

"Key takeaways from entrepreneur's keynote about making money for the sole purpose of giving it all away."

"Philanthropies' Most Elusive and Eligible Bachelor, Businessman Osgood Finlandian gives away $6.3bn to women's rights charities in the Middle East."

"Humanitarian receives highest honour by Her Majesty the Queen."

Well, that's a relief. At least I know he's not bullshitting me about who he is. I click on the 'images' tab and regret it almost immediately.

The first picture is Oz with a beautiful, tall blonde. The caption says her name is Dr. Pippa Imperialus. I want nothing to do with a man that's taken. My jealousy gets the better of me and I open a new tab to search for her name. My shoulders sag in relief when I see a wedding photo where he is the best man at Pippa's wedding—it looks like she kept her last name, too.

I decide not to look at any more images of Oz, just in case I find something that causes jealousy to rear her ugly head again. Instead, I check my email and respond to collaboration requests from brands. I schedule blog posts for the next few weeks; Where to Stay in the Amazon, How to Spend a Day in Duluth, Unusual Foods You Must Try in Peru, and How to Hire a Guide for the Amazon River.

When I finish, I think about why I came home. I need to figure out what happened to my mom, even if the things I find out unsettle me. Who am I to say no if Oz wants to help me? I grab some of my nicer clothes, more toiletries, and shoot him a text that I'm ready whenever he is.

～

Oz INTRODUCES me to his driver, who takes my backpack and places it in the trunk of the black Range Rover and opens the backseat door for me. I thank him as I slide in and shut the door. The opposite door opens and Oz settles in next to me. I'm happy he's joined me in the backseat, and he slips his fingers through mine.

My cell phone buzzes, and I take it out of my backpack. It's my best friend, Hannah.

> I MISS YOU! Come see me? CJ is with his dad next week.

Not wanting to let go of Oz's hand, I respond with one thumb.

> Sorry! Might be going out of town for a bit with my neighbor. Lots to explain. On my way to find clues about the note from D.

Her response comes immediately.

> IS HE HOT??

I grin. She knew he was male because I deliberately said nothing more about my neighbor. I've kept pretty quiet about him, unsure what to tell her. 'Oh hey, vampires are real, and your best friend is a witch? Surprise!'

> I stayed at his place last night,

I respond instead, followed by three fire emojis.

> Oh. Em. Gee. Fill me in when you can! You never stay at a man's house.

She's right. Hannah has always been the one to stay at people's houses or have someone warm her bed with little thought to it. While it makes me nervous, that same quality made us fast friends; her ability to trust quickly and take me under her wing when I was most broken did more than save me from my downward spiral—it gave me a renewed sense of purpose.

As I re-read the text, Oz shifts next to me and I sense a change in his emotions. I glance up at him, and he looks satisfied.

"What?"

He says nothing but grips my hand a little tighter before looking out of the window. Can't miss the smile on his face.

I doze off during the ride to the airstrip, and I startle awake when Oz enters my mind to tell me we've arrived.

Sorry. I hate to wake you when you're sleeping so peacefully.

My door opens, and I step out. Oz meets me with my bag, and we walk towards the landing strip. The sun is bright but a cool nip in the air reminds me winter will arrive soon.

"You said you have a plane." My eyes grow bigger as we move closer to it. "This isn't a plane, Oz. This is a jet. A *jet!*"

He shrugs. "Sorry."

As a travel blogger, I've always wanted to ride in a private jet. I can't help but squeal with delight as we climb the steps to *his jet.* A middle-aged steward greets us and takes the bags from Oz. Then, the pilot steps out and gives him a bear hug, lifting Oz right off his feet.

Vampire.

"Lana, please meet Wren Highlandburg. We've been friends for a couple of thousand years, I think."

"Pleased to meet you, Wren." I shake the pilot's hand.

"Likewise. A Sahira?" He raises an eyebrow and glances at Oz.

I'm not sure what to say to this, so I give my assent and take a seat in the plush cream-colored leather seat. Oz situates himself in a seat next to me and buckles in.

Within minutes, we take off and shortly after, reach cruising altitude. I can hardly believe I'm in a private jet with *vampire.* So much has changed in the last week.

"I will bring your breakfast out in a few minutes." The flight attendant disappears behind the galley curtain.

I turn towards Oz. "I'm living in a dream. I'm going to be so mad if I wake up from this."

"Me, too." A unique aroma emanates from him this time. It isn't spicy, it's more like warm vanilla and sugar, like freshly baked cookies. This is new for me, but I love the way it seeps right into my heart and settles there.

The steward raises a table in between us, and Oz shows me how to swivel the seat with a small lever, so it faces the table. The flight crew then brings an assortment of foods, from omelets and pastries to tropical fruit and cereal. I blink my eyes rapidly at the enormous amount of food spread out on our table.

"I wasn't sure what you were hungry for, so I asked for a little of everything."

"I'll say." My eyes scan the assortment in front of us and I shrug. "I'm not picky."

With that, I place an omelet on my plate and several pieces of honeydew melon. He grabs two omelets for himself, a bowl of cereal, an English muffin slathered in peanut butter, and a bagel with lox and cream cheese. He witnesses me biting back a smirk, to which he reminds me, "I don't get full."

In between bites of food and sips of mimosas, we discuss D's letter and the possibility of getting more clues about what happened to my mom from this mysterious "D." Whoever this person is, they must know my mom is a witch.

The steward clears the table for us and lowers it back into the floor. Oz unbuckles his seat belt and asks me to join him in the back. I unbuckle, stand, and brace myself on his muscular arm when we hit a small patch of turbulence. I anchor against him as we stumble towards the back, and I'm grateful Oz is so tall. At 5'10", I'm used to men hovering near my height, and I enjoy having to look up at him rather than down or straight ahead.

At the back of the jet is a bedroom, and Oz closes the partition door to give us some privacy. I grin and stand on my tiptoes, wrapping my hands around his head and pulling it closer to mine. He leans in for a deep kiss.

"We're landing soon. I just wanted you all to myself for a few minutes without prying eyes." He grabs my ass to pull me in closer.

The thickness of his hard length against my stomach weighs heavily on me, and I'm satisfied at the evidence of his arousal.

Wren announces over the intercom we'll be landing in a few minutes and should return to our seats. I steal another passionate kiss from Oz before we make our way to the front. Heat floods my cheeks and neck when we bump into the steward in the aisle as we emerge from the bedroom.

The jet touches down on a private airstrip right outside of Salem, and we meet a black Mercedes to pick us up and take us to Maeve's lab. The lab is in the basement of an old colonial home in a residential neighborhood with manicured lawns and fall décor at every lamppost. There are no signs to show a business operates here, but Oz navigates us to a back entrance. There are cellar doors, and he reaches down to swing one open and beckons me to follow him down the steep steps.

The inside of the lab looks nothing like its colonial accommodations; it is pure white and sterile, with what looks like very expensive state-of-the-art science equipment.

At the far end of the lab, a petite woman with straight hair so black it almost looks blue, works at a computer. She has black grunge boots on with a thick heel, black leggings, and a Ramones t-shirt under her black lab coat.

The woman beams as she watches us walk in and she's at Oz's side lightning fast. *She must be a vampire.* She throws her arms around Oz and picks him up in a bear hug.

I stifle a giggle when she gives me a bear hug, too.

"You must be Lana!"

She reminds me so much of Hannah—her enthusiasm is infectious. This can't be who gets ornery in the afternoons, but deductive reasoning tells me this is who Oz told me we're meeting. "You must be Maeve."

She puts her hands on her hips and strikes a power pose.

I think I'm going to like this woman, Oz.

I knew you would; he responds in my head.

She can't read my mind, can she?

No, I'm the only vampire who can.

"Did you bring it?" I assume she's referring to the note.

As I unzip my Super Souls backpack, Maeve opens a low cupboard and shows me an identical bag. "I was at Super Soul Sessions at UCLA, too!"

"That's amazing. I love Oprah." I pass her the letter from D and the box it came in. Considering how cranky my mom got when I played with her Ebbswick key, I figure I should keep mine on myself.

"Perfect. I'll work on this. You two have fun now."

CHAPTER FIVE

When we reach the front of the house, our driver is waiting. "Where are we headed now?"

"We're going to Ropes Mansion."

"Ropes Mansion?" We put ourselves in the back of the SUV.

"You might've seen it in the movie Hocus Pocus."

"I love Hocus Pocus! That was my favorite movie as a kid, and I must've watched it a hundred times over the years. I love it the same as I did then."

Wow, I've got to reel it in here.

Oz squeezes my hand affectionately. Before long, we pull up to the mansion, and I marvel at seeing a genuine piece of my favorite movie in real life. Oz grabs our stuff from the trunk, and the driver takes off.

I cock my head to the side in confusion. "We're staying here?"

"For the night, yes. I'm friends with the trustees of the museum who own this mansion. Unless you prefer to stay somewhere else?"

Of course, I want to stay here.

"Everything is quite historical, and my friends will have a fit if anything gets damaged, so we'll need to be careful."

Understood.

Oz and I spend most of the day and night looking at artifacts.

Many times, I need to stop and ask what they used a tool for. I might've loved history class if taught by someone who actually lived through it. He never tires of my questions. Instead, he takes great delight in answering every query passing through my thoughts.

The mansion has nine bedrooms, and we can have our pick; each boasts a 19th-century bed with a canopy. I choose the one next to the bathroom with a deep soaking tub after remembering Oz enjoys taking baths. Butterflies flutter in my stomach at the prospect of joining him in the tub.

After ordering takeout, we eat at the dining room table before heading upstairs to the bathroom to bathe. I draw the water and slip out of my clothes, never breaking eye contact with Oz, who remains with his back leaning against the wooden bathroom door.

The scent of his arousal intoxicates me, and I shut the water off before walking over to where he stands with hunger in his eyes. I grab one of his wrists, willing him to cup my breast while I plant a kiss on his cheek. Continuing to hold his hand in place, I help him knead my breast while his other hand slides between my thighs.

He purrs in pleasure when he has the evidence of my arousal on his fingers, and he plunges two into my core while still working at my breast with his other hand. I release my hands from his, allowing them to do their work. I've never been this ravenous for a man, I think, while I undo Oz's belt and then his button. Slowly, I unzip his zipper; his jeans drop, no longer held in place.

In slow and measured movements, I slide his boxers down his ass, revealing his large, throbbing length. This time, I purr—half from the work his hands continue to do, and half because of his size and girth. I stroke it a few times before lowering to my knees.

I tease the end with my tongue, and he lets out a low growl. Before meeting Oz, I would've recoiled at a man growling at me in the bedroom, but not with him. A bead of moisture forms at the head of his penis, and I slowly flick my tongue to lap it up. His hands now free, he pulls off his shirt and runs his fingers through my hair as I take him into my mouth. He moans as I work my hands around the shaft, pulling while I work my tongue and mouth around the tip.

Fuck, he moans in my head. This time his accent is much heavier than usual. *I need you, Sahira. I want to take you. Now.*

So, take me, I command.

In one swift motion, Oz scoops me into his arms and carries me into the tub. His legs cradle me, and we both face the waterspout. The room cloys with the scent of baked cookies again, and waves of raw emotion hit me. Just as fast as it started, it stops.

"I can't, Sahira." He sounds tortured. "I cannot take you now. I'm sorry. The stakes are too high, and I don't want you regretting any of this."

Oz can sense the rejection in my heart.

Please understand, he begs inside my head. I want you more than anything.

He moves my now-wet hair to one side of my neck and plants a tender kiss on my exposed neck. Sensing my arousal at his touch, his erection stiffens against my back. Oz nips at my ear and growls softly. With one hand, he kneads my breast and thumbs my nipple, which stiffens at the attention. He commands me to bend my knees, and my legs fall wide open for him when I do. Reaching around my waist, he grabs my warm mound before his fingers find their way into my core.

I am lost in ecstasy as I grind against his fingers. He keeps going until my legs quiver and I find my release and let out a soft moan.

"I love hearing the little noises you make, Sahira."

Quite satisfied, I flip over and begin stroking his already stiff cock. I want to make him come—if not in me, for me. I want to take him to the brink of ecstasy like he's taken me repeatedly; satisfy his arousal and ride out his orgasm in my arms. Working him with both hands, the water provides me with natural lubrication.

Oz tilts his head back and rests it on the lip of the tub. His eyes are closed now, and I take quiet satisfaction at the pleasure written on his face and the way his abs contract. Victory will be mine soon. We are weightless in this water, neither here nor there. A rush of exotic spices fills my nose, and he moans in quiet pleasure, as though he doesn't want to be too loud.

I want to hear you; I direct him in my head. *Louder.*

He grunts with each pull and tug of his thick length, and his hands grip the sides of the tub as if bracing for impact. He climaxes and triumph settles in my chest, as though I've slain a beast, or at least conquered one. His eyes remain closed as I turn to nestle between his legs while my fingers delicately trace the outline of his abs.

"I've never had abs," I interrupt the moment. "I mean, I'm sure they're under there somewhere."

Oz smirks and opens one eye to look at me. "You're perfect, Sahira." He mutters under his breath and then closes his eye again.

After a while, I am chilled. Oz's body acts like an ice cube and the water's no longer hot. I climb out of the tub and towel off before putting my clothes back on. The lower half of my waist-length curls are wet, so I pull it into a messy bun using a black elastic I keep on my wrist.

"You can use my shirt to dry your hair."

Taking any opportunity to force him to go without a shirt, I happily oblige. Oz grins at this thought and says in my mind, *man-eater.* I toss his denim jeans at his head in protest, and they fall into the water.

"I suppose now you'll be without pants, too." I grin. "Keep it up, and you won't have boxers to put on either, *vampire.*"

Oz gives me a sultry look. *Don't tempt me, Sahira.*

"Watch me."

Oh, I have been, Sahira, and I like what I see.

I give him a devious grin, pick up his boxers, and leave the room with them before he can protest. He meets me in the hallway in a flash and drips water at my bare feet. In one swift move, he picks me up by my thighs, hoists me over his shoulder, and carries me across the house.

One of his hands wraps around my thighs, and the other grips my butt, holding me in place over his shoulder. I protest but stop when I realize I have an excellent view of Osgood Finlandian's perfect naked ass as he carries me to the bedroom.

He lowers me so I'm sitting upright on the bed in front of him. He's still buck naked when I notice something I haven't seen before.

On the upper part of his rib cage is a thick, angry-looking scar. It looks more like a brand, and it's shaped like an old key, with what resembles an intricate knot on one end. I trace my fingers around it, and Oz flinches, then steps away from me.

"I-I'm sorry. You don't have to talk about it if you don't want to."

Oz says nothing but turns to rummage through his gingerbread-colored leather weekender bag on the footstool in the room's corner. His movements are slow and deliberate while he removes a pair of heather gray sweatpants and a crisp white shirt. He dresses in silence, and the air in the room is somber. When finished, he pulls me into bed with him without saying a word.

This time, he nuzzles in the hollow between my breasts, and I wrap my arms around him. I wish it were me who could read minds. He is quiet—almost pained—as his head moves with the rise and fall of my chest. Despite our physical proximity, he's miles away from me.

Most of the day, we've acted like horny teenagers with free rein in a mansion without adults present. Except intercourse is off the table. Oz refuses to have sex with me, despite assurances he wants to. I hope I find out why sooner rather than later.

And now, something is bothering him. I don't want to pry, but it hurts me to see him like this. My entire life, I've been a fixer, a problem solver. I'm powerless, not knowing how to help, or even if I should.

There's still a rift between us when I drift off to sleep, and I wake alone.

"Oz?" I sit up on my elbows and clear the sleep from my eyes. Slipping out of bed, I put on one of his t-shirts and it hangs to my thighs.

I pad to the bathroom to relieve myself before checking the rest of the bedrooms upstairs. Despite my best efforts to remain calm and collected, my breathing shallows and my hands tremble while I descend the stairs. I call out for him again but receive no response. Everything is quiet. He's not downstairs either.

He wouldn't have left me here ... right? I *knew* we were moving too fast; men always freak out when this happens. Now I'm going to have to figure out how to get my letter back from Maeve, book a flight, and rent another car from the airport to get back to the cabin. Disappointment creeps into my chest and settles in my gut while I climb the stairs. I dress and shove my clothes in my bag.

My gaze catches on the messy bed and I know I should probably make it but fuck it and fuck *him*. This is why I don't get close to people. With the sleeve of my shirt, I brush my tears away. I sling my bag over my shoulder and shut off all the lights in the house before pulling the front door shut. A hard lump constricts my throat, and I try to ignore the gnawing ache in my chest. On our way here, I spotted a coffee shop about half a block away. They'll have Wi-Fi so I can see about getting a flight home today.

Right before I step onto the sidewalk, I hear my name called, and I whip my head to the sound. A brief flutter of hope blooms inside me at the sight of Oz jogging my way from the backyard.

Protect your heart, protect your heart, protect your heart. I straighten my spine and school my features. "Yes?"

"Where are you going?"

"Home."

Hurt flashes across his face and he puts his hands in his pockets. "I'm sorry for shutting you out last night."

"Oz ... you don't have to tell me anything. You owe me nothing. I'm not your girlfriend."

He blinks. "Aren't you?" He toes his shoe against the gate. "I thought maybe we were more than that. A lot more."

My heart thrashes in my chest as I take in his vulnerable eyes. We haven't had the exclusivity talk yet, and though none of us are seeing anyone else, being *his* is everything I want right now. So when the next words come out of my mouth, it shocks even me. "I'm only now coming into my witch powers after thirty-four years, and my emotions are all over the place. I don't know what's gotten into me, but maybe we need to pull the reins back, because I don't want you to hurt me." The words are mine, but I'm not entirely sure I mean them.

He's been *so* good to me. I'm safe with him, and he's helped me understand more about my abilities. I don't *want* to pull back but think I should before we're in too deep.

Lana, I can hear your thoughts, Oz reminds me in my head.

I don't even care anymore. Sometimes I can't articulate everything I want to say in the right way. This is what's in my heart: I'm afraid of drowning in you, but I don't want to stop because I want to be in over my head. I enjoy having you near me, and it pains me when you hurt. You asked me to trust you before I even knew you, yet I felt it in my bones I could. I want to understand you, your heart, and everything that makes you, you.

A torrent of warm vanilla and sugar invades my space; the aroma is heady and clings to the air between us.

Will you say something?!

I don't want to pull back, Sahira. I need to map every square inch of your body, heart, and your mind, and I want to share all my secrets with you. Some of these have implications far bigger than you or me, it isn't that I'm keeping anything from you; I'm trying to figure out how to do it in a way that doesn't drive you away from me.

Our fingers intertwine, and I rest easy knowing we agree.

～

Oz and I descend the steps to Maeve's lab, and I take a deep breath before I motion for him to open the door.

"Are you ready for this?" Maeve nearly hops up and down.

"What did you find out?" Oz pulls out a stool for me to sit on and I take it.

"Okay, so the paper from this letter comes from a printing company in Iowa called Buston. They mainly ship their products in the US. However, they predominantly sell church bulletins locally. I checked, and there are a hundred and sixty-seven churches within a twenty-mile radius of Buston. That would not work for me, so I scanned their site for what messaging they typically include on this specific type of paper." She gets more and more excited the longer she speaks.

"I determined they use this specific paper for visiting pastors at nursing homes. So, I called Buston and acted like an arrogant secretary to the pastor, demanding they print the exact bulletins we had on the Sunday before this package shipped. They have zero security protocol, so when they went to confirm my shipping address, they gave it to me instead of the other way around."

My mouth drops open. I don't entirely understand how she arrived at her conclusion, but she's confident in her results, and Oz seems to agree.

She slides a piece of lined paper to me with an address on it, and I take it with trembling hands.

"This is the nursing home you need to go to. Whoever sent you this package attended a service here."

Windhaven Senior Living

3141 E Main St

Tripoli, IA

"Wow, Maeve. You have me speechless." I try to fight back the tears. Instead, I give her a big hug and thank her.

After we finish our hug, she responds, "Are you kidding me? I live for this! Err … I mean, I don't actually live, but it gives me purpose. I hope you find your mom."

CHAPTER SIX

"$\mathcal{D}$o you want to take a road trip before we go to Iowa? Wren is with his boyfriend for the weekend, but he can fly us from anywhere." Oz asks me over breakfast in bed of French toast, mimosas, and sliced tropical fruit. He spent the morning letting me sleep in and surprised me by making us breakfast.

"I love road trips!" I cut a small corner of French toast. "Where are we going?"

"I have a place in Mont-Tremblant I'd like to take you to."

I set down my fork. "Just how many places do you have?"

"I'm immortal. This means I have to assume a new identity fairly regularly not to arouse suspicion from humans. It's a lot easier to do this when I have many properties throughout the world I hold in the name of corporations." He takes my hands in his. "Don't worry. The properties aren't always sitting empty. I create a lot of jobs for people in areas that might not otherwise have them. I treat my staff very well, and for that, they're loyal."

After breakfast, we spent an hour putting the museum back the way we found it. I linger a little longer in each of the three pantries, trying to memorize all the old gadgets Oz showed me.

We load up the Jeep and embark on our five-hour drive to Montreal, stopping at a New England clam chowder food truck for lunch and a little boutique next door to buy some much-needed clothes.

About ninety minutes after leaving our last shop in Montreal, I am rendered speechless as we pull the Jeep into a ten-car garage attached to a towering stone chateau overlooking the water. The rest of the garage is empty, except for a few snowmobiles, a ton of skiing equipment, sleds, and a pickup truck outfitted with snow tires.

"I sent the staff home to be with their families for the rest of the week." Oz shuts off the vehicle. "I hope you don't mind."

"And have you all to myself in another enormous house? I wouldn't have it any other way."

From the garage, we enter a large foyer where we remove our coats and shoes. We leave our things here so Oz can give me a grand tour of the place. I count seventeen fireplaces, nine full bathrooms, four half baths, eleven bedrooms, a gym, a formal dining room, a parlor, an in-house spa, a home movie theater and two kitchens on the first floor alone.

"You said your properties don't sit empty. Who lives here when you're away?" I'm curious, not judging.

"No one takes permanent residence here, but I allow the staff and my friends to use it as a vacation home or party venue for charity and private events."

"The place is lovely." I admire the vaulted ceilings with wooden beams across the top. Brilliant beams of orange and red fill the walls as the sun goes down, and a chandelier leaves beautiful prisms on the floor.

"Wait 'til I show you upstairs. Hurry before the sunset goes away." Oz grabs my hand to drag me upstairs.

We race to the top of the stairs, down the wide hallway, and into a bedroom facing the West. He leads me onto a balcony off the bedroom overlooking the water, and I weep at the magnificent beauty before my eyes.

Stunning.

Oz slips his arms around my waist, and we remain silent as we take in the last bit of the sunset. A chill runs through my body, so he leads me inside to warm up.

"I love the way your mind works, Sahira."

"And I keep waiting to wake up from this dream."

Me, too.

We head to the kitchen to figure out food for tonight. "When I was in Paris for the first time, I was so broke I could barely afford to buy a baguette and butter." I examine the shelves. "My friends took pity on me and treated me to the most incredible meal of my life at our Airbnb. It was Coq Au Vin Blanc with Foie Gras. I'm not a fan of the method used to obtain Foie Gras, but I love it so."

"We can make it if you'd like?" Oz leans against the pantry door-way. "I've made the dish at least a couple hundred times over the years."

I throw my arms around his neck and plant a kiss on his lips. *I believe I could get used to this.*

Me, too. The recipe Oz knows by heart takes a little over two hours. While cooking it, we enjoy some of his wine.

"Where does the name Finlandian come from?"

Oz chuckles and says he needed an easy way to keep his story straight when changing his identities. The most recent time he had to do so, he was living in Finland. Apparently, one of his vampires, Gideon, helps create an entirely new identity for everyone approximately every fifty years. They have funerals for everyone, too.

I laugh at the simplicity and brilliance of the explanation. It makes sense. I ask what other names he's had throughout history.

He goes through a list of some names.

Arnold Germahny

Eugene Zealander

Romeo Italiano

Atticus ... a few times

Alastair Polander

Augustine St Michael

"What's your real name? And did you ... or do you ... know anyone famous?" I set my glass down. "Are *you* famous at any point in history?!"

"I don't think you can make it through even a few thousand years without crossing paths with poets, dictators, presidents, actors, royals, scientists, and other notable people in life," Oz leans back in his seat, and I admire the peak of his abs when he stretches. "You've probably stumbled across my work throughout the various occupations I've had over the years—I've had a long time to do some cool things. As far as my real name goes, I promise I'll share it with you in time."

"Anything you'd like to share with me?"

"I'd rather show you if you'd like?" Oz leads me to the grand piano in the formal dining room.

I sit next to him on the piano bench as he plays Clair de Lune. He leans into the music as though it is harnessing him, and Oz is merely but a vessel through which it flows. This is a complex piece to play, but he appears as though he's been practicing it for a century. I have goosebumps watching him immerse himself in his work.

"Isn't that by Debussy?"

"Ha! Claude was a friend of mine, and we worked on this piece together. He argued it was only fair he got to take credit for it entirely if I got to live forever. This way, he could live forever, too, but through music." Oz gazes absently at the keys, as though lost in thought. "Why he insisted on this piece, I'll never know; considering he had plenty of his own work to immortalize him. He was brilliant."

"Wow. You are incredible." I'm very fortunate to be sitting next to someone with so much creative aptitude. I wish I had half the talent he does.

"You've only been on this Earth for thirty-four years, Sahira." He closes the lid to the piano keys. "You have so much ahead of you. Besides, you have other, more impressive talents."

A hint of spice hovers between us as Oz stops playing and takes my hand in his. As fast as it came on, it disappears.

"Let's eat." He tugs me up by my hand. "Then, we play."

I have to resist the urge to wolf down the meal we spent so long making. Oz's amused expression studies me, hearing me debate in my head about what he meant when he said we can play after dinner. Did he mean we're going to play the piano? A board game? Soak in the hot tub? Or the pool? Shoot, I didn't bring a bathing suit.

Butterflies dance in my stomach when the idea crosses my mind maybe Oz meant we'd do something a little more adult-oriented. The idea of it stirs a warmth at my core.

"We'll get to that," Oz smirks, "but I think we need to address a few things first. Now you're aware you're beginning to use your magic, many other creatures in this world can harm you, and I want to teach you how to defend yourself for when I'm not around. Before, you were simply a witch whose power they bound. And now any magical being within a hundred yards of you will know how powerful you are. They'll feel threatened."

His words sting a bit. It's ridiculous to assume I'd spend forever with Oz, let alone we'd be in each other's company 24/7, 365. Am I only in the right place at the right time? My mind flits to college, when I'd had my heart crushed in the worst possible way.

"Hey, hey now." Oz laces his fingers through mine. "The bastard who hurt or betrayed you and made you think you're not worthy of everything should die a miserable, lonely death. I don't think of you as just a fling, Sahira. I like you far more than I'm willing to admit out loud."

"What I meant to say," he squeezes my hand, "is should some other vampire or witch try to hurt you when you're not in my company, I need you to control your magic and defend yourself. You've got this huge magic ready to burst out of you, but uncontrolled, it can seriously hurt you."

"And you can teach me this?" I'm skeptical.

"Yes, I can teach you," Oz softens his features. "And I'll be happy to. The better you can harness your magic, the easier it will be to find answers about your mom."

My eyes tear up at hearing this. I've spent most of my life with abandonment issues. Not knowing what happened to my mom, I've come away a little messed up. I suppose it is why I sometimes spiral when I think about what I mean to Oz and what his intentions are. I don't want to hurt, and I don't want to hurt him, either.

Oz is wearing only gray sweatpants, and I warn him he might be a distraction—a welcome one—but a distraction, nonetheless.

"That's alright. We'll play in due time."

"The first thing we're going to learn is a proper defense." Oz crosses the room. "I want you to show me what happens when a random stranger attacks you in an alleyway. Okay?"

I straighten my shoulders. Oz lunges for me, and I pitifully swat him with my arms. He does a full belly laugh.

"Are you laughing at me?"

"Yes, Sahira. I'm laughing at you." He kisses me on the forehead and I slide out of his arms and cross the tile. "I said you can't hurt me, so don't be afraid to try."

With no hesitation, he lunges at me again, but this time he tries to distract me by leaping towards me as he gets close. I dodge out of the way with a quick swoosh.

"Good. Trust your instincts. That is what they're there for." Oz circles me. "Now, most of the newer witches are going to need to use spells to cast magic. For you, this isn't the case. Otherwise, you wouldn't have been able to dodge a vampire as old as me. Right?"

Right.

"I'm going to move in like I'm attacking you. Your job is to lay me on my ass or make me face plant. Don't hold back, or you won't play tonight." He cocks an eyebrow in warning.

My mouth drops. "That isn't even fair! I've been doing this all but two minutes, and you've been doing this for over five thousand years!"

Then don't hold back, Oz teases in my head.

Fuck! Okay, I can do this.

Oz comes at me, and I lift my arms in the air and slam them down at my sides, almost like I were an eagle giving a brief flap of her wings. In a single blink of an eye, my hair blows back, and I'm weightless. My hover is wobbly, and my stomach plummets when I fall, landing on his back right as he reaches me. It catches him off guard, and he falls to the ground.

"Did you see that?" I scramble off the floor and give a fist pump in the air. "I can actually fly!" Holy shit. My chest heaves and adrenaline surges through my body. This is nothing like the dreams I've had about flying, where everything was perfect and I soar through the air; this was more or less controlled falling than anything, but with more practice I *know* I can do more.

Oz chuckles. *I suppose you can, Sahira. Good work,* he says in my head as I help him up.

"I didn't hurt you, did I?"

"What did I say? You can't hurt me."

I grin when I think about this for a second. Tell me, Oz. Does this mean you like it rough?

Okay, you want to play now? If you can catch me, you can keep me.

He takes off in a blur before I can even stop him. I'm conflicted. Of course, I want what he's offering, but dammit I can freaking *fly!* I don't think we're celebrating my incredible feat enough.

"Oz! Get back here and help me practice flying."

"You're right, Sahira." I whip my head behind me and he has a smirk on his face.

I saunter over to him and wrap my arms around his neck. With a small grunt, I heave myself up to wrap my legs around him. "Caught you." I whisper in his ear, and he chuckles.

"You tricked me."

"Nope, this way I get both things. I can fly *and* play after." I hop down and make to run upstairs before he darts in front of me.

"You will not jump off the gods damned balcony, Lana."

I cock my head and feign innocence.

"Don't even give me that look, Sahira. I saw in your head what you planned to do."

I huff and roll my eyes. "It isn't like you wouldn't have caught me if I were in any real trouble." I grab his hand and drag him to the kitchen, where I climb onto the counter.

Oz stands back and I jump but I get distracted by the way he casually leans against the wall like he's Adonis or something. I wince when pain shoots up my ankles at the impact.

"Aren't you glad I didn't let you jump to your death in the back-yard?" The bastard cocks an eyebrow at me.

I scowl at him. "You can't stand there looking like that," I gesture to his body, "and expect me not to get distracted. Maybe you need to wear more clothes. Or a sleeping bag."

His pupils blow out, but in a single blink, they're back to normal.

"How about we meet in the middle: you fly from ground level, and I'll stand behind you in case you run into any trouble. You won't even know I'm there unless you need help."

I slide an arm around his waist, and he gives me a kiss on the head before leading me to the foyer, where I'll have plenty of room to fly—or fall. With one deep breath, I slowly raise my arms before bringing them to my side fast. This gets me off the ground, but I still wobble, and my ab muscles are on fire, trying to keep myself upright. I'm more of a hovering, wobbly ...

Umph. I land in Oz's arms and am thankful I don't hit the ground.

Again, he tells me in my head. I slide out of his arms and ready myself with a few deep breaths. This time, I close my eyes, and imagine I'm in the clouds; a light breeze blows against my hair, but I'm otherwise in complete control and weightless.

Frustrated it didn't work, I open my eyes and startle. *Holy shit.* Oz is below me with an enormous grin and I'm near the ceiling, just *floating* like a gods damned ghost.

"Oz! How do I get down?" I panic; heart racing, hyperventilating, and I flail my arms and legs. Immediately, I feel gravity take hold and I plummet—fast—and I let out a scream.

"I got you." Oz jumps to meet me to help lessen the impact of my falling into his arms.

My entire body trembles as he carries me to the bedroom. I never realized I'm afraid of heights.

"It appears as though the key to you controlling flight is to remain calm and envision how you want to fly. We'll practice another day. You've done well."

I rest my head against his chest. "Another day. I think I shot my nerves for the night."

"Lana, I'm going to have to feed tonight." He traces a delicate finger along my shoulder. "I haven't fed in almost a week, and I can't risk losing control around you." His eyes return to their normal, piercing blue color.

"Will it hurt?" I'm more than happy to give him blood, after all. He's been feeding me for several months. It only seems fair.

"I'm not feeding on you, Sahira."

"Oh. Alright." I try not to sound wounded my blood isn't good enough for him. "Who will you feed on then?" I'm trying not to read into anything, but I can't help my feelings. I am not the jealous or controlling type. Most of the men I've dated have said I'm too distant and unattached; perhaps that was self-preservation. Maybe this whole witch thing has recalibrated my hormones.

"It isn't like that, Lana, I promise," Oz tries to reassure me. "The Canadian Alpine Ski Team will be at the ski lodge nearby, so I'll be able to find a male athlete or two to feed on. I won't need to feed for another week after tonight, and I'll be back before you even wake up."

Oz is cautious to specify he'll be feeding on males instead of the females, and I appreciate this courtesy.

"You won't hurt them though, right? What if they call the cops?"

"A bite only hurts if I let them hurt; otherwise, they won't feel a thing. Not even a mosquito bite, I promise. When I'm feeding, they're in a dream-like state with no recollection of what's happening."

"Okay."

We take quick, separate showers. My emotions are so over the place I needed a bit of space before saying anything else crazy. Maybe going to sleep by myself tonight will allow things to cool off a bit between us. Sometimes I feel like Icarus; the god who flew too close to the sun.

After crawling into bed, Oz kisses me and says goodnight.

Once he leaves, I have trouble falling asleep. I replay the last few days on repeat in my mind. Did I imagine all of this? I am surely living inside of a dream.

First, I'm a witch. Second, I'm with a very rich, ancient vampire who doesn't look a day over forty. If he had gray hair, I'd say he's a silver fox. But his hair is like onyx, and so are his eyebrows. He's got the most beautiful eyes I've ever seen, especially paired with dark hair. He treats me so well and isn't stingy in bed. Come to think of it ... have I been the stingy one? At this thought, I cringe and try my hardest to drift off to sleep.

❧

I STIR awake when a heavy weight on my legs crawls towards me.

"Oh, I'm so glad you're home." I smile, eyes still closed.

"Well, hello, little poppet. I'm so glad I'm here too." This comes from a voice I don't recognize.

My heart leaps through my chest, and my eyes fly open to a beautiful woman with long, black wavy hair falling into her face. Her eyes are as black as coal, and there are no whites on them. A cruel, fanged grin crawls across her crimson lips.

Vampire, I panic.

I don't have any time to react when I am yanked by my arms out of bed and thrown against the wall like a rag doll, and something snaps. The pain is immediate and unbearable, and as I lay crumpled on the floor, I realize my femur has punctured through the skin.

I try to pull myself up while holding a hand to my leg, but the pain is unbearable, even through the adrenaline, and I cry out in sheer agony. There is blood pooling under my leg, and I'm woozy.

"Ugh. You are pathetic, little witch," the vampire hisses. "I like to play with my food before I eat it, and you're spoiling my appetite."

The atmosphere is bitter and palpable, and swirls of black and red consume the space between us. The vampire drags me by my broken leg through my pool of blood and into the hallway. I shriek as she pulls me to the top of the stairs, hoists me over the banister, and dangles me above the landing.

Blood rushes to my head, and the pressure in my brain and pain in my leg is too much. My familiar buzzing sensation slides in like a heavy blanket and builds to a deafening roar.

This is how I'm going to die.

I will never find my mother. Hannah will never find out I'm a witch. I will never marry, and I will never have children. And I will never take Oz in my arms again.

My heart breaks into a million tiny pieces, realizing he will be the one to discover my lifeless body. He will have to tell my best friend what happened to me. And she will have to tell CJ his auntie is dead. Will Hannah believe Oz?

It will destroy them all.

CHAPTER SEVEN

The vampire's grip releases my ankle and I fall. I am weightless, tumbling in the air when I have a sudden, coherent thought:

I know how to fly.

I can barely muster the energy to think about flying, but as I do, I sense the ground pull away from me. The wind whips my hair and I hover just above the floor.

"Well, well, little poppet," the vampire snarls. "You can fly. Good; now I may eat."

She leaps over the banister and slams into my back, and I let out a scream when we hit the ground. The impact is jarring; a metallic tang accompanies the throb of my tongue where I bit it. Anger fuels me, and I claw at her face—catching her eye—and she shrieks.

I'm losing blood fast, but adrenaline keeps me going. I won't go down without a fight. When she recovers, she grabs my good leg to pull me back from where I've scooted across the floor, and I put all of my power into a kick to her face. This sends her sailing back, but not for long; she's pinning me down before I even know what's happening.

The vampire grips my hair and yanks my head back, exposing my neck. Searing pain chokes me as she rips at my throat, sinking her teeth into my neck. As suddenly as the pain began, it has stopped, and the darkness closes in.

The last thing I hear is the front door open, and Oz bellows in his rage and agony as he tears across the foyer. Despite my eyes being closed, my third eye opens in a last protest of the approaching dark, and I catch a brief vision of Oz ripping the throat out of the trespassing vampire. I smile in quiet satisfaction before my world goes black.

❧

MY THROAT STIRS to life as sweet, metallic nectar coats my tongue and drips down the back of my throat. Copper permeates the air. I am so cold, and every inch of my body screams in pain. I take a while to register Oz is cradling me in his arms, and we are on the floor of the foyer. He is sobbing, and he presses his wrist to my lips.

Drink, he begs. *Drink, damn it!* His thoughts in my head are like a roar, shaking me awake. The liquid warms me, and I can sense my heartbeat thumping in my chest. Slowly, but it is there. "I couldn't hear your thoughts anymore, Sahira." Oz's anguished sobs will haunt me forever. "I thought I lost you, and I would've died right with you."

Tears spring to my eyes hearing this. I try to talk, but I can't because I'm too weak, and Oz's wrist is still in my mouth. I realize now the nectar in my mouth is his blood.

Will this make me like you? I ask in my thoughts. The air between us cloys with warm sugar and vanilla. It's a welcome scent. I didn't think I'd ever smell it again.

No, Sahira. You did not die, but you were close, he replies. *I need you to keep drinking, and my blood will help you heal enough so I can move you. Then, I will need to call Maeve's sister, Pippa; she's a surgeon. I used to be one, but I'm afraid I've been out of practice for a while.*

I drink Oz's life force until he can move me. He sets my femur so it's no longer poking through my skin. It's agonizing, even with the spell he taught me to help lessen the pain. He cuts my blood-soaked pajamas off me and carries me to the basement. There is a full surgical suite here, and I'm confused as Oz dials someone on speakerphone.

He is frantic, asking the woman on the other line to take the chopper immediately for surgery. Oz hooks me up to an IV and explains I will need more than just a spell and his blood to heal me. With the femur break alone, I've lost at least 1,500 ml of blood. With the tear at the neck, I'm at risk of dying. Terror quakes through me. How can a leg break can be so detrimental?

Minutes later, a woman enters the surgical suite. She looks as though Taylor Swift was born a Kardashian. Poking out of her fuzzy white hat is her long, blonde, curly hair. Pippa's chiseled features are even more beautiful with her impeccable makeup, and with her boots on, she's almost as tall as Oz.

Pippa introduces herself to me as she hands Oz her coat and washes up. Her demeanor is kind and full of compassion, and when she checks my vitals, her touch is cold. Her icy vampire stare dances across my injuries as she inspects them. Only when Oz is confident I am comfortable alone with Pippa does he excuse himself from the room to gather more supplies. A pang of grief stabs at my chest when I realize he has to pass the evidence of my assault every time he leaves the room.

"I'm so sorry it took so long for me to arrive. A snowstorm just hit. I'm also very sorry about what happened." Pippa scribbles notes on a clipboard. "Oz has done an excellent job of taking care of your injuries. My team will be in shortly, and we'll need to put you to sleep. Oz told me you were on the very brink of death when he found you, and you're still not out of the woods."

I knew I was going to die when the vampire had me dangling from the landing, and it was the thought of the absolute heartbreak they'd all endure that gave me the energy I needed to fly. Had I not flown, I would have died when she dropped me.

Thinking about this, my eyes water, and my breathing shallows while I try not to cry in front of my surgeon.

"I'm sorry to trouble you, Pippa."

"Had he called an ambulance, you would've been dead by the time they arrived from La Annonciation." Pippa speaks gently by my side. "And even then, if you had lived, how would he have explained your injuries? The femur break would've been a lot easier to explain than the wounds on your neck. It's why he called me. After imaging, we'll have to put you under."

Oz accompanies the team in the room, and he holds my hand as they inject something into my IV. Red tears spill down his cheeks, and everything around me goes black before I can comment on it.

When I wake, I'm in a recovery room in the basement. It's a lot warmer than the surgical suite, and it isn't like a hospital anymore. Oz is at my side, and his clothes have blood all over them. The look on his face is a mixture of grief and relief. He takes my hand in his and kisses it. When I try to swallow, my throat is raw, and when I try to speak, Oz shakes his head. I want to tell him he needs to go clean himself up.

"You need rest, Lana." He gives my hand a gentle squeeze. "Pippa had to do what's called an external fixation until you're well enough for a second surgery. You had a lot of soft tissue damage."

Second surgery?

Between the spell and my blood, you should be ready for that by morning.

Who did this to me?

"Her name was Mayim-Willow Flametree." His eyes have gone black again, and his fangs protrude from his mouth. "She was an auction house curator in London, though why she came here? We're still figuring that out. There's no way she would've attacked you had she known you were here with me. I have my people looking into it."

I SLIP in and out of sleep most of the evening.

Between the sedatives and the spell Oz helped me cast to control the pain, I have a hard time arranging my thoughts into a coherent pattern. Speaking is difficult, and sometimes when I try to open my mouth to speak, I sob instead. I keep having flashbacks of this vampire dragging me through the hallway, and the look on Oz's face is tortured as he watches me relive those moments in my mind.

I can't eat, so Oz opens his wrist and has me drink from him.

"My blood will heal you." He encourages me to take more and more. Taking his blood doesn't gross me out at all, and every time I do, I'm surprised it's pleasant. His blood is thick, like maple syrup, and easily slides down my throat.

My thoughts drift to the painting he has of the naked woman hanging on his wall in Minnesota. It had to have been a recent painting because it bore the name O. Finlandian in the corner. I realize while, on the one hand, it's like I've known him all my life, on the other—I don't know him at all.

"Quinn Kennedy commissioned the painting for her husband as a fiftieth wedding present. They died in a terrible accident not long before I went to deliver the painting to their house. I couldn't bear to part with the painting after learning there were no family members to pass it on to, and I had the Kennedys buried in my family mausoleum in Croatia."

Guilt spreads like an inferno in me, and I realize I'm a terrible person for having even thought this beautiful woman was some secret lover of his. Lord knows I've had my share of rendezvous over the years, and after living for over five thousand years, no doubt Oz has had many lifetimes of his own.

"I don't mean to talk about past relationships, but you should understand this about me. I carry a lot of grief. I had a wife when I was still human, and they killed her and my son before I was turned."

Oh ... Oz. I'm so sorry.

I can't fight the tears pouring down my cheeks. I don't know what else to say because I've seen the way Oz reacts when someone he likes gets hurt, and I can't imagine the profound grief he deals with every day having lost his wife and child.

THE FOLLOWING MORNING, Oz wakes me for my second surgery. This surgery will take much longer than the first, but to me, it will be as though I close my eyes and open them again. He transfers me to a cot and wheels me into the surgical suite, where Pippa and her team wait.

They explain the surgery to me and how I might feel afterward. This differs now I can use magic and have a ready supply of Oz's vampire blood to help me heal. Within minutes, I'm put under.

It's dark when I wake in the recovery room. Oz has Helen Jane Long playing quietly on the stereo speakers overhead, and the scent of warm vanilla and sugar permeates the air. He bites open his wrist and places it to my lips, and his blood is thick as it pours onto my tongue.

Pippa's team arrives for more x-rays. Changing positions hurts, and I'm grateful for the painkillers in my body. It's difficult to turn my neck, both from the pain and from the stitches I received. They said I'd lost a lot of blood, so I'll take at least a few days for both his blood and my magic to heal my wounds. This surprised me because I lived my entire life without knowing magic or mythical creatures, and injuries this grave would've killed me or left me incapacitated for months.

If it weren't for Oz, I would be dead. Whatever the future has in store for us, I owe him my life. I've spent so much time trying to push him away because my feelings for him are so strong. When I'm recovered and in the clear, I vow I will not run away from my emotions and instead will share them with him.

After the x-ray technicians leave, Pippa returns to give me some medicine. "I want you to try walking this weekend. It will not be easy for you, but Oz has explicit instructions to see to it you walk several times. By Tuesday, you should almost be healed, and then you're free to travel. I don't want to risk any further injury. For now, he has what he needs to care for you."

"Thank you again, Pippa. Please thank your team for me, too."

"It's no trouble at all, Lana. I'm glad Oz has someone in his life." She gives my hand a squeeze. I'm not sure what Oz told Pippa about me, but hearing her say, 'someone in his life' makes it seem like I'm important to him. This comforts me because he's important to me, too.

After Pippa leaves, I doze off thanks to the increase in medicine she put in my IV. I have vivid nightmares about my assault and of a man carrying me through the woods.

Early the next morning, an aroma of warm vanilla and sugar breaks through the recesses of my slumber. When a hint of ice dances on my eyelids, I open them to Oz sitting in a chair next to my bed. I'm so heavily medicated I didn't realize he was holding my hand.

"Oz?"

"Yes, Sahira?"

"Why do you sometimes smell like cookies?" I slur my words. While I am semi-coherent, fighting against the grip the increase in medicine has on me, I am numb.

I close my eyes, and Oz responds in my thoughts.

The scent is the aroma I give off when I am in love.

CHAPTER EIGHT

The sun illuminates a flower bouquet on the nightstand and a large glass of blood when I wake. I'm no longer in the recovery room. Instead, I'm in a room on the first floor of the chateau. I'm getting much better now, despite the restless night, and the vivid nightmares.

We spend the rest of the week in a routine. Oz feeds me his blood, whether by vein or in smoothies. He says his blood will provide far more nutrients than solid food, and I need my strength. We spend our evenings playing card games like UNO and Phase 10, and I beat him most of the time, though I think he lets me.

"I think today we'll have you walk to the bathroom where I can bathe you." He gathers some dishes from the nightstand. "You have no broken skin anymore, so you can submerge yourself."

The idea of taking a proper bath sounds heavenly. Oz did his best to clean the blood out of my hair, but there is only so much you can do with a washcloth, especially with how much hair I have.

"Will you join me in the tub?"

"If you'd like me to, although Pippa told me in so many words your body needs time to heal." He raises an eyebrow at me.

Understood. I'd still like you to join me, though.

A slight poke makes me grimace while Oz removes the IV from my hand. A small pool of blood appears, and he covers it with a flesh-colored bandage. My hand aches from the large bore IV, but I'm glad not to be attached to the thing anymore. I go to swing my legs out of bed when I realize I'm connected to tubing and a sharp pull tugs near my groin.

I have a catheter in. Oh, gods. I haven't gone to the bathroom at all this week, and I'm mortified at the thought of someone having to insert the catheter and dispose of my urine.

"Sorry, Lana." He winces. "I had to."

I want to crawl in a hole or throw myself off a cliff at the sheer embarrassment of it. Oz reassures me he's been around for a very long time and practiced medicine in a hospital for years. It wasn't his first catheter placement. Oz having to be the one to handle my most intimate parts in such a clinical way makes me cringe.

"I'm sorry, but I'll have to be the one to remove it now, too."

Jiminy Christmas. Shoot me now. If one could die because of sheer humiliation, this is my time. Somebody hand me a shovel; I'll dig the damn hole myself.

Oz smirks. A little dramatic, no?

"Do you know me as anything but?"

"It will be over in a millisecond, I promise."

I lay down, throw the sheets off me, and cover my eyes with my arms. Oz's chilly hands lift my nightgown and part my legs. *Take a deep breath*, he says in my head. I do as I'm told, and it helps me through a tug and a slight burning sensation as the catheter slides out of me. I grit my teeth.

Please don't let me see it, take it out of here, I say to Oz in my mind while keeping my eyes closed. I don't need to add to the humiliation of actually seeing the medical device he just pulled out of my urethra.

When he returns, the water runs in the tub, and I can't bear to look at him while he helps me out of bed. I lean on him as I try to steady myself. My leg is sore, and it won't be easy to walk. I shuffle my feet and sweat at the effort while we make our way to the en suite bathroom.

I'm sorry you have to do this, Oz.

"Nonsense. I'd rather it be me than anyone else."

Once we reach the tub, which took far longer than I thought it would, he helps me out of my nightgown and into the tub. The water is warm and is so soothing to my muscles. I close my eyes and lean my head on the lip of the tub when he joins me. This causes the water to rise, and I float off the bottom of the tub. He shuts off the water, and we soak together in silence.

While I'm lost in my thoughts, Oz grabs a loofah and soap before positioning himself behind me, so I'm wedged between his legs. His moves are slow and deliberate as he lathers the soap on the loofah and rubs my skin with it.

"Oz, how come you smell like cookies sometimes?"

"I worried you might not have been all there the last time you asked me."

"I'm sorry. I don't remember asking you anything. It must've been the medicine."

"You've been through a lot this week. And besides, it isn't a conversation I wanted to have with you while you were medicated, but you asked, so I answered."

Okay. What's the answer, then? I've smelled it regularly lately. It isn't your regular scent of earthy elemental that reminds me of a thunderstorm. And it differs from when you're aroused—the same, but with hints of spice. Your arousal scent is powerful, but nothing compares to the sugar cookies. It overpowers me in the most pleasant of ways.

"Sahira, I told you as a predator, I can sense emotions like fear and sorrow, and I can also smell hormones like arousal." He stills his hand. "Just the same, my body gives off a scent. As a witch, you can smell this."

"Yes, I understand that." Why's he dancing around a simple answer? "But what am I smelling? You're not baking Christmas Eve cookies!"

"Love, Lana," he blurts out. "I've been in love with you since the moment I met you, and I've tried so hard to withhold my scent, but it's just too overpowering, and I can't control it now. When I saw the vampire feeding off your limp body, I lost my mind, and all I saw was red. I almost lost you, Sahira, and it would've killed me if you died not knowing what's in my heart."

By the time he finishes speaking, I can hear anguish and despair take over his voice.

"I love you, Oz." I mean every word. He's like a drug I only meant to dabble in. I have fallen in head-and-heart-first, unable to escape ... because I don't want to. He consumes me in the best of ways.

I know, Sahira. Oz replies in my head. *I figured it out right before the assault when your scent changed when I touched you. I didn't want to say anything until you recognized what that feeling was. When I first realized you love me, too, I felt like the luckiest man alive. I wanted to take you and make you mine. I planned on telling you that night when I got back from feeding, but then everything changed. Every bone in my body told me I had to tell you, but I didn't want to do it when you were out of it.*

An array of emotions swirl in me. Grief over remembering what happened that night, love for Oz, and gratitude he loves me back. He grabs the conditioner and adds a large dollop to his hand before lathering it on my head and rinsing it off.

A chill sends goosebumps up my flesh, so Oz scoops me out of the tub and brings me to the bed. He dries me off before helping me into his sweatpants and t-shirt. A lot of my body has bruises, and the looser clothing is better. It's still morning, but I ask Oz to lie in bed with me and hold me. His cool body soothes my skin now that I'm dry.

"Oz, does it scare you we've fallen in love so fast?"

"No, my little dove." He kisses my head. "You are a witch, and I am a vampire, and we are doing what we do best: we feel. Our emotions help drive us. Never mind the humans who say you need to think with your head. Your intuition is the smartest thing you have, and your heart doesn't make a decision without consulting it first."

He's right. Ever since my witch powers have started, my emotions have been a little all over the place, and I've spent so much time denying my feelings. And when I listened to my head, I hesitated, and I nearly died because of it.

If I had run with my intuition, the vampire never would've been able to lay a finger on me. I would have used the powers I was born with to kill her, just as I was born with the ability to breathe. It's never something I have to think about. My body knows how to survive; it is my head that gets in the way.

"Does this have anything to do with why you won't sleep with me?"

"Because I'm in love with you." Oz trails his finger along my arm. "I won't be able to control marking you if we make love."

"Marking me?" I furrow my brows.

"It tells every creature and witch you ever come across you are mine, Sahira," he stills his hand. "Mated, for life. Think getting married, except the only escape is death."

It makes sense why he doesn't want to sleep with me. You've got to be sure you want to spend the rest of your life with someone, and it's hard to do if you've only known each other for a brief moment. I might be a terrible housekeeper, or don't want children. I could have a ton of debt, or a bad credit score. I could even be a serial killer with bodies buried in shallow graves across the world. One can never know.

"None of that matters to me, Lana. You don't have to clean because I have staff. If you have debt, I could pay it off, no matter the amount. Your credit score doesn't matter because I have more cash than you'll ever need. I've also killed people, so do you think it matters if you're a serial killer? And as far as children go, if you want them, then so do I."

Oz shares an image in my mind of me chasing around little ones, and I have a big round belly in front of me. I can't fight the warm curve of my lips at this sight.

"Mating with a vampire, especially one as old as me, doesn't come without risks. Many bad people in this world would give anything to hurt a powerful vampire like me, and they'd stop at nothing, including hurting my mate or anyone I've sired."

"I am not withholding sex for my benefit. It is for yours." He laces his fingers through mine. "If you told me you wanted to spend the rest of your life with me, I'd take you right here and now, Sahira." His eyes turn light blue at this prospect.

The idea of spending the rest of my life with Oz both excites and terrifies me. I love him, but my vanity worries about growing old. I will be old and wrinkly, and he will remain his flawless, otherworldly self. Lana Chapman-Sawyer will be but a blip on his infinite timeline, and maybe one day forgotten altogether after I'm long gone.

The air in the room shifts suddenly and becomes palpable. I can sense Oz is angry. When I look up at him, his eyes have turned black.

"I can never forget you, Sahira." He tries to contain his anger. "When you die, my life will be over."

I raise my hand and rest it on his cheek, and the air shifts again. His features soften, and his eyes return to a piercing blue. "Then I'll have to live forever." I remember I can learn how to become immortal in Bedlam. "Or you can make me a vampire."

"You are never becoming a vampire, Lana." His tone is firm. "We are blood-thirsty creatures who kill without hesitation, and I will never turn you into a monster."

"Then I must find a way to Bedlam, so we can live forever together. And for the record, I don't think you're a monster." I consider everything Oz shared with me this morning, and I still have questions. "You told me once you won't feed on me. Why?"

Oz kisses my knuckles. "If I feed on you, I'm afraid I may not control myself, and I can never risk it. After having almost lost you, it is a risk I'm not willing to take."

"You told me yourself you're an ancient, powerful vampire. Let's say you could control yourself. What would it be like for me? Would it hurt like when Mayim-Willow took my blood?"

"When a vampire takes blood from its mate, it's never at the neck. It is on a thoracic vein on your breast. I would know every single secret you have, and there would be no hiding anything from me. It is the most intimate experience you could ever have with a vampire. Most often, this occurs while making love."

"Have you ever had a mate?" The question alone sends a jolt of pain to my chest. "As a vampire, I mean?"

"No. I have never taken a mate."

I consider this a moment. "Why would you deny me the experience of having you feed from me? Isn't it my choice to make?"

He is quiet while he considers my objection. *Yes, Sahira. It is your choice*; he responds inside my head.

Then, when I'm healed, please take me, Oz. I want you to have me and mark me; everyone should know I am yours and you are mine for all eternity. I love you, Osgood Finlandian.

"I love you, Lana Chapman-Sawyer." Oz's voice is but a whisper, but I can sense a smile in it. "Nothing would make me happier."

I doze off in Oz's arms, thinking happy thoughts about what it will be like to call him mine.

～

Are you ever bored just watching me sleep?

Oz holds me and nuzzles against my hair. The lights are off outside the house, but a faint glow from the moon reflects on the snow now piled up along the windowsills. The crackle of the fireplace across from the bed comforts me.

"I said I don't need to sleep, not that I can't." He kisses my head. "Besides, your dreams keep me entertained for hours."

Of course, he can see my dreams if he's in my head! I have a moment of alarm, wondering what kinds of crazy, uninhibited things I've dreamed about since we've been together. Most dreams I don't remember, aside from one where I'm carried through the woods while dying and the person carrying me, glows. It is a dream I've had almost every night since I was a little girl.

"Before the attack, your dreams mostly comprised of us ..." Oz clears his throat. "Playing. Since then, though, you've had a lot of nightmares, and I try to influence them and steer them in a different direction. I haven't ever tried to do that before."

The rumbling of my stomach interrupts us, and I'm happy my appetite is back.

Oz kisses me on my forehead and heads downstairs to start on supper. I stare into the fireplace for a bit before deciding to call Hannah. So much has happened since I've been home, and I have to figure out how to tell her. She's the most open-minded person I know;

she convinced me to sell everything to travel the world, didn't bat an eye when I told her I was swearing off all men and joining a female monastery, and when I decided the same evening maybe I wanted to date Bobby Leonard, she fully supported my decision.

After four rings, she picks up the phone.

"Lana! Hi!" She has a high-pitch voice. "Is he there? Tell me everything."

You wouldn't think this was the voice or personality of a thirty-something-year-old, but Hannah Mae Yeung is the most positive person in the world. Her enthusiasm and zest for life are infectious, and I clung to it when I went through the adoption process and the subsequent loss of my parents as an adult.

"Hey Hanalei." I refer to the nickname I gave her when we were kids. We were obsessed with Puff the Magic Dragon then. "I'm actually in Mont-Tremblant with him now." It is so good to listen to her voice, but I hesitate. She might worry when I tell her everything that happened here.

"You're in ... Canada? Are you skiing?"

"Not skiing; we took a road trip after we were in Salem."

"Wow, that sounds like fun."

"Yes, it was. We took his jet to Salem so his friend could help us figure out who might've sent the package to you."

She is quiet for a moment. "Did you say his jet?"

"Yeah, Hann, I did. I have so much to tell you."

"I'll say! So, shoot. Tell me everything. I just got CJ some supper, so I've got time."

I start from the top; meeting Oz, the private jet, going to Salem, finding out I'm a witch, the road trip, vampires, almost dying, surgeries, and how Oz had to put a catheter in me.

"My God, Lana. I'm so glad you're okay." I knew she'd believe me and wouldn't judge. "But ... did you just say you're a witch? And he's a vampire?"

I'm quiet, and that's all the answer she needs. She knows I'd never lie to her.

"Jesus Christ,"' she breathes. Over and over again, she repeats herself. First, an exclamation, then a question, then resounding defeat. "This explains so much."

"It does?"

"You win everything, Lana! You know when the phone is about to ring. You knew what you'd find when you heard Ross in the other room."

My breath hitches and I wince. "Yeah," I whisper.

"You know I have some questions for Oz."

"Alright."

He must've heard our conversation, because he pads into the room with his hand out to take the cell.

"Hello, Miss Yeung."

I don't hear her side of the conversation, and I try to glean what they're talking about based on his responses to their discussion. "Sorry, Hannah. Yes, the security company notified me immediately once they tripped the alarm. I came here as fast as I could. I do, more than anything. That is the plan. I'd love that, thank you. I'll have Lana give you my number. No, never. Understood."

When they finish, he hands the phone back to me, and I eye him while I say goodbye to Hannah and tell her I love and miss them both.

"I can gather she asked you about the security alarm from the night the vampire attacked me, but what about the rest of the conversation?"

"Hannah asked if I love you. She's going to help me with something, so I'll need you to text her my number. She asked if I planned on turning you. And she said she'd spend the rest of her life hunting me down if I ever hurt you." He has an amused grin on his face.

I chuckle at this shocking show of aggression from her. She's a tall, thin woman, but I bet she could still kick my ass despite my having a good forty pounds on her. That she threatened a five and a half thousand-year-old vampire who is at least 6'4" and two hundred and forty pounds of solid muscle amuses me, though, and apparently, it amuses Oz, too. She's seen me go through my fair share of heartbreaks, so perhaps it's why she's so protective of me now.

After texting Hannah Oz's phone number, she responds with two texts:

I love him.

Be safe!

I shake my head and put my phone back on the nightstand.

"She took that ... remarkably well."

I shrug. "That's Hannah for you. She's something else."

Oz disappears downstairs for a while and brings a large tray holding two bowls of chili, oyster crackers, and several cornbread muffins. I glance at the King-sized white duvet cover on the bed and then suggest we move to the small table near the window.

Good idea, he says in my head. He helps me out of bed, and I decide to go to the bathroom since I'm up. I'm putting less weight on him tonight, but I still need a lot of help.

I sit on the toilet for several minutes, and Oz asks if I'm doing alright from outside the door. "Uh yeah, it ... burns. I'm trying to pee."

"Yeah, sorry. It will be like that for a few days. I had patients who said having a catheter made it difficult for them to find the 'button' to pee although though they had to."

"That's exactly what it's like. I can't find the damn button, but I need to!"

This conversation has taken our relationship to a whole new level. If he can still love me through this, we can face anything together. After sitting here a while, I finally figure out how to pee, and I'm able to hobble over to the sink and wash my hands myself.

He scolds me once I reach the door.

"I wanted to keep whatever little dignity I have left, Oz."

He helps me to the table. Little does he know I'm determined to heal sooner rather than later.

While he and I finish supper, I ask him more about his life. How many times has he been to school? What are his favorite foods? How'd he learn to make wine? What motivates him?

"I've been a student all my life, but only formally occasionally, like when I went to med school. I didn't see the point in a lot, considering I lived through most of civilized history and have read far more books on about every subject under the sun. It was entertaining hearing the theories they teach at university, but it was hard to hold back when they got it wrong. I love pasta, cheese, bloody steak, and fruit. Wine was one of the first things I ever learned how to make in Sumer. My father taught me."

He takes a sip from his glass. "And as far as what motivates me, that's a good question. My motivations have changed over the years. When I was younger, I wanted to be powerful and wealthy. Now I'm both, and for thousands of years, I've been in search of something missing, and I never knew what it was until I found you."

Butterflies soar in my belly, and I can't help but tear up. "I'm certainly not as old as you, but all my time in foster care, I just wanted a family to love me. When that was taken from me, I started traveling in search of something missing too. I didn't feel like I had a home, and so I spent so much time going from hostel to hostel, hotel room to hotel room, wandering aimlessly; wherever the wind, or a flight deal, could take me. I did these crazy things to feel something." Using my sleeve, I wipe tears away. "Then, in a matter of days, the entire trajectory of my life changed when I got the Ebbswick key and went in search of clues where I might find my mom. I think everything we went through in life brought us to this very moment, Oz."

Oz pushes his chair back and stands up, and I do so, too. He's at my side to help me, but I tell him I want to try walking to the bed myself. I want to gain my strength, and that won't happen if I don't try. He holds my hand rather than taking my arm so I can walk. There's still some pain in my leg, but there is an itch where the spell works to repair all the damage. I hope by tomorrow evening, I will be near total recovery.

Once I reach the bed, he helps swing my legs into it. After covering me with the duvet, he clears the table and brings back some macarons we still have from Salem.

We enjoy these in bed together. Oz always eats the witches, and I always enjoy the vampire bite macarons. I sense love when I'm with

Oz most of the time now, and I ask him what I smelled like when he realized I was in love with him.

"It's still vanilla and peaches, but now you also smell like home." He traces his finger along the curve of my arm. "In Sumer, sometimes we would make mead, and we got our honey from bees next to a cardamom field. This would make the mead have notes of cardamom, and that's what you smell like now. Vanilla, peaches, honey, and cardamom."

This is all so fascinating, and I love when he tells me about Sumer. I think a lot about what he was like back then and all he went through to become the man he is now.

"Oz, how come you know so much about magic?"

He takes a deep breath before answering, and I tense up. "I used to be a witch, Sahira."

My mouth gapes, and I stare out at the moon outside the window and follow the snow falling down, unsure of what to do with this news.

Oz, a witch.

A huge part of me wants to know what happened and why, but I don't want to pry. At least his mom had to have been a witch for him to be one. But who turned him into a vampire, and why? Was he in the wrong place at the wrong time?

"I'll tell you the full story of how I became a vampire. After all these years, I still have a hard time articulating it, so please bear with me." He looks down at the duvet covering me. "A time-traveling witch killed my wife and son."

The look in Oz's eyes holds so much pain. When I rest my hand on his cheek to comfort him, he blinks, spilling bloody tears out of his eyes and onto the white duvet. He has known so much heartache; I cannot imagine losing my spouse and child, and it would tear me in two.

"It did," Oz responds to my thoughts. "I lost my mind and ended up killing the witch in revenge. When she didn't return to her timeline, her husband sent his time-traveling sister to Sumaria to find out what happened to his wife. She found out I killed that witch, and she consulted with the Edimmu to mete her revenge."

"The Edimmu? Is that like a deity or something?"

"People now believe he was a vampire, but he wasn't. He was a demon, and the witch sold her soul to him. In exchange, he made me what I am today: a vampire." He turns his head away from me, and the anguish on his face kills me.

Were you ... the first vampire? Is this why all those Sumerian statues have blue eyes?

He drops his head. "Yes. I spent at least a hundred years after becoming a vampire either killing people in a blood-lust or turning them into vampires. No one could guide me; I'm directly or indirectly responsible for the death of millions, Sahira," he chokes out through tears. "This is something that haunts me every day of my life. And until recently, it consumed my every thought."

I swallow but I can't keep the bile from rising to my throat at the scenes I envision in my head: Oz raiding villages full of innocents, leaving nothing but death in his wake, and oh gods ... *children.* Nausea roils through me, and tears pour down my cheeks.

Oz's face contorts with grief, and he pulls back from me before turning his head away. I reach out a trembling hand to his shoulder and he meets my eyes.

"I never should've shared that with you."

I shake my head in anger. He's been alive for five and a half thousand years, most of which he has shouldered the burden of every death at the hands of every vampire. No one person should ever carry that kind of responsibility. My heart bleeds for him, and I try to find the words to comfort him, but they escape me. What he did was *terrible,* and I know he had no control over it, but the facts don't make the gravity of what happened any easier to swallow.

I know he will never turn me for this very reason. Together, we both cry fits of sobs until we both fall asleep holding each other.

CHAPTER NINE

"*D*o you want to share who came to the chateau today?" My fingers dance along his arm, and I take pleasure in the goosebumps that follow.

No. Oz's sly grin disarms me.

Osgood Finlandian, are you up to no good?

He simply pulls his lip between his teeth, and the room fills with the scent of sugar cookies. "You're adorable when you're told 'no,' Sahira."

"I love you, even when you're hiding something from me."

"I love you, too."

I kiss Oz and remind him I'm almost healed. His eyes shift to a light blue, and I catch a hint of spiciness in his scent. His fingers trace along my collarbone, and his erection grows below me.

"I know, my love." His voice is thick and silky now. "I've been waiting patiently. Slowly counting down the days, hours, and minutes. I can see the network of your life source working on knitting your wounds closed."

"You can?"

"It was one of the many skills I had as a witch. I've been able to keep most of my witch abilities through the years. Some abilities died out over time as I used them less and less. I still have my mother's grimoire, though, and it has some ancient spells I've forgotten. It isn't like any you'd have nowadays, and it was on a tablet."

"Your mom had an iPad? Was she a time traveler?"

Oz lets out such contagious laughter I can't help but laugh, too. "No, Sahira." He tries to stifle it with a smirk. "Like a cuneiform clay tablet."

I wince. That would make a lot more sense.

We continue talking about his life in Sumer until I'm cold. Oz puts some logs in the fireplace, and it doesn't take long before I'm warm again. That will take some getting used to, but I imagine having a vampire around during the summer is an enormous asset. I would've loved to have had him with me in the Amazon.

"Lana, there is something we need to talk about."

My stomach drops and I think about all the terrible things he needs to tell me. I'm wondering if he is going to tell me he's thought it over and I'm not quite cut out for being his mate. I panic inside when I think of him leaving me.

Hey now, Sahira. None of that nonsense. He gives my hand a reassuring squeeze. "Do you want children?"

Not only can I smell his affection for me, but I can feel it, too.

"Oh ... ah ... okay. Yeah, we need to discuss that." This caught me off guard, partially because I wasn't sure if Oz could have kids. I mean, he's not alive, right? Can vampires and witches have babies together? I'm also thirty-four, which is on the older end of my child-rearing days, so that further complicates things.

"Vampires can't produce children. But, because I was a witch before I became a vampire, I can. It's pretty rare for a witch to be turned, but because I was the first vampire, I didn't know what happened until it was too late. You're not on birth control, otherwise I'd sense the chemicals it emits in your body. You don't need to decide now about children unless you want one now. Pharmacies are closed because of the weather, and I figure you'd want us to enjoy each other before it clears."

I take a deep breath as I consider what he's asked me. Me, a mother. Wow. Okay. I can be a mother, right? Would I be a good one? Children are a tremendous amount of work. Although, the idea of growing and nurturing a baby he and I can then raise together? It would be an incredible honor to give Oz a baby.

"I'm pretty sure I want a baby with you. But I think I'm going to need some time to mull the decision over." My head spins at the thought of becoming a mother. A memory of my mom French braiding my hair sneaks its way in, and a bittersweet pang spills into my chest.

"Absolutely, I'm only asking because we'll need to take precautions if you don't want to get pregnant now. In the meantime, I'll make you herbal birth control tea. You only have to drink a cup of it a day. I thought I should also let you know as a vampire, I can't actually catch anything; I'm clean."

"Oh, uh, thank you for letting me know." I have a mini internal panic attack trying to remember when my last test was, and if I had any sexual encounters since then.

Oz bares his teeth. "You're clean, too, not that it would matter, considering I can't catch anything."

"Well, that is a relief, I suppose." I don't even want to ask how he knows that.

It leads me to think of all the mistakes I've slept with; not a single one was worth it. The men always treated me like just another hookup and were selfish in bed. Zero foreplay, and as soon as I met their needs, they were content to quit. And then, there was Ross ... my chest clenches at the memory.

"Lana, there is no way for you to change the past. What's important is we're together now, and I will spend the rest of my life loving only you, and whatever children we bring into this world—if that is what you decide." He runs his hand along my curls.

"How many vampires have you sired who are alive now?"

"Oh, there are lots. Thousands, but few who keep in contact with me. They have their own families. The ones I sired in the beginning aren't around anymore, aside from a few, but over time, I created vampires with a lot more care. It is very rare for me to turn anybody; I learned a long time ago sometimes, we need to let nature take its course. You've met Wren Highlandburg, who was our pilot. You've also met Maeve and Pippa Imperialus. Then there is Gideon Cathal ... and Auguste Grey. They are part of my court. If anything should ever happen to me, you can trust them implicitly. They will keep you safe from all harm."

"I suppose that makes sense. Who are Auguste and Gideon again?" I remember him mentioning the latter, but not the first one.

"Gideon handles a lot of our family's affairs. Financials, properties, records, antiquities, passports, name changes, etcetera. His expertise is invaluable; he helps keep track of our family's name changes and locations, too. He's the best tracker in the world. Auguste can do a lot of that, too, but mostly focuses on security."

Wow. That has got to take a lot of careful planning and maneuvering to keep everything straight. *I'd love to meet them.*

"We will meet with them soon enough, don't you worry," he replies to my thoughts.

The irony I spent most of my life desperately wanting a family, only to have one thrown in my lap, doesn't escape me. I'm a little nervous about whether they'll like me, considering I'm a witch and all. Oz reassures me they'll love me, and I smile, still unsure of myself.

THE FIRST SPELL Oz teaches me helps guard my mind against intruders, as well as from myself. The simple spell involves me mentally building a house inside my head out of bricks. When there are things I'd rather not think about, I place those thoughts in a safe in the house's basement. He says this will help keep me from having such vivid nightmares and flashbacks of my assault.

Oz warns there will be no way to keep him out once he feeds from me, even if I build a house and keep the door locked.

"When we mate, our bond is irreversible. Because you're a witch, I will have no secrets from you, either. You will know every terrible thing I've ever done, and I share my burden with you. Are you certain this is a commitment you're willing to make?"

"Yes, I am." I have zero doubt in my mind Oz and I are meant to be together. The idea of knowing everything and not having secrets between us chips away the ice I've spent years building around my heart. Trust was always a big issue in previous relationships, and I've had my fair share of heartache after men have cheated and lied.

I work to build a house inside my mind to test out the spell, and I ask him to guess what I'm thinking. His eyes are light blue when he says, "You're thinking about sleeping with me, which you've thought about damn near the entire time we've known each other."

"Damn! I thought this house-building business would be easy."

"Try to think about the finer details of your house after you've put the bricks in place; the way the sun penetrates the living room, with shimmering dust particles dancing in its beams. Or how the house expands and contracts with the changing pressure of the weather."

Within the confines of my mind, I am standing in the middle of my living room. The white curtains flop thanks to the ceiling fan humming above. I smell the waft from sugar cookies baking in the oven, and suddenly a knock sounds on the large wooden door.

I peer outside the tall, thin window next to the door frame. Oz is outside, asking to be let in. While I mosey away from the door, the phone rings on the end table next to the sofa. I glance at the caller ID: Oz.

I answer the phone to Oz's smooth voice. "You did very well, my love." After, I lower the walls in my mind and come back to the present. I'm giddy enough to throw my arms around Oz and give him a big kiss. He laughs and says it was weird not hearing my thoughts after hearing them nonstop for weeks now.

"Does this mean I'll be able to keep out everyone else, though?"

"I don't know about any other mind readers, other than some royal fae in Bedlam, so I'm not sure you can keep them out. They're strong." He tells me to build the basement and the safe for my assault. Handling these thoughts in my mind causes me a bit of anxiety while I view the flashback, but before long, I have them tucked away safely into the dark recesses of the basement's safe. I use my gem-encrusted Ebbswick key in my mind to lock the memories away before retreating up the steep wooden stairs to the first floor. I lock the door behind my memories in the basement and return to the present.

I nod at Oz as though to tell him, "Mission accomplished." Together, we walk hand-in-hand to the foyer, and I look up to where Mayim-Willow dangled me by my ankle. The house in my mind vibrates. As we slowly climb the stairs to the top of the landing, memories slam against the insides of the safe in my mind's basement, threatening to break free.

"You are safe for as long as I am with you." We make our way down the hallway and to the bedroom I was in when the vampire yanked me out of bed and threw me against the wall like a rag doll. By the time we reach the bed, the memories in the basement have gone quiet. I breathe a deep sigh of relief and wrap my arms around Oz's neck.

Despite the flurry of snow, brilliant orange, yellow, and red beams pour in the balcony door and interrupt our quiet celebration. He grabs the thick duvet off the bed and wraps me up before opening the door so we can view the blizzard from the balcony. He picks me up, covers and all, and carries me outside. Snowflakes fall on my cheeks and instantly melt, and I laugh when Oz has to keep dusting his away.

You might've noticed, snow is a pain in the ass for me as a vampire; the flakes just won't melt, he says in my mind.

I rest my head on Oz's chest, and we observe the ancient ceremonial exchange between sun and moon. This is but one of the greatest love stories of all time:

I will die for you tonight so you may live until morning.

Love is a lot like that. We each make sacrifices and compromises to keep each other happy. With any luck, people who spend their entire lives searching for love find their soulmate, like Oz and I have.

After our time outside, we retreat to the kitchen. Oz shows me how to make a healing elixir to be used with the spell already at work in my body. The elixir glows, and the flask hums as I palm the liquid in my hand. I glance at him, and he assures me the vibration is perfectly normal. I swallow the contents in their entirety, and the liquid tingles on my tongue and down my throat. Butterflies take over my belly, and then they disperse towards the still injured parts of my body, flapping their wings and encouraging the spell to knit faster.

I'm amazed I can see the injuries heal in real-time, thanks to my third eye. As soon as my body stitches its last injury, I grin.

"I'm ready." I drag Oz towards the foyer so we can go upstairs. I don't have to encourage him at all, and instead, he scoops me into his arms, and we're in our new bedroom within seconds.

CHAPTER TEN

My heart races both from the speed at which we arrive at our bedroom and for what we're about to do. We've waited for this moment for a long time.

Using my magic, I shut the door behind us, and Oz slows his approach towards the bed as though he's trying to savor the moment. He shows incredible restraint while he places me on the plush covers, his eyes wild with anticipation of what's to come.

I sit up to remove my shirt, but he shakes his head. Instead, he slowly removes it for me, revealing the new black lily lace demi bra we got in Montreal.

He bites his lower lip as his eyes admire my body. The sight of his fangs elongating while his eyes feast on my form turns me on. With my help, we pull off his shirt, and I run my hands through the dark hair on his chest before tracing the scar on his rib cage.

I sit up and kiss the key before Oz lays me back down so he can slide my leggings off. I lift my hips, and he purrs when he sees my matching black lily lace panties. He lays next to me and wraps his leg over mine so he can run his finger along the curves of my body, giving me goosebumps. My heart gallops in my chest.

I turn towards him so I can unbutton his jeans. The belt is thick, so

I have a hard time, but this gives more opportunities for him to kiss me. I have to use two hands to undo the button to his jeans, and my heart beats even faster when I unzip his zipper.

Oz pounces on top of me and grabs my wrists as if to say, stay put. I pin him with my gaze, breathing heavy in anticipation. He hitches his thumbs in the loops of his jeans and slides them over his butt, taking his silk boxers with them. He slides out of his jeans and boxers, and I grip his sex in front of me.

Oz grabs my wrists again, this time with one hand, and holds them in place. He kisses me deeply, and I want to touch him, but I can't. The weight of his body on mine makes me ache for him.

When I keep my arms in place, he flips me over to be on my stomach, which sends the pillows falling to the floor. One by one, he unhooks each of the three clasps holding my bra in place. I writhe, trying to arch into him. He bends over and plants kisses along my bare back before reaching my panties, and occasionally his stiff cock brushes against the back of my legs.

As though I weigh nothing, Oz slides one hand over my hip, and I think he's going down the front of my panties, but instead, he flips me again so I am on my back. His fingers run under the band of my panties to tease me, and grips the lace with his teeth. He uses these to pull the panties off, and I'm left exposed for his eyes to take in.

Oz grabs both of my heels with his hands, causing my knees to bend. One hand slides up my calf so his fingers rest on my knee while the others part my legs. He trails down the length of my inner thigh until reaching my soft mound. He moves in closer, and I'm overpowered by the scent of static electricity and spice of him.

With one finger he wets with his mouth, he traces the outline of my outer folds. I move my hips to arch closer. He places the finger in my opening, and I let out a quiet moan. I am so wet for him already; he can add another finger. His movements are slow and deliberate, relishing the pleasure on my face while his fingers work to conquer me. I whimper softly, and Oz lets out a quiet, hungry growl before kissing my heat.

He kisses my pleasure again before parting my lips with his

tongue. Both his tongue and his fingers send me just to the brink, and I beg him to keep going. He keeps his fingers in place and positions himself so he now has one arm wrapped around my waist to bring me in closer. I'm so close to climaxing now, and he watches my face as I contort in pleasure.

Sahira, he says in my head. I will take you now if you let me.

I am on the edge now, and he slows his fingers so I don't climax. My body craves release and I beg him to take me.

Have me. I am yours, and you are mine.

Oz pulls his fingers out and grabs his shaft so he can guide his velvet length to my opening. He rubs himself against my swollen lips, and I arch my pelvis to move closer. The head of his penis presses against my opening until she gives way, granting him safe passage. We both let out a moan as his sex plunges into me and my core stretches and fills.

He rocks his hips slowly until he is sure I can handle his size. I hitch my leg so my heel rests against his buttocks, pulling him in to loosen the tension; beckoning him to go faster. His thrusts pick up speed, and he positions me so I'm sitting in his lap with my legs wrapped around his waist. I'm sweaty now, and my thighs glide over the tops of his easily. His arms wrap around my waist completely, gripping me tighter with each thrust of his hips.

Right when I'm about to climax, Oz slows down, bringing me back from the brink. He doesn't want me to release yet. In one smooth movement, he hooks his arms underneath my legs so he can control our speed. He glides slowly in and out of me while resting his head against my chest. He unhooks one arm so he can caress my breast, and I let out a purr at the attention. I'm lost in pleasure when his lips press at the curve of my breast.

Please.

A brief stab of pain clutches my chest when Oz sinks his teeth into my flesh. Immediately following the pain, waves of pleasure so intense I weep consume me.

I have an overwhelming sense of love for this man. I would give my life for him. We are but one flesh, two sides of the same coin. A tight tether binds us together, settling in my bones, and granting me immeasurable bliss.

I ride the wave of ecstasy until the euphoria crescendos, and I have my release. Every secret I carry pours out of my body and into his, and every one of his comes to me. The pleasure overtakes us both now, and Oz moans as he spills his seed in me. His hips pulse until we both collapse into each other, satisfied.

We remain entangled, neither one of us wanting to move so we don't break the overwhelming sense of love and passion between us. When my breathing returns to normal, Oz strokes the long, dark strands of my hair.

"I love you, Sahira, and now, everyone will know you are mine, and I am yours."

"I love you, Osgood Finlandian," I lean into his kiss.

At first, I was afraid of knowing every one of his secrets, but now I do, I'm grateful. Everything he holds in his head has made him the man he is today. I love him more now there is nothing between us. When I downloaded Oz's secrets into my mind, there were so many my brain worked frantically to categorize and rearrange them.

"I think we should spend the weekend here before we go to Iowa. We're getting another snowstorm tomorrow, but by Monday every-thing should be clear."

"That sounds good to me. I'm so grateful to you, Oz. Not sure what we're going to find in Iowa, but the fact you're willing to help me look means the world to me."

"Lana, I would yank Hades out of hell if it meant something to you."

Now who's being dramatic, I say to him in my mind while I give him a peck on the nose.

My body is tired, so I pull some pajamas out of the armoire for both of us, and we dress for bed. After I return from brushing my teeth in the bathroom, Oz asks me to come over to the balcony door. The moon takes up most of the horizon, and he pulls me into his arms so I can rest my head on his chest. I'm so engrossed in the moon I'm not aware of him pulling away from me.

Emotion pummels me from all directions, and the air is as though I walked right into a cookie factory. Smiling, I turn towards Oz and realize he is down on one knee.

"Lana Chapman-Sawyer, you are the love of my life, my far better half, and my mate for all eternity. Will you do me the honor of also becoming my wife?"

I imagine the look on my face is that of an ugly cry when I answer him. "Yes!"

My hand trembles while he slides the ring on my finger, and an electric spark jolts my finger. Oz takes my hands in his to steady them before kissing me deeply, and when I come up for air, I am smiling through the tears pouring down my face.

"Will I be a Finlandian? Or do we pick our new names?"

"Foremost, you will be an Ankida. That is the first last name I ever chose, and you are always under the protection my name bestows. However, if you'd like to pick another name to use, we can do that. Know you're always an Ankida—it means where heaven and earth meet. That is how I think about home."

I shake my head no. I want your name, Oz.

He presses his lips to mine and smiles against them before pulling back. "My full, original name is Enlil Ankida. Enlil essentially means "storm god.' Don't worry, though, I'm not the penal god notorious for destruction, and I never married a goddess—until I bound myself to you."

He gives me a sly grin.

You trying to butter me up?

His eyes go half-lidded.

He scoops me up and takes me to bed, where we settle underneath the covers. I can hardly believe I'm engaged. And *mated*.

I sit up and reach for my phone on the nightstand. *I've got to tell Hannah we're engaged.*

"She already knows," he grins. "I asked for her help with the ring and told her I planned on proposing. She helped me work with a jeweler in town to create this ring for you. That's who came to the door."

I hold up my hand and admire the gold ring. The center stone is oval-shaped and is a brilliant deep blue gemstone. On the outside of the center stone are diamonds and red gemstones, and the red gems look a lot like the ones I have on my Ebbswick key. This must've cost a fortune.

This was my mother's ring. Hannah helped me make her ring a little more modern.

Hannah was always great at design, which is why she opened a flower shop.

"The center stone is a lapis lazuli, which was most prized in Sumer, even above gold. People believe the stone helps bridge a connection between the physical and celestial planes. I thought it fitting, considering you're a witch, and I'm a vampire. Lapis lazuli is also supposed to aid in protection and give connection to spiritual realms. The red gemstones are carnelian." He gives my hand a squeeze. "Hannah had me add diamonds to keep up with modern tradition."

"This ring is so beautiful, Oz." I can't stop staring at my hand. "I am so honored to wear your mother's ring, and I promise to be worthy of it."

He wraps me in his arms and pulls me tight against him.

You are worthy.

CHAPTER ELEVEN

"We don't have to rush things, but I'd love to get married before Bedlam. Just in case you change your mind when you see it and decide not to come back."

Wait a minute, I panic, eyes wild. "You're not coming with me to Bedlam?"

He tucks a dark curl behind my ear before holding my hand to his chest. "I can't, Sahira." There is sorrow in his voice.

Oz sits up, takes off his shirt and places my hand on the scar on his rib cage. *This. This is why I can't.*

Using the back of my other hand, I wipe tears away from my eyes. "I don't understand!"

"I told you to gain entrance to Bedlam, you need three things:

A grimoire

A Bedlam Moon

An Ebbswick key

When I became a vampire, my Ebbswick key burned itself into my skin. I'm neither here nor there, Lana. Without a key, I can't get in."

Tears still spilling down my cheeks, I grab his hand. *This isn't fair.* He's been robbed of so many opportunities because of vampirism. I'm distraught I have to go to Bedlam without Oz.

On one hand, I want to go there so I can learn how to live forever, so I can be with him for all eternity. To go to Bedlam, I have to leave him. I don't know how long it will take me to learn what I need, but I'm a novice at magic, and some witches never return. What if I return from Bedlam, and he's moved on?

Tears spill over my eyes and down my face like a torrent from a broken dam. They consume me, and I am drowning in my grief; lost of all hope.

Please make me a vampire, Oz. I cannot leave you; I beg in a moment of clarity and promise.

"Sahira. I love you more than anything, but I can't make you a monster." Tears gather in his eyes. "I cannot destroy the best part of me, which is you. I will wait for you, and you will come back to me. There isn't a doubt in my mind about it."

He holds me as I weep. Profound grief crushes my chest, and it's as though the darkness closes in on me.

Oz hums Somewhere Over the Rainbow to me. My mom used to sing this to me when I was sad, and it has an instant soothing effect.

I wake several hours later. He holds me still, stroking my hair. My eyes swell from crying so hard and a rumble in my stomach demands sustenance. We haven't eaten yet.

Let me feed you, I say in my head as I drag Oz out of bed. I've always been a comfort eater, which explains why I'm not thin despite being active.

He is more attentive than usual, no doubt because of how badly I'm hurting. He has complete confidence in my returning from Bedlam. I'll face all kinds of trials, and the thought I might not make it back is difficult to think about.

I decide to make chicken and dumpling soup, which is one of the very first recipes my mom taught me as a kid. Oz chops the carrots, celery, garlic, and onions while I work on searing the chicken before placing the ingredients in an enameled Dutch oven of salty water. My eyes burn from the onions he's chopping, so I open a window above the kitchen sink to let in some air. The air is chilly, but it's a welcome respite from the warmth of the stove.

Oz eyes me while I add the chopped vegetables to a cast iron pan with flour, butter, and sage. I have him shake the pan for me—my wrists are no match for the heavy cast-iron pans in this kitchen. Once the vegetables have flour, I add chopped thyme, salt, and pepper to season the roux.

"Sahira, do you understand why this comforts you?"

I shrug. "My mom used to make it for me."

"To an extent, yes. But your mother was teaching you magic."

I pause what I'm doing to look at him.

"Thyme, for wisdom and bravery. Salt for protection. Sage, to aid in sleep and letting go of anxiety." He picks up a leaf. "And let me guess, you're going to make the dumpling dough with flour and ... lemon olive oil? Or heavy cream and lemon balm?"

"Actually, I will steep lemon balm in evaporated milk for a few minutes ..."

He inclines his head. "Lemon balm, for peace." He picks up the wooden spoon and stirs the food for me. "I watched you add each of these ingredients, and you circled your hand above the pan three times clockwise with every element of your recipe. I thought it was just a fluke at first, but then you kept at it with the rest of the recipe."

The sudden revelation my mom taught me magic sends a chill up my spine. This is the first real concrete proof I have she was a witch. Why didn't she tell me we were witches?

Oz approaches me from behind and wraps his arms around my waist to comfort me. *Whatever her reason for not telling you, Sahira, we will figure it out together.*

"No wonder she made this every time I was sad. It always made me better because of magic!"

I ponder what other magic my mom taught me without my knowing. All the tiny little rituals I do throughout my day—do they have a deeper meaning?

"If we can find your family grimoire, it will answer a lot of our questions."

"DHS moved me around to so many foster homes. Once I was with the Sawyers, I had very little of my own things left." I drag a stool over to the stove and sit on it. "They were so good to me, the Sawyers. I didn't want for anything, and the inheritance they left me allowed me to travel the world. Mom and Dad Sawyer would've loved you."

I'm sorry they can't be here, Sahira. They sound like they were great people.

"We have to find out what happened to my mom, Oz. Do you think she went to Bedlam? I can't believe she would have, but I can't rule it out."

Possibly, but we can't figure it out without you going there yourself. No matter how much I want to keep you here with me, we have yet another reason you have to go. His eyes water at the very thought of me leaving for Bedlam.

Whatever the reason, even if it's the last thing I do, we'll find out what happened to her, Sahira, Oz says in my head.

Instead of eating at the table, we take our meal to the living room on the other side of the foyer. Comfort food calls for fireplaces, so Oz builds a fire. He pulls the square coffee table close to the hearth so we can set our food on it and sit on the rug in front of the fireplace.

As soon as I eat the chicken and dumpling soup, calm seeps into my bones. While I don't like the idea of leaving Oz, the benefit of going to Bedlam is far too great to pass up. I will be with Oz for all eternity, and perhaps my mom *is* there. If she is, I can convince her to come back here.

"Oz, do you think we can take a picture together?" I'm afraid of what his answer might be. Early in my twenties, I asked a guy I was dating to take a picture with me. You would've thought I asked him to marry me with how fast he moved away from me. It wasn't until he ghosted me that I realized he was seeing someone else and didn't want photographic evidence.

"Of course, we can take pictures together." He tucks a curl behind my ear. "I'd love to."

I think about what outfit I want to wear for pictures, and how I want my hair and makeup. Oz interrupts my thoughts. *We'll have plenty of time for those kinds of pictures later.* I look at him, puzzled. He leans in and his lips brush my ear when he speaks. "I want to take pictures with you when your hair is wild, your eyes, satisfied; and your skin glowing."

An intense rush of both sugar cookies and spice invades my senses, and I know exactly what he means as he slides the coffee table away from us.

CHAPTER TWELVE

*O*z informs the staff about what happened while they were away and when I come downstairs, he introduces me to them. There are many vampires and witches among the staff, as well as a few humans; the witches and vampires are very kind to me, but they avoid eye contact.

We're both marked, Sahira. None of them want to risk making it look as though they want to bed you when I'm around. The mark is very strong the first couple of days—they won't always avert their eyes.

I didn't realize how obvious it was to everyone else Oz had marked me. While we've been near-inseparable since meeting, it's like there's a cord between us now we're mated; we're but two lovers, orbiting each other thanks to some gravitational pull so strong, nothing can divide us. My eyes constantly seek him out, and my heart longs for him to be near.

Oz gives the head of staff our rental car keys from our road trip, and they gather our things and take it to the car waiting out front.

When we climb the stairs to the jet, Wren greets us at the door. His eyes bulge when he sees me, but he says nothing and diverts his eyes.

He knows, doesn't he?

He does now. Oz gives my hand a squeeze.

~

Tripoli is a sleepy Main Street town with a tiny creek running through it. We pass a visitor's center, a post office, city hall, and a pizza place before turning by the school. Next to the school is a gravel track with small stands for spectators. We're just a block away from the nursing home now, and the familiar buzzing sensation intensifies as we near the facility.

Oz parks the Audi in a parking space in front of the nursing home. Noticing my trembling hands, he opens my door for me and asks if I'm alright. I have a difficult time speaking, so I take his hand. Together, we strut through the front doors and the buzzing sensation takes over. Wisps of magic thread through the hallways, and we walk until we come to a four-way crossing.

They have set the nursing home up like a cross. The crossroads between all four sections is where the nurse's station is, but no staff are present. The nursing home is small, so they must be making their rounds. I sense exactly where we need to go.

I follow the gossamer of magic to the right, and it leads us to a resident's door marked Alphie Bennett.

It doesn't start with "D." Do we just go in? Or do we knock?

We'd better knock, just to be on the safe side. Oz does the honors, and a man yells for us to come in. The extra-wide door swings open, and across the room is a man wearing a flannel long-sleeved shirt, dark gray sweatpants, and fuzzy peach-colored hospital socks. He doesn't look old enough to be in a nursing home, although he is pretty frail. He is sitting in a brown recliner with his feet up. These magic wisps dance around his body and shimmer as he moves.

The handsome man must be in his late sixties, and he looks vaguely familiar, as though I knew him at some point in my life. His eyes are blue, and his hair is mostly gray.

Sahira, this man is related to you.

My heart races and butterflies churn in my stomach. I move closer to the stranger across from us, and he speaks.

"I've been waiting for you, Lana. I knew you'd come."

So, this is 'D.'

"Who are you?" I'm still trying to place where I know him from. He invites us to sit down on his bed next to his recliner, and we do.

"I'm your dad." He has a hint of regret in his voice.

"My dad?" I whisper, trying to blink back tears. Oz holds my trembling hand and tells me things will be okay. "I don't understand."

He gives me a sympathetic tilt of his head. "Gods, Lana. Had I known about you, not a thing in this realm could've stopped me from giving you the world. Are you happy?"

All the air escapes my lungs, and my tears come barreling down my face. I can't speak—emotion chokes me—so I nod instead.

"I'd love to hear about your life."

I take a deep breath before responding. "Tell me about my mom. Why would she keep me from you? Were you good to her?" I wrestled with these thoughts my entire life; why did she never tell me who my father was?

"I loved your mom dearly, Lana. I met her at the bowling alley in town. Her laugh captivated me. She had graduated from college, and I had been a farmer for quite a while." He takes off his glasses and puts them on his side table. "I didn't know I had gotten her pregnant. I tried to be the best man for her, and I thought I was. She lived with me right outside of town, and one day I came home and her stuff was gone. The only thing she left was a note and the key I sent you. Although, the note was a goodbye letter to me, and I don't think she meant to leave the key behind. I found that in a box under the bed."

I am in shock. I had hoped for news about my mom's whereabouts, but my *dad!* The recognition I saw in him were some of my own features.

"I only recently found out about you after I did an Ancestry DNA test. It said you were my child, Lana. So, I had help from the staff here to help me find your address. We couldn't find it, but they could find Hannah Yeung's address."

"There are so many questions. Where do I begin?" I fight back tears. "Thank you for giving me the key. I'm hoping I can use it to find my mom."

My dad looks sad and tells me he found the articles about her while they were trying to track me down. I'm grateful Hannah and I figured out my ancestry before I took off on my travels; the plan was to go to my ancestral roots. When I did that, I kept on traveling. I never imagined it would help me find my dad.

"I'm sorry I wasn't around." Tears spill from his eyes. "I wish she had told me. I wanted to marry your mom, and I still don't understand why she left. Not a day goes by I don't let the guilt consume me."

"I don't know either, but please don't feel bad." I try to reassure him. "Eventually, a wonderful couple in Minnesota adopted me. They were great for me. Unfortunately, they've since passed."

"I'm sorry to learn they died; I would've loved to thank them for taking care of my girl when I couldn't. I'd like to make up for lost time and get to know you and your husband."

"Oh, he's not my husband yet. We just got engaged." I fidget under his amused stare.

"Well, you're more than married in the eyes of a vampire, Lana." He has a wry grin. "I'm a witch, too. I knew he was a vampire the moment you two walked in."

Both my parents are witches! I am near giddy while I explain to my dad I didn't even know I was a witch until recently. In fact, it was the Ebbswick key that set in motion the recent discoveries of my roots.

"How long have you been here?" I refer to the nursing home.

"Just over a year now. I'm on hospice."

The air expels from my lungs, and I can't stop the tears from spilling down my cheeks. I've only just met my dad and now I'm going to lose him? If he's been on hospice for over a year, it is only a matter of time. More often than not, people go on hospice too late, rarely ever too early. I have so many questions, and an entire lifetime to make up for.

He puts his hand on mine and pulls me in for a hug. We hold each other for several minutes before letting go.

"How long?" I fear his answer.

"Six months ago. There are some maladies that can't be fixed whether or not you're a witch."

So, he's overdue. I ask if drinking vampire blood helps, and both he and Oz respond with a resounding 'no.'

I ask Oz in my head if he'd mind if I invite my dad to stay with us. He responds he'd love to have a relationship with my dad.

"Dad, how would you like to join Oz and me for Thanksgiving? You can spend the rest of the week with us in Dubuque at Oz's home, and we'd love to have you stay in our home—permanently. We can bring on a medical team to attend to your needs there." I won't have my dad alone for the holidays; he should be with family.

"I would love to, thank you." He pushes the call light attached to his chair. A CNA comes in a couple of minutes later and her eyes widen when she sees us sitting on his bed. When she realizes I'm the daughter they'd been looking for, she can't contain her joy. She pages the rest of the staff to come meet me and help us get my dad ready to come with us.

They wheel my dad out to the Audi and see us on our way. I sit in the back with my dad, and I am still so in shock we're together. We spend the entire two hours talking about our preferences in foods, TV shows, music, and movies. There are so many things he likes that I do, too. We were both never fans of goulash but loved my mom's chicken and dumpling soup. While his body is certainly failing him, his mind is sharp and witty.

He asks how Oz and I met, and I'm a little sheepish about explaining how recent it was. I tell him anyway, and he can sense the reluctance in my voice while I share the story with him.

"Nonsense, Lana. Witches and vampires, that is what we do; we feel. When the heart knows, the heart knows. Your mom and I were the same way. We met on a Friday night, and I'd moved her in by Tuesday morning. Actually, she just never left ... until she did." His voice quiets at the last part, and I know I need to find out what happened to my mom before he dies. He needs closure, just as I do.

～

"I'M WARNING YOU NOW, it can be a little rowdy with the family all under one roof." Oz looks back at us through the rear-view mirror.

"Nothing I can't handle; I once took in a group of fae for an entire summer."

I whip my head towards dad. "No way!"

He simply grins. "Back in my prime, I acted as an agricultural liaison for the new fae in the state; I taught them how to grow Earth food."

Wow. The fae. I don't think I've seen one, but Oz describes them as huge, ethereal creatures with superior strength and even more cunning personalities. They're who gave witches magic.

The scenery gets hilly once we're close to Dubuque. Oz turns into a wooded driveway just before the bluff, and we travel until we're at the top. The house has a Romanesque stone exterior with several gables across the front. I laugh when I think about how Oz said the house wasn't too big; sure, after spending time at the place in Mont-Tremblant, this place is small. But it is still quite large, as a lot of French colonial houses are.

A medical team greets my dad by the car and helps him into his wheelchair. They take him to his room so he can settle in.

Before we go inside, I wrap my arms around Oz and thank him. He has given me the best gift a girl can ever ask for—an opportunity to have a relationship with my dad. I spent so much of my childhood wondering what he looks like and whether he was even alive. And here, he didn't know about me. A small part of me has animosity towards my mother for leaving him in the dark and denying me the opportunity to have a father.

We all convene for supper around the dining room table. The staff made us chicken and wild rice soup, tea party sandwiches, and a large Mediterranean salad. The room is jovial when I ask my dad if he's done any traveling.

"The farm kept me pretty busy, but every once in a while, I'd travel to Europe or South America for a week at a time. It wasn't easy finding someone to look after things while I was away."

"Do you have a grimoire?" Perhaps if we had our family tree, Oz may recognize a name.

"I do, and you're welcome to have it, seeing how I won't be needing it soon."

I am both happy he has one, but also sad because he won't need it.

"You can find the grimoire upstairs in my room. I bring it everywhere with me. Never know when I might need it."

"Thank you, Dad. I wish we had more time together."

"Me, too, kiddo."

We move into the parlor to continue our conversation. "Do you remember the last thing my mom ever said to you?" I wonder if it would reveal any clues.

"I must've performed the Memorall spell six hundred times, trying to look for a reason she left."

"Memorall?"

"It's a spell that allows a witch to replay a scene from their past. Sometimes, our memories miss little details, and this spell helps us view it again."

"Do you think you can teach it to me? I want to re-live the scene when my mom left me at the cabin. Maybe I missed something."

"You might've missed something, honey, but are you sure you want to drag out those memories?" He takes a bite of his cookie. "They can be incredibly painful to relive, particularly with something so traumatizing. You were a little kid, and the Memorall spell isn't like watching a movie. You're actually reliving it as though you're experiencing it right then."

"I'm certain, Dad. Oz taught me how to guard my memories. I can always lock away the memory after we figure out what happened. Besides, because he can read my mind, I'll have an extra set of eyes on my memory as I relive it."

Oz interlaces my hand in his to reassure me. Although these men entered my life only recently, they are the most important men in my life. I'm so grateful to have them here.

My dad agrees and has me locate his grimoire in his room. The book isn't on his bed where he said it should be, though. I move the pillows, lift the sheets, and look under the mattress. I sandwich myself to the floor and shine my cell phone under the bed; not here either.

"Everything ok?"

I scoot out from under the bed and rest my elbows on my knees. "Babe, I don't know where it's at."

A small breeze flutters my hair and I stand and cross to the window. I quirk my head to the side and pull it shut. "Oz, why would dad leave his window open in these kinds of temperatures?"

"Let's go ask, I don't have a good feeling about this." I follow him down the stairs and into the dining room.

"Dad, did you leave the window open in your room?" Sure, he could've stood to open it, but it sticks and isn't very easy to do in his frail condition.

"No, honey, I didn't. Why?"

I look at Oz before turning my gaze back to Dad. "Your window was wide open when I went in there. You said your grimoire was on the bed in plain sight, but it's not there anymore. I think ... I think someone might've stolen your grimoire."

He eyes me over the rim of his glasses. "We can't let it get into the wrong hands. A grimoire has all of our spells, secrets, and list of magical abilities. Anyone looking to do our family harm can use it against us."

I quell my rising dread. "Okay." I pace the room. "You haven't been down here long, so whoever took it can't be far. I don't know if this will work, but I'm going to try. Can you explain what your book looks like?" One of the first things Oz taught me was how to do a homing spell after I lost my retainer I wear at night. I'm betting the spell will also work on dad's grimoire.

Dad nods. "There are loose scraps of paper sticking out from the book. It also has a deckle edge. Its cover is leather and obsidian in color, aside from the large golden honeybee in the center. As my blood daughter, you should feel a pull to it."

I close my eyes and envision what the grimoire looks like, how heavy it is, and the pull I feel when I'm near it. Instead of murky black behind my eyelids, the image of the book forms. Along with this vision is a man, clinging it to his chest while he darts his eyes around him. He's in a hurry when he sets his sights on a tall building ahead.

Surrounding the entire building is a shimmer of sorts, like a force field. My eyes fly open and I grab onto Oz's sleeve.

"I know where it's at!"

He shakes his head in warning. "Don't do it, Lana. It could be a trap."

"No, I see the trap ahead several blocks. I have to go now before he reaches the warded building. I'll snatch it from his hands and be back before he even knows what happened."

"No!"

"Trust me, please."

Oz hesitates, but I see his expression change the moment he decides, however reluctant. He squeezes his eyes and pulls me in for a chaste kiss. "Go."

In my mind, I work to build the city block in front of the thief. Snowflakes swirl in the air, and the wide streets provide little cover from the wind. Cars idle at the traffic lights and the smell of exhaust fumes fills my nose. A small crevice in the ground opens and I slip through.

Once I'm to the other side, I duck into a small alcove to keep out of his sights, and to block the breeze—I have no coat on. The way magic pulses from him, I know he's a witch. I wait for him to pass in front of me before I step out and place a hand on the book and yank it out of his hands. With but a few thoughts while running, I've built the dining room in my head and slip through just as the man stabs my shoulder.

The pain is blinding, and I stagger through the dark expanse towards the slip of light that will take me home, all while taking shallow breaths. My landing is far rougher than normal, but I make it. Oz and dad slump their shoulders in relief and Dad looks to the ceiling and whispers a short prayer.

My mate puts his head in his hands and he runs them through his hair. He whips his head to me and his nostrils flare before he stands. I crack a big grin and hold the grimoire up just as I stumble into the table and hit the ground.

"Ow." I reach to my shoulder and probe the wound with my fingers. "Fuck, I think I've been stabbed."

Oz bolts to my side in a panic and Dad yells for his medical team to come help. He picks me up and lays me on the table face down so he can get a better look at the damage. With gentle hands, he examines my injury. "Thank the gods; they missed your arteries. Lie still and I can heal this for you."

I'm not going anywhere, I wince.

My shoulder pain ebbs, and the telltale healing magic itches while my wounds stitch together. Once there's only a slight ache left, Oz helps me sit up, and I dart my eyes around to the mess I've made with my blood.

"Sorry, babe. I'll clean it up."

He whips his head to me. "Are you really apologizing for getting blood on *our* floor because you were stabbed?"

I crack a grin.

Oz makes me rest for the rest of the afternoon, despite my protests I'm back to feeling fine. I regale them with my brief adventure, emphasizing how much bigger the other guy was compared to me. The only regret I have is not getting a good look at his face; I don't think I could tell who the witch was if I saw them again, although he had a distinct, sour smell.

That evening, I place the huge book on the wooden table in front of dad. "This is beautiful."

"Your mother had one similar to it." He traces the markings on the cover. "Instead of black, it was a beautiful blue color. There is a golden honeybee on the front of hers, too, and it has gold embellishments all over the cover. There are also two gems on the front corners. I'm pretty sure it's the same gem that's in your ring." he gestures towards my hand.

"It can't be a coincidence you both had honeybees on your family's grimoires, can it?"

"Hard to say. I used to think it was divine intervention we both had similar grimoires, but then your mom left. I kind of stopped believing in such things after that."

My dad turns the cover on his grimoire and a small whoosh of air escapes from it. He flips through the pages until he's about halfway through the book. After adjusting his glasses to the bridge of his nose, he leans in close to the book to have a better look. He turns a few more pages. "Aha! Here it is!"

He turns the book around and slides it across the table towards Oz and me. The page is worn vellum and has a spiral symbol at the top. It lists several ingredients I recognize; ginkgo biloba, lemon balm, rosemary, and rose water. I'm not sure what eye of newt is or where I can find it, though.

Mustard seed, Oz says in my head.

I gather the ingredients from the pantry, and we bring them to the hearth. Oz opens a large wooden cupboard to the right of the fireplace and takes out a massive metal pot. This must be the cauldron.

"The last ingredient we need is something from that day." Dad adjusts his glasses. "Do you have anything?"

"Oh goodness, I doubt it." My shoulders slump. "Most of the stuff I've ever had got lost between foster homes."

"Lana, you used to have police tape in your coat pocket. Is it still there? They would've put those up the day it happened."

"I do!" I run to the closet and locate my coat. Oz bought me all new winter gear in Montreal, so I never emptied the pockets of the coat I wore the night we met.

I place the faded police tape on the table.

"We better cut just a piece of the tape in case we need to do this more than once."

"Good idea." Oz hands me a pair of scissors and I snip a three-inch square from the tape.

Oz stills my frantic hands. "Do you want me to watch these memories?"

"I want you there because I'm going to need you when I'm done. I'm about to undo twenty-six years of therapy reliving it all again."

He squeezes my hand in understanding.

The instructions have me place all the ingredients in the cauldron and stir it clockwise three times. I look at Oz and my dad for reassurance before lighting the fire in the hearth, and they both motion for me to proceed. I strike a long match against the back of the hearth and drop it on the tinder across the logs. Then, I recite the spell:

"Rewind the hands of father time,
fill in the blanks of the crime.
Make my eyes see what's missed,
release the memories that resist."

CHAPTER THIRTEEN

"$\mathcal{H}$oney, I'm going fishing. You coming with?" Mom pulls open the curtains. I open one eye to look at her and shield my face from the light. She has a yellow sundress and her baby blue rubber boots on. Her dark brown hair is French braided and there are white flower buds between the braids. Mom never leaves the house without a full face of makeup on, even though she doesn't need it. At the cabin, though, she doesn't wear it at all. I like her best like this; it makes her seem more like mama and less like what others expect her to be.

I roll over and pull the covers over my head, and grumble. She let me stay up late last night so I could finish reading my favorite book, *The Fairy Rebel*, and I'm paying for it now. Mom likes to fish early for bluegill, but I prefer to go in the early evening. I've always been more of a night owl.

"Can you take me fishing later?"

"Sure thing, Lana. Try not to sleep too late." Mom sits on the edge of the bed and her perfume reaches my nose. "Head on down to the pond if I'm not back by the time you wake. I'll try to pick some raspberries while I wait for a bite."

"Thanks, Mama."

Mom kisses me on the head even though I'm covered in a blanket, and I tell her I love her. "Love you, too, my little honeybee." The cabin door pulls shut and I listen to the sound of her picking up her fishing rod, camp chair, and tackle box off the porch.

By the time I wake, the cabin is quite warm. I kick the covers off with both legs and sit up on my elbows. The cottage is quiet—Mom must still be fishing. I pull on my rubber boots next to the bed and run outside, eager to use the bathroom. No dew coats the grass while I walk to the outhouse, so it has to be late morning by now. After using the outhouse, I wash my hands at the station set up with jugs of water, soap, and a towel.

I head back into the cabin and pull an oatmeal chocolate chip cookie from the glass cookie jar shaped like a beehive. After finishing the cookie, I look around before grabbing three more. I take these cookies with me to the kitchen table, and I pull out a chair to sit. My feet don't quite reach the floor, and without mom around, I carefully tip the chair back, so the front two chair legs are in the air. She hates when I do this. She says I will either break my neck or a chair leg.

After eating the cookies, I dig in the big blue cooler under the table for a can of Sprite. Mom will be mad I had cookies and Sprite for breakfast, but it serves her right for taking so long to fish. I open the can and leave the cabin again—this time, to head to the pond. The water is not too far, although I might finish the Sprite before she sees me.

I round the bend before our fishing spot on the pond, and Mom's fishing pole leans against a Y branch sticking in the mud. The line is still in the water, and the tackle box is open next to her camp chair. She must be picking berries, so I plop myself in her chair. After there are no bites for a while, I reel the line in to discover no bait on it. Darn it, those little buggers took the worm.

I don't particularly enjoy baiting hooks with live bait, so I dig through Mom's tackle box to find a fishing lure. She taught me to make these earlier this spring, and I loved tying the colorful threads to the lures. Sometimes, we even got to use real feathers. I take the hook off the line, switch it with the fishing lure, and cast it to the pond. I can't quite cast as far as Mom, but I'm still good at it.

I should see how Mom is coming along with those berries. After propping up the fishing pole, I run along the edge of the pond and back where the bushes are. Mom's bucket is there, and it has a couple of handfuls of berries in it. Where's Mom? Did she have to go to the bathroom, and I just missed her going to the outhouse?

I grab the bucket and start picking more raspberries, trying to go for the big plump ones. The smaller, lighter colored ones are usually too tart yet.

When the bucket is half full, I bring it back to the pond and set it next to the camp chair. The line is taught, and the end of the fishing pole curves under the weight. I don't bother sitting down, and I jerk the rod to secure the hook before reeling it in. It's a nice-sized bluegill, but I hate taking these off the hook. I dangle it in the water so the fish won't die, and I look around for Mom. The mosquitoes are bad by the pond, and I'm mad I have to search for Mom while I'm getting eaten alive.

Where is she? Ugh, I hate doing this. Maybe her fishing gloves are in the tackle box. I search the box and find a pair of black fishing gloves and put them on. They're far too big, but at least I won't get stung by the fish barbs, and I don't need to deal with any stinky hands. I grab the fish and use the fishing pliers to pull the lure out of the fishes' mouth.

Woo-hoo! I got the fish off the hook all by myself. But shoot, where's the bucket Mom usually brings to keep the fish in? I scan around the area but can't find it. Instead, I take the little yellow fish stringer, thread it through the fish gills, and toss it in the water. This way, the fish won't swim away, and I can pull it in when I find Mom.

I take the gloves off and toss them next to the camp chair. I better find Mom and ask her for help. It doesn't take me long to run along the trail back towards the cabin and knock on the outhouse door. The door swings open. She isn't here, so I check inside the cabin. Not there, either. The car is still here, so she didn't go anywhere. Where in the world is she?

Maybe she's in the garden? I run to the other side of the property and open the little garden gate. Mom loves gardening and grows about everything you can think of. I can't quite see over the top of some of the plants in here, so I go down each row.

"Mom?"

Silence.

After not finding her in the garden, I check behind the cabin where we cut firewood. There are several felled logs, but she's not here either. I run to the front of the cabin and start down the drive-way. Maybe she went for a walk? Strange, she wouldn't have done that here, though. I turn left out of the driveway and walk along the dusty logging road. The woods are kind of spooky, even though the sun is out.

The canopy of trees reaches out over the road, and little light peeks through its leaves. I sing You Are My Sunshine to keep my eyes from wandering towards the woods on either side of the road. I always have a strange sense of being watched when I'm out here.

When I finish, I sing what I can remember of Somewhere Over the Rainbow. The mosquitoes aren't as bad on the road, but my rubber boots keep kicking up dust, and it gets in my eyes and mouth.

I enter a break in the canopy, and the sun bakes my neck, but I don't want to put my ponytail down because it's too hot. I should've brought water, and Mom shouldn't have left me at the cabin by myself. What if she's hurt? What if I got hurt and there's no grown-up to help me? I need to find her.

My legs hurt from walking, and the boots chafe my calves. I'm getting worried now. Maybe Mom is hurt. What if she got eaten by a bear? Or a wolf? Oh, gods. Here I am, mad at her my legs hurt, and she could be dead. I am a terrible daughter. Maybe this is why she's gone. I didn't deserve her. Only good kids keep nice moms like her.

I use my t-shirt to wipe my tears away when I hear a car coming. Not only is the gravel loud, but the car is, too; it sounds like a real hunk-a-junk. I move to the grass right off the gravel road so the vehicle can pass. The car goes by fast, but the brakes squeal as the driver slams on the pedal. The car backs up, and a woman leans out from the passenger side window. Her hair is blonde, definitely from a bottle, and she's smacking the gum in her mouth.

"What are you doing out here, honey? Do your parents know where you're at?" She looks around. "These woods aren't safe for little kids by themselves."

The driver shuts the car off, and the back door opens. A girl a little older than me pokes her head out.

"There are bears in these woods. Wolves, too."

I don't like how bossy she sounds.

I'm madder now than I am sad. "Don't you think I know that! I'm not a little kid. I'm looking for my mom. She was supposed to be fishing, but when I woke up, she wasn't at the pond, but her stuff was."

"How long has she been gone?"

"Since early this morning, I guess."

The woman talks to the driver for a moment before stepping out of the car. She walks up to me and crouches down, so she's at my level. "How about we take you to the ranger station, and they can help find your mom?"

I adjust my clothes and slide in next to the girl in the backseat.

"I'm sorry you can't find your mom." The girl holds out her hand. "I'm Cassie; what's your name?"

"I'm Lana." I fight back the tears and shake her hand. I don't want to cry in front of these strangers.

"How old are you?" Cassie asks me while she hands me a stick of Fruit Stripe Gum. I tell her I'm eight, and she says she's ten. We're the same size, even though she's two years older than me. I've always been the tallest in my grade, and I love being the tallest ... usually. I hate I never got to go inside the Berenstain Bear's treehouse at Valley Fair because I was always too tall to go in.

"Where do you live? Why are you out here?"

"We live in Minneapolis, but we have a cabin here. We live here all summer when I'm not in school."

Cassie tells me about how they were at a campground all week, but they turned the wrong way out of the campground when they left, and that is how they ended up further in the woods before turning around.

"Dad doesn't like to use a map." Cassie's voice is but a whisper in my ear.

"Wouldn't matter, anyway. These old logging roads aren't on any of them."

The drive takes forty minutes to reach the ranger station on the main road. The mom explains to the ranger how they found me walking by myself down a logging road and my mom has gone missing. I am about as big as an ant the way they all keep peering back at me. Their stares make me self-conscious, so I keep adjusting myself in my seat.

The ranger walks over to me and takes off her wide-brimmed hat as she crouches down in front of me. "My name is Ranger Turner, and I'm going to help you if you're okay with that." I decide I can trust her and nod my head in agreement.

Cassie hugs me before her family leaves and wishes me luck, and I thank them right before the ranger door closes.

Ranger Turner brings me into her office and lets me sit in her swivel chair while she gets out her lunch box from the mini fridge across the room. Plumes of dust dance in her wake.

She unzips her lunch box and asks if I like turkey sandwiches, and I tell her I do. She brings the sandwich to me, and I wolf the food down like I didn't eat a bunch of cookies this morning. Next, I guzzle a bottle of water she places in front of me.

Ranger Turner asks me what my mom's name is, and I tell her Annabelle Chapman. She also wants me to tell her everything I can remember from this morning. I explain Mom woke me up early to go fishing, but I was up late, so I wanted to sleep in. I looked for her on the property but couldn't find her.

"Oh no! I left the fish on the stringer in the pond." I can't stop the panic rising inside me. "The fish is going to die!"

"Oh, I think the fish will be alright for now. I'm going to call for some other rangers to come to help me look for your mom. Can you wait here for a minute?"

I tell her I'm not going anywhere, and she leaves the room and closes the door.

Her voice is too quiet, so I can't make out what she's saying on the radio, but I can tell she's right on the other side of the door. Why couldn't she have radioed from in here?

When Ranger Turner finishes radioing the other rangers, she returns to the room. "Do you think you can show us where the cabin is?"

I nod.

~

I SPOT the entrance to our driveway and point it out to Ranger Turner. At the mouth is a sign I made a couple of months ago—NO TRE3PA33ING, and there's an alien ship on the board attacking a person. This way, bad guys will think twice before coming on to our property. The ranger smiles when she sees the sign, and she parks her truck behind my mom's car.

She has me walk through my entire day, and I show her exactly what I did this morning, including the cookies and Sprite. I take her to the pond and the berry bushes, and she radios the rest of the rangers to give our position. By nightfall, I told the same story at least a hundred times to different people, and the entire property is crawling with people in uniforms from the U.S. Forest Service.

They have police tape around the cabin now, and I blubber when I see it. The tape reminds me of the show Rescue 911, and now I know things are serious. The last vehicle to show up is a black car, and a woman with a black skirt suit steps out with a sparkly teddy bear.

I'm too old for teddy bears, but I bury my head in the stuffed animal and sob when she hands it to me. The bear is soft, but it doesn't feel like any stuffed toys I've ever had before.

"Where is my mama?"

This stranger wraps her arms around me and holds me while I shake. A rush of calm washes over me, just like what happens when mama hugs me, and the woman explains she is here to make sure I'm taken care of while people try to find mom. She explains I'll be staying with her tonight, but then tomorrow I'll go to another home to stay with a family until they find my mom.

I fall asleep after several hours in her car, and I wake once we reach Minneapolis. It's weird driving through places my mom took me with a stranger. We pass by the McDonald's next to the silos where mom used to stop for ice cream cones.

The buildings seem unfamiliar now as we enter a friendly neighborhood. The houses are big and far from the road, and lawns are much nicer than ours; they don't have any weeds or brown patches.

Katie turns into one driveway and pushes the garage door button on her sun visor. We pull into a garage big enough for three cars, and she explains this is her home and I have a bed made for me upstairs.

The house is quiet when we enter her home, and our footsteps seem to echo while she shows me to my room. There's a small bed, a trash can, a desk, and a bookshelf in the room. Outside the window, flickers of lightning light up the night sky as a storm approaches. I've always loved storms, although most of my friends at school always scream when the thunder cracks.

Miss Katie gives me a pair of pajamas, a new toothbrush, and a comb, but I don't think this will even go through my hair. Mom used to chase me around the house so she could brush through my snarls. I wish I had straight hair like my friends, and they don't have curly, ugly hair like me. I thank her anyway, and she shows me how to turn the light on in the bathroom that's attached to the bedroom.

"Our job is to do everything we can to find your mom." She leans against the door frame. "Your job is to keep your chin up and tell us anything else you think of from this morning, no matter how tiny the detail might be. Everything matters."

"Okay." I tuck the blanket up to my chin.

"Is there anything else you need tonight?"

You can bring me my mom and drive us back to the cabin, and you can wake me up from this nightmare.

"No ... thank you."

She closes the bedroom door, and the silence is making me scared.

I'm left alone with my thoughts, and I'm worried. What if my mom died? Where will I go? Who will take care of me? How will I pay for her funeral? I have no one.

I don't bother brushing my teeth, but I keep the bathroom light on for a nightlight. The pajamas fit fine, and the bed is nice and cool when I crawl under the sheets. My legs still hurt from all the walking and running today, and I should probably take a bath, but I don't want to; I only want my mommy.

I want her to tell me everything will be okay; I think as I cry myself to sleep.

CHAPTER FOURTEEN

ears pour down my face, and Oz wraps me in his arms. I nuzzle into his chest because I'm dizzy from my return to the present. My knees buckle, and he cradles me in his arms and carries me up the stairs to our bedroom. Dad must've gone to bed already, as the spell lasted all day and night.

Oz wraps his arms around my waist, and we both lay in bed, unsure of where to even begin. Seeing my mom again was incredible, but reliving the moment also broke my heart again. Her scent still lingers, and when I close my eyes I can picture the way the light hits her eyes just right; they almost twinkle in the sun. Grief overwhelms my senses as I cling to every fractured memory I had forgotten until now.

I miss her, I say in my mind to Oz while I cry harder. I flip over and bury my head into his chest, and I wail. The pain is unbearable. It crushes me both as a little girl who has lost her mother and as a woman who has just witnessed the trauma again. The memories assault my mind and pour out of my eyes in a deluge of tears. Why? I scream in my head. *Why?*

Oz continues to hold me, and then he hums Somewhere Over the

Rainbow to me. He's quiet at first, as though he's afraid of saying or doing the wrong thing. As my sobs grow quieter, he is louder.

My mom used to sing me this when I was little, and the melody was one of my go-to songs I sang when I couldn't sleep because of the monsters in my closet. When he finishes, he kisses me on the forehead, and I thank him for helping soothe the ache in my heart.

"I love you, Lana. I don't have the right words to say, and I don't yet understand how to make things right. All I can say is I love you more than anything, and I will stop at nothing to find out what happened to your mom."

I use my sleeve to wipe the tears off my face.

"I love you, too, Oz."

We fall asleep, and it isn't until late morning we make our way downstairs.

Dad's at the table, enjoying an early lunch of chicken noodle soup and turkey and cheese sandwiches.

"You doing okay there, pumpkin?" He adjusts his flannel shirt. "The first time I did a Memorall spell, I was out for a whole two weeks. One of the hardest things I'd ever gone through. It isn't easy reliving the most painful moment of your life."

I pull up a chair next to him at the table. The dining room is warm, thanks to the logs in the fireplace. I take off my cardigan and drape the sweater over the back of my chair.

"It was good to see Mom again. She was wearing a yellow sundress and her baby blue rain boots. Her hair was braided, and it had little white flowers in it. She knew I loved when she put flowers in her hair."

Dad loses himself in thought before he fights back tears. "When you're ready, you can tell me all about it. But first, you need to eat. Casting spells is hard work, especially one's like these."

I scoot my chair back to head to the kitchen, but Oz tells me to sit tight, and he'll feed me. Gods, I love this man.

"Thank you for showing me this spell, Dad. It was hard seeing her again, but it was a gift all the same. I hope together we can all piece together what happened to her."

"Me, too, pumpkin. Me too."

The nursing staff gives dad his medicine, and he makes a sour face as he tosses a handful of his pills back. He chases the mouthful of pills down with a glass of apple juice.

"Apple juice is my favorite, too." I catch a little twinkle in Dad's eyes.

Oz enters the dining room with a big tray of food and I'm overwhelmed with love. If Hannah and CJ were here with my mom, it would fill this room with everything I care about in the world. He kisses me on the head after setting the tray down on the thick wooden table.

Today is a comfort food kind of day, so the tray has peanut butter sandwiches, bowls of chili, and lots of oyster crackers. I like to add so many oyster crackers to my bowl there's hardly any liquid left. And then, I dunk my peanut butter sandwiches in the chili. Hannah thinks I'm vile for doing this, but I'm happy to see Oz does this, too.

"Your mom liked to eat her chili like that." Dad gestures to my bowl with the spoon in his hand. "It's nice to see you've taken after her in so many ways, and you're a spitting image of her, too."

I relish this compliment. As a little girl, my mom was my hero, and I thought she was the smartest, most beautiful woman in the world. To hear I'm like her brings me happy tears.

After we finish brunch, we all head to the parlor. There's a giant chandelier in the center of the room, and below it is a tall coffee table. Two couches are on either side of it, and then there are several chairs. Oz scoots a chair out of the way to make room for Dad, and he and I take up residence on the couch facing him.

"Did you witness anything you think you forgot about?"

"Actually, yes. The lady I stayed with from the state—she's a witch, and I felt her cast a spell on me to help calm me down."

Oz laces his fingers between mine after he pours us all coffee. I plop ten sugar cubes in my mug, and both men smile knowingly at me but say nothing. They take their coffee black and smirk while I pour a lot of creamer into my coffee.

"I caught that, too." Oz sips his coffee. "The teddy bear was also enchanted."

Having Oz in my head helps. At first, I didn't like it, only because I couldn't hide salacious thoughts from him, but that was very short-lived. He can sense my feelings anyway, so who cares what he witnesses in my mind. I've never felt closer to anyone ever before.

"Other than the witch, I noticed nothing out of the ordinary. We know she made it to the fishing pond and started picking berries, but then she just vanished."

"Maybe we can try to track down the witch and see if she remembers anything from the investigation that might help us. They've got to have records of who you stayed with."

"I can have Auguste look her up for us." Oz takes his cell out of his pocket. "He handles all the security data projects for the family, including the tracking down of people and antiquities. He learned everything from Gideon."

Oz excuses himself from the room to place a phone call to Auguste. Dad takes a plastic container of cookies out of the saddlebag he keeps on the side of his wheelchair. He wheels himself over the ornate purple and red rug and offers me an oatmeal chocolate chip cookie.

"Thanks, Dad." I take a big bite. My sweet tooth must come from him. "These are just like the ones Mom used to make me."

"Who do you suppose taught me how to make them?" Dad cocks an eyebrow at me.

After we finish eating a few cookies each, Oz returns to the room and sits next to me.

Dad asks to see my right hand, and he takes it in his. His hands are very soft—probably far different from what they were when he farmed. He studies my hand and asks Oz to shine his phone light on my palm so he can see better. I didn't realize my dad could read palms.

"You have water hands, Lana."

"What does that mean?" I glance at Oz before turning my attention back to Dad.

"See how long and slender your fingers are? And your palms are long, too." I'm a little self-conscious about this because I've always had enormous hands. "You're both intuitive *and* creative."

When I was younger, I spent a lot of time drawing. Although now, I have little time for it. I have nowhere I can keep my artwork when I'm traveling full time. I regret I create little anymore.

"Huh, that's interesting. Mom used to call them piano hands."

"I can tell you've spent a lot of time denying your intuition, though." Dad traces a line on my hand. "See how this line feathers out a bit here? Potential courses through the nerves in your hand. You mustn't turn your back on it, Lana." His eyes bore into mine.

He's right; I have spent a lot of time trying to deny my intuition and feelings. I didn't know I was a witch, and I've spent most of my life second-guessing myself when things didn't seem logical. How far along would I be with my magic if I had known?

A huge part of me is angry my mom never told me. Why did she keep such a huge secret from me? And why did she bind my magic?

"Dad, how come you never went to Bedlam?" He didn't meet Mom until he was in his thirties, so I'm curious why he didn't want to live forever.

"Well, your grandparents never did. So, I didn't either, and I never had a reason to. The magic I have now has been more than enough to live with all these years."

If I can go to Bedlam and learn how to live forever, I can spend eternity with Oz. Not only that, but I can also learn spells that might better help me figure out what happened to Mom. Maybe she's there after all.

"Do you think Mom went to Bedlam?" We haven't found her grimoire, and the key Dad sent me was mine. Mom's pearl-like Ebbswick key is missing, too.

He shakes his head. "She'd never leave you. Not willingly, anyway. Me? We never married, and she apparently didn't share the same feelings when she left me."

This makes me sad. I want to prove to Dad that Mom loved him and wouldn't have left him under her own volition.

"Is there anyone who didn't like Mom when you were together?" Maybe she had enemies or secrets that got her into trouble.

"Everyone loved your mom. I can't imagine a world where anyone would ever want to hurt her."

CHAPTER FIFTEEN

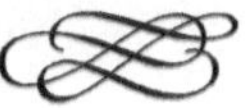

$\mathcal{E}$arly Thanksgiving morning, Oz and I wake before the sun so we can start on preparing a feast for family and staff. Because this is our first holiday together, I wanted to be the one to help make food rather than leave it for the staff to do. Besides, I enjoy cooking with Oz. With our extrasensory perception, working with him in the kitchen is like being two sides of the same coin.

Oz and I both wear aprons—mine, very feminine, like the wallpaper in this French colonial home, and his, all black, but with copious amounts of flour on the front. He might also have two flour handprints on the backside of his slacks.

Bonnie Driscoll, an old witch friend of Oz's, is coming for Thanksgiving, and she will be here in a few hours. He also invited his court, so we will have a full house. For once, I'm grateful to have such a large house to entertain in. I want to learn about everyone important to Oz.

Hearing my thoughts, he folds me in his arms and kisses the top of my head. He told me he can hear most of my thoughts when I'm near him, and any louder thoughts when I'm far.

"You two make a fine couple," Dad says from the entryway to the kitchen. He has a smirk on his face. Oz dusts off the handprints on his behind, and a blush creeps up his cheeks. I giggle at getting caught.

Dad eyes the pies lining the counter. Two of each; sweet potato, pumpkin, and pecan pie. I reach for the tray of cookies on the other counter and toss him one. He beams as he catches the treat midair. This is one thing he and I share—a fondness for cookies, no matter the hour.

"Bonnie Driscoll will be here soon. She has been to Bedlam! Maybe she can tell us a thing or two that might help in our search for Mom. And Auguste will probably bring what he knows about the witch who works for the state."

"Everything's coming together. I'm sure lucky to have you two in my life."

He's been looking rather gaunt over the last few days, and it saddens me he won't be with us much longer. He's been able to maintain his appetite, even if a lot of what he eats is sweet. The doctor said at this stage, he's better off eating what he wants, as nature will run its course no matter what he eats now.

"We're thrilled you're here, Dad." Oz echoes this sentiment and shares he's happy to have Dad here as long as he desires to stay. After all, he's family.

Oz HEADS to the front door when he hears a car come up the driveway, so I join him and peer through the curtained window on the door.

Wren Highlandburg is here, although I'm uncertain who is in the passenger seat. Whoever his guest is, he's definitely a vampire. He's roughly as tall as Oz when he comes to the door and is arm and arm with Wren.

Oh! This must be Wren's boyfriend he was visiting while we were in Mont-Tremblant.

We exchange hugs, and Wren hands me a bottle of Moscato d'Asti. I thank him. He must remember I like this wine after I had several glasses on the jet.

Wren introduces his boyfriend as Sebastian Talbot and says he also likes sweet wine like me. As a result, they always have some d'Asti on hand. I put the wine in the fridge and show them to the parlor. I realize this is kind of Wren's place, too, so I feel silly afterward.

Of course, he can find his way to his own parlor. Wren doesn't embarrass me about my flub, though.

Next to arrive are Maeve and Pippa Imperialus. Elliot, Pippa's mate, can't make dinner—they're on a dinosaur dig in Spain. It's nice to see these two again and given the bear hug each of them gives me, I'd say they agree. These two have so much joy in them their glee is infectious.

Dad entertains our guests with tales of the nursing home while Oz and I make our way upstairs to shower. The shower is big enough for both of us, and we bathe fast, so we have time for a quickie before more guests arrive. Having sex in the shower is a little more awkward, and I'm reduced to fits of giggles several times as we try to keep quiet. We find our rhythm and move together until we both come.

Oz gives me a quick kiss on the lips before I use a t-shirt to scrunch my hair. He's already dressed in a sharp suit and goes downstairs so as not to invoke suspicion. I put on a red wrap dress and black velvet pumps. He bought me a black pearl necklace that goes well with this, and I wear it because of the special occasion. To complete my look, I finish my makeup and add strip lashes; I love the way these make my blue eyes pop, especially in contrast to the red dress.

I walk down the hallway carefully, as I haven't worn heels in a while, so I cling to the railing while I make my way down the stairs. My heels click with each step, and Oz meets me at the bottom of the stairs. His eyes grow wide when I come into view, and I can't fight the salacious grin crossing my face when he climbs a few steps to take my hand and help me down the rest of the way.

"You look radiant, Sahira." I'm enveloped with a scent of both sugar cookies and spice. I kiss him on the cheek and wipe the smudge of red lipstick off with my thumb.

"Not too bad yourself, Osgood Finlandian." I take his hand and hook my arm in his. I tremble as we round the corner and work our way towards the parlor. My nerves threaten to swallow me whole, and I have to keep wiping my hands on my dress on account of sweat. The opinions of Oz's family mean everything to me—after all, they're my family, too.

A familiar voice is the first thing I notice. The second: a tall, thin woman with thick raven-colored hair standing in the center of the room. I throw a hand to my mouth and cry. The bangles on her wrist jangle as she rushes towards me, arms outstretched.

"Hannah! What are you doing here?" I throw my arms around her. I'm going to have to re-do my makeup, but Hannah is more than worth it.

"Wren and Sebastian picked me up in the jet!" She is beyond giddy. "Oz and I have been keeping this secret for days. It's so hard to surprise you, Lana Chapman-Sawyer! I've been waiting in the car this whole dang time."

This is the best surprise ever. My best friend here to meet the rest of my newly gained family is just what I needed.

"CJ is with Chad the rest of the weekend, so it worked out perfectly to come to visit."

"But what about the shop? Thanksgiving is one of your biggest holidays!" I refer to the huge amount of floral arrangements that usually go out of her shop for hundreds of miles around. Her town is pretty rural, and hers is the only flower shop in Shelby.

"I hired some help, and I'm glad, too. I needed free time."

"Well, this is just getting better and better." First, Oz. Then my dad, and now Hannah.

When she heads back to the parlor to converse with the rest of our family, I throw my arms around Oz and thank him profusely while squeezing him tight.

I'd do anything for you, Lana.

I would do anything for him, too. He has breathed so much life into me, and things almost seem perfect for the first time in a very long time; the only thing missing is Mom.

How can I ever repay Oz for everything he's done for me? He has given me so much, and I've given him so little. That will change when

I go to Bedlam and come back immortal. Together, we will live for eternity, and even then, it won't be enough. The love I have for this man is worth a thousand immortal lifetimes.

The doorbell interrupts my thoughts, and when I answer the door, a thirty-something-year-old man bigger than Oz towers in the doorway. He has a black trench coat on, and my pulse quickens as his sapphire blue eyes shift to a gunmetal blue and bore into me.

Vampire. Definitely a vampire.

"You must be the Sahira." The man has a heavy Australian accent. His skin is olive-toned but a couple of shades lighter than Oz's, and his dark eyelashes are full. "I'm Gideon." The air in the entryway is thick, and cinnamon invades my nostrils.

"Oh, please come in." I'm flustered as I step aside. I extend my hand, and he ignores it.

Oz is at my side now, and he shakes Gideon's hand and pats him on the back. "Nice to see you, Gideon. I see you've met my mate, Lana."

Gideon walks straight to the parlor where the rest of the family is.

I don't think he likes me very much. I wince as I speak to Oz in my head.

Wrong; he likes you very much. Oz shares a quick flash of what he saw in Gideon's head when I answered the door. My eyes dart around, unsure what to say to the image of me pinned against the wall, with Gideon's teeth sunk into my breast. I gulp and close the door.

Cinnamon must be the scent Gideon gives off when he's aroused. Duly noted.

Being able to read minds is both a blessing and a curse, he says in my head. *People aren't meant to be privy to every desire that flashes across one's mind on a whim.*

I never once thought about what it might be like for Oz to witness his mate be the object of another person's dark desires, or even their ill intent, especially when this person is someone he's sired. Sometimes, being unaware of someone's feelings towards you, especially when they're malignant feelings, can give them an opportunity to change those feelings and you're none the wiser. Oz never has the opportunity. It must be exhausting.

I can see how it might even be dangerous for Gideon, considering how strong the mark is when a vampire mates. Maybe this is why he treated me so coldly—he's trying to keep himself in check so as not to piss off Oz. I will need to tread carefully with him because I don't want anyone hurt.

While I help dad fiddle with his new phone, I see Oz escort Gideon into the living room. He looks pissed off, while Gideon is more resigned. They're in there for a good twenty minutes before they both come back into the room.

"Lana? Can I speak to you for a moment?" Gideon asks.

I give a tentative look at Oz, and he inclines his head, so I follow Gideon into the kitchen where we can have some privacy thanks to the loud vent over the stove. I lean against the counter and tuck my arms around my middle. What does he want to talk about?

"I'm sorry for being cold to you when you tried to greet me at the door. You were kind enough to invite us all to Thanksgiving, and I disrespected you." He fidgets with the rolled-up sleeve of his button-down shirt. "I promise my behavior had nothing to do with you, but everything to do with me ... kind of. Never in my life have I had such a visceral reaction to a woman, and I didn't want any distractions, so I reacted poorly."

Oh. It's my turn to fidget now. "No need to apologize, Gideon. I'm really glad you're here. Oz thinks so highly of you, and I'd really like to get to know the family."

He gives me a heart-stopping grin. "I'd like to get to know you, too."

I take a deep breath, and after checking on the duck roasting in the oven, the doorbell rings again. I hesitate briefly after what happened earlier, but excuse myself to answer the door, anyway.

Bonnie Driscoll greets me. Her gray hair and squinty eyes lend her age, but she's spry and sharp. She wears a brown and teal wool shawl over a long, patchwork dress adorned with hand-sewn flowers. The magic dances around her clothes, and the petals to the flowers open and close rhythmically.

"Hello, dear. Thank you for having me!"

I offer her my arm and show her to the parlor.

Now, we're just waiting for Auguste. I light the candles on the table and adjust the silverware for the thirtieth time. I can't remember the last time I cooked for a crowd. I hope I've done a good job.

Oz joins my side after hearing my internal doubts, and he grabs my hand before I can micromanage another unnecessary adjustment of the silverware.

"You've done a wonderful job. Besides, the food we cooked for the staff was well-received. Now, they're home with their families so we can enjoy ours."

He folds me in his arms, and he hears a car pulling up the drive. I follow him to the door, and we open it as soon as we see the man approach. This man is wearing an all-white suit, and he quickly averts his steel-gray eyes away from me as we open the door to greet him.

"Lovely to meet you, Auguste." I offer my hand. He has a very viking-esque look to him.

He takes my hand and kisses the top of it, catching me off guard. When he raises his head, his eyes are now a pale blue, and my core stirs in recognition. The entryway smells of cloves, and I quickly usher him into the house and to the parlor.

My Gods. Between Gideon, Auguste, and Oz, we'll have a blood-bath before we even make it to dessert.

Hannah and Maeve cozy up nicely together, and I can't help but chuckle to myself. Hanalei is quite a little vixen, but I do not doubt Maeve can keep up. It might take a vampire to be equally yoked with her.

"SHIT!" How did I burn the toasted nuts? I checked them several times. Auguste pops into the kitchen and asks if I need any help.

I give him a wilted look and show him the pan. "Can you un-burn these?"

He smirks. "No, but I can toast more if you want to take the duck out of the oven. I can sense you've cooked it perfectly."

"Thanks, Auguste." I take the ducks out of the oven just as Oz walks in.

"Mm, looking good in here, Sahira." He kisses me on the cheek. While I check on the other food, he carves the fowl. Between him and Auguste, we have everything on the table just in time.

When I enter the parlor, everyone stops chatting, and icy vampire eyes dance across my exposed skin before settling on my bust. "Dinner is ready; you may take your seats."

The guests file their way into the dining room, searching for their names on the handwritten placards on each plate. Oz sits at the head of the table, and I'm to his right. Dad is next to me, and Hannah is next to him. Then we have Maeve, Pippa, Bonnie, Wren, Sebastian, Auguste, and Gideon. I've never been more thankful for an oversized table.

I lean into Oz, and he meets me halfway to see what I have to say. "Just wanted to say I love you." I squeeze his hand, knowing full-well every vampire in the room can hear me plain as day.

"I love you, too." He kisses me full on the lips. I flash an image across my mind of him taking me right here on the table, spilling the side dishes to the floor. He smirks at this and sits upright in his seat, satisfied.

"Have you two discussed a date for the wedding yet?" Sebastian puts a forkful of food in his mouth while he waits for our response.

"Ah, not exactly." I shift uncomfortably in my seat, feeling the full stares of every vampire in the room. "We want to marry before I go to Bedlam."

The rest of the conversation at the table stops.

"You're going to Bedlam?" Gideon glares at Oz while he slams his wineglass down on the table. Thankfully, it doesn't break. I've deduced he is the more outspoken one of the family.

"I think it's a lovely idea," Bonnie pipes up from the end of the table.

"Why don't you just turn her?" I can't miss the accusing tone of Auguste's voice. "Surely that is better than her going to Bedlam. What if she can't come back?"

Oz's lips form a tight line, but he tries to maintain his composure in front of my dad, Bonnie, and Hannah. No doubt this would be an entirely different conversation if it were just the vampires and me in the room.

Before he can speak, I try to take the brunt of the blame. "I'm going there to learn what happened to my mom. She disappeared and left me at our cabin all alone when I was just a kid."

"You're going with her, right?" Gideon looks at dad.

"In his condition, he wouldn't survive the portal."

Dad clutches my hand to comfort me when tears spring to my eyes. I blink them away as I build the house in my mind, safely tucking away Mom's memory in my safe in the basement. Pippa and Maeve pass side dishes around to help defuse the tension in the air.

"Surely Gideon and I can track her down, or at least figure out what happened to her," Auguste leans in. "There is no one in the world better at tracking than we are. And besides, I got information on the DHS woman you wanted."

I look at him with a renewed sense of hope and ask what he found. Everyone listens intently as he dishes out the details of the witch who looked after me the night my mom disappeared. The DHS lady works as a supervisor now in the state of Minnesota. She still lives in the same house, and is married for the second time, but has no kids.

Hearing this news, my heart flutters, and both Auguste and Gideon zero in on my chest.

"This is fantastic news!" My voice comes out louder than I intend because I'm unable to contain my excitement and it startles them out of their gaze. "Thank you so much for looking into this for me; it means a lot."

Auguste sits a little taller in his chair after my praise.

"We can visit her on Monday. This way, you can still spend time with the family before most of them head out," Oz says.

Sebastian, Wren, and Hannah will leave Sunday night, so she's back in time to pick up CJ from his dad's house.

"Thank you, Auguste." Dad sets his fork down. "This might bring us one step closer to figuring out what happened. Any help you or Gideon can provide will have me forever in your debt."

Both men are eager to appease Dad and offer to do whatever they can.

Bonnie interjects, asking if my mom may be in Bedlam. My dad and I quickly refute that. She's not someone who would abandon her family unless forced to, and you have to be willing to go to Bedlam to get in.

"That just leaves two logical conclusions." Gideon leans back in his seat. "Either someone has taken her somewhere else, or she's ..." He doesn't finish his sentence. The rest is far too painful for my dad and me to hear.

We knew there was always a possibility she wasn't alive. The very hint she could be dead causes the house's basement in my head to groan under the pressure. The memories of my mom threaten to break through, but then Oz enters and sits down next to me in front of the basement door. He holds me as we brace the bulging door with our bodies. His very presence causes these memories to retreat to the deep recesses of my mind's basement.

Bonnie shares how it took her twenty years to emerge from Bedlam, and it causes me to panic. I'm thirty-four, and I don't want to be old when I return. People stare at us in public as it is. I can only imagine the looks of disgust I'd receive with a younger man on my arm. No doubt my adrenaline is surging now.

"If we find out what happened to your mom, Lana, then you can become a vampire and won't need Bedlam." Auguste must sense my discomfort it took Bonnie so long to come back.

I am hopeful about this but am also aware of Oz's feeling about turning me.

The vampires shovel spoonful after spoonful of food into their mouths, giving little grunts of pleasure, showing they enjoy our cooking.

"If he doesn't turn her, I will." Gideon leans in conspiratorially, and I have a brief vision of the image Oz shared with me earlier; pinned to the wall, Gideon's teeth sunk into my breast, and now I turn to feed from him in return.

A flame roars to life at my core, and Gideon's eyes flash as he senses my arousal. Before I even know what's happening, Oz has Gideon by the throat, pinning him to the wall. His fingers dig into Gideon's skin, and blood wells up at each finger.

"The hell you will!" He snarls only inches from Gideon's throat. I rush over to them both and place a hand on his shoulder tentatively. Oz is more beast than man now, and we're all in a dangerous position with him like this.

Come back to me, my love, I urge gently in my mind. I can feel the eyes around the table, observing me. Flying too close to the sun—it's what I do best.

Oz turns his head towards me, and his eyes are black as the night before they soften and turn blue again. He releases his grip, and I take him by the hand and excuse us from the table for a moment while we step outside for some fresh air.

I can still sense Oz seething with rage inside, so I gently place my hand on his cheek. Compassion envelops us both, and I know I am using magic now. The magic dances where my hand rests, and when I pull it away, his beast has retreated to its home.

"You shouldn't have intervened, Sahira." Oz's tone isn't something I like. "I could've killed every one of you." He stares out over the bluff at the Mississippi. It's too dark for me to see much, but I can make out a barge based on the spacing of the lights on its deck. The breeze sends a few flurries between us, and I nuzzle in closer.

"But I knew you wouldn't." I turn towards him. "I may be new to the world of vampires, but I am yours, and you are mine. Forever. I would rather snuff the light from my soul and take the breath out of my lungs than live another moment without you as my mate."

Oz folds me in his arms and holds me close when my body involuntarily chills from another sudden wind gust. "How do those two think they can challenge me? It makes little sense. They know better than that."

I look into Oz's eyes, and he softens. "Do you think it has anything to do with the fact I'm the mate of the first vampire? You've never had one before, so maybe it makes me far more palatable instead of the opposite."

Sure, it was a bit of a stretch. But things might work entirely different with Oz considering who he is. Mortal men do crazy things in the name of desire and love, and I imagine it's even more heightened in vampires. In wolf packs, it's a fairly common occurrence for beta males to challenge the alphas for rank and status. Maybe vampires are similar? Can these men be staging a coup?

"Did you just compare us to wolves?" He raises an eyebrow.

"Am I so far off?"

Fair point, he says in my head.

Are you okay, or do I need Bonnie to come out here and show me how to enchant myself, so I look like a hairy old man? I'll do it! I ask Oz in my head.

A grin softens his features, and I surprise him by jumping on him, wrapping my legs around his waist. He purrs and holds my ass as I give him a long kiss to let him understand I mean business.

"We better head inside before I catch a cold." He sets me down and wraps his arm around my waist while we walk inside. The family has moved to dessert and they barely look up when we come into the room, save for Gideon and Auguste, who immediately zero in on me.

Oz grabs a slice of each pie, and I take a handful of cookies back to my seat before I remember to drink the herbal birth control tea Oz made me. I grab a mug of it and bring it back to enjoy with my cookies.

Auguste and Gideon give a cursory glance at my mug before scarfing down their pie.

Your period starts tomorrow, Sahira. I had the staff fetch supplies for you this morning, and you'll find them in the bottom drawer of our bedroom's bathroom, Oz says in my head.

I look at him with wide eyes. *Don't tell me you can sense that.*

The shrug of his shoulders and wince on his face tell me all I need to know.

Hannah helps me clear the table while Oz talks with Gideon and Auguste outside.

"You doing okay there, hon?" She rinses off each dish and hands them to me to place in the dishwasher.

I tell her I'm so happy she's here, and that she got to meet my dad. I fill her in on Oz and my conversation outside. She doesn't quite understand vampire dynamics yet, either.

"Would it be weird if Maeve and I ..." She looks nervous, and I chuckle before she even finishes. "I mean, that *is* weird, right? Oz is her sire and does that make you kind of like the stepmom? Oh gosh. That sounds so creepy when I say it like that."

"Oh, Hanalei. I'm so glad you're here." When I finally stop laughing, I give her the green light. I adore Maeve, and the two of them would be great for each other. She practically dances to the dining room, where she collects more dishes for the dishwasher.

"Ah, Hann. I forgot to tell you vampires have super hearing. She's probably heard this entire conversation. She could be outside, sitting on a boat on the Mississippi, and could probably listen to our conversation in this noisy dining room."

Hannah's eyes grow wide, and it looks as though she's seen a ghost. "That is why Oz and I have a lot of conversations in my head."

"I'm cool with it." Maeve grins from the doorway, and Hannah whips around, wholly mortified. I chuckle and leave those two alone in the kitchen while I sneak a couple of bites of pie from the dining room table.

The three vampire amigos return from their conversation outside and catch me red-handed. "Oh, hello." I speak with a mouthful of pumpkin pie. Gideon is the first to come in the doorway to the dining room, and he nudges at his nose as if to show I have something on mine. Auguste is the next to see, and I quickly wipe whipped cream off my nose as Oz files in behind them.

You have pie on your chest, Sahira, Oz says in my head. All three vampires gaze at my chest now, and the room smells of spices like cinnamon, cloves, and cardamom.

CHAPTER SIXTEEN

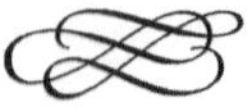

*a*fter Bonnie leaves, Dad retires to his room. The rest of us pile in the parlor, and Sebastian throws some logs on the fire. It crackles and sparks while we take seats.

Maeve and Hannah are on the floor together, while Oz and I share a love seat we dragged in from the sitting room. Auguste, Pippa, and Gideon share a couch, and Sebastian joins Wren on the other couch.

"Lana, how did you and Hannah meet?"

Oz pops a cork on a large bottle of Finlandian and pours everyone a glass before wrapping his arm around my shoulders.

"Well, I think it was the summer going into the sixth grade, right, Hann?"

She nods.

"The Sawyers had just adopted me, and they took me to the Mall of America to go on rides at Camp Snoopy. They were too old to enjoy going on rides, and so I couldn't go on a lot of them as a solo rider until I spotted this girl my age in the same predicament. We must have spent the next four hours riding rides together. We ended up being in the same classroom in the fall, and no other friendship was a match like ours."

Hannah smiles at this memory. We'd been through so much

together, and I'm thrilled she's here with me now. After the Sawyers died, she helped me sell everything, and then she moved to Montana after Chad got a job working on the railroad there. It wasn't too long after when they divorced.

"She's the best friend I've ever had. Although, we sure got in a lot of trouble, didn't we, Lana?" She has a mischievous gleam to her.

Gideon leans forward. "Do tell." I catch a flare of something sultry behind his eyes.

We enjoy another glass of wine while sharing stories from our childhood. The vampires have much scarier stories to share than Hannah and me, but we enjoy them all the same. I particularly enjoyed hearing about how Oz smooth talked their way out of being hanged in New England in the late 1700s.

I imagine it would've been tough for them to explain the failed hanging. You can't exactly choke a vampire.

Oz throws his head back, roaring with laughter at this thought in my head. Everyone's heads swing toward us, eyes darting back and forth to discern what just happened.

"Sorry. I thought you can't choke a vampire, and Oz thinks it's funny."

The room erupts in laughter.

"While true," Gideon leans in, and his cinnamon scent tickles my nose. "They sure try." He winks his gunmetal blue eye at me.

A flick of fire stirs at my core, and both Auguste and Gideon's eyes flash in response. I'm surprised by my body's reaction to this, more so because I want to drag Oz upstairs. My goodness, why is my body reacting like this to *them*?

"I'm quite tired, aren't you, Hannah?" Maeve redirects the conversation, and I'm relieved. Hannah grabs her hand, and the two of them make their way to one bedroom on the first floor. Knowing full-well vampires never *need* sleep, I consider whether Hannah understands this.

Oh, she knows.

One by one, the rest of the vampires retire to their bedrooms. Oz and I climb the two flights of stairs until we reach our floor; I hit the one floorboard that creaks—he never does. I faintly hear the TVs on in both Auguste and Gideon's rooms as we pass them. No sooner do I shut the door to our bedroom does Oz undress me. His movements are swift, barely giving me time to catch a breath.

"I've been waiting all night for this." He tosses me on the bed as though I weigh only as much as a sack of potatoes. He grabs my ankles and pulls me to the end of the bed, situating a thigh on each side of his head. His appetite is ferocious, and he greedily devours me like a man starved. I come quick and hard, bucking my hips as I ride his face.

"I want to taste." I pull him by his collar up to my face and kiss him hard, my tongue detecting the faintest bits of peach and cardamom. My fingers work to unbutton his shirt, and he rips it off, sending buttons flying all over the bedroom. Some roll under the bed, and one bounces off the wall. He is quick to unbuckle and rid himself of his pants and boxers.

Oz scoops me into his arms and carries me to the center of the bedroom, where he enters me while I'm carried. I have my arms wrapped around his neck, unable to move, so he does all the work. My breath is shallow, and I let out a moan with each fast thrust. This drives him wild, and he walks forward until he has me pinned against the wall shared between our room and Gideon's.

His thrusts cause artwork to fall off the wall, but we are too in the throes of passion for caring. Oz is a lot more vocal than he usually is and grunts with the effort of each drive into my throbbing sex. His pace is faster now, and we're nearing the peak.

He sinks his teeth into my breast, and I let out a loud moan, both from the force of it and the pleasure it gives me. This is the ecstasy my core has been aching for all night. He sucks hard, and his release fills me as he thrusts his hips several more times in succession.

Oz lays me down on the carpet below us, never removing his stiff shaft, and picks the pace up again.

"You are *mine*, Sahira," he snarls possessively as he drives into me.

What the fuck? He's acting like this because he's *jealous*?

With one shove and a turn of my leg, I am on top of him now. I grind my hips into him, and dig my fingernails into his chest.

"And you are mine, but you will never use me as a pawn again, or I will eat your heart." I dig my nails deeper into his chest, drawing blood. Heat hovers around my fingernails now, and I pull them back, witnessing little purple flames dancing at their tips. "Do I make myself clear, Osgood Finlandian?" I thrust my hips deeper and harder.

There is a brief flash of fear behind his eyes, and he nods. "Say it."

"Yes, Sahira. Clear." I can tell he's half terrified and half turned on at my sudden display of aggression. His moans aren't so forced anymore, but they still are audible as I give into my pleasure.

"Good." I ride him until we both come again.

My legs and arms are weak by the time we finish, and I collapse onto his chest. I'm out of breath, and my heart races from the effort. Once I catch my breath, I put on the robe Oz bought me in Montreal and I saunter to the bed. I use my magic to turn out the lights and fall asleep quickly.

IT's late morning when there's a knock at the bedroom door. I sit up and notice Oz's side of the bed is untouched.

He never came to bed last night? This wounds me.

I slide out of bed and tie my robe tight as I make my way to the door. I peek my head through the doorway in case Auguste or Gideon are at the door, and I'm relieved to see Oz on the other side.

What are you doing out there? I ask in my head, and I pull on his sleeve and fold him into my arms. He doesn't look well.

I wasn't sure if you wanted to be with me anymore, Sahira, he says in my head. A moment of grief grips my chest, and I cling to his shirt.

I love you, Oz; I snarl in my mind.

Sure, I was mad at him last night for his display of dominance in the bedroom, only to show Gideon and Auguste who I 'belong' to. But that doesn't mean I want nothing to do with Oz. He is my mate, and soon, he will be my husband. I love him.

Oz stares into my eyes, and I search for understanding. Is this wounded pride?

"I'm sorry." His voice breaks. "What I did last night was uncalled-for."

I pull him in and hug tight while I tell him I'm the one who should apologize, and he winces. I step back with suspicion and cock my head to the side as I study him.

Then, I notice it.

Ten small red crescent moon shapes on his shirt.

I inspect them closer and panic when I realize the shapes are blood. I tug his shirt off and tremble. Under his shirt, you can still see the deep wounds my fingernails made in his chest last night.

"Why haven't you healed?"

"I-I ... I don't know, Sahira."

I lay him down on the bed and throw open the curtains above to bring in more light. When this isn't enough, I turn on the sconce on the headboard and shine it on his chest. After closer inspection, threads of magic dance deep at the core of each wound.

What in the world?

Never would I have done anything like this if I knew it would have left you wounded.

"Hey, are you two kids—oh, uh? My bad," Auguste goes to pivot back out of the room. I hadn't remembered to shut the door when Oz surprised me a few minutes ago. He bumps into Gideon, who also stands in the center of our bedroom.

"What the hell did y'all do last night?" Gideon surveys the scene and his eyes widen as he moves closer to see the huge wounds in Oz's chest. "You freaky, Lana?" His gunmetal blue eyes shift to the lower half of my butt cheek exposed by the short robe I have on. Auguste's eyes dance along my thighs, too, so I toss the comforter over my lap.

"Icarus, you might need to have that looked at," Auguste places a hand on Oz's shoulder, referring to the god who flew too close to the sun. I always joked I flew too close to the sun with Oz, but truth be told, I am his fire, and he is my ice.

"Pippa!" Gideon calls down the stairs, his eyes not leaving the scene.

It takes but a moment for her to enter the bedroom and see the desecration of Oz's chest. I place a trembling hand on his forehead. He's warm; too warm. I am beside myself when she asks me to tell her exactly what happened.

"Um, we were ..." I clear my throat and continue, "making love, and I was far too rough with him. I dug my nails into his chest, and when I pulled them out, there were little purple flames at the ends of my fingers."

The room is heavy with the smell of cinnamon and cloves, and I can't believe Auguste and Gideon are horny now. I don't know what the hell happened, but I hurt Oz. It actually pisses me the fuck off.

"Were you ... angry?" Pippa has no hint of judgment in her voice.

"I was." I turn my eyes back towards Oz.

"About?" When I hesitate, she continues, "It matters *why*, specifically."

"I was mad he was being loud and possessive in the bedroom only as a display of dominance over Gideon and Auguste." Using the back of my hand, I wipe tears out of my eyes. "I threatened him never to do it again."

Both of the men have amused looks on their faces. Oz looks worse by the minute.

"Water hands with a fire heart." Pippa's voice is barely a whisper, and the room goes silent. "There is a prophecy about this, but I never believed in the ravings of a mad woman until now."

Auguste and Gideon look at Pippa, eyes wild. "No. No freaking way."

"There is an old stalkerish vampire witch who used to tell a tale about a queen who kills her king, but we all thought she was mad. The queen is a witch with water hands and a fire heart. Her king is a vampire, who is on most cellular levels—ice. Her water hands can penetrate his ice, much like a swiftly moving river underneath a glacier. This allows her fire heart access to kill him by accident. The legend says the queen kills her king while making love, and no one believed it."

"Okay, but I'm not a queen?" I cycle between fear and a glimmer of hope. "And Oz isn't dying ... is he?" Hysteria sets in, and I have a difficult time trying to assuage the guilt.

"Oz is the king of vampires, and as his mate, you are his queen. I ... I ... don't know how to stop this." she motions to his chest.

The magic wisps have grown underneath his skin now, connected like a sinister web. They flicker like a flame and turn the flesh it touches purple and black as it weaves itself in and out of the ice inside him. Oz's skin is like fire now, and I can no longer feel him inside my head.

Why can I no longer feel him in my head? Panic grips me, cleaving my chest in two.

Oz! I scream silently, trying to reach him while giant, hot tears pour down my face.

My familiar buzzing sensation overtakes my head like a torrent, and it is almost deafening now.

Oz! I scream again. More silence.

"Oz!" I let out an audible, blood-curdling scream as I claw at his chest, trying to tear the magic wisps overtaking his body.

Both Auguste and Gideon have to pull me back from him, and the whip of the wind drowns my screams out, swirling in a furious rage in the bedroom. The rest of the art falls off the walls, and the house shakes.

I bellow in sheer agony and my chest feels as though it's cleaving in two. My soul is ripping right out of me.

The mating bond. I don't feel our bond.

It's gone.

My love—my entire life—is dead.

CHAPTER SEVENTEEN

"**B**ack away from her, or you'll all be killed!" Dad's in his wheelchair in the doorway.

Gideon and Auguste hesitate.

"Let her go!"

Both men let me go and back away slowly.

The wind dies down as I throw myself at Oz's chest and sob as I work furiously to pick threads out of his limp body. Each wisp comes apart in my hands, and I cry out in despair. This can't be happening. *Oz!* Sorrow grips my throat, and then a hand is on my shoulder.

"Focus, my dear child." Dad's voice sounds heartbroken. "Water. Conquers. Fire." He punctuates each word.

"Help me get him in the tub!"

Gideon and Auguste rush over and drape one of Oz's arms over their shoulders, and I grab his feet. Together, we carry him into the tub, and I turn on the cold water.

I climb into the tub with him and splash water on the wounds on his chest. Some of the fiery wisps sizzle and lick back in protest as though to proclaim they are Dante's inferno, and I am but a child with a squirt gun.

"No! You are *my* fire, and you will obey me."

I use my magic to direct the water flow from the tap so it pours into Oz. Unsatisfied with this, water runs out of my hands and over him, as though I am an ocean, and he is but a vessel for me to command. The magic threads flow upstream and back into my body. A current flows out of my hands, trying to take him out to sea, but I command him to come back to me.

A song of sirens pours out of my throat, and it beckons the rest of the magic threads back into me. When the last thread has left Oz's body, the air shifts suddenly, and he turns cold. The water returns to my body just as swiftly as it went, and I pull Oz close to me.

Inside my mind, I am sitting on the couch in my house, waiting, watching. Pacing. Not even bothering to wipe away the tears pouring down my cheeks and checking the clock on the wall.

Tick. Tick. Tick. Tick.

I hold my breath, afraid that if I breathe, I might miss something.

A knock comes to my mind's front door, and I fly to the door and throw it open so hard and fast it flies off its hinges, and it splinters into a thousand pieces as it hits the ground. Oz stands there, scorched and sopping wet. I sob as I throw my arms around his neck.

You came back to me.

Sahira.

"I told you she was into some freaky shit." Gideon glances at Auguste, and I snap back to present reality.

Oz folds me in his arms, and we are both soaking wet in the tub. By now, everyone present in the house is in our bathroom, and I can feel the wary vampire stares on my back. My teeth chatter from the cold.

Let's get you dry; Oz says in my head.

Hannah helps me out of the tub, while Gideon and Auguste help Oz out. He is weak but on the mend.

"Dude, you died. Again." Gideon raises both brows at Oz. "But like, died-died. Six feet under, stick a fork in him; he's done."

Maeve slugs him in the arm to stop.

"The prophecy was true," Wren's voice is wary. "What they didn't count on was the queen being a necromancer."

The room quiets, and the air is palpable.

"A necromancer?" Hannah helps me into a set of Oz's gray sweat-pants. I don't even care about my dignity now—I just need warmth.

"A witch who can bring someone back from the dead." There's a haunted look on Auguste's face. "I've never heard of a necromancer who can *actually* do it. The only ones I know of can only speak with the dead." He eyes me with suspicion, wondering what other tricks or spooks I might have up my sleeve.

"Well, he was already dead. And now he's ... less dead? I thought we could only die by beheading or a stake to the heart." Gideon pokes Oz. "I mean, he's still a vampire, and a witch, far as I can tell."

Oz swats at Gideon's hand.

I turn around to face the wall when I remove my robe and put Oz's sweater on me. Several vampire eyes dart around my bare back just before I do, and I can bet I know who's watching.

Hannah asks Sebastian to put some logs in the fireplace in the bedroom, so I can warm up. The fire roars to life as he does, and I welcome the sweet relief the warmth brings to my bones.

"The two of you need to rest." Dad wheels himself out. "The rest of you, out now," he shouts as they follow him out the door.

Hannah is the last to leave, and she whispers she loves me before shutting the door behind her.

Oz crawls into bed with me, and I cry into his chest.

"I am so sorry, Oz. I *killed* you. You weren't in my head anymore. I felt our mating bond break."

"I'm already dead."

You know what I mean.

Never mind the fact I'm a *necromancer*. I killed the love of my life. I would sooner throw myself off a cliff than ever hurt him, but I did. They should shackle me and cart me off to prison or hang me for my crimes. The words in my head are like a poison, festering insidiously.

Hey, hey now, Sahira, Oz interrupts the verbal assault in my head. I am your king, and you are my queen. I love you, no matter what. Our bond is back; we're okay.

"My intuition was wrong this time, Oz. I wasn't thinking; I just acted. And I killed you. I said I would kill you, and I *did.*" By now, I am inconsolably hysterical.

If I am a queen, and you are king, they should hang me for treason. Please take me to the gallows? If you don't kill me, the guilt will eat me alive.

"Lana, they prophesied this before you were ever born. Even in the prophecy, it said the queen killed her king by *accident.* That is all this was. The vampire witch tried to warn me about this thousands of years ago and several times since. Not a witch, nor vampire, hybrid, faction, or prophecy could have ever stopped me from falling in love with you."

"Why didn't you tell me about this prophecy?"

"It was the ravings of a madwoman, Lana!" He sits up in bed to face me. "It was never a secret. If it were, you would've seen it the moment we mated. No one believed this crazy vampire witch or her followers they call the *Lapis Templar.*"

"She has followers?" I shrink down into the bed. The very thought a group of people is so invested in our relationship freaks me out. They must hate me if they're such staunch followers of this prophecy.

"Wait a minute." Dread snakes its way through my body. "Do you think this could've been who attacked me in Mont-Tremblant?"

"There is no way it would've been the vampire witch who prophesied it. I don't think she's even alive anymore. But it could've been a loyalist. I'll have Gideon and Auguste look into that possibility now we know the prophecy is true. What we need to do is keep you safe. The best way to do that is to figure out how to control your magic. I've been a witch for thousands of years, but a lot of what I do is strictly intuition-based. I don't have a formula or spell you can follow. Sure, I have some spells on the cuneiform tablet from my mother, but I never thought to keep a grimoire because I didn't have anyone to pass it on to. It wasn't like I expected to have kids."

Oz takes my hand in his and massages it. A sense of calm washes over me—I didn't realize I had been wringing my hands nervously. Things seem like they're so out of control, but his touch helps ground me.

"Maybe we should make our own grimoire or book of shadows?

We can combine what we know and copy some from my dad's grimoire. This way, we can pass it on to our children." The air between us smells of sugar cookies, and I'm overwhelmed with love for this man. Through all this, he still loves me.

"I like your idea, Sahira." He brings my hand to his lips and holds it there before continuing. "I will *always* love you. There isn't a thing you can say or do to change that. In the meantime, I don't want to risk you or anyone else I love getting hurt; Hannah and your dad included."

"I agree. But what can we do? My dad is dying, Oz. I wish there was something I can do to fix this." I turn over to face him. "Now we know I'm a necromancer, do you think I could bring him back to life when he dies?"

Oz's eyebrows furrow and his eyes glisten. I don't think I'll like his answer.

"No, Lana, we can't risk that. We don't know what the toll will be for bringing me back. I'm sure it wouldn't be as heavy of a price considering I was already dead but bringing a witch or human back to life is entirely different. What if the toll is *your* life? Or Hannah's? We can't risk it, I'm sorry."

I hadn't thought of this. One of the very fundamentals of magic is power is an exchange. Performing magic can drain, especially for powerful magic. Bringing back an entire person from the dead has got to be one of the most difficult things you can do. And apparently, no one knows of another witch who has actually done it. I'm not sure what the implications of this are, and the idea haunts me. No matter the price, though, I would have gladly paid it a million times over just to bring Oz back.

The rest of the day, Oz and I both nap. I sleep in fits and nightmares consume me.

Knowing I so easily killed him terrifies me.

I terrify me.

AFTER SUPPER, I ask Oz to take a walk with me on the property. The sky is dark, but the lights from the river move smoothly across the water. The expansive view makes me feel small.

Ever since I was a little kid, I've been afraid of the dark. I always felt like someone, or something, was watching me.

I realize the likelihood someone *was* watching me is high. The Lapis Templar would've known I was the future queen destined to kill her king. My intuition as a kid told me I should be afraid, so I was. The real question, though, is why didn't they act then? Surely it would've been so much easier to kill me off as a child than as an adult. If the person who attacked me in Mont-Tremblant was part of the Lapis Templar, and they can drag a sleeping woman from her bed, I wouldn't put it past them to hurt a child.

"Lana, I think your mom had a protection or sentry spell on you as a child. It might explain why you had those buzzing sensations the closer you got to me. If I were your parent, I would've done the protection spell on you until you met the vampire witch you're supposed to mate. She knew we were going to marry before you were even born."

I think about this for a moment. "But why wouldn't she have kept the protection spell on me for life?"

"It takes an enormous amount of energy to do something like this." He slides his fingers between mine. "Her priority would've been protecting you, Lana. Not me. She would've known I could protect you, so she did what she could until then." Well, it makes sense. The buzzing sensations began at the airport when I neared the Ebbswick key. Then, the attack happened in Mont-Tremblant.

Fear courses through me now. They could be out there on the river, watching us. Panic rises in my chest and reverberates up my throat. My heart races, and the darkness closes in. Then, Oz's cool hand rests on my cheek and peace pours over me, chasing away every worry.

"When I marked you, Sahira, that was also like a protection spell. None of it—your mother's spell or my mark—is fool-proof, but it would be a suicide mission for anyone to try anything, lest they want to meet my wrath."

I pause our walk and face him. "I don't want to be a witch anymore." The risks far outweigh any potential benefit it brings me. "Please make me a vampire."

"No. Even if I made you a vampire, you'd still have your powers. You'd be an even bigger threat—you'd need *blood* to survive. And what happens if you can't get blood? You'd take it from someone you don't want to, like your dad or Hannah. The first *hundred years* I was a vampire, I was an evil killing machine. Sure, over the millennia we've honed the training, so recovery takes but a few months until you can be around humans again. I also understand you're a far more powerful witch than I ever was, Sahira, but I will *not* turn you into something you'd hate."

"Then I have to learn how to control this." I hold up my hands and stare at them. My hands are dangerous, and I don't want to hurt anyone else, and I don't want to *kill* anyone else.

"Sahira, *you* are magic. I could tie your hands up right here, and you could move the wind with your mind to sweep me off this cliff. You only need to learn how to control it. Tomorrow, your dad and I can teach you what we know about control."

Oz wraps his arms around me. My hair gently blows in a slight breeze, and I smell warm vanilla and sugar. *I love you, too;* I tell Oz in my head.

I know.

"Lana, your cycle is here. Head inside." His voice is soft, and I groan while dragging him inside with me. The family is in the parlor, and all the furniture is in the hallway. Gideon has Auguste in a half nelson, and it looks like Hannah is taking bets with Dad and Sebastian.

That isn't a sight you'd see every day, I muse. Gideon gets distracted when he senses me, and Auguste uses the opportunity to step back and reach down to grab Gideon's ankle, and he pulls, sending Gideon to the floor with a gigantic crack. The floorboards have busted.

Cheers erupt from Dad and Sebastian, who obviously placed their bets on Auguste.

Always a gentleman, Auguste extends an arm and helps Gideon to his feet. "I would've won had you stayed outside for another thirty seconds, Lana."

"Uh-huh," comes Auguste's reply as he high-fives Sebastian, then Dad. In no time at all, Dad uses magic to fix the floor. Gideon's nostrils flare as we pass by, and I try to ignore the icy tingling sensation I feel on my behind as I round the corner and go upstairs.

I have difficulty opening the bottom drawer in the bathroom because they stuffed it full of period paraphernalia: pads, tampons, menstrual cups, and period underwear. There are several types of each kind, like organic pads and cloth pads, and applicator-free tampons, and ones with plastic applicators. I stare at the drawer, half amused, half terrified of what Oz thinks my periods are like. There are enough supplies in here to supply a whole all-female boarding school for a year.

When I emerge from the bathroom, Oz has a mug of birth control tea waiting for me on the end table. Folded at the end of the bed are a pair of black drawstring sweatpants and one of his gray hooded sweatshirts, and I change into them. There's just something so comforting about wearing his oversized clothes—it makes me want to snuggle up next to a fire and watch sappy movies with him.

"We can arrange that." Oz hands me a box of chocolate truffles.

"Oh, babe! You didn't have to but thank you." I take the box from him and kiss him on the cheek. Seriously, what did I do to deserve a man like this?

Affection coats Oz's face. "I like when you call me babe. It makes me feel like we're a millennial couple with everyday problems."

"One of us *is* a millennial, babe. Do you want to see if anyone else wants to come to the movie room?" I feel bad for having slept most of the day and night.

We make our way downstairs. I'm in the mood to see *The Secret Life of Walter Mitty*, but the men want to watch *Insidious* or some other thriller. I concede and decide to make stovetop popcorn for all of us while they pick out the movie.

$$\sim$$

AFTER THE MOVIE, we go to our rooms for the evening. Having slept most of the day, Oz and I decide to stay up and work on some magic. We weren't going to start until tomorrow, but he wants me to learn a few things in preparation for Monday's beaver moon and penumbral lunar eclipse. He says this is when the sun, earth, and moon are aligned, and my magic will be amplified. Because we're going to see the lady from DHS that day, I need to be very careful.

Oz explains some witches are born with inherent abilities that make them unique, like his ability to read minds. We already know I have the gift of necromancy, the ability to sift to other places, water hands, and fire heart. There may be other gifts I've yet to discover. Some witches only have one gift, like canis nasum, or hound's nose, which enables them to detect maladies and cancers by smell. Rare gifts like time travel and second sight are usually kept secret by the witch who possesses these powers for fear it will be used against them.

"What special abilities do you have, aside from the ability to read minds?"

I sit cross-legged on the bed, and Oz has his head in my lap. I stroke his broad shoulders and think about how lucky I am to be his mate. It is as if the gods hand-picked him from all the celestial stars in the sky and made him mine.

His eyes and scent betray a more sensual response to my question, and he doesn't even need to tell me his answer is his abilities in the bedroom. I know these first-hand, and I love them.

"I don't think you understand, Sahira. The only reason you think I'm amazing in the bedroom is because we're mated. And before we mated, I knew I wanted you the moment I saw you. It wasn't because you weren't wearing a bra, your hair was wild, or your skin was glowing from chopping wood. We are destined to be together. Don't you see? Vampires are notoriously selfish in the bedroom, but all I want is to please you. I could spend millennia lying in bed with you, listening to your little moans as I satisfy your needs. My thirst for you is never satiated."

I lean down and kiss Oz on the forehead.

"Time for magic, Sahira. You've learned how to protect your thoughts, fly, dodge me, and move things with your mind. Considering what we witnessed this morning, you also definitely have a harness on air and water magic. I'd like to show you some earth magic now."

Oz procures a few seeds from his nightstand drawer. He places one in the palm of his hand, closes his eyes, and whispers something to the seed. His fingers close over it, and he uses his other hand to weave a magical thread through the back of his closed hand. When finished, he opens it, and I watch a seedling sprout. He loosens the magical thread on his hand, and the sprout grows taller and taller until he holds a plant full of ripe tomatoes where the seedling stood.

My mouth drops, and my eyes ... they must deceive me. There is no soil, yet Oz just grew an entire tomato plant from a seed in his hand. I weep from the splendor of it. I've always loved plants but had a hard time getting them to stay alive, no matter my grandiose plans with it.

Oz hands me an apple seed. The tiny black seed sits in the well of my palm, and I close my eyes and gently whisper, "grow!" to it before closing my fingers over the seed. I use the magical wisps to anchor it to the back of my closed hand with my other hand. I open my hand, and the tiny black seed becomes a seedling. It doesn't stop there, though: within seconds, the seedling becomes a giant apple tree that grows so heavy I drop it on the floor.

The old wooden boards creak under the massive weight and tree limbs shatter through the window above the bed and along the far wall. I scramble to Oz, and he holds me as I look on in horror at how out-of-control my magic is. Our bedroom door flies open, and all the vampires, my dad, and Hannah run into the room to defend against whatever creature could have been in the room. Well, dad doesn't *run*. Hannah pushes him in the wheelchair.

They stare in bewilderment when they see the giant apple tree has now busted its way through the roof. Little flecks of frost whirl through the air from the broken windows and ceiling, and the house groans under the pressure put on the floor.

"What in the hell happened here?" The situation amuses Gideon. "More freaky shit?" he stares at me.

"I was practicing growing a seedling. I guess I screwed up?"

Gideon erupts in laughter, and the rest of the room isn't sure how to react because I'm clearly panicking. "I'm so sorry, Oz. I will fix your house."

"Hey now, you're alright. This is just a house, and the place is *ours, not just mine*. Are *you* okay?"

I just broke his house, and he's asking if *I'm* okay?

Dad reaches into the pouch he carries with him and draws out a wand. With a few flicks of his wrist, he cuts and stacks the entire tree in a pile by the fireplace. Then, threads of magic shoot from his wand, and they work to mend the windows and the roof. In under five minutes, the room looks normal and not as though I grew a monstrous tree in the bedroom. The only evidence this ever occurred lies stacked against the wall and the giant pile of Fuji apples on the bed.

"Dad!" My eyes grow even wilder watching him fix damage this significant with magic. "First, thank you. And second, can you teach me?"

He smiles with a little twinkle in his eye. "Sure thing, hon."

CHAPTER EIGHTEEN

The smell of incense wafts up my nose when we enter the metaphysical store in town for Small Business Saturday.

My eyes slowly peruse the white wall of gemstones, crystals, and minerals, stacked in see-through plastic boxes and nailed to the wall. I recognize lapis lazuli, amethyst, and quartz, but that's about it. Oz hovers his hand over several of the important crystals and gemstones.

"As a witch, you don't need these things, but they can help amplify the effects of your magic or help guide your intentions." Oz tosses a stone in the air and catches it. "I perform most of my magic without the use of tools, but I've been doing this for thousands of years. Although, I can't say I've needed repair magic in at least a few hundred of them, so I'm glad your dad is around to show you how to do that. I'm afraid I'm a little out of practice. But, with you in my life, I'll have your dad show me it, too."

I give him a playful swat on the arm. "Well, lucky for you Osgood Finlandian, I sure look cute when I make a mess."

That you do. He puts an arm around my waist, and I grab a velvet-lined tray to place some crystals and candles on.

Oz and I pause in front of the big row of books, and he raises his eyebrows at a few before dismissing them. I spot a book on tantric sex and flip it over to read the back cover before thumbing through some pages.

He leans his head over my shoulder, and I'm very aware of his presence when my senses become overwhelmed with spice.

We don't need a book on that, Sahira. What you and I have is written in the stars.

I turn around and pull him in for a kiss.

I interrupt our kiss when the heavy wooden door to the shop creaks open, and the bells around the doorknob jingle gleefully as it shuts.

"Hey," Gideon spots the title to the book I hold in my hand. He saunters over and runs a hand through his dark chocolate-colored hair. "May I?" He reaches to inspect the book's contents. I nod and he takes it from my hand.

"I didn't take you for needing any instructions, Lana. Don't think I can't hear ya both." Gideon eyes shift to a gunmetal blue. "Unless you think Oz is the one who needs some instruction. In that case, I'm happy to demonstrate how to please you." His nostrils flare, and the smell of cinnamon takes over the space between us.

"Unnecessary, Gideon, although I applaud your gallantry." I snatch the book back from his hands. "Why play little league when I'm already fraternizing in the majors?"

Gideon clutches his chest and acts wounded. Oz grins at my dig and pulls me in a little closer by the waist. *Man-eater,* he says in my head, and I tighten my hold on him.

"Well, you just let me know whenever you tire of this old man and want to have a go at it." I roll my eyes. They're *both* old.

After we pay, the five of us check out a few more shops before joining the rest of the family at the tree farm to pick out a Christmas tree for the house. We might not be here for Christmas, but the idea of decorating a tree with most of the family was too good to pass up. Gideon quickly zeros in on the biggest tree at the farm, and I have to talk him down.

"I'm uncertain it will fit." I size up the tree.

"Oh, that is what they all say, but we always make it fit!" Gideon has a feline grin and scoops up a ball of snow to toss in the air.

I'm glad Dad isn't within earshot, otherwise he'd probably give him an earful. Instead, I redirect Gideon to a tree a little shorter than he is. This way, we can fit a topper on it. Everyone gathers around the tree and agrees this is the one. The evergreen is full, and not too big. The men make quick work to cut it down and strap it to Wren's SUV.

After stopping at a cafe for lunch and returning to the house, Dad needs to rest a bit before teaching me, so he takes a nap. He grows more tired as the days wear on, and each interaction I have with him leaves me longing for more time.

The men haul the tree inside while Maeve and I rearrange the furniture in the parlor to make room for it to sit in front of the large picture window facing the Mississippi. Oz steadies the tree in the stand while Auguste tightens the screws to secure the tree upright.

I sweep the pine needles off the floor, then take Hannah to the attic where the decorations are. Oz says they're stacked in large gold plastic totes with green lids. The loft is a walk-in room right off the bedroom Gideon stays in. As soon as we open the door to it, his room smells strongly of cinnamon, and I don't even want to think about why. I use my Ebbswick key to unlock the attic door, and Hannah is speechless as she watches its magic.

"I can't believe what my eyes are seeing! Can you imagine the trouble we would've gotten in when we were in high school with one of these things?"

I turn the doorknob and push the attic door open. It creaks, and the room reeks of dust and mothballs. Across the space is a large circular dormer, and light spills in streaks across the attic floor.

I locate a pull-string light hanging from the center of the room and pull its cord. Dust particles dance in the sunlight beaming through the window and stir as we make our way to the row of plastic totes against the far wall. I can make out a very faint buzzing sensation as we near the totes.

The Christmas totes are exactly where Oz said they'd be. Each of us grabs a golden tote, but my eye catches a small wooden box in between the studs of the unfinished attic wall. I set the tote down so I can pick up the light box. The buzzing becomes a hum once it's in my hands. When I blow the dust off it, it reveals little magic threads wrapped tightly around it. There appears to be some inscription on the front of the box, but I can't make out what it says. It doesn't seem to be in any language I know.

"Huh. I wonder if Oz knows this is here?" Hannah peeks around me and asks what it is. "I'm not sure. I'll bring it downstairs and see if he knows."

I set the small box on top of the Christmas tote, hauling them both down the stairs. When the vampires see the box, they grow quiet and dart their eyes to Oz.

"Hey, babe. I found this little box in the attic, and it appears to be enchanted." Oz's focus falls on the box, and he rushes over to me and clutches it in his hand.

"Where did you find this?" His shoulders turn in while he traces the inscription on the side.

"Wedged behind the totes and in between the studs in the wall. What's in it?" The magic threads wrap tightly around the entire box, so I didn't want to try opening it.

Oz sits down on the couch nearest the Christmas tree and holds a hand over the box. "This has been missing for at least two or three hundred years." His voice is barely above a whisper. "I enchanted it to keep it away from prying eyes, and that also meant I couldn't use a locator spell to find it when I lost it." He slides his fingers underneath the magic wisps and gives a slight tug. The magic threads fall apart and on the floor before disintegrating into the air. With a small shove with his thumbs, the thin wooden lid slides off into his lap.

I can't see what's in the box until he lifts it out. It's a small clay boat with a little hole at one end—presumably where one might tie a rope to it. He flips it over, and I can make out five rust-colored smudges about two inches long along the bottom. Oz blinks away tears, and the air in the room shifts.

Grief hangs thick in the air, and I kneel next to him, unsure of what to say because I don't know what's going on. I don't want to push him to tell me in front of everyone, but I want to hold space for him if he wants to share.

"Mendalla." His accent is heavier than usual. "I made this for him the night he was born."

"Mendalla?" Hannah glances towards me.

"My son." No one speaks, and instead, we share in this moment of grief with him.

Horror shoots through me when I realize the rust-colored streaks on the boat's underside are from a small, bloody hand. I knew Oz's wife and son were killed, but I don't know the details.

So many secrets and memories were revealed to me when he made me his mate, but there were so many I couldn't keep up with them all as they flooded my mind. I didn't feel it was my place to ask for any details, and now I feel like a crappy mate for not knowing the most painful parts of Oz's story.

Do I even have a right to know? Perhaps I don't, and I certainly wouldn't hold it against him if he keeps this one close to his heart. Besides, the details don't matter in the grand scheme of things. This was a tragedy by any right.

Oz takes a deep breath and turns the boat over in his hands. "I'm just now piecing things together. It was the Lapis Templar."

I feel as though I'm intruding on a private thought and not a spoken conversation. He is here, but his mind is distant as he works to arrange his thoughts.

"I woke to terrible noises from the cattle. It sounded like a predator was attacking them. I ran barefoot to the barn and there was utter chaos; it moved so fast, I never saw what it was, but the animals dropped one-by-one until everything stopped. I was so distraught, trying to save animals that were already dead. They were our livelihood, and my family would starve otherwise.

It was then their screams pierced the night—first, Mendalla, and immediately after I heard Anunit, half-sobbing, half-screaming until she went quiet. I was too far away. It might've only taken me sixty seconds to get back to the hut using my witches' speed, but every step felt like I was trudging through mud. I couldn't ..." he wipes his tears with the back of his hand. "I couldn't get to them fast enough. She slaughtered them like animals. A woman stood over them, speaking in a language I didn't yet know. For thousands of years, I tried to make sense of her last words before I killed her.

'You will scorn her, and that will be your undoing.'

Even when I learned English, I didn't understand, until just now."

The agony splayed on Oz's face is haunting: harsh lines, deep grooves, and bloody tears. All the peaceful smiles, raised eyebrows, and joy have leached from his being. I can't reconcile the gap widening right in front of me; I feel like a trespasser—an interloper—having stumbled upon a love *I have no right to.* The more I witness the journey he's taking; the more ominous and precarious things feel between us.

"They killed my wife and son because of the *prophecy*, but it was their mistake. I was still human and not yet a king. Anunit was *never* a queen." Heartache hangs thick on his words. "They weren't supposed to die." Oz shields his face now as sobs take over.

I don't know the right words to say because I have never lost a child or spouse, despite knowing profound grief. The weight of every-thing I *should* say crushes my chest, and I hyperventilate as panic and despair grip my throat and threaten to devour me from the inside out.

I am the reason Anunit and Mendalla are dead. If it weren't for me, there would be no vampires, and with no vampires, there is no prophecy. Oz would've died in Sumer, happily surrounded by those he loves, *thousands* of years ago. Every vampire I love would've lived normal, human lives free of the burden of bloodlust.

I am the curse.

Suddenly, I know exactly why my mom left my dad. I know it killed her to do it, just like it will me, but it had to be done.

"I love you all. I'm sorry."

Please forgive me; I beg Oz in my head while fat tears roll down my cheeks.

I squeeze my eyes tightly and think about my dad's farm in Tripoli. I so desperately wish to be there in November 1985. My mind works to build his farmhouse along a dusty gravel road between Readlyn and

Tripoli. Mom kisses Dad on his scruffy cheek as she wishes him a safe trip to Minnesota for his appointment. She sends him off with a sack lunch and tells him she loves him.

As I fill in more details of the house and time, the ground beneath my feet shakes where reality and the past collide. The earth has opened up just enough for me to slip through a crack, and I lower myself down and slide through the gaping void.

I love you, always—I have to make this right. I let go of the floorboards and fall.

"No, Sahira!" Oz reaches for me, but I vanish right before him.

CHAPTER NINETEEN

TRIPOLI, IOWA; THE DAY BEFORE
THANKSGIVING, 1985

*D*on't cry. Don't cry. The sun sits high in the sky, but it doesn't warm the bitter cold I feel without a jacket. The wind whips my curls across my face, and I say a little prayer Mom is home. I'm eager to be somewhere warm. I peer in the slit between the curtains on the door's window, and I see her sitting at the table while she reads the newspaper. I knock gently, so I don't startle her.

Standing on the porch, I shiver without my coat or warm clothes. When Mom opens the door, she gets one good look at me before looking to the driveway, presumably searching for my car. I have to resist the urge to wrap my arms around her and cry. It has been over two decades since I've seen her or felt her hug. I'd never let her go.

"Can I help you?" She narrows her eyes.

Fuck. What do I tell her? I'm older than she is, and no doubt she's wary of some strange woman without a coat and no transportation just appearing at her door when there's an inch of snow on the ground.

"Annabelle Chapman." I stutter her name out, whether from the tremble in my voice or the chattering of my teeth, I can't be sure. I clear my throat and quickly blink the tears out of my eyes. "Mom."

Her face drains of any color, and the eyes roll back in her head. I catch her just before she hits the floor. *Crap.*

I drag her just far enough for me to shut the door from the cold. What the hell am I going to do now? I pace frantically and decide to grab a small decorative pillow from the couch and put it behind her head. She comes to, and her eyes are huge as she stares at me, trying to find her features in mine.

"But I only just found out I'm pregnant this morning." she squints her eyes. "I haven't even told your dad yet."

Shoot. I was hoping I'd travel to just before they conceived me so I could convince her to leave dad so I wouldn't be born—I'll have to work with this.

"I'm from 2020." She believes I'm her child, but will she believe I'm a time traveler? She sits up and runs a hand through her long brown hair. "Ah, yeah. I figured my offspring would time travel. I named you Lana, didn't I?"

I nod and cry for so many reasons. Relief she doesn't think I'm crazy, anguish over what I have to do, and grief over leaving everyone and everything I love behind. I don't have all the answers, but I have to make this right.

"Oh, sweetheart," Mom grabs my hand. "What's the matter? Why are you here? You must be careful traveling through time, or you can get lost."

"I've made such a mess of things, Mom. Vampires are real because of me. I'm why millions of people are dead. I'm why the love of my life had his own ruined. Please help me fix this." I help her off the floor, and we move to the living room where I tell her everything. I start from the top and leave nothing out.

She straightens her shoulders, and I see a thought enter her mind. This is when she realizes what she has to do, too.

"Mom, see that I am never born. Millions of lives depend on it."

She's crying now, and the sacrifices she and I both have to make breaks my heart in two. I had to leave Oz to spare him from the burden I brought. If I am never born, then there is no prophecy. There are no vampires and no king for me to kill. No murder of an innocent child and his mother. People don't have to live through unimaginable heartache at the hands of vampires. It kills me I will never come to know Oz, enjoy his touch, or bask in his warm vanilla and sugar when he looks at me.

The ache is unbearable, and I know my mother feels the same way. After all, I know now the reason she left my dad all those years ago was that I came to her and told her what was at stake if she didn't. She has to abort me and leave this life behind.

AFTER MAKING an appointment with the abortion clinic in Waterloo for early this afternoon, Mom spends the rest of the morning sobbing. I feel like the worst person in the world for bringing this to her. I know how my dad felt when my mom left, and it kills me to have to be the reason to put him through that.

I wonder where Oz is in this place in time. Is he in the US? Perhaps he's in Colombia, practicing his Spanish with the locals. Or maybe he's in the Middle East.

Fear strikes me when I remember he may be in the middle of the Iran-Iraq war. I'm having a difficult time recalling his whereabouts through time. There is no real way to look him up—I'm not sure what name he's using now. My heart longs to be near him, so much so, it physically aches.

Mom writes a letter for Dad and places the envelope under the flower vase on the table. She cries as she puts on her winter jacket, and grabs me a spare one, too.

Briefly, I consider telling her no. After all, I won't need a coat in another hour or two if the abortion is successful. But the weather is freezing outside, much colder than usual this time of year. I brave a stoic face for her, lest she have second thoughts while we drive to Waterloo.

BEFORE GOING TO HER APPOINTMENT, Mom drops me off at an Italian restaurant downtown. She takes a couple of twenty-dollar bills from her purse and hands it to me so I can enjoy one last meal. I try not to cry while I bury my face in the crook of her neck. "I love you, Mom."

"And I've loved you since the moment I knit you in my womb." She wipes a tear from her face with the back of her hand. Mom hops in her car and drives away, and a torrent of tears falls to my chest, knowing it won't be long now. These are my last moments on this earth, and I am alone once more. I allow this brief cry before collecting myself and heading inside the restaurant.

The maître d'hôtel asks me to follow her to a small table next to the window. The menu is extensive, and I breathe a sigh of relief when I see Moscato d'Asti available under the white wine section. I order a glass and manicotti and wish Oz were here to enjoy it with me. I think back to the first time he and I met and how he knew I loved sweet wine.

I remember all our other shared moments; teleporting to his bedroom, watching the sunset, him saving my life, becoming his mate, finding dad, killing Oz, and subsequently bringing him back from the dead. These memories roll down my cheek, and grief chokes me. He means everything to me, but I know I have to do this for him to give all those I love a chance to live a normal life free of their burden.

The server checks on me several times over the lunch hour. I don't have a watch on me and no cell phone, but surely Mom's appointment is over by now as the lunch rush came and went long ago. I fully expected to vanish during her appointment, having ceased to exist.

A sinking feeling in my gut tells me I've got things wrong. Mom didn't leave Dad in 1985 because I told her so I would never be born. I wondered why she didn't seem surprised I'm a time traveler.

It's because *she* is one, too.

My hands tremble at this realization. She left because she couldn't face aborting me. Instead, I bet she traveled somewhere in time. That is why I was alive in the future, and why she left Dad suddenly one day.

I have to find her in time so I can stop her from giving birth to me.

If I can do this, then there is no prophecy, and millions of people's lives will be spared. The only problem is trying to find where Mom went in history or the future. If I were in her shoes, where would I go to ensure I could give birth without risking running into my time-traveling daughter? Nothing comes to mind. I do know one place, though.

I throw back my second glass of Moscato d'Asti and leave both twenty-dollar bills on the table before walking to the bathroom. Closing myself in a stall, I lean my head back against the door, trying to remember the scene right before she vanished. I build our cabin's property in my mind; the path of worn grass leading to the pond, towering maple trees, chirping birds, and raspberry bushes plump with juicy fruit. Mosquitoes buzz about my exposed skin, sweat causing my curls to cling to my neck, and wildflowers sway in the breeze.

The floor below the bathroom stall opens up, and I slip through it. I don't waste any time letting go this time around, and I fall. I can't distinguish which way is up as I tumble through time. I can see what my mom meant by getting lost here. I have to right myself before I find myself somewhere I don't want to be.

Gaining control of my arms, I bring them to my side quickly, and float into the void. Now that I'm no longer tumbling, I can see which way I need to go. I have to follow the magic thread to the fissure behind me.

Slipping through the opening is easy now I kind of know what I'm doing, and I have to turn my body to the side as though I'm passing between two chairs in a crowded restaurant.

When I teleported to Oz's bedroom the first night I met him, I had an inkling I could do much bigger things if I concentrated hard enough.

A race through time to intercept my mother is the most effective skills test I could ever face.

CHAPTER TWENTY

JUNE 1994; FINLAND, MINNESOTA

twig snaps under my feet when I land near the raspberry bushes. It is still morning, but the summer heat is quickly rising. Crickets and birds make their beautiful songs, completely oblivious to my entire world falling apart. Mom has several berries in her bucket already, and she startles when she sees me.

"Mom." I stretch my hands towards her, afraid she'll slip through time again. "Please don't leave. Hear me out."

She sets her bucket down and speaks instead. "I knew I'd see you sometime this year, but I wasn't sure when. I've kept magic from you so you'll never have the occasion to know Oz."

Well, this explains the binding of my magic.

"That changed nothing! It only made me out of control when my magic emerged. I killed Oz *because* of my uncontrolled magic. Had I known magic from the beginning, I would've been able to control myself by the time I met him."

Mom considers this for a moment as she swats a mosquito on her arm. "We're in a huge, confusing loop of space and time, and things are getting muddled. Where exactly did things go wrong? Don't ask me to go back and abort you or prevent your birth in any way—it will never happen."

We stand in each other's presence while we both try to make sense of things. The sun bakes our skin, and the heat feels appropriate considering the turmoil we both face. She's right, though. All of this time travel mess has muddied things, and I can no longer see clearly. My intuition doesn't know the right course, and part of me wonders if it would be better to just let it go.

"I don't know how to make this right, Mom. This stupid prophecy has caused so much irreparable harm." I drop to my knees and bury my face in my hands. She kneels next to me and wraps her arm around my shoulders, holding tight, and I'm flooded with a sense of calm. I put my head up to look at my mom and see her eyes are closed. The feeling of peace quickly turns to dread as I watch her vanish right before me.

This was when Mom left me, but I don't know where in time she went. I leave the bucket where it sits, walk back to the pond, and sit in her camp chair. It will be a couple more hours before little me wakes, so I have time to figure out when and where to go from here. I wrestle with the guilt of leaving eight-year-old me to fend for herself, but in reality, I turned out alright.

At a young age, I knew profound grief far beyond my years. I went through unimaginable trauma that shaped who I am today.

As I aged, though, I also came to know profound love. Love for the Sawyers, Hannah, Oz, his sires, and Dad. My heart wretches at the realization of what I let go of. To spare Oz and the world from pain, I've hurt all of the people I love.

Will they even want me back if I go?

Hot tears pour down my face while I work to build the house in Dubuque in my mind. It should be easier now I know the specific date, although I'm unsure of the specific time. We were so busy with the tree, but I know it was in the afternoon. I can try to show up in the early evening just to be on the safe side.

After building the house, I work on the inside—the Christmas tree is in the parlor, and two large golden totes sit next to it. On the couch is the little box containing Mendalla's clay boat. Everyone is in their separate bedrooms before supper, and I have Oz sitting on the lounge chair in the tower, staring over the Mississippi.

The Earth quakes below me, and it opens up just a sliver. I pull clods of grass from it so I can slip in, and I let go. The entrance to the present place and time is familiar to me, having left it only hours ago. As I approach it, a buzzing sensation reverberates from the opening. I step inside quickly, and the vibration stops.

CHAPTER TWENTY-ONE

Our room is trashed. The couch; in splinters. Picture frames shattered. Feathers everywhere from our pillows. My eyes immediately find Oz with his head in his hands in the tower. I am silent but know the sounds of my heart, mind, and scent give me away far before I ever make a peep.

He looks up in a daze, and I can see he's been crying. His sweater is soaked in blood from his tears. As soon as he sees me, he hesitates before scaling the distance between us.

His arms wrap around me, and I am off the floor, his cushion to sob on.

You came back to me, Sahira, he says in my head.

"I'm so sorry, Oz. I tried to fix things, but I think I only made them worse." The pain inside of me is sharp and dark, as though my body is working furiously to knit the hole that appeared when I left him. "I just wanted to stop the prophecy from ever happening so Anunit and Mendalla would've never been killed, and you would've grown old together."

This causes Oz to sob harder and hearing him breaks my heart again. The door to the bedroom flies open, but he doesn't move, just holds me tighter. I can sense the other vampires watching our exchange now. They're only in the room a moment before leaving and closing the door behind them. I have a lot of explaining to do, but they're allowing Oz and me time to work through what happened.

Oz carries me to our bed and throws back the trashed covers before laying us down under them. The look on his face is one of heartbreak, and I am gutted to witness it. He holds a hand to my cheek as though I am not here, and he has to touch me to know I have gone nowhere else. I can imagine the trauma I caused everyone today. So foolish. How will we heal from this?

Will you say something? I plead with him in my mind.

"Where did you go?" His voice is hoarse. For a vampire, this means he's been crying far worse than any human might've.

"1985. I tried to get my mom to leave Dad before they ever conceived me, but I screwed up and arrived after the fact." Oz holds me while I explain the rest of what happened and how Mom took off for 2018 instead. I also explain how Mom left in 1994 while we talked, so we've solved that mystery. We just need to figure out where in time she went.

"Where do you think she went?" He's no longer crying, but there's hesitation in his voice as though I will disappear again.

"I don't know. The last thing I told her was how much harm this prophecy has caused."

"Do you think she'd try to stop the prophecy? Wherever she went, she never returned. This can't be good."

I'm not sure. I only knew my mom for a moment in my life, and she kept so much from me to protect me from the prophecy. Where could she even go to stop it? She wouldn't stop my birth. What else is there to do? We don't know the identity of the Lapis Templar followers.

"You talked about a vampire witch. The one everyone said was crazy. Who is she?"

"Dolphina Darling." His tone has a hint of anger in it. "No one has seen or heard from her in at least a thousand years. Maybe two thousand." Oz pulls me in close to him, and I just want to be near him. It was agony being separated, and I never thought I'd ever see him again.

Lana ... Oz says in my head. You broke all our hearts today. I know you thought it was the right thing to do, but you must understand I made peace with what happened thousands of years ago. I never got over it, but I eventually learned to live again. What you witnessed today when you found the clay boat was merely me finding a small piece of my past that I used to cope with. Seeing it again sent a rush of old memories back. It doesn't mean I regret being with you or wish you'd never come into my life. Do you understand?

I bury my head in his chest, and sob. I've brought so much pain to everyone I love only because I tried to do the right thing. It was logical to me that if the love of my life is hurting, I should fix it, even to my detriment.

"You are my mate. The only one I've ever taken." His voice breaks. "Life doesn't matter without you. Do you realize what I would've done as soon as your dad passed away?"

Grief grips my chest like a vise, and I have difficulty breathing under the pressure. Oz would've taken care of Dad, and then he would've killed himself as soon as he died. All this would've been for naught.

"I'm sorry, Oz. What I did was so screwed up, and I've made such a mess of things. I don't know how to fix this, and I don't expect you to forgive me for it. I just hope in time you can heal from my betrayal."

I love you, Sahira. Please don't do this again, he pleads in my head.

He still loves me, even after all this. "I love you too. I promise I will never do this to you again."

We are a mess of limbs, holding each other until sleep takes us.

A knock on the bedroom door wakes us not long after.

"Come in." Dad opens the door and wheels himself into the room, asking for a few minutes alone with me. Oz heads downstairs to work on supper for everyone.

"Dad, I'm sorry. I am *so* sorry. Mom left you because of *me*." My voice is hysterical. He wheels himself until he reaches my bed, and he leans over to hug me. I wrap my arms tightly around him, and he speaks while I sob in his chest.

"Lana, there are many lessons you learn in life. This is one of them.

Trying to change the past has consequences, and often, fate intercedes anyway." Dad strokes my hair, and a magical wave of calm envelops me.

"Had I never gone back in time, Mom would've never left you, and she never would've left me. She is somewhere in time, and I think she's trying to stop the prophecy. If she hasn't returned after twenty-six years, I'm worried something has happened to her." The look on his face tells me everything I fear. Wherever she went, she probably didn't survive. Depending on the year she traveled to, being a woman is difficult or extremely difficult. Never mind the fact she's a witch. Entire centuries could be very dangerous for her.

Dad sighs. "I'm afraid I don't know a lot about time travel because your mother kept this a secret from me. I don't blame her, as that information could be detrimental on many levels if it got into the wrong hands." This surprises me Dad didn't know about Mom. She was in love with him, and he with her. Even if Oz couldn't read my mind, I'd still tell him everything.

"I suppose everyone is upset with me, aren't they?"

He winces. "We realized what happened as soon as you disappeared, and Oz filled us in with the rest. I've seen no one love as he does."

He is so good to me. Far better than I deserve. Once I get to Bedlam, I'll have eternity to show him how much I love him. For now, I've got a lot of making up to do on the home front: Oz, Dad, Hannah, and the vampires. I'm afraid to even to go downstairs now, but know I'll need to face the music. Maybe I can have Oz send them upstairs one by one, so I can apologize.

Dad goes downstairs and lets Hannah know I'd like to talk to her.

When Hannah enters my room, she is heartbroken.

"I'm sorry, Hanalei. I screwed up." Fat tears mar my face, and I use a scrap of the comforter to wipe them.

"I forgive you, but I'm more upset you didn't talk about this with anyone. We would've talked you out of it."

"That is why I did it. I thought I was doing the right thing." I cast my eyes to the ground at her feet.

She crawls into the bed and holds me. "I don't know what I would've done without my best friend." She's so understanding, and I deserve far worse than she's giving me. "You should've seen him, Lana. I was afraid for his safety. His sobs will haunt me for the rest of my life."

"Thank you for being there when I couldn't be. I don't know how I'm going to make this right, but please know I'm sorry."

"I already said I forgive you; the boys might have a few more choice words."

I figured as much. They're more vocal than the rest of the family. I might as well deal with the repercussions of my actions. I tell Hannah I'll be down in a bit, but first, I should shower. First, I was in the cold, and then I was in the dead of summer today. I'm a mess.

Oz SITS on the bed while I towel off. Understandably, he doesn't want to be far from me after what I put him through. My movements are slow and methodical, allowing him time in my presence before facing the rest of the family. When I'm dressed, I wrap my arms around him and breathe in his scent. We don't say a word when I grab his hand and open the bedroom door.

"Do you mind if I speak with Lana? We'll meet you downstairs." Auguste leans against the hallway wall. I look hesitantly at Oz, and he nods to support it. Oz collects Gideon from his room, and they head down the stairs for supper.

I'm nervous about what Auguste has to say to me, so I decide to speak first. "Listen, Auguste—I'm sorry. What I did today was uncalled for. I thought I was doing the right thing, but I was wrong."

He switches on the stereo and turns it up before speaking his piece. "Have you *any* idea what you've done to Oz?" Usually, Auguste is quite reserved, but today, he is spitting angry. "He came unhinged, Lana. I've never seen him like this, *ever*. Do you know what it does to a vampire when something happens to someone he loves? He lives with it forever."

Tears spring to my eyes, hard and fast now. I'm like a schoolgirl being reprimanded in front of the entire class, and the more he speaks, the angrier I get.

"You may as well have tied him up and drove stakes through every square inch of his body and poured acid in the wounds." He paces the room. "Losing a mate is like losing your body, mind, and soul on repeat, and it's torture."

"*I* was tortured, watching *my mate* relive the worst moment of his entire life! Not just a few decades of pain, but millennia. I'm the only person who could go back and stop it. Wouldn't you do anything for the one you love, even if it meant your life?" My chest heaves and I don't even care about the tears pouring down my cheeks.

"Enough, Auguste!" Oz bursts into the room. He takes me by the arm and brings me out to the hallway, and I lose it. I knew it would upset Oz if something happened to me, but I didn't realize it would drive him to madness. Then again, I love him so much I would sacrifice myself to stop his pain.

Auguste follows us to the hallway and uses a gentler tone this time. "I'm sorry for coming unhinged. You just ... you wrecked us, and most of all, you wrecked Oz. I'm going to get over this, but it might take him some time. Go easy on him, and for the love of all things, do nothing stupid like this again."

"I'm sorry." He motions his hand towards the stairs, and we meet the rest of the family in the dining room. They are quiet when I enter and they just look at me, unsure of what to say. I'm not sure what to say either, so after I sit down, I begin my apology.

"Today, I made a huge mistake." I fidget with the cloth napkin in front of me. "I want you to know how sorry I am and hope in time, you can learn to forgive me for this. What I did was unconscionable."

Pippa is the first to speak. "Lana, we all make mistakes, and you did what you thought would help, and no one ..." she looks directly at Auguste before continuing, "can fault you for it. Love makes us do foolish things, and no one knows that better than Auguste."

Auguste shifts in his seat. He's loved before? The room is quiet when he speaks.

"I took a mate once, and she was human. She worked as a nurse in an infirmary, and it was love at first sight. We married in a small church just outside of Chicago. I made the mistake of not turning her before I was called away to WWI, and word reached me on the battlefield she succumbed to the Spanish flu."

"Oh, Auguste, I'm so sorry." Words don't seem quite enough, and nothing could stop the tears from flowing.

This is why he lost it on me. His wife died, and he knows exactly how Oz felt today. Not only did I hurt the love of my life tonight, but I hurt the rest of the people I hold so close. To make matters even worse, I reminded Auguste of what he lost, too.

"We're just happy you're back, Lana," Sebastian holds my stare. The rest of the table gives their agreement before digging into the tacos Oz prepared. I expected far more scolding than I received, but I doubt anything could compare to the way I feel about myself.

The air is somber tonight, and for good reason. This isn't how I wanted to spend our last night as a family since Hannah, Wren, and Sebastian go home tomorrow. It'll be quieter without them here, but I'll sure miss them all.

MY FIRST DREAM IS HIM. Nuzzled against his warm chest and listening to the steady thump-thump of his heart while his swift feet pad through thick woods far faster than any mortal. I am bloody and gravely injured, but this man isn't my captor. No, he's here to save me.

I cannot smell this man. A warm glow comes from his skin comforts me, even in my dream state. I never see his face, just his muscular arms and the soft luminescence of his body. The way he speaks is always the same; his deep voice is like a balm to my soul.

"Stay with me. We're almost there."

I can't fight it. Sleep takes me, and I immediately find myself in a nightmare with the Lapis Templar again. This time, I encounter them while wearing two babies strapped to my chest with a long dark cloth.

The streets are cobbled, and the leather sandals I have strapped to

my feet provide little protection from the cold. I'm looking for someone. No, I'm running away from people chasing me. There is no electricity, and I sprint past many shops with worn canvas awnings. As I
round the corner, I run into a woman wearing a head covering and
her lips in a sneer. I'm startled, and she snatches the babies right off
my chest.

How did she grab them both? The babies—*I must save the babies.* I
fall trying to get them from her, and the Lapis Templar catches up
with me. One of them rips my dress open and sinks their teeth into
my neck. The pain is intense, and I get no pleasure from it like I do
when Oz feeds from me. No one hears my screams.

The last thing I see is the kidnapper handing the babies off to a
blonde woman. I don't see her face, just a flash of her nearly white
hair before she disappears around a corner.

CHAPTER TWENTY-TWO

I'm still in the movie room when I open my eyes, except now I'm lying down on the couch. The vampires, my dad, and Hannah hover over me, and I'm weirded out.

"Hi ...?" Why are they all staring at me? I sit up and put my feet on the floor.

"You were screaming, Sahira. I couldn't see your dreams."

I give a detailed play-by-play of my dreams—the first one when I'm in the woods and someone is rescuing me. Then, the next dream; the old-looking village, my shoes, the babies strapped to me, the kidnapper, and the vampire from the Lapis Templar. The surroundings didn't look familiar at all, and I suspect it wasn't exactly modern times, either.

"It isn't unusual for witches to have vivid dreams as we approach a full moon." Dad pats my hand. "With a penumbral lunar eclipse in two days, I imagine dreams are even more heightened."

It makes sense, but why is it Oz can never see my dreams when they're about the Lapis Templar? No doubt he might recognize some of their faces or even the settings I encounter them in. He never sees the man carrying me through the woods, either.

"Sorry for falling asleep on you guys; I've had a long day. I'm a bit more rested now, though; if anyone wants to catch another flick?"

They laugh and say they've already watched three while I was asleep. Goodness, I suppose I was exhausted. Oz helps me up from the deep couch, and we all file upstairs to our rooms. I pass the grandfather clock in the dining room just as it chimes two gongs.

One great thing about being with a vampire is any awkward sleep schedule doesn't bother them at all. Oz is ready to go if I want to play a game in the middle of the night. Or, if I want to do some baking late into the evening, he's more than happy to.

IT SEEMS like so much has happened these past few days, and Oz and I haven't connected. He grabs a bottle of Finlandian from the fridge and two wine glasses on our way upstairs. We open the tower curtains and sit on the couch so we can view the Mississippi. Oz smells good—his usual aroma, and now he has some cologne on. After pouring us each a glass, he puts his arm around me, and I rest my head on his chest.

"I love you." I take a sip of wine. The drink mellows me out and I feel so close to Oz now.

"I love you, too." he kisses me on top of my head. "What do you suppose the babies in your dreams meant?"

We've talked about how I want a baby with him, and we'll have to have children sooner rather than later, thanks to my advancing age. Would we get pregnant before or after I go to Bedlam? What happens if I don't come back for twenty years like Bonnie Driscoll?

"I don't know, but I could tell they were ours. They smelled like us and had olive skin." The tower smells of warm vanilla and sugar now, and I nuzzle Oz. Even after all this, he still loves me. That reminds me, though. I can't recall if I've had my birth control tea tonight.

No, you haven't. Oz answers my thoughts. He runs to the kitchen to make me some and is back upstairs in just a few minutes.

We should talk about the wedding before we decide on babies. It's clear

Auguste regrets not having turned his mate, so we need to talk that over once more, too. Oz shifts his body to face me and takes my hand.

"Sahira, if you tell me you want to marry me tonight, I'd summon the nearest officiant in the next ten minutes. You and I are already married under vampire law, and my marrying you in human law only serves as a public display of our nuptials. I think it would be ideal to marry sooner rather than later, so your father can give you away."

A sharp ache in my chest at his suggestion feels bittersweet. We are on borrowed time with dad, and I'd love him to walk me down the aisle. "Do you know where you'd like to get married?" I don't exactly have a large family or a ton of friends to invite to the wedding, but Oz certainly does. We'd need a large venue, but it might be difficult to find one on short notice.

"We have a villa on Nahuel Huapi Lake in Patagonia that would make a splendid setting for our wedding."

Hm, Arizona. Sure, that could be beautiful, and the copper state is close enough, it wouldn't take more than a couple of hours' flight for most guests, I'm sure. I chug the tea Oz made me.

"No, not Arizona. Argentina."

My mouth drops. That is one place I haven't been to yet. I've been saving Argentina for when I go to Antarctica.

Argentina. "*Yes!*"

Oz has a self-satisfied smile. "Do you think we can plan a wedding in less than a month?"

Hell, I'd marry him tomorrow if I could.

"Whenever, wherever, as long as we're together, we can make it happen." He plants a kiss on my lips. I pull him in closer and linger longer. Spice invades my senses, and I wince before I pull away.

Sorry babe, I'm on my cycle, remember?

He sits back and gives me an incredulous look. "That doesn't bother me in the slightest, Sahira. In fact, I know I'll enjoy making love to you no matter what. Provided you don't mind?"

Most men I've ever encountered have treated women as though they're infected with the plague at the mere mention of being on their period. And now, I'm about to marry a man who not only doesn't care but still desires me when I am.

"I mean, I guess I don't? First time for everything, yeah? Although I think I'd prefer it in the shower for easier cleanup."

Oz scoops me into his arms and carries me to the bathroom. I give him a quick kiss after he sets me down, and I tell him to wait outside so I can get in the shower. The last thing I want to do is take out a tampon in front of him.

After I'm in the shower, I tell Oz he can come in now. He undresses quickly. I watch the way his smooth muscles move in the light, with thick, corded power. He's like an ancient marble statue come to life, and I can still hardly believe he's mine. When he is close to me, I can see the newly acquired scars I gave him the other night. On his rib cage is the Ebbswick key scar and a few more minor keloid scars along his back.

A gush of cool air takes over the shower when Oz opens its door, and goosebumps line my skin. My nipples tighten from this sudden chill, much to his delight. He moves close against my skin, and his firm sex presses against my core.

Oz hooks an arm under one of my legs and wraps it around him while bringing me in tight with his other arm. He kisses me hard, and I grip around his back to hold on. With my free hand, I arch my pelvis forward and guide him into me. We both let out a small moan as his thick length fills me.

The warm water falls on my back as we move in tandem against one another. He fits me like we're two pieces of a puzzle. Together, we are whole and separate, our edges are jagged and incomplete. I press my face against his chest, and my breath is warm against his skin as we embrace. My hold on him gets tighter as I climax, and Oz purrs in delight as I'm vocal about it.

I kiss him as I cross my raised leg over his stomach and place it on the ground so I'm facing away from him. Oz moans at the sight of me as I bend over and anchor my hands to the floor.

"I want you to pound me."

He clenches my waist tight and grunts with the effort of driving hard and fast into me. My breasts bounce in rhythm as I look at the rust-tinged water falling at our feet. From this angle, Oz hits my G-spot, and I beg him not to stop. I order him to slap my ass, and he does as he's told. An image flashes across my mind of him sticking his thumb in my backdoor.

Do it, I beg. He massages it before his thumb slides into me. Between this and his cock, I am full and near climax again.

I can tell he's getting close by the way his moans have become shallower.

"Pull my hair when you come with me."

He hesitates before grabbing the hair at my nape. This causes me to arch my back, so he is even deeper, and he grips my ass with his other hand while his thumb anchors to me, and he pulls me in tight.

"I'm coming!" My breath hitches with each drive against my hips.

Oz lets out a groan as his warm release fills me. His come is the only warm thing about him, and a welcome conclusion to our love-making. He gives a few more slow pumps and holds on the last one before releasing his grip on my hair and ass. I stand and face him, and he takes me into his embrace.

"So, you do like it rough."

And I love hearing that pretty little mouth talk dirty to me, Sahira.

Oz is inhumanly strong, and it helps in the bedroom. I'm pleasantly surprised how much I enjoy having sex while I'm on my period. I think I'd like to try period sex outside of the shower, too. I never seem to get enough of him.

After we thoroughly wash up and towel off, he grabs a dark towel from the cabinet and brings it over to the bed. *In case you'd like to have another go at it on dry land.*

You certainly don't have to ask me twice; I think as I drop the towel from around me and rush over to the bed. His appetite is just as hungry as mine, and he barely has enough time to lie down the towel before I tackle him.

Oz HAS to make a few phone calls about the wedding, so I head downstairs, following the pleasant aroma of breakfast. Pippa has an assortment of food on the table, and Gideon eyes me curiously as I reach for a blueberry muffin and sit next to him. The only thing he wears is gray sweatpants, his natural tan on full, unabashed display.

"What?"

"Nothing." His gunmetal blue eyes bore into me, and the room cloys with cinnamon.

"What's going on?" Hannah enters the room. She takes a bite of a lemon poppy seed muffin while she looks at Gideon, waiting for him to fill her in. Her hair is in a high ponytail, and she's wearing yoga pants with a long black sweater. We have similar styles and would share clothes if I weren't twice her size. Comfort, always.

"Oh, you have missed nothing." Gideon winks. "Other than more confirmation Lana is freaky. Those two were up all night and morning."

I nearly spit out my apple juice, and I'm grateful Dad isn't in the room. Hannah chuckles, but she was privy to my college sexcapades. None of this is new to her. Although, we should move Gideon to another floor if we're going to keep this up. Not that it matters much, considering he's a vampire with super hearing.

"Look, all I'm saying is I'd storm the gates of hell for a roll in the hay with you." Gideon's voice has a lover's purr as he leans towards me. I roll my eyes at him. "Hell, I don't normally swing that way, but if you guys want a third, I'm game."

"Sorry, I don't share. Besides, you're not my type." The heat of my core betrays me, and I avert my eyes, but not before I catch a flash of knowing behind his gunmetal stare.

He leans in and whispers into my ear. "Your arousal tells me otherwise, *kitten*. Just say the magic words, and I'm all yours."

"Careful vampire, or I'll have your heart."

"It's yours," he calls after me as I leave the table and put on a coat to go outside to escape his proposition. I don't look back, but his icy stare settles on me as I leave the house.

I'm not interested in anyone other than Oz, and I certainly don't need one of his vampires complicating things. I round the corner of the house and startle when I see Auguste on the footpath. "Oh! Sorry, I didn't see you there." My heart rate is still elevated, and no doubt I'm flustered.

"Are you alright?" He doesn't have a jacket on, although he doesn't need one as a vampire. He's wearing a gray cashmere shawl-collar sweater and dark blue slacks. It doesn't matter what vampires wear; it appears they're so put-together.

"I'm fine." Although I'm pretty sure he can tell I'm lying based on the unconvinced stare he gives me. The silence between us makes me uncomfortable, so I continue. "Actually, I'm not sure why Gideon is so obsessed with me, to be honest. He's going to get himself killed."

Auguste gives me one of those half-opened smirks and runs his tongue along the bottom of his upper teeth. He has a young Marlon Brando way about him, and he collects himself so he can speak politely. "Well, Gideon has never been shy about his feelings, especially if a prophecy is involved."

"You mean about the queen who kills the king? While the prophecy came true, I brought Oz back to life? What more is there?" I stare at him, confused.

"There are many prophecies, but one of them is where he falls in love with a time-traveling witch, and she has his babies. Gideon seems to think you're her. I wouldn't be surprised if he's already in love with you. You have that way about you."

I chuckle and then break into a laughing fit. Auguste watches me, amused, as tears spring to my eyes from laughing so hard.

"First, he's a vampire, so he can't have babies. Second, Oz is my mate; I don't want anyone else."

Auguste takes a deep breath before telling me how the prophecy goes. Apparently, a witch travels back in time where she falls in love with Gideon, and they have babies before he's ever turned. Why he thinks this is me, I don't know, and it isn't happening. I don't go for men like him. Looks-wise he's my type, but not in personality. I value confidence over cockiness, always.

I'm happy to understand Gideon's behavior, at least, but I'll need to nip it in the bud. "Thanks for telling me this, Auguste. Any other crazy prophecies that may or may not involve me?"

Auguste takes another deep breath. "There might be one or two more, but we haven't heard from the witch in millennia." He kicks around some loose rocks on the walking path. "I think one is about the queen sleeping with the king's vampires, too." The air between us smells of cloves.

"Does this prophecy say the queen loses her mind? If not, this will never happen. But thank you for letting me know." I hope Oz isn't going around thinking I'm going to cheat. The idea of Oz cheating on me makes me ill, so I had better talk to him to reassure him.

Auguste follows me inside, and Gideon is still at the table, shirtless. Dad is awake now, and Maeve is pouring him a cup of coffee.

"Good morning, Dad! How are you doing today?"

He reaches across the table to get a muffin, and Gideon pushes the basket closer to dad to make it easier.

"I'm feeling a lot better this morning than I was yesterday afternoon."

Yeah, I suppose I deserve that.

Oz enters the room, and he has a big smile on his face and whispers in my ear. "Come with me. I have news."

I shrug my shoulders at Hannah when Oz takes my hand and leads me outside. I snag my coat on the way and put it on as soon as we're out. "Somebody is happy!" I love seeing him like this.

"What do you think about getting married on December 21st? This gives us a little over three weeks to plan everything. The 21st is on a Monday, but a celestial event called the *Great Conjunction* not seen since the Middle Ages happens that night. This is when Jupiter and Saturn are so close it looks like a double planet in the sky."

Goosebumps radiate from my head to my toes hearing this.

"Wow, that sounds ... incredible. Do you think we can pull it off?" Three weeks doesn't give me much time, even if I don't have many people coming from my side. Some women spend their whole lives planning their wedding down to the finest detail. On the other hand, I just knew I wanted to marry a prince, and I didn't care about the finer details.

Oz's eyes glaze at the thoughts running through my mind. "Would you settle for a king, Sahira, or should one of my vampires step in?"

I let out a giddy scream and jump into Oz's arms and wrap my legs around his waist. He plants a big kiss on my lips, and all is right in the world. The wedding details don't matter to me, only that I get to spend eternity with him.

After I come up for air, he continues to hold me around my waist.

"Oh, Babe, I'd like to discuss something with you." I'm pretty sure my thoughts have given away what I need to talk about, but a conversation is crucial all the same.

He sets me down, and we go for a walk.

"Auguste told me about a couple of prophecies that might involve me." I fidget with my coat. "One prophecy explains why Gideon is so obsessed with me, and the other is concerning because I don't want you to think I'd ever do it." Before I can even elaborate about the prophecies, Oz slips his fingers through mine and faces me. He holds our hands up to his heart before kissing them.

"Lana, I'm well aware of what the prophecies say, and it still doesn't change the way I feel about you. You are the fire in my veins. My existence doesn't matter without you."

This, I understand, but it would gut me to walk around knowing some prophecies paint me as a terrible queen he should steer clear of. Worse, that I'd love another man or sleep with one of his sires. The very idea is unconscionable.

And then, to make matters even more complicated, I am attracted to these men. Not like I am to Oz, but they're pleasant to look at. No doubt the entire room of vampires senses my arousal when in their company, and I have terrible guilt over it. They're beautiful—men and women alike.

The reason you find them attractive, Sahira, is because they're my vampires. We're mates, and my blood runs in their veins, no matter how much blood they take from other people, Oz explains in my head. "You couldn't help it even if they were grotesque, hideous monsters. I promise on my life; I don't hold it against you. It is not uncommon for vampires to share their mate with their sires. Our bond is new, so I'm a little more territorial than I'll be later on. I'll do what I can to make sure my jealousy doesn't impact you."

Well, I'm certainly relieved, and I'm also grateful our bond is so strong, despite being new. I imagine a weaker woman might give in to the charms of someone like Gideon or Auguste. They're both completely different from each other—one is a gentleman, and the other reminds me more of Casanova.

Funny you should mention that.

My eyes go wild, and my mouth drops. *No,* I mouth inaudibly from the shock. *Gideon was Casanova?!*

"No, no, he wasn't," he chuckles.

Who was it, then? It couldn't have been Auguste; he's far too much a gentleman.

"No doubt Gideon taught Giacomo a few things; those two were friends until Casanova started scamming people and doing other unsavory things. Gideon might be a terrible flirt, but he never pretends to be something he isn't. He's always been one to lay all his cards on the table."

I've noticed this. There's something honorable about his honesty, although I will have to address his constant blatant and open propositions. "He's in love with you, Sahira," Oz's voice is quiet. I'm not sure how this can be; I only ever sense cinnamon from him, and that's his arousal.

"As soon as you leave the room, his scent changes as he longs for you to be in his presence again. The aroma is nutmeg and ginger. His thoughts give it away, too."

Huh, I think. He'd have better luck trying to convince a porcupine to marry him than he would me. "How could he if he understands we're mated? The mating bond is for life." I understand little about the vampire and witch world.

"Yes, we're mated, and soon we'll be married. But you can't change the way your heart feels. His being in love with you may be a good thing, and he can keep you safe when I'm not around."

My stomach lurches. "What do you mean Osgood Finlandian?" I try to hold back the fear in my voice.

"I only mean when I can't accompany you places, like if I'm busy fighting off hordes of your admirers and he needs to take you to a safe place."

I slug him in the arm. *Not funny.* Besides, Oz is the king. Just look at him—he's a perfect specimen of what it means to be a man.

You don't give yourself near enough credit, he says in my head. He tucks one of my stray curls behind my ear before resting the back of his cool hand on my cheek. My breath hitches in my throat as he trails his finger along my jawline and then over my neck. He tilts my chin and leans in for a kiss. *You, Sahira, are the most beautiful woman in the world. Not only that, but your scent is irresistible to my male vampires.*

Maybe that's why Oz and I are together. I have some kind of siren-like scent luring him in, and he can't get away. It would certainly explain why these god-like men fawn over me.

"I don't know why you don't see yourself as worthy, Lana." His eyes soften. "Whoever made you feel less than perfect doesn't matter anymore. All that matters is there are people who love you for far more than just your beauty. It is only fitting you and I marry during a rare celestial event. Fate hand-picked you for me, and I am the luckiest man in the world." Oz bends down and pulls me in.

CHAPTER TWENTY-THREE

Hannah leaves today. I rap my fingers on her door. "Come in!" Her suitcase is rainbow, and despite her best efforts, she's struggling to fit everything in it. I sit on the luggage while she zips it.

"I have a favor to ask you."

"Sure, what's up?" She's always ready for an adventure, no matter what I ask of her. I sit her suitcase upright and ask if she's alright to pack again in a few weeks.

"Sure. What's up your sleeve Lana Bo Bonna?" We used to make up little rhymes with our names as kids. When I wasn't calling her Hanalei, I'd call her Hannah Bo Bana. She folds her arms across stomach, waiting for me to divulge.

I clear my throat. "Hannah, it would make me the happiest woman alive if you were my Maid of Honor."

She screams and throws her arms around my neck. "Yes! When? Where?"

I laugh and tell her we're getting married on December 21st in Argentina.

"Everything alright in here?" Dad's in the doorway. He must've heard Hannah shriek. Behind him are the vampires, who no doubt heard our exchange. They allow me the courtesy of telling Dad the plan.

"Dad, Oz and I have set a date. It would be my honor to have you accompany me down the aisle in Argentina on December 21st." I take his hands.

Tears well up in his eyes. "I never thought I'd ever have the privilege to walk anyone down the aisle, and the honor is all mine."

I also ask Pippa and Maeve if they'd be bridesmaids, and both eagerly agree.

The room seems small with everyone in it. Gideon looks depressed, and Auguste puts on a cheerful face for me.

"Let's give her some space, shall we?" Oz appears in the doorway. "Gentlemen, if you could join me downstairs, please." He kisses me before he ushers everyone out.

Hannah and I sit on her bed and reflect on how nice it was to have her visit. "Thank you, Lana. Truly. It means a lot you trust me enough to let me into this wild world of vampires and witches. And this entire family is incredible. Dad, too. Let's FaceTime tomorrow, and we can hash out wedding details."

My heart warms when I witness Dad hug Hannah. Most of these people weren't even in our lives months ago. Now, I can't imagine my life without them. Oz and I walk them to the car and give one more round of hugs. "See you soon!"

I'm pulled into his arms while we watch the car drive away. I turn around after they've left and search his eyes. "Thank you, Oz. This was such a wonderful gift." I drink in his scent of warm vanilla and sugar until I'm dizzy.

Let's get you inside before you catch a cold.

We spend the afternoon and evening working on a guest list. Auguste made everyone homemade pizza, and Pippa made a salad to enjoy while we worked on logistics. The main house in Patagonia has eight bedrooms to house the immediate family, and then there are several guest houses across the small island. Oz struggles with how he'll pare his list down to just the essential guests—he's made so many close friends over the years and has many sires.

Each of the vampires left in the house gives their opinion on who should stay on the guest list and who is safe to omit. There are many high-ranking officials from governments worldwide, royalty, celebrities, and family members whose names I struggle to pronounce. The list started with over five hundred names, and we've got it down to two hundred and twenty-seven now. With plus ones and children, that still means an enormous wedding.

"Let me check with the hotels around the lake, and it shouldn't be a problem to buy them out with enough financial incentive." Auguste stands.

Oz heads to his room to make phone calls while Auguste excuses himself to the backyard.

"Do you think people will come to a destination wedding with this late of notice?"

Pippa and Gideon laugh.

"This is no ordinary event, Lana. Yours is a royal wedding. Not just *a* royal wedding, but *the* royal wedding. The people have waited for this for thousands of years, and they'd sell their souls to get an invitation."

Wow. Butterflies take flight in my stomach and careen up my throat. I shove my chair back and run out the front door, leaving it open as I heave on the frost-covered grass. Oz rubs a hand across my shoulder blades to comfort me. I wretch the contents of my stomach at our feet before using my sleeve to wipe off my mouth.

Sorry, I say to him silently.

"Lana, we don't have to have a wedding; we could get married this week just in front of a judge." Oz folds me into his arms.

I don't get to respond before Pippa speaks from behind us. "You must have a wedding, Oz! We'll never hear the end of it if you don't!"

Forgoing a wedding is out of the question, especially if the ceremony and reception is as big a deal as they say. I shake my head. "I want to have a wedding, Oz. I'm just nervous, is all. Not about marrying you, just about being in front of all those people. I'm worried I won't measure up."

"Nonsense. You are already my queen, and this is simply for theatrics." He ushers me inside to get cleaned up.

"Everyone will love you, Lana." Auguste gives my shoulder a small squeeze as we pass by him.

My feet are heavy as I climb up the stairs. I plop down on the edge of the bed, and Oz hands me a wet washcloth, warm but not too warm. After I wipe off my face, I groan as I drag my feet to brush my teeth in the bathroom. I have zero energy now.

"You feel that way because the penumbral lunar eclipse is tomorrow. And you're on your cycle."

Huh. Who knew? Oz understands a lot about this stuff. I don't know if I'll ever understand everything—there's so much to learn.

"There was a time when I was the only doctor in the village. I *had* to know these things." So many talents; I can't wait to discover them all.

"Do you think you could teach me?" I mumble; my mouth is full of toothpaste. I spit into the sink, run the water, and see him nod as I look up in the mirror.

"We'll have eternity to learn and grow together, Sahira."

This makes my heart swell.

I worry my lip, thinking about leaving Oz for Bedlam, even if I'm only there for six months. Any amount of time away from them is torture. I wish he'd just turn me.

Rinsing off my toothbrush and putting it in the holder on our vanity, I dismiss the ache in my chest. On the bed, Oz and I both sit cross-legged with a large college-ruled notebook between us. I scribble at the top of the first page:

Ceremony to Forever

He tells me he likes the sound of that. "Although, if you want to be technical, that happened when I marked you."

I scribble below it, "Part Deux," and he chuckles.

We need to decide on a color scheme, and I propose carnelian red, lapis lazuli blue, and gold—especially considering how prized each of those was in Sumer. I want to pay homage to Oz's lineage.

"What about yours?"

I never considered honoring my ancestors during the wedding. It isn't easy to honor a family I never knew, and I always felt like I was neither here nor there—a lot like Oz with his vampire and witch blood. Although, I think we can honor both my mom and dad. They have honeybees on their grimoires.

"You say I smell like Sumer: vanilla, peaches, cardamom, and honey. Do you think we can do little jars of vanilla and cardamom-infused honey with those cute little honey dippers for favors? Or do royal weddings not have favors?"

Oz's eyes light up. "That is a great idea, Sahira. And spiced peach mead as a signature drink; a perfect blend of the two of us. It takes months to make, but we can use a little magic to speed it along in time for the wedding."

As we dream up these ideas, I scribble them down and circle the ones we know for sure. We'll have little canvas bags monogrammed with our initials, the wedding location, and the date. Aside from the honey jars, we'll add bottles of water, sachets of herbal tea, iced sugar cookies with our monogram, and bags of popcorn to the canvas bags.

"Do you know where you'd like to spend our honeymoon?"

I guess I didn't realize destination weddings have honeymoons. Going to Patagonia was always on my list. Maybe we could spend our time hiking in Argentina and Chile before going to Antarctica.

"Have you ever been?"

"A few times," Oz pulls open his phone to show me pictures. "Can't think of a place I haven't been yet."

This makes me giddy. As a travel blogger, I've always wanted to see and do everything. Now, I'm marrying someone who has and can show me his favorite places. If I'm going to hike, I will need to train rigorously now, which is something I want to do anyway, in preparation for the wedding; I want to look my best.

He gives me that look again—the one that says I'm fussing too much about not being good enough. "I just don't want you to have to carry me up every mountain we climb."

I wouldn't object, Oz says in my head. I roll my eyes and give him a quick peck on the lips. I suppose I could always fly if I were too tired to use my legs, I muse.

This causes Oz to shake his head. I wonder if I could fly and carry him at the same time? That would be a sight to see.

∼

HAIR FALLS over Oz's eyebrow, and I use my fingers to tousle it. He kisses me on the nose.

"I love you, Sahira."

"Mm, not near as much as I love you."

Uh-huh. He takes off his shirt, and I lay in the crook of his arm. My fingers trace his abs, and he puts his knee between my thighs.

Oz lifts the white t-shirt I'm wearing just enough to slide his hands down my sweatpants. I let out a soft moan as he kneads my mound. His touch is cool against my heat, and I hook one of my hands around his shoulder so I can be closer to him. I don't care that I'm on my period. I just need him in me. My breath is warm on his chest, and my heart rate rises as I arch my pelvis to take more of him. He uses his knee to spread my legs apart further before his finger finds my opening and slides in. I am already ripe for him, but he is slow and methodical.

I want to hear you, Sahira, Oz tells me silently. He inserts another finger, and I moan—both from the pleasure and the fullness of it. My hips buck against his body, and my breath quickens as my release builds.

"I want another finger." He works to get another one in, and I am full now, and have both pleasure and pressure from it. He uses his thumb to rub my clit, which sends me over the edge, and I clench as I ride the wave of pleasure.

"Come here." I give him a feline grin. His arousal is strong as I reach into his pants and stroke him until a bead of moisture is on the tip. My thumb collects the evidence of his arousal, and I rub it between my fingers. I bring my hand to my mouth, and my tongue rolls against each finger. I take his hand and slide it under my shirt to rest on my bare breast when I am through. While I work on sliding off my sweatpants, his fingers caress my nipple. I sit up, and he helps me take off my shirt.

"Only if you beg!" Gideon shouts from the other room, and I stifle a laugh using Oz's shoulder.

I roll Oz to his back and sit just below his abs while he lifts his butt to slide off his sweatpants. After he watches me let down my hair, I run my tongue from my palm to the tips of my fingers and reach out to his already erect sex, and I stroke it several times before sitting up and guiding him to my wet core. We both moan as his steel length enters me.

My hips rock slowly at first, savoring every heightened pleasure. In one swift move, Oz flips me over so I'm on my back and he's on top. He is slow but drives into me deep with each thrust. A wave of spice and control washes over me, and I know this familiar scent is his mark. He nor I can control it now, and his desire for me matches my own for him.

Oz sinks his teeth into my breast, and there is no pain, only ecstasy. He draws from me in a long steady cadence, and his hips rock with each draw. Memories pour out of me as he feeds—the first time I felt his touch, how his heart soars when I make love to him, the way his dark hair shines when the light hits it. His memories come at me fast, and I catch a few—when he knew I was the one for him, how he felt when I said I'd marry him, and also how he felt when I left. I weep as this memory crosses my mind, and Oz stops feeding to hold me.

Please, don't stop, I beg him. The pleasure of him feeding from me is worth the pain some of his memories bring up. After a little more reassurance, his teeth pierce my breast again. Instead of memories, love and peace mark our rising pleasure. He brings his mouth to mine when he is satiated, and I taste my lifeblood on his lips.

My legs wrap around him, and my heel rests in the crux of his thighs, and I use them to pull him into me deeper before his fingers intertwine with mine. In one smooth motion, he sits me up, so I am cradled in his lap. I can rock my hips easier now, and my fingers run through his hair as I pull him tighter into me. My abs burn under the effort of rocking my hips, but I don't want to stop because I'm getting close.

"Come with me."

"Let me hear you." My breath is shallow and fast, and my moans become louder than the sound the headboard makes against the wall.

"I'm coming!" Oz grunts, and together we ride wave after wave of release.

Loud pounding on the wall across the room interrupts our moment, and Gideon yells, "If you two don't pipe down, I'm coming in there!" As if he couldn't hear us if I were quiet.

"You're only mad it isn't you," Oz yells through the wall, and Gideon curses.

"You know, Gideon offered to be the third wheel." I hop off his lap and head towards the bathroom to shower. Oz raises an eyebrow and looks at me in disbelief.

"And what did you say?"

A bedroom grin spreads across my face. "I simply said I don't share, and he's not my type."

"Did he believe you?" Oz slides the shower door open for us. I reach in to turn the hot water on and test it with my hand before pulling him in with me.

"Of course, he doesn't believe me. He might be good-looking, but he'll never measure up to the love of my life."

Well, that is true, he says in my head. *He thinks that is the way the prophecy of you sleeping with my sires comes true, or he's relying on the fact vampires often share their mate with their sires.*

We shower quickly before changing back into sweats. In another hour, the penumbral lunar eclipse will peak. Oz says the eclipse will look like a regular full moon, but I will tell the difference. He makes me a mug of my birth control tea while I rearrange the couch in the tower so we can view the moon out the windows. The eclipse will last just shy of four and a half hours. I'm not sure I'll stay up for it, but I'm going to try.

He made me a London Fog with my herbal tea and made himself a

London Fog using peppermint and almond milk. I take a sip and sigh. "This hits the spot, thanks, babe."

"I seem to do a lot of that, don't I?"

That you do, I tell him in my head as I lean in for a kiss.

"Do you think I may wake up with new magical powers?"

"I'm almost certain of it. Celestial events amplify powers and manifest new ones for newer witches."

Part of me is nervous. What if I don't like this new power, or the magic is out-of-control like when I killed Oz? He squeezes my hand to reassure me.

I take Oz's hand and lift his arm over my shoulders and rest my head in the crux of his shoulder. A very faint humming sensation comes from within me, and he senses my alarm.

"Are you alright?"

I tell him the humming came back for a moment. Oz can never listen to my thoughts when the sensation is around. We're not entirely sure what that means, but this time, it was very short-lived.

The stillness of his chest reminds me of how I almost lost him, and it's unsettling. "You have lungs ... right?"

He chuckles. "I don't have to breathe, although I have lungs and occasionally use them when I need to look normal around humans. They may not regard it outwardly, but their subconscious sends off alarms if something is moving and not breathing next to them."

If I needed CPR, he *could* resuscitate me. And, if he wanted, he could even have labored breathing while making love to me.

Oz is quiet for a moment before shaking his head in amusement. "Yeah, I suppose I could. Never even considered how much I enjoy hearing your breath and how you might enjoy listening to mine, too."

I smile and nuzzle back into his side.

"Do you think we can do a little hiking tomorrow after we finish spell-casting?" My cardiovascular condition won't be able to keep up with him. "I want to get in as much exercise as possible before the wedding."

He tells me about the Horseshoe Bluff Nature Trail, which isn't too far from here. The trail isn't quite what I need to condition myself for hiking Patagonia, but it's about the closest we can get to any kind of elevation gain in the area.

The moon outside is full, but I can faintly make out most of it is darker than the other side of it. It's not as noticeable as a total eclipse or anything, but it's still beautiful to understand what's taking place in space.

"There are people who practice witchcraft who don't have inherent magic like us, and you must understand the distinction. For human-born witches, an eclipse can be a negative thing for them. They lose energy and the protection of the Luminaries. They have to rely on crystals, herbs, and manifesting to access anything resembling magic. We still treat them as witches—I've never been too fond of the gatekeeping between humans who practice witchcraft and born witches. There is room at the altar for all."

CHAPTER TWENTY-FOUR

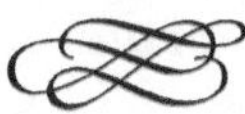

Birds sing their song outside our window, and the heat from the fireplace causes sweat to slick my skin. Ice dances across my eyelids and I open them to see Oz lying next to me in bed.

"You were dreaming." Sleep is thick in his voice. "I carried you to bed last night because you fell asleep on me during the eclipse."

I must've because I don't recall coming to bed. "I don't feel any different today; I don't think." I hold out my arms and examine them, and he laughs.

"That is not the way it works. Although we should get up and work on your magic now. There is no better time of the month to do it."

I glance at my phone and groan. Seven am?

I roll over to get out of bed and see a mug of tea on my nightstand. "Thanks, babe." I drag myself to the bathroom to shower.

Oz throws a towel on the warmer. Today is a crisp morning, so he also tosses a couple of logs on the fireplace in the bedroom. By the time I finish my shower, the room is toasty.

"We're FaceTiming with Hannah at 11 am. What should we work on before that?" I plop down on the just-made bed and sip on my tea.

"I thought we'd try scrying. It will help with your intuition. Some witches use crystal balls, water, or even mirrors, but you don't need any of that. We'll do pyromancy today."

Oz takes my hand and ushers me over to the fireplace. He places an armchair three feet from it and has me sit. The fire is warm on my legs but not hot.

"Think of a question you've wanted answered for a while. Try to start with something simple and easy-to-digest; you don't want to ask the universe why we have free will or anything complex yet."

I want to know what new magic I've manifested overnight, so I'll start there.

"Now you've set your intention, meditate by watching the flame to clear your mind. Keep your eyes open and relaxed. Think of your intention and let the images flash in your head. Don't chase them or control them—you will know when you have your answer." He dims the lights, and I focus on the flicker of the flames at the top of the fire. They dance and disappear, only to have new ones reappear just as quickly.

My breathing slows, and I relax my face. *What powers did I gain last night?* I ask the flames. A blurry image flashes in the fire, but I can't make it out. The fire pops and crackles, and another image surfaces. This time, the shape moves too fast for me to make out what it is. I grow frustrated and command it to stay still, despite Oz having warned me not to control it.

The image protests and small flames spit at me. I can sense he is about to intervene, but he observes instead. *Still yourself,* I command again. The image steadies, and it is a person, but it has no face. I stare at it, trying to discern what this means and who this is.

Show me your face, I command. The small figure shudders in the flames, and familiar faces flash in succession. First, it is Oz's face, then Gideon, Hannah, Dad, and the rest of the family. Then, I see faces of people I don't recognize before it cycles back to the beginning.

I'm dizzy from watching the faces rotate, and I tell it to stop. It hesitates for a moment before its face goes blank again. My familiar buzzing sensation takes over, and I know my answer as I blink and look to Oz. I stand and walk to the tower before turning around to face him across the room.

"Let what happens happen, okay?" He eyes me, no doubt wondering what I've got up my sleeve and if he should be worried. He can't read my mind because the buzzing is a roar now.

Gideon, come here and kneel in front of me, I command. Not a moment later, the bedroom door swings open, startling Oz, and he's surprised to see a stark-naked Gideon at the door. My attention naturally drifts to below his waist, and I throw my hands up to cover my eyes. I didn't think he slept naked.

His icy stare looks back and forth at both of us as Gideon scales the room and kneels in front of me. He looks up at me, confused why he's here, and I sense his love for me now he's uninhibited.

Now shake Oz's hand for me, please, I command silently, eyes still closed. Gideon slowly gets up and sticks out his hand in front of Oz, who is now in the tower with us. Confused, Oz shakes Gideon's hand before looking back at me, waiting for me to explain what the hell is going on. *Thank you, Gideon. You may have a seat now, but cover up,* I compel him. He takes a seat on the couch next to me and uses a throw pillow to cover his lap.

"Control. I can control anyone, just like the man in the flame. I was confused at first because the man's face kept changing, but then I instinctively knew."

Both men stare at me in shock. Had they not seen it with their very eyes, they might not have believed me. Now I have this power, I must be careful with it. I imagine compelling someone to do something they don't want to do when I'm angry; I don't want to be that kind of person.

"What else can you make me do?" Mischief dances in his eyes.

For starters, you can put on some clothes, I command him.

Gideon saunters over to the armoire and yanks one of Oz's t-shirts from a hanger and puts it on. He slips into a pair of Oz's sweatpants, too.

"Hey!"

"Oh, this could be very fun!" Both men eye me and shake their heads. "Oh, don't worry. I'm just having a little fun. You can take off Oz's shirt but leave the pants on until you can get a pair of your own on."

"If you want me to undress, you don't have to ask," Gideon purrs, and I roll my eyes at him. "You're the one who compelled me here this early in the morning," he continues with that bedroom grin of his. "Did you want to take me up on my offer?"

Oz glares at him, and he just smirks in response. Gideon reaches his hand over his shoulder and grips the shirt before pulling it over his head, purposefully flexing his taut muscles as he does it. He tosses it at Oz, and cinnamon wafts from the shirt as it meets its target.

Gideon crosses the room and back to the tower. "Well?"

"No."

Gideon takes a deep breath and looks at me with longing before returning his attention to Oz. "And what if your bride wants to? I can hear her heart race from here."

I try to compel my heart to slow down, but it refuses.

I don't have time to speak before Oz intervenes. "If Lana wants to introduce our court to our bedroom, that's up to her."

My head whips to Oz incredulously before settling back on Gideon.

"I don't want to sleep with you, Gideon. I'm sure you're a great guy, and any woman would be lucky to have you on her arm. But I am your queen, and Oz is my mate. Soon, he will be my husband. Whatever prophecy you believe involves you and me *together* is *wrong*." He looks wounded but tips his head towards me before walking to the bedroom door.

Gideon pauses and turns around to speak. "The gates of hell, Lana," he closes the door.

"What's that supposed to mean?" Oz quirks an eyebrow at me. I take a deep breath before responding.

"Gideon told me he'd storm the gates of hell to be with me if I let him. I'm sorry, I didn't know he'd be naked when I compelled him in here." I hope I didn't give Gideon renewed hope for his unrequited love.

That is your first lesson, Oz warns in my head. You must be careful with magic because even the smallest detail can have unintended consequences. I'm okay if you have feelings for him, it's not uncommon in our situation. He picks at a string sticking out of the comforter. "I'm sorry you had to witness Gideon in all his ..."

"Glory!" Gideon screams from the other room. Oz and I both cackle at Gideon's eavesdropping.

Despite the terrifying new power I've gained, and the potential consequences of it if used wrong, hope blooms in my chest. "Do you think I can use my power against Dolphina?" I lay my head in Oz's lap, and he strokes my hair.

"I worry she may resist your magic, and I'd hate for you to go in there thinking you're invincible, only to get crushed because she's an old, powerful vampire witch. Don't underestimate her."

We say goodbye and head downstairs to make brunch. Dad is sitting at the table, playing cards with Gideon, Pippa, and Auguste. "What are you playing?"

"Pinochle," Dad takes a card from the deck.

"You guys hungry? We're thinking about brunch; we've had a busy morning."

Gideon eyes me with satisfaction and a knowing smirk. "I could eat." He stares at me with a coquettish look.

I glance around at the rest of the table, and they all look eager to indulge.

"Alright, we'll get to work. You can keep playing,"

Oz and I scan the fridge. We have a bit of duck to use up, so I dice the rest of it for omelets. He grabs a loaf of brioche from the bread cupboard to make French toast. The medical staff pops into the kitchen to get some of dad's medications from the fridge, and I ask if they're hungry. They thank me but say they are stuffed. Pippa was up early and made them a large breakfast. Sounds like her, I think; she's always taking care of others.

I bring a bowl of fruit and silverware to the table, and Oz comes in with the French toast and plates for everyone. I set out a rectangular wooden trivet in the center of the table for the large platter I have full of omelets I took from the warm oven. Oz taught me how easy it is to cook for a crowd this way.

"Thanks, you two." The rest of the table echoes his sentiment while I call Maeve downstairs to join us.

Gideon doesn't take his eyes off me the entire time he eats. Auguste joins in, no longer able to distract himself with food. Although they already ate a huge meal for breakfast, vampires do not get full and partake in any food whenever available.

"Did Gideon fill you all in on my new power?"

Gideon's eyes flare and his cinnamon scent overpowers my senses. "I sure did."

"Your power will come in handy in the event you're ever in trouble again," Pippa volunteers. "Use it only when necessary, though."

"I didn't mind." Gideon shrugs and I roll my eyes.

"I didn't take you for a beta in a relationship," I tease, and the table laughs.

"Oh, so we're in a relationship now?"

I squirm under his attention.

"No, but she's your queen, so I suppose that makes you a beta either way." Auguste leans back in his seat and rests an arm on the table.

"Whatever it takes." Gideon's chair scrapes on the hardwood floor and he leaves the room while staring at Oz.

I cast my eyes down at my plate and fidget while I finish both the fruit and omelet.

"What's on the agenda today?" Dad asks, and I look at him, thankful for the reprieve.

"Oz is taking me to Horseshoe Bluff in case any of you want to come along," I say. "The trail has a wheelchair-accessible area." Dad shakes his head. He said his staff are taking him into town to get supplies for our wedding gift.

"Oh, Dad, you don't have to. You are a gift enough." I mean every word.

"Nonsense, let me do this for you two." he tries to stab a grape with his fork.

"Okay."

"I'm not much of a hiker." Maeve stands.

"Me either." Pippa joins her. Auguste and Gideon want to join us.

After everyone cleans up, we head to our rooms to change into hiking clothes. At just thirty-four degrees out, I'll need to wear a couple of layers.

~

It doesn't take us very long to complete the Horseshoe Bluff Nature Trail, so we head for the two-mile Calcite trail. Lead mine pits are all along the path, so I've got to be careful not to trip. The vampires, not so much. The first trail was very easy, but the Calcite trail was steep. I push on and try to hide my huffing and puffing as we climb.

You okay, Sahira? We can stop. Oz has the courtesy to ask me in my head.

Never. I grin.

"Auguste, would you mind taking a picture of Lana and me?"

They can all hear my labored breathing and racing heart; no doubt Oz asked for my benefit. He pulls me in close to his side as we smile for several pictures taken on Oz's phone.

"I have a tripod in my backpack. Let's all get in the picture."

Oz hands me the bag and I pull out my telescoping tripod and fit my phone in it. I keep the Bluetooth remote clipped to the base and unhook it before moving into position on a rock above us. He flanks my right side and puts his arm around my waist, while Gideon puts his arms around Auguste and my shoulders. I slide my arm with the remote around Oz's waist, and I click the button several times; our first hike as a family is something I want to remember.

"This weekend, why don't we hit up Maquoketa Caves?" Auguste stoops to pick up what looks like a geode. "The park is just a half-hour drive and there are some pretty good hiking trails."

We continue climbing the trail, and I stop to pick up small, pretty rocks. Oz holds them for me in his zippered pockets, and I'm surprised they're functional. It becomes obvious after a while why they call this trail Calcite—these little translucent mineral rocks are everywhere.

Oz and I lead the pack, while Gideon is behind us, and Auguste takes the rear. They look as though they're taking a leisurely stroll around the block while I try to muffle my labored breathing. We take pictures of the view, and I take photos of the men doing crazy stunts. We're a bizarre bunch, but they fill me with a sense of home and belonging.

"Auguste, where do you stay throughout the year?"

"I'm in either Chicago or New York City, although I have homes in both Shanghai and Berlin. Every once in a while, Gideon invites me to Sydney."

I hardly remember Gideon handles all the family financials; properties, name changes, records, and everything else those entail. It seems more like a job Auguste would enjoy. Gideon reminds me of a reckless bachelor and not a responsible, high-functioning finance expert. It could be his Australian roots—they are more laid back there ... I think.

Don't let the accent fool you. That is a recent adaptation Gideon took on a couple hundred years ago. He's from the Dolomites, Oz tells me in my head.

The sun is setting, so we head to the house after we complete the Calcite loop. After Gideon parks the car, I thank him for driving us.

"Thanks for the view," he offers in return.

CHAPTER TWENTY-FIVE

After a week of daily hikes, the day we leave for Argentina is here. My nerves about trying to impress hundreds of people at our wedding consume my thoughts while we make our way to our seats on the jet.

"Did we remember to get my dress?" My fingers tremble while I work to unscrew the lid to my water bottle, and I get sympathetic looks from Maeve and Auguste behind us.

"Yes." Oz settles his hand over mine and steadies me. "Pippa has it in the back, and don't worry, I didn't see it."

Last night I had a nightmare we forgot my dress at the seamstresses' house, and I had to wear a flour sack down the aisle.

"And you and the men have your tuxedos?" I plop down in the leather seat.

He sets the bottle down so he can take my hands in his. "Even if we forget anything, we still have two weeks before the wedding. Everything will work out exactly as it should."

I turn around in my seat to see Dad already taking pictures from the window. He's like a little boy on Christmas who was just given a toy train. This is his first time on a private jet and watching him marvel at all the little details makes my heart swell. He catches me watching him, and I say, "Wait 'til we're up in the air and the flight crew brings out lunch."

He grins and pats his belly. "I'm ready."

This jet is bigger than the one I'm used to flying on. I'm pretty sure they just took a regular-sized plane and converted it to a luxury private jet, because this one is huge. It has a dining room, a lounge, several bedrooms, many bathrooms, and even a meeting room.

I peer out the window and see several dark SUVs pull up. The sun is bright, so I cup my eyes to see better. Butterflies threaten to fly up my throat, and Oz takes my hand. Before I know it, calm washes over me like a gently lapping lake. He stands, and I follow him to hug our arriving guests.

First to board are Juliette and Alexander Van Horn, who are sired by Pippa. Their skin is fair, and their clothes are nice, but unassuming. They give Oz and me a kiss on each cheek before making their way to a back room.

A woman with skin and eyes as dark as the night boards, and an internal warmth radiates from her when she smiles at me. Clad in a long, golden dress, she wears a headscarf colored like lapis lazuli. "I am Makeba Musa, and I have been waiting to meet you." She embraces me. Her touch is cool but leaves an impression of peace and warmth on my skin. Auguste sired her.

"I'm thrilled to meet you, Makeba."

She inclines her head towards me and takes her seat.

Next is Elliot, who prefers the pronouns they/them/theirs. Their hair is long on one side and shaved on the other. A small stud adorns their nose, and I learn Maeve sired them, which surprises me. Pippa is their mate. The two of them met in the 1930s just outside of Boston.

Oz, help me remember names. I'm going to meet a lot of faces over the coming weeks. With all the trauma I've been through in my life, my memory is shoddy. I try to repeat names back to the person as soon as they say them, but that doesn't always help.

Don't worry, Sahira, you'll learn them all soon enough. I can teach you a spell to help remember details.

Oh, that would solve about ninety-nine of my problems in life.

He chuckles.

Some of the family traveled from other airports throughout the country to meet us in Iowa, but for others, it made sense to fly straight to Chile, or even Argentina. The vast majority will arrive the day before the wedding with the rest of the guests, but for now, we've got plenty of help.

Oz excuses himself to show dad some of the seat's capabilities, and Gideon saddles up next to me.

"Nervous? It isn't too late to back out now."

"No." I'm not entirely sure that is true. I'm not nervous about getting married to Oz. I'm just nervous about making a great impression on the family—and the dignitaries—and all the other people coming to the wedding.

"You're a terrible liar, Lana." His lover's purr tickles my ear and sends a shiver through me. "I can smell it on you." I roll my eyes at him.

"Heartbroken yet, Gideon?" I reapply my red lipstick and smack my lips.

"Every day. I can ask Oz to be my best man and I can be the one waiting at the end of the aisle for you. He's already your mate, let me be your husband."

"Here's the great news, Gideon. I love you only as your queen can." I absently pick at the stitching on the armrest. I love Gideon, but not in the way he wants me to. My love for him is the same love I have for my dad, Pippa, Wren, and Maeve ... right? I grow more uncertain of my feelings the longer I'm in his company.

"Well, that is certainly a start. I can't wait till we get to the part where the hot queen seduces her husband's younger and much-better-looking best friend. Then, they steal every opportunity they have to make love."

"You watch far too much porn." I roll my eyes again.

"Funny enough, I haven't needed it since you and Oz pretend to sleep in the next room."

If looks could kill, Gideon would be dead now. Oz leans against the TV stand, eyeing the exchange. Gideon clears his throat before standing and putting his hands up in surrender. "Just heading to my seat."

What do you think it will take for Gideon to stop pining for me?

There is no end, Sahira. You're irresistible.

We take our seats near dad so I can take pictures and videos to commemorate this experience for him while we take off. He snaps several of Oz and me, knowing I'll want to remember this moment forever.

DUBUQUE IS A SMALL AIRPORT, so it doesn't take long for Wren to taxi before liftoff. When we're in the sky, we push Dad in his wheelchair back to the dining room. The room has a large oval table in the center with a glittering chandelier above it.

Little wisps of magic threads dance around each piece of glass on the light fixture, and I suppose that keeps the glass from breaking during turbulence. Oz nods at the thoughts in my head as I take in the rest of the room.

"Well, I'll be!" Dad marvels as he transfers himself from his wheelchair to the padded leather captain's chairs. He swivels the chair to face Oz and me. "I could get used to this." Dad spent his life working hard on the farm, and he absolutely deserves to spend the rest of his days being pampered.

"Happy looks good on you, Dad."

"The folks at the nursing home don't know what they're missing." I blink back tears, and grief threatens to break down my walls, knowing we're on borrowed time.

Oz and I have discussed delaying our departure after the wedding so we can spend as much time with Dad as possible before cancer takes him.

Gideon eyes me from across the table, and his expression is one of knowing instead of the usual amorous look he throws my way.

The entire room can sense my grief, despite the joy on my dad's face. They don't let him in on the silent elephant in the room and instead, allow him these pockets of peace and happiness. I sit down in a chair next to him and grab his hand. "I'm so happy you're here, Dad."

"Me, too, pumpkin."

The flight crew interrupts our moment when they serve drinks. I opt for a glass of Finlandian, and eye the menu in front of me.

I read the names of the courses. So many of these Oz and I have enjoyed making together. They come with special memories that seem forever ago, but in reality, it only *seems* like I've known Oz forever. "Consider this a menu tasting. I think it'd be fun to serve our wedding guests recipes you and I have enjoyed together."

"I *love* that idea!" Warm vanilla and sugar invade my senses now, and he kisses my hand.

By the time I reach my eighth course, we touch down in Miami. I'm shocked I made it this far, this fast. The vampires are impressed, but not near as impressed as I am Dad is on his tenth course. All this excitement sure gave him an appetite.

I decide to take the hour we're on the ground to recover from eating so much. Oz introduces me to our Miami guests, and some of them join us and the Van Horns in the jet's lounge for takeoff.

Juliette Van Horn sits next to me after we reach cruising altitude. "Lana, wedding tradition says *something borrowed* should come from the longest-married couple in the family," she says. "We brought our cake serving knives if you'd like to use them."

I give her a big hug.

"Yes! Thank you. I've been so worried about what to borrow, and who we could ask." Both she and Alexander smile at me. We chat for a bit before I practically float over to Oz, who is reading Proust's *A LA Recherche Du Temps Perdu.* That's a book I've always wanted to read but haven't found the time to do so.

"I've read it nineteen times. I prefer to savor it, rather than skimming it. It is a magnum opus."

When you don't *have* to sleep or eat, you have all the time in the world to read whatever you want and learn whatever you want.

"Would you like to head back to the dining room? I've got a few more courses to finish."

"Don't have to ask me twice." He sets the book on his lap and stands. Oz loves food as much as I do. He folds the book in his hand and sets it back on the shelf before putting his arm around my waist. Together, we stroll down the corridor to the dining room. Dad is there, polishing off his twelfth course, Gideon cheering him on.

My mouth drops, and I ask dad where it all goes. "I may have performed a belt-loosening spell for such an occasion." Dad has a Cheshire grin on his face.

"You didn't!" Oz chuckles and shakes his head.

"*Don't* teach me that one, Dad. I'll never fit through a doorway."

This must be what's kept him around so long after they put him on hospice. A lot of cancer patients go on hospice far too late, and waste away. If Dad charmed himself to consume food, even when his body didn't want or need any more, the spell could extend his life. Sure, if he did it for thirty years, it would have the opposite effect, but in this case, it was a good thing.

Dad gives me a kiss on the cheek as he wheels himself by retiring to his room. "Love you, Dad."

"I love you, too, pumpkin."

I check the time and glance at my mate. "Shall we head to bed?"

Before Oz can respond, Gideon volunteers, and I roll my eyes.

"I'm only in the next room in case you change your mind. I'd love to welcome you to the club."

I raise my eyebrow at him, but this time, Oz intercepts before I can speak.

Mile high club.

"Not interested in your hazing, Gideon. I have a different initiation in mind." I grab Oz's hand and drag him out of the room with me. His scent responds to my proposition.

We race through the corridor to reach our bedroom. This is the first time I've been in it, and there are rose petals all over the bed. It looks like a five-star hotel suite, and you'd never guess you're on a plane if you could ignore the hum of the engines and the vibration at your feet.

"I was going to surprise you, but this works, too," Oz says before I shut the door and pin him to the wall. I stand on my toes to kiss him while my fingers work to undo his buttons.

Using magic, I turn on music to help drown out our exploits. It's not the usual piano music. No, I don't feel like tonight is the night for slow ballads, either.

First, Nine Inch Nails, then Powerman 5000, and finally Rammstein pour over the speakers, and I've never seen Oz so thrilled. No, tonight, I don't want to take things slow and soft. I want to hear Oz, and in a plane full of vampires, we need something to cover the sound. Surely, only the room next to us will hear Oz and me, but the rest of the plane won't be able to discern what's going on behind closed doors with music going.

I don't plan on getting a lot of sleep till the wee hours of the morning, anyway. Let 'em talk. This is our wedding month, and we get to commemorate my joining the mile-high club however I want.

Oz's eyes go wild at my thoughts. He scoops me up and tosses me on the bed.

Let's go.

CHAPTER TWENTY-SIX

The flight crew opens the aircraft doors, and the panoramic views take my breath away.

"Hey Alphie, would you like to ride with Pippa and me to the docks?" Gideon points while we approach the line of black SUVs waiting to take us to the boat.

What does Gideon need with Dad?

Not sure, he's singing a song and I can't make out what he's got planned. Oz gives my hand a squeeze.

"Be safe!" I call out before sliding into the next car.

Auguste and Maeve slip in the back, and we follow the SUV in front of us.

Most of the car ride follows the huge lake, and these are some of the most breathtaking views I've ever experienced. There's something about the Andes Mountains that just makes you feel there's got to be a higher power in charge of this all.

A yacht is waiting at the dock, and some cars are already unloading. Dad looks to be in great spirits, and Oz pushes his wheelchair up the ramp for me.

"Thanks."

After the boat ride, we gather our things and head to the lower deck so we can disembark on a wooden dock. I can tell the dock was freshly stained a rich mahogany color. I hand my bag to Auguste, and Oz hops down and takes my hand.

"Thank you." He grabs my bag from Auguste and slings it over his shoulder.

Gideon offers to push Dad, and I thank him, too.

Oz slips his fingers in mine as we make our way up the ramp. At the top of the landing, a wooden slotted sidewalk divides different parts of the island. We go straight towards the larger stone house and wave bye at our guests. We've all had a long journey, so we'll reconvene for supper to go over the game plan for this week and next.

Oz shows Dad to his room, and I trail behind them, taking in the fine details in the artwork on the walls, and peeking through windows to see which rooms have the best views.

"Hey, Dad!" I stop in his doorway.

"Hi honey, just about to lie down for a nap. Wake me when it's time to eat."

I grin and shut his door for him. Whenever I'd fly, I tell the flight crew to wake me for food and drinks. I never skip a meal, if I can avoid it, and know that is a trait I get from Dad.

Oz and I find our room, and I plop on the bed, and he snuggles up beside me.

"We're getting married," I whisper, as though Oz will disappear if I speak any louder. If I am dreaming, someone just end it all now because I can *never* recover from this.

He takes my hand in his and brings it to his mouth. "It's you and me, Sahira, till the end of time." He presses his cool lips to the back of my hand.

Oz strokes my head, and I soon fall into a deep slumber.

"KNOCK, KNOCK!" A woman raps her knuckles on Dad's front door. She has an ethereal quality to her with her creamy, blemish-free skin and blonde hair

so light, it's almost white. Her piercing green eyes might be beautiful under the right circumstances, but the look in them is unsettling.

Dad swings the door open and gives a tight smile at the woman before stepping aside to let her through. The scene appears harmless, but I can't fight the clawing fear gripping my chest. Who is she? Did my dad date after my mom left him?

The woman swings a large bag onto his kitchen counter and starts rummaging through his cupboards. She pulls out a crock pot and begins assembling ingredients while they talk about corn prices. It feels platonic between them, but I still don't like her, nor the familiarity she takes with his things.

"Would you be a dear and run over to my place? I forgot the roast, silly me."

"You don't have to do this for me, you know."

"Oh, please—it's the least I can do. You plow my driveway every time it snows!"

Dad sighs before slipping on his coat and grabbing his keys. "I'll be back in a Jiffy."

My attention goes to the woman; she watches out the window for several minutes before running back to the kitchen and pulls a vial out of her pocket. I can't tell what's in the bottle, but she uncorks it and dumps the entire contents in the crock pot. A purple, noxious plume nearly touches the ceiling before she slams the lid down to contain it.

I jar from my sleep in a wild panic.

"Are you alright? I couldn't see your dreams, but you look like you've seen a ghost."

It might as well have been a ghost. I replay the dream as I remember it in my mind for Oz to see.

"Who's the woman?" I'm uneasy about the pained look on Oz's face.

"There's no mistaking it, Lana. The woman in your dream is Dolphina Darling."

Violent tremors rack my body and bile rises in my throat. Dolphina is the vampire witch behind the prophecy.

"I ... I have to see Dad." I scramble from the bed and run to the door. Oz is right behind me when I knock to wake Dad.

"Come in." Sleep mars his voice. Dad sits up and transfers to his wheelchair, and he has a concerned look on his face. "Everything okay, pumpkin?"

I shake my head as I cross the room to sit on his bed.

A deep breath doesn't quite prepare me for what I'm about to ask him. "Dad ... did anybody ever cook you food regularly?"

He has a puzzled look on his face. "All the time? I was a single, good-looking farmer who worked long hours in the fields." He grins. "The neighbors would drop off goodies for me, I ate out a lot, and ladies at the Farmer's Market would bring me home-cooked meals sometimes. Why?"

"Lunch is rea ... Oh, my bad." Gideon back peddles out of the room.

I return my attention to Dad. "Was there a tall, blonde woman with light green eyes? She was part-vampire, part-witch, but looked like an angel?" There isn't any other way to describe her. She is ethereal and stands over six feet tall.

"My neighbor, Dee, used to bring me over meals every Sunday. Enough to feed me supper for the week, but she moved when I went on hospice."

Grief clutches my chest and spills down my cheeks.

"Dad, Dee is *Dolphina Darling*," I choke out. "She was poisoning your food with *cadmium*."

She's the reason dad has pancreatic cancer, and why I'll lose him only after having him in my life for a brief moment. My tears are angry, and they sting my face.

"The vampire witch behind those prophecies?" Dad's voice cracks in disbelief. "Why would she do such a thing?" He looks so frail now, and my heart breaks to witness the betrayal he feels.

"We will find out, Dad."

Oz gives Dad's hand a squeeze before cupping the back of my head and giving me a kiss. "I'm gonna go see if Auguste and Gideon and I can sort this out. Maeve might figure things out, too."

I hold Dad in my arms and sob.

After it seems like I have no more tears left to cry, Dad's stomach growls.

"Let's eat." I wipe my tears off with the back of my hand and straighten out the scarf at my waist.

He nods and unlocks the brakes on his wheelchair so I can push him to the kitchen.

GIDEON RETURNS in the early evening, but Oz, Auguste, and Maeve are nowhere to be found.

"Everything alright?" I eye him warily.

"Yes, they're just taking a little longer than we expected. They should be back in an hour." Gideon tilts his head to the side. "I actually came back here because I need to talk to you."

A sense of dread takes over me. I always feel this way when someone says they need to talk, because it is never good news.

Panic surges throughout my body. Oz has sent Gideon because he can't face me himself and he doesn't want to marry me—and all my problems. Or worse, they found Dolphina Darling in all her gorgeous splendor, and he'll be with her instead.

Gideon senses my panic and puts his hands up. "Hey, it's nothing bad, I promise."

The fear subsides a little, but I'm still apprehensive.

"I want to talk about my wedding gift for you. Well, a gift your dad and I are giving you."

What on earth could Gideon and my dad be collaborating on?

He grabs a bottle of Moscato d'Asti and three glasses while tilting his head towards the living room.

"Sit." I take the bottle from him.

"Okay ..." He disappears into another room.

I attempt to uncork the bottle of wine but am unsuccessful.

"Aye, let me help with that." Gideon returns and sets the wine glasses down and Dad trails in after him.

"Thanks." I hand him the bottle. He makes quick work of removing the cork and I steady a glass for him to pour. I pass it to Dad, and then Gideon pours two more.

The room smells of nutmeg and ginger when he speaks. "I've been racking my brain trying to figure out what to get you for a wedding present, you know, because you don't want me meeting you at the end of the aisle."

I give him an unamused look.

"I didn't figure it out until we were on the plane, and I saw and felt how painful it is for you to know your dad is dying and there isn't anything you can do to stop it. Your heartache is the same I had when my parents died."

I fight back tears, but I can't keep them from spilling. Having my dad in my life after all these years has been the best gift, and also most painful. To know and love him for such a short time, knowing he's dying, is unbearable. And now, to learn Dolphina poisoned him, likely because of a *stupid prophecy,* makes my blood boil.

"After the wedding, I'm turning your dad into a vampire."

All the air leaves my chest, and the wine glass drops out of my hands, shattering on the floor and splashing wine at my feet. The buzzing sensation grows deafening, and I can't hear what's being said. It's as though I'm underwater, unable to make out any discernible sounds.

Gideon waves a hand in front of my face, but I stare right through it. He puts his hand on my knee, and it jolts me back to present. "You heard nothing I said, did you?"

I blink my eyes to clear them.

"Ah, no. Sorry. You're turning my dad into a vampire?" My voice chokes on a sob and I throw my hand to my mouth. "Will he survive the transition?" I hold my breath, afraid of his answer, but hoping.

"Well, that's why I brought Pippa into the fold. She's run just about every test imaginable on him to see if there is a way she can cure him conventionally, and this is our only option. We're confident he'll turn with my blood, considering I'm the oldest vampire in the family willing to turn him. I'll teach him how to survive being a vampire while you and Oz are on your honeymoon. Shouldn't take more than a couple months."

I am speechless. Oz is the strongest, oldest vampire. He'd never turn Dad. He despises what he is and would never make someone he loves a vampire. That leaves Gideon, although I didn't know he was the next oldest. Based on his mannerisms, I'd peg him as the youngest of the family.

"You're okay with this?" I look at Dad, not wanting to get my hopes up. I want him around forever, but only if he's willing.

"Meeting you is the best thing that has ever happened to me, Lana. I have a lifetime to make up for." He fights back tears. "I will be strong and healthy again, although there isn't much I can do to change how old I look. Unless I use one of those glamor spells Bonnie Driscoll is so fond of."

I weep happy tears and laugh as I hug Dad in his wheelchair. By the time I'm done hugging him, I am ugly crying. Rainbows and sunshine threaten to burst out of me because I'm so happy.

Paying no attention to the glass still at my feet, I throw my arms around Gideon and bury my face in his neck. "Thank you. This is the best gift you could've ever given me." My voice is barely a choked whisper.

His arms envelop me, and I continue to sob into his chest. Nutmeg and ginger fill my nose, and I breathe it in deep. For the first time since knowing him, I'm actually okay with that. I love Gideon, too.

"Lana, you're bleeding." Gideon pulls away. I stare down at my bare feet and wipe my tears—no doubt mascara streaks down my cheeks. Blood pools at my feet, and when I take a step to sit down on the couch, I slip.

"Whoa, easy there." He catches my fall and helps me sit down. "Stay put, I'll grab Pippa."

"She's across the island gathering herbs and medicinals, but there should be a med kit in the pantry." Dad wheels himself towards the kitchen. I helped Pippa supply damn near every room in this house with a kit. She figured if we've got vampires, witches, and humans all under one roof for a while, we'd better be prepared.

"Top shelf, red bag." I point.

I get woozy, and the adrenaline from my surprise wears off. Gideon puts my feet in his lap, never minding the fact he's now getting blood on my favorite couch. I wince.

"Never mind the couch, Lana. Oz will have my head if I don't fix this. And don't worry, I will not bite you unless you want me to." He waggles his eyebrows at me.

Gideon uses a bottle of water to wash away any debris before he tears open a little packet and pours powder on the bottom of my feet.

I brace myself for stinging, but it doesn't hurt at all. He packs the powder into my cuts and applies pressure to my wounds, which causes me to grimace.

"Sorry. Oz would kill me if I gave you my blood to heal this." He is gentle with his words, and I'm seeing a far more tender side of him than usual.

If my life were in danger, I know Gideon would give me his blood anyway, and I know Oz wouldn't hold it against him.

"Thank you." He brushes away the excess powder and bandages my feet.

"Sorry for getting blood all over your pants."

"Want me to take 'em off?" He quirks a brow and I roll my eyes. "Here comes trouble ..."

The door nearly flies off its hinge as Oz rushes to kneel at my side. "You're bleeding!" His angry eyes dart to Gideon.

"Yeah, I dropped my glass and stepped on it. He fixed me right up. I was just about to do a healing spell to take care of the rest." I put a hand on his shoulder and the air shifts. Oz is visibly more relaxed now.

"Thanks."

"Yep, don't mention it." Gideon stands coolly before Auguste comes with a broom and dustpan. We watch Gideon drop his blood-soaked pants and boxers at his feet before folding them neatly over his arm and disappearing into the hallway, his sculpted ass and thighs on full display.

At first, Oz doesn't take it very well Gideon will turn Dad. Not because he's turning him, but because he didn't think to consult Oz first.

I agree it should've been discussed with the king first, but I'm grateful all the same.

"Don't be hard on him about it, please." I lean into his kiss.

"I won't, but only because I know how much this means to you. Gideon will make a great sire for your dad. There are few I'd trust to do so." His words comfort me.

CHAPTER TWENTY-SEVEN

My stomach is so full from supper I remove my swimsuit and put on the light robe Oz got me in Mont-Tremblant. I crawl on the bed and lay my head in his lap while he strokes my hair. He looks down at me, and the room smells like a cookie factory.

"I love you, too. What did you find out today?" Most of the court were out for such a long time, and I'm hopeful they have some answers.

"We haven't figured out why Dolphina was trying to kill him, as her beef is with you, not him. But we know she's responsible for what happened to you in Mont-Tremblant. Mayim-Willow was simply a crazed follower of the Lapis Templar."

I suck in a deep breath before I speak. "After our honeymoon, I'm going to Bedlam. There, I'll learn where Mom went in time, what I can do to bring her back, and how to become immortal. Then, I come home and will find and kill Dolphina Darling."

Oz shakes his head and flexes his jaw. "You will do no such thing. Bedlam, yes, but you may not go near the Lapis Templar or Dolphina Darling. They've spent thousands of years scheming and organizing with one goal in mind: *to kill you*. We will take care of her and her followers. We'll declare war on the Lapis Templar following the wedding, and anyone aiding them will stand trial for treason."

His tone is far different from one he's ever had with me before. It's like he's speaking to one of his subordinates and not his equal, and it makes me uneasy. Tears form in my eyes, but I blink them away. We're bound to disagree sometimes, but I don't enjoy feeling scolded like a child.

"I'm sorry," Oz responds to the thoughts in my head. "I shouldn't speak to you like that." Sometimes, his ability to read my mind is helpful, like now, when I don't quite have all the words to articulate how I feel.

"No, you're right. I'm foolish to think I can take her and the Lapis Templar on by myself. I just didn't enjoy hearing it."

When I sit up, I turn to face him. I've always felt couples fail because they can't communicate, and I want to make sure Oz and I never go to bed upset with each other. The last time I went to bed mad at him, he *died* the next day. That is a mistake I will never repeat. I don't care if I don't sleep for fifty years.

"It's not that I think you can't take her, or them. You're the strongest witch I've ever met." He takes my hand in his. "I just don't want you doing it alone, because I would never recover if they killed you."

This, I understand on a profound level. Oz died, and I brought him back to life, but a part of me will never heal from that. It was the single most tragic thing I've ever endured. *I killed a man.* Not just any man, but the love of my life.

"Are we ..." I hesitate. "Are we okay?" Between our disagreement now, and my asking him to go easy on Gideon, I want nothing left for interpretation later.

"Yeah, we're okay." He kisses the top of my head.

Oz closes the space between us but is tender with his touch when he reaches me. Chills course through my body, causing goosebumps to dot my arms. Time stops. His fingers brush my hair behind my shoulders, and he traces my collarbone, the lightest touch sending a jolt straight to my core. My breathing shallows in anticipation.

Take me.

He takes me into his arms and carries me to our bed. "I have one condition." He sets me down on the duvet.

"Okay ..." He's hesitant about what my request might be.

"I want to hear you breathe when we make love. Not just tonight, but every time."

"I think I can manage that." Oz puffs up his chest when he takes a deep breath. I giggle and pull him towards me. His lips press into mine, and I take in his scent. Spiced sugar cookies.

Tonight, like many other nights, we are one. My sweat cools on his skin, and we become nothing but arms and legs, and now breath and rhythm. I open my chest to him, allowing his teeth to sink into my breast. His draw is deep, and it sends waves of euphoria through me with each pull.

Hours pass, but they feel like mere minutes. Oz is satiated, and I've come several times. Finally, I collapse on his chest, unable to handle any more. He kisses my forehead before grabbing his phone from the nightstand.

"I want a picture." I rest my head on his chest and turn towards the camera. He frames both of our faces in it, and I laugh before sticking out my tongue for another one. Oz snaps several more—my wild hair and bedroom eyes, the curve of my breasts, and my miles of leg. Each picture is more suggestive and risqué than the previous.

"I want pictures, too." I reach for my phone.

He puts one arm behind his head and flexes his whole body for some pictures. "Careful, or we might not sleep at all tonight."

I raise an eyebrow at him. The soft light from the bathroom high-lights his muscles—his thick forearms, strong jawline, and washboard abs. Then, there are his obliques that cut sharply across his hips. He is *exquisite*, and he's *mine*.

Oz chuckles at my salacious thoughts and pats the duvet next to him. By the time I crawl to him, he's got the covers pushed back for us. "We have forever," he says. "For now, you must have your rest. I fed from you for a long time, and you'll need your strength. We'll take a rain check, though."

I groan. I am not an early riser.

I WAKE when I feel Oz stir under me. The sun intrudes on our slumber, so I pull on my robe so I can get a good look at the mountains from the balcony off our room.

"Morning, sunshine."

I'm startled because it isn't Oz's voice. Instead, it's Gideon's. He's on his balcony reading the newspaper, which is right next to ours.

"According to this poll by an online dating site, Australian men make the best lovers." Gideon brings the newspaper closer to his face before setting it on his lap. "Care to give one a spin?" His eyes flash gunmetal blue and the aroma of cinnamon wafts in my direction.

I roll my eyes at his proposition, but don't have time to respond before Oz steps out on the landing.

"You're not even Australian."

"I'm more Australian than any person alive!"

"Yeah, only because you've lived there for the last couple hundred years, ya old goat."

Gideon acts wounded and tips the newspaper towards his head in a salute before going inside his room. I eye the placement of the chairs on each balcony and shuffle ours a bit to match his. After sitting down in the chair, I turn towards Gideon's room. I can see right to his bed.

"We didn't have the blinds closed last night." I panic.

Oz maneuvers himself to where I sit, and we both hear Gideon cackle from his bedroom.

"Don't worry, I saw nothing I haven't seen before," Gideon yells. "But I do want a copy of those pictures, Oz!"

I tighten my robe and go back to our bedroom.

I RETREAT to the balcony in our room to work on my vows. How does one measure the love between two other-worldly people? Our love isn't like human love—ordinary and linear. Our love is deep, and it's wide, and all-consuming. The kind of love that leaves you breathless any time we fix our gaze upon each other. It isn't just about looks, though. It's being willing to give up everything you have and love so as not to hurt the other.

I picture Oz, and think about everything I went through, and put him through, because of the depth of my love for him, even if it was a little misguided. Words flow out of me and onto paper so fast, my mind nary has the chance to read what I put down.

"Lana?" Oz stands in the doorway, startling me. I slam the book shut. He's covered in dirt, and only has sturdy work pants on. Holy hell, I bite my lip and undress him with my eyes.

I stand and greet him with a press to his mouth, not caring he's filthy. "Hey babe, just working on my vows."

He peeks over my shoulder, and I swat at him. *Nope!* I tell him in my head.

"Well, that's no fun. We've got the extra dock all put together. Thought I'd see if you want to do a bit of sailing before the sun goes down? Wren and Sebastian are going."

I dart to the armoire and start changing my clothes into something a little warmer. "Do I ever!" I've sailed many times throughout my travels, and I can't get enough of it.

"Alright, I'm going to hop in the shower quick. Can you make the rounds and see if anyone else wants to come with?"

Part of me wants to hop in the shower with him, but I know we're crunched on time, so I give him a quick kiss before leaving him.

The first stop is Gideon's bedroom. I rap my knuckles on the door and he's in just a towel while using another one to dry off his hair.

"So, you've finally decided to give it a go?" He wets his lips, and the cinnamon pours off him and wallops me in the face.

"No, but if you want to come sailing with us, we leave in a few minutes." The heady feeling when I'm in his proximity just does something to me I'm not ready to admit, so I step back.

He shrugs his shoulders, "Sure."

Next, I knock on Auguste's door. "Hey, would you like to come

sailing with us? Oz, Wren, Sebastian, Gideon, and I will leave in a few."
I lean my head against his doorway.

His hair is still damp from showering, and his khaki shorts hang low on his hips, no shirt or belt. He has tattoos, and that deep V ... I try not to ogle—there's no way I'm going to give into baser urges.

I smell cloves on him, and he hesitates for a moment before agreeing to come with. His eyes are a pale blue now. It felt like he was about to touch me for a moment, but the feeling passes, and his eyes shift back to their normal steel gray.

"Are you alright?" I wait for him to respond.

"It's just ... I'm not sure what to get you for a wedding present. Gideon has thought of the best gift you can give a daughter who's losing her dad. I just don't know if I can top that." Auguste looks distressed.

"Look, Auguste, I need nothing. I promise you. Just having you in my life is enough. I don't have a need for anything other than family. Please understand this."

His eyes seek the truth in mine, and I can sense a certain sadness in them. It's a feeling I'm familiar with.

"Alright."

I can tell he's still reserved.

"May I hug you?" I've always been a hugger, and it looks like Auguste could use one now. He tells me he's worried about my gift, but I have a feeling that isn't quite what's on his mind. I bet he's missing his mate. We embrace, and his hug is strong but tender. I take a deep breath, and I sense sorrow and love from him.

Footsteps in the hall interrupt us, and Gideon and Oz pause their steps.

"I'm just going to grab a shirt and I'll meet you guys outside." Auguste turns on his heel and shuts the door.

"Did we interrupt anything?" There's a jealous tone to Gideon's question.

"No, he just looked like he could use a hug, so I gave him one." I don't need to justify anything, and Oz knows my intentions. He can read my mind to know there's nothing more to it than that.

CHAPTER TWENTY-EIGHT

*O*ur island has transformed over the last week and a half. Staff added a beautiful stone waterfall to the pool and brought in hundreds of full-grown native plants and trees. Natural walk paths now line the property and connect the houses, rather than the cement that badly needed repairs.

Part of me is anxious because I'm worried I'm not doing enough to get things ready for the wedding. Oz reassures me the staff have it all covered, and any changes or decisions that need to be made will be ran by either him or me. We have spa staff flying in tonight to pamper us. Then, on Friday, I'll get waxed and primped for our ceremony on Sunday.

"I need your opinion on something." I sit on the edge of the desk.

Oz is busy working on his laptop, but he closes it to give me his undivided attention.

"Sure, what's up?"

"As you know, I'm getting waxed on Friday. Brazilian, or nah?"

Oz grins at this question and pauses before answering. "I thought it was going to be a question like, 'Is Die Hard a Christmas movie or not?'" He taps his pen on the notepad next to him as though he's deep in thought. "You have a lovely mound of hair, which I prefer over bare."

Well, that answers it. No on the Brazilian, but I might get a full bikini wax, my legs, and armpits.

He leans back in his chair and studies me. "Do you think I need a wax? Or a Brazilian?"

I can tell he's fighting back a smile. He's messing with me.

"No Osgood Finlandian, I like my men hairy. Although, when I was a little girl, I said I would never be with anyone who has hairy arms, legs, and armpits."

He chuckles and shakes his head.

I attended one of those sex toy parties a coworker threw years ago, and I was so surprised to learn how many women like their men completely smooth. The sales rep joked if you trim the hedges, it makes the tree appear larger. Oz doesn't need to look any bigger than he already is; it's intimidating enough. His self-satisfied grin changes into a look I can't decipher.

"Thanks, I think." Oz pauses, as though he's not sure if he should continue. "What toys did you get?" The dramatic shift of air in our bedroom and the aroma of spices tell me he's ready for any answer I could give him. He's got just one thing on his mind.

He shrugs as though it's inevitable.

"Well, I was single, so I got a couple of vibrators ..." Growing up in the Midwest, sex and body positivity weren't a thing. Having this conversation makes me squirm. "There was also a jeweled butt plug." I move to the bed and sit cross-legged on the edge, and Oz sits next to me and takes my hand in his. I intrigue him.

"Have you ever done anal?"

I figured this question was coming. "Not on purpose. Wrong hole." I shrug. That has happened a handful of times, unfortunately. The first time was in high school, and I was dating a bull rider my senior year. I thought I was in love with him. We were having sex in my bedroom, and it slipped, and I did the only thing I could—I kicked. It sent him flying into my dresser across my bed. He was so startled, and I just sobbed from the pain.

"It doesn't have to hurt. If you want to do it, we can. In fact, I'm open to anything you want to try."

I've used plugs before, and I enjoyed the experience because I was in control. I imagine I could enjoy anal sex, too, provided it doesn't hurt. The nice thing about sex with Oz is he can read my mind, so every single move he makes in the bedroom is exactly what I need. I trust him completely. "Yeah, I'd like to try it, but maybe we can start with plugs to ... prime myself first?" I hesitate.

He brushes my hair behind my shoulders. "Okay. I'll have to order it in. I think the nearest toy shop has to be in Bariloch. Unless you want to go there today to pick some stuff out? Our schedule is clear all morning and afternoon. We could go there for the day, check out some of the chocolate shops, too?" He knows the way to my heart.

I change into a red sundress and slip on black flip-flops. Oz wears khaki shorts, a white button-up shirt, and boat shoes. Everything he wears is so effortless. I sure hope our kids inherit his impeccable style and good looks.

"If they're lucky, they'll look like you," Oz responds to the thoughts in my head. I style my hair and makeup. Might as well look cute if I'm wearing a dress. Ice bubbles to the surface of my skin, and I take pleasure in knowing Oz likes what he sees.

When we exit our room, Gideon and Auguste are in the hallway.

"Heard we're going shopping?" Gideon steps in line with us as we walk.

Remind me to have private conversations in my head and not out loud.

Although, maybe if those two come to the sex toy shop, they won't pine for me near as much. They'll be too busy offing their rocks themselves.

It doesn't hurt to try.

"I suppose if you two are coming with, we should see if anyone else wants to go to town." Oz makes the rounds, and no one else wants to go, although we have several requests to bring home lots of chocolate. That came from Dad, CJ, and Maeve.

"See you tonight!" I give hugs around.

Hannah lent me her oversized tote bag. I pack this full of bottles of water and snacks. I'm certain the men will appreciate it.

The boat ride to town was smooth. The only ripples or waves in the water came from passing boats. After docking, we hail a cab to take us to the toy shop. I'm sandwiched between Auguste and Oz in the backseat, and Gideon takes shotgun with the driver. No matter who I sit between, there would be no room either way—these men are giants.

It wasn't easy finding the shop as it blends in with the upscale clothing and jewelry boutiques. I expected obtrusive signage and raunchy mannequins that scream *get your dildos here!* When we enter the doorway, a cashier greets us from the register. I'm impressed. The place is spotless, and it makes me feel like I'm buying diamonds and not butt plugs and vibrators.

Oz slides his hand in mine, and takes me to a wall full of toys, while Gideon and Auguste peruse separate sections of the store. The fingers on my free hand glide over some toys, and I land on a butt plug set. The set has four glass plugs, each designed to work your way until you're ready for anal sex. He picks up the package and turns it over.

This'll do.

I spot some lubricant and grab a bottle of it.

Anything else you want to try out? He takes me to the BDSM section and holds up a leather bondage set.

Let's get it.

I don't like pain, but I love being spanked. I'm open to exploring new horizons.

The store has several lines of luxury lingerie brands. A couple of them I recognize from our trip to Montreal.

"Pick something out for me." While Oz scans the selection, my eye catches a big black seat resembling a saddle two aisles over. It has ridges in the center and several rubber attachments.

"*That* is a Sybian." Gideon's voice is a lover's purr in my ear.

I'd never heard of one before, and it surprises me he has. The display says it's used for couples.

"You sit here," he points to the ridges. "And use this remote to rotate, vibrate, or both." There is also a stool for the partner, to embrace whoever is using the Sybian. Interesting. Oz and I could both use this. "Let me know if you want a demo," he finishes while I walk away to see if Oz found anything.

Hey babe, have you ever heard of a Sybian?

He shakes his head no, and I tell him about the device. He's intrigued, so I take him over to see it. *We could both use it, whether you ride it, or I do.*

Alright, Sahira. Oz goes to the cashier to arrange delivery for the device while I look at handcuffs on a nearby stand. I'm uncertain any of these would fit his wrists, although they'd fit mine.

Gideon strolls over to me with a tall, rectangular box. "You should do this." He hands it to me. "Until I can convince you two to let me in." I examine it. It's a kit to make a silicone mold of my lady bits, attached to what looks like a masturbator for men.

"Well, that would indeed be the only way you're getting close to her." I quirk a brow, referring to my more intimate parts. "And besides, I told you I don't share."

"Who said anything about sharing Oz? Think about it—two handsome men worshiping and pleasing *you*. It's not uncommon for vampires to share a mate. Hell, entire clans have shared a mate," Gideon continues in a whispered frenzy. "Besides, you know how I feel about you, and I know how you feel about me. It doesn't make your love for Oz any less or any different. He'll say yes if you tell him you want to."

The idea of any other man having me makes me sad, because I love Oz, and it would devastate me if he asked me to share him with anyone else.

No, it would destroy me.

I'd feel inadequate, and it would eat me alive. I love Gideon, but I love him like I love Pippa, or Auguste, or Maeve. There isn't a thing I wouldn't do for any of them, but my heart, body, and soul belong to Oz now. Forever. The *only* way I'd ever let Gideon in our bedroom is if Oz wants to share me with him. Some guys get off on that, but I'm far too possessive to watch him have another person.

"Gideon, I know you think you're in love with me." I bring him in conspiratorially. "But Dolphina Darling is wrong about this prophecy about you and I falling in love and having babies. She's wrong about the prophecy about me sleeping with Oz's vampires, too. It's true I love you, yes. I would die for you, just like I would for any of his family. But I don't love you in the way you want me to, I'm sorry."

He looks like I just broke his heart, but I don't know what other way to tell him. I enjoy Gideon's company. He's entertaining, and he's honest. I never have to wonder what's on his mind, because he'll tell me, often without my even asking. He's smart, protective, and he's kind.

This man offered to do for me what no one else would—not even my mate. He's going to turn Dad. There isn't a better gift he could give me, and for this, I am forever in his debt. But I cannot share a bed with him; I belong to Oz.

"Another time, another life, things could've been different for you and me." This isn't the faux-facade vampire revealing his feelings to me. It is what's underneath all that—the man made up of blood, bone, and feelings other than jealousy and desire. He's raw and vulnerable.

I try to imagine how I'd feel, watching the person I think I'm in love with love someone else. It would be difficult. Gideon places the rectangular box back on the shelf but pauses before releasing his hand. "I know you don't feel worthy of being queen. But I want you to know you alone are the best possible person we could ever hope for. Then, now, and forever. After you gave up everything you love to save the man and people you love, you showed you're more than worthy of being our queen. We're undeserving of you."

Our conversation took a much different turn than I expected. Was he testing me? I don't think so. Was what I did ... brave? All I thought at that moment when I went back in time to stop the prophecy was how these people suffered because of me. What other choice did I have? In hindsight, I see how it was foolish—Auguste said as much. Now Gideon praises me for it.

"Oz gave me so much more than a kingdom of vampires to help him rule. He gave me a family. You, Auguste, Pippa, Maeve, Wren—and everyone else—I mean it when I say I love you all. You've given me purpose. And now, you're giving me the best gift of all: my dad. I don't know what more a girl can ask for."

Gideon winks at me before looking over my shoulder. I turn around and see Auguste perusing books.

"Find anything you didn't already know?"

He takes my teasing in jest and holds up a book featuring a woman strapped to a door swing.

"Whatever do they need this for?" The puzzled look on Auguste's face is priceless. Gideon and I try to hold in our laughter, but we fail.

"Some men, believe it or not, don't have super strength and need help to lift their partners." I can't keep a straight face.

Auguste puts the book back, and we meet Oz at the register.

"All set?"

"They're delivering it this afternoon. I figured you didn't want the staff coming to pick it up for you."

"Ah, good point." I bite my lip. "Let's have lunch." The men are eager for this, and we spot a little cafe with a magnificent view of the lake. The eatery is small, but it has outdoor seating on a patio right on the water.

Oz and I look up at the stars dotting the horizon just above the mountains in front of us. I am dozing off, so he carries me to our bed. To keep with tradition, we won't be in each other's company at all before our ceremony tomorrow, so we revel in each other's touch tonight. Sleep, be damned. I don't have to be awake until noon, so we've got time to play.

Instead of using toys, it is just him and me; Naked, crinkled sheets, and magic. When we finish, I am exhausted straight down to my bones. It is my last night as a Chapman-Sawyer, and sleep comes fast for me while I lay on Oz's chest.

We wake just before noon to a knock on the door. Oz answers it in his boxers.

Gideon and Auguste have brought us brunch in bed.

"Nope, you stay put." Gideon eyes me, and I hike the duvet up to my chin. He has my tray, and Auguste gives Oz his.

"Thank you! This means a lot to us." I guess we'll spend a little time together after all, and I'm grateful these two bought us more time together.

Auguste snaps several photos of us eating our brunch and heads downstairs.

Oz and I savor the quiet before the hustle and bustle of the rest of the day's activities. He has a full plate of waffles, fresh tropical fruit, bacon, eggs, toast, and hash browns. I have a lighter fare of an açaí bowl, scrambled eggs, and an espresso. Also on the tray is a large glass of apple juice. Gideon knows I love it so.

We steal several kisses from each other before parting ways.

"See you at the bridge, babe."

"I'll be waiting for you, Sahira." He steals one more kiss before going downstairs and letting the ladies know they can come up now.

I shower while Pippa, Maeve, and Hannah unload their things in Oz and my bedroom. The men have Gideon's room next door, and the wedding party will always check the hallways to make sure Oz and I don't accidentally see each other before tonight's ceremony.

EACH OF OUR rooms has a photographer and videographer to capture the entire day. They're pros, and after a while I don't even notice they're here.

After a while, a knock sounds on the door.

Pippa cracks it open and peers through it. "Come on in, Alphie" She opens the door wide enough for him to wheel in.

"Hi, Dad." I'm still in the chair I've occupied for several hours.

"My, my." He blots a handkerchief to his eye. "I wish your mother could see you now. You look beautiful, Lana." He gives my hand a squeeze.

"Thanks Dad, you look very handsome in your suit. I wish Mom could see you now, too."

She would be here if it weren't for my meddling in the past. Perhaps one day I can take him back in time to see her—I owe him that much. Even if I can do it for a day; they both need closure. And who knows, maybe he'd decide to turn her and she can bring them both back to live forever.

Dad doesn't stay long because he's going to take a brief nap before he's needed anywhere. Shortly after he leaves, a massive vase of flowers arrives. Red and blue peonies dot the arrangement, and they place golden branches between long strands of eucalyptus. Maeve puts them on the coffee table and hands me the little card attached to it.

I'll be waiting for you at the bridge. Love, Oz.

I text Oz to thank him for the flowers. They're breathtaking.

"I didn't think peonies came in blue?" Hannah marvels. I can see her wheels turning in her head now. If Oz has a connection to blue peonies, she'd get orders from all over the world. I flip over the little card and see a handwritten scribble on the back.

Tell Hannah they're enchanted. Sorry.

I show her the message, and she groans audibly. "Darn. We could've cornered the market on this." I'm sure there are other ways Oz can help her with her business.

She checks her watch. "Almost showtime. Are you nervous?"

My hands are clammy when I tell her I am. Not because I'm getting married, but because there are many people watching me.

What if I trip? Or do they think I'm not attractive enough or thin enough?

Hannah reassures me and asks if I'm ready to get in my dress yet.

"Now or never," I breathe. Maeve helps Pippa take my dress out of its protective garment bag, and I step into it.

Hannah zips it up for me. I was nervous my recent indulgences here would've made the fit tight, but I'm relieved. The dress fits perfectly. There isn't a dry eye in the room as they take me in.

"Okay, ladies, you're going to make me cry. Enough of that."

Oz, if you're listening—keep occupied while I look in the mirror, so it doesn't ruin the surprise for you, okay?

Alright, I'm headed downstairs, anyway. See you soon. I'll be waiting for you at the bridge. I love you.

I love you, too.

The girls help me slide into my shoes, and I see something pinned to the back of the left heel. Oz's sixpence, set in a vintage cameo design with lapis lazuli and diamonds, adorns my heel. "He thinks of everything."

"That is not all." Pippa moves the curtains in front of the window to reveal a medium-sized box.

The box is light blue with a gold ribbon on it and is far heavier than it looks. I slide the ribbon off and lift the lid. They lined the inside with silk, and I uncover its inner cloth. I damn near wheeze. Everyone crowds around to see, and they let out a collective gasp when I take it out of its box.

This is a crown. Not just a crown, but one with hundreds of diamonds, crystal beads, pearl beads, and white gold filigrees. My hands tremble holding it. This must be worth a fortune.

Pippa helps me pin it to my hair, along with my veil. Hannah looks inside the box and notices there are matching earrings. I put them on, and see magical threads woven into the details.

They're enchanted. They'd have to be, otherwise the weight of them alone would cause them to fall out of my ears. Sure enough, when I put them on I don't feel a thing. Same with the crown, and I sigh a breath of relief. I'd have a sore neck for the next month wearing this all night had he not done that.

Finally, I look at myself in the mirror. I hardly recognize what I see —in a good way. Dare I say it, I look ... regal. A wave of relief washes over me and I stand taller. The spray tan I had a few nights ago gives me a healthy glow, and I look like I belong.

"I'm ready." I emerge from the bathroom. My bridesmaids help me down the stairs and out the doorway before they run ahead to take their spots on the bridge. Dad waits for me next to the house, and I wheel him towards the towering gate built for the entrance to the woods. Soft music and lively chatter from our guests fill the island.

"I'm going to walk you down the aisle."

"How? I thought you were too weak to walk any long distance." I give him a confused look.

He asks me to face him and hold his hands. Faint whispers encircle us, and magical threads lift him out of his wheelchair and affix themselves to his legs. He chuckles with joy and gives his legs a few kicks.

"Oh, Daddy." I blink back tears and hug him.

"This is what I went into town for that day." He straightens his tie. "I went to get ingredients for this spell Oz taught me. It will only work for twenty-four hours. Enough time for your wedding."

The gifts keep coming. I fold dad's wheelchair and place it out of the way. A member of our staff comes and offers to take it to his room. Another member of staff helps me undo the bustle of my cathedral train.

Dad positions my veil to cover my face. "Ready?"

I hook my arm in his and grip my bouquet. My palms are slick with perspiration. "Ready." Staff speak quietly into their radio, and the music changes to someone playing the piano. The song is Clair de Lune.

"This is our cue." We enter the arch and wind down the petal-covered path through the woods. Vines full of flowers hang from the ulmo trees, and the woods are whimsical and enchanted. Lights float in the trees to look like fireflies. When we reach the first row of benches, we pause, and everyone stands. The hush over the crowd is palpable.

There are so many people here, and Dad reaches around to place his other hand on my forearm. A sense of calm hits me and I thank him quietly for the magic. We stroll down the aisle, and I spot Maeve at the end of the bridge. As we get closer, I spy Pippa, and then Hannah. Their golden gowns shimmer through the light filtered through the trees. The women all have huge smiles on their faces.

My heart beats fast as I feel hundreds of vampire stares dance across my skin.

Then, I see him. My vision tunnels and everyone else falls away.

Every bone in my body wants to weep at the sight, but I hold back my tears. Instead, my breath hitches in my throat. Oz is so noble in his suit—a blue sash runs from his shoulder to his waist, and it holds all kinds of medals and badges. Atop his head is a crown that sparkles brightly when he adjusts his stance.

Gideon, Auguste, and Wren each have their own medals bedecking their suits. It makes sense now. These men have all lived for so long, they've probably fought in hundreds of wars.

Dad accompanies me to the stone bridge and gives me a hug before taking his place behind Wren. I give my bouquet to Hannah before facing Oz, and he lifts my veil carefully. Our eyes meet, and his water as he takes me in.

You are the most beautiful woman of all time; he says to me in my head. I'm so lost in his stare I'm startled when Lorraine asks us to join our right hands.

"They gather us here today to witness the union between two souls—Osgood Finlandian Ankida and Lana Chapman-Sawyer." She turns towards Oz's side of the bridge and inclines her head towards Gideon. The look on his face is one of duty and honor, and nutmeg and ginger radiates off him when he steps forward and faces us. "Do you, Gideon Cathal, bless this union?"

"I do." Gideon places a blue cord over Oz and my hands before returning to his position on the bridge.

"Alphie Bennett, do you bless this union?"

"I do." Dad drapes a gold cord on us and takes his place behind Wren.

Lorraine turns to my side of the bridge. "Hannah Yeung, do you bless this union?" She passes my bouquet to Pippa and steps forward with a red rope in her hand and lays it over the other ropes.

"I do." She walks back to her side.

"Each of these colors represents what the couple wishes to bring into this marriage. Gold, for longevity. Blue for patience and trust. Red means passion, love, and courage." She grasps the three cords with one hand and ties a knot with them so our hands are bound. With our free hands, we each grab a dangling set of three cords and pull as we slide our joined hands out of the rope. This creates an infinity knot, and a cheer erupts from the crowd before quieting down.

Lorraine holds the rope for us while Oz takes my wedding band from Gideon.

"Since the moment we met, I knew I loved you. All the fae, gods, goddesses, and magical creatures predicted our love would signal the birth of a new chapter for all. They smile upon us now, knowing together, we are better. Our people will come to know this day as the beginning of a story—one of hope, love, and magic. Today, I give you my last name, and the rest of my heart for all eternity."

Oz rights his shoulders. "You are selfless, and it is an honor to join my life with yours. To love you is a gift. I promise to be worthy of that gift and not bind you to my will. Will you allow me to be your husband?"

I can't even speak around the emotion clogging my throat, so I nod vigorously. Oz slips the wedding band on my finger, and a small buzzing sensation hums around the ring and a sense of peace settles in my bones.

"I will. Osgood Finlandian Ankida, the night we met, you quite literally swept me off my feet. I've spent months now thinking I just got lucky, and we were in the right place at the right time to fall in love. But now, I recognize it wasn't luck at all. Instead, it was fate that brought us together. I choose to share my life with you, to be your bride, your queen. I swear my oath to you now, Oz. I am yours, forever. Do you accept me and all that I am?"

"I will." I slide Oz's wedding band on his finger. The look in his eyes is one I want to capture forever. It is of pure, undying love and devotion.

"I now pronounce you husband and wife. You may kiss your bride." Lorraine turns to the crowd. "Her Majesty the Queen Lana Finlandian Ankida and His Majesty the King Osgood Finlandian Ankida!"

Oz wraps his arms around me and plants a kiss on my lips.

The crowd's cheers grow loud when he pivots his feet to dip me while we kiss, and the noise fades away. I am anchored to him, completely safe in his grip. He rights me so I can come up for air. His fingers slide between mine, and together we run down the aisle, hand-in-hand, while guests erupt even louder. Tiny white petals fall from the trees above us. These petals feel suspended in time.

When far enough away from the crowd, Oz steals a kiss from me. It is just him, with my back pressed against a tree, lost in his kiss. *I love you, Lana Finlandian Ankida.*

I love you forever.

The noise of the crowd draws closer, and our wedding party finds us before they do.

"Alright, time for pictures." Pippa claps.

Music plays while guests enjoy refreshments before the reception. Many of the photos we take are candid, but there are also the obligatory posed pictures. I enjoy the candid ones a lot more. We take some where it is just me and Oz's groomsmen, and he takes one with just my bridesmaids. Then, each of us takes photos with dad before taking them together.

AFTER PHOTOS, we head on the path towards the reception. The guests are lively and celebrate our arrival, and I have a hard time taking my eyes off my husband, but manage to pull my attention away. It's the first time I get a real good peek at who is here.

"Oh, my gods." I grab onto Oz's forearm. For a moment, I forget he can hear my thoughts. It doesn't take long for him to register who has me starstruck. *Is that ... Stevie Nicks?! Did I miss her name on the invite list!?*

He grins at me. "I'll introduce you two later. We go way back."

She isn't a vampire, is she?

No. Human, but an ally to the supernatural.

Stevie Nicks is at our wedding reception. I don't know whether to cry happy tears or try to act normal. I'm not one to fangirl over anyone or anything, but this is the reigning queen of rock-and-roll. She's a little before my time, but my mom listened to her raspy vocals on repeat every single day, and I listened to it every time I needed to feel close to her after she left me. It never got old.

Gosh, if only Mom was here now.

We seat ourselves at the head table, and I'm happy to see someone brought the flower arrangement from our bedroom. I take a moment to see the three empty seats at our table. There is a picture at each seat with a lit candle—one of Mom, one of Daniel Sawyer, and another of Claire Sawyer. I throw my hand to my mouth and fight back tears. Whoever did this kind gesture, it means the world to me.

Auguste.

"Thank you." I grab Auguste and pull him into a hug.

"You're welcome."

I don't think he realizes just how touching this is; it's the perfect gift.

THE SOUND of microphone interference interrupts the song before the music stops. Gideon has the mic, and he taps it twice to make sure it works. Speakers broadcast him loud and clear, and he stands before proceeding with a speech.

"Thank you all for coming here to celebrate Oz and Lana's commitment to one another." His Australian accent is thick tonight, which likely comes from the couple of shots I just saw him take. Alcohol doesn't stay but a few minutes in a vampire's system.

"I'm Gideon Cathal, and I'm His Majesty the King's best friend. There isn't a person alive that has known him as long as I have, and that means I'm *also* older than dirt." Everyone laughs, which only encourages him further.

His megawatt smile and piercing eyes fall to me. "If I'm the best man, why are you marrying *him?*" Oz and I just laugh and shake our heads until the audience quiets down.

"I've watched Oz go from being a young vampire thrust into leadership to someone worthy of leading men and women into battle. I have seen him conquer and topple dictatorial regimes. He makes a formidable ally in combat and an even greater King of his people. You've witnessed his philanthropic efforts and personal contributions to the arts, sciences, technology, and medicine. He's unmatched in business acumen, and I wouldn't be half the man I am today if it weren't for him."

I can see Oz's eyes gloss, so I slip my hand in his under the table.

"So, when Oz first told me about falling in love with Lana, a witch no less, I worried she'd upset the delicate balance of the throne. The moment I met her, though, it was easy to see I could not have been more wrong."

Now, my eyes water.

He addresses me. "Lana, you are by far the best thing that has not only happened to Oz, but to this family. You've taken my title as the best-looking Ankida, and I'll forgive you in time for that." Mischief dances in his eyes and the forest erupts in laughter. When they've quieted, his face takes on a more serious look and he gets down on both knees.

"It isn't just good looks that make you the perfect Queen. You gave up *everything* you know and love for not just our people, but all humanity. Most will never know this, but if it's the last thing I do, people will come to know you as a selfless Queen worthy of their undying love and devotion. You already have mine."

I dab at my eyes with a napkin while Gideon stands, turns to the crowd at their seats, and raises his champagne flute. "Cheers to the newlyweds." He hands the microphone to Hannah.

Guests clink their glasses and drink merrily, and we do the same. Gideon gives Oz a tight bear hug, and I hear Oz thank him for his kind words and tell him he loves him. It's my turn for Gideon's embrace, and I also get a bear hug.

"Thank you, Gideon. I love you."

"I love you, too." He gives me one more brief squeeze before taking his seat.

"Hey, hi!" Hannah has the mic, and I catch her fingers tremble. She's still bubbly, but there is a hint of trepidation in her voice. "I'm Hannah, and Lana is my best friend. We met at Mall of America when we were in sixth grade, and I've had the pleasure of watching her go from being a frizzy-haired tween with a questionable fashion sense to this stunning, curly-haired goddess of a woman who makes even yoga pants and hooded sweatshirts look Trés chic."

Everyone laughs, and I think back to when her and I first met.

I'm pretty sure I had on Dr. Martens sandals a size too small with white socks, too-short, flared jeans with pin striping down the sides, a black spaghetti strap tank top and little butterfly clips in my hair. Let's not forget the puka necklace and purse full of Tamagotchis. I think I even had a My Secret Diary on me then.

"Lana spent a good chunk of her life feeling abandoned, unloved, and unworthy. She gave people everything she had. In fact, she's the whole reason I even have a business." Hannah and I are both teary-eyed. "When her parents died, she gave me a lot of her inheritance, so I could fulfill my dream of starting a flower shop. I didn't find this out until almost a year later—she concocted an elaborate scheme to convince me an anonymous donor gifted me this money."

I take a sip of my champagne to steel my nerves.

"After she got rid of most of her possessions, she kept a few keep-sakes and papers at my house while she traveled the world to find herself. The only reason I found out was because she had me scan some of her documents and email them to her so she could do her taxes. That's a secret she would've taken to her grave."

I had no intention of telling her, although I felt bad about lying to her. She never would've taken the money otherwise.

Hannah continues. "Her heart is so big, and she gives so much to others—all without seeking recognition or acclaim. Lana tells me she's the luckiest woman in the world to have Oz and her dad now. That's where she's wrong. I'm the luckiest, and I'm a better person because she's in my life. No doubt Oz has an impressive list of accomplishments, but the best of all is snagging Lana. Together, they make even the stars want to shine brighter. Congratulations, you two." She raises her glass, and so does the crowd, before taking a sip.

"I love you." I pull her into my arms and squeeze her tight.

"I love you, too."

Oz gives her a hug before taking his seat.

"I love you, Sahira. Thank you for making me the happiest man in the world."

"I love you, too, babe. I hope I continue to make you happy." With every fiber of my being, I want to spend the rest of my days growing in our love together.

Music plays in the background while we plow through course after course. Then finally, it's time to cut the cake. We had to order an enormous one, so Oz and I make just our ceremonial cuts using the Van Horn's serving knives. We each stab off a tiny forkful and feed it to each other for the cameras.

I thank the gods Oz didn't slam it in my face like I see some grooms do. I cringe at the waste of makeup every time I see one of those.

Never, he says in my head. Glad we're on the same page.

Caterers whisk away the cake for cutting, reserving the top tier for our anniversary. Pippa takes the microphone, and asks us to find our way to the dance floor. Lights hang down from the trees above us, so it makes it easy to see. Pippa sings Christina Perri's "A Thousand Years" with the orchestra for our first dance.

"May I?" Oz holds out his hand with a bow. "You may." I take his hand, and he folds me in close to him with an arm at my waist, and his other hand holds mine. While I sense many eyes on me, it's as though

Oz and I are the only ones here. Sure, Pippa croons beautifully in the background—she has a very Adele-like quality to her voice—but time stands still when I'm in Oz's arms.

I rest my head on his chest, soaking in the comfort of his embrace, hearing the steady thump of his heart in tune with mine. Tears track down my cheeks when Oz coos tender words in my ear.

When the song ends, the familiar notes of "Somewhere Over the Rainbow" sounds on the speakers. Dad cuts in for our father-daughter dance, and Oz takes over the microphone.

"Huh, I didn't know Oz has pipes."

"I didn't either." I look at Oz crooning in the mic near the musicians. He's hummed to me on-key a few times, but he's never actually sang. It shouldn't come as a surprise, though; every Finlandian I've met is so musically inclined. It makes me wonder what else he's good at I don't know about yet. Also, because I can't carry a tune in a bucket, he'll have to sing to me the rest of eternity. His voice is so soothing.

"Thank you, Daddy."

He gives me a look as if to say, for what?

"Thank you for sending me my Ebbswick key. I never would've met Oz if you hadn't."

"You're welcome pumpkin. I knew I had to get it to you as soon as I found out about you."

I've missed out on so much with my dad, but—it's like I've known him my whole life. So many of his mannerisms I see in myself.

Oz finds me when he finishes, and I scold him for keeping his voice from me. He takes me in his arms and we sway to the music.

The dance floor is crowded now, and people ask to dance. I can hardly keep up with all the names and faces, but still enjoy myself.

"May I cut in?" Gideon places his hand on my hip and his other holds mine out. A faint buzzing sensation emerges when our hands touch. The look on his face tells me he notices it, too, but he says nothing.

"You Are the Reason" plays, and I can't help but think of the coincidence this is playing when he asks me to dance.

"You look beautiful."

I get dizzy from the scent of nutmeg and ginger while we dance.

"Thanks. And thank you for those kind words you spoke about me."

He sidles me in closer before speaking. "I mean every word. You've brought us back together. You're why most of our court lives under one roof."

I don't know any ballroom dances, but he does such a great job leading. I'm pretty sure we're doing something similar to a waltz. He's taller than Oz, so I focus on the medals on his chest so as not to strain my neck and cause the crown to fall off. The metal jangles when we spin, and I make a mental note to ask what they're for later.

When the song winds down, Gideon links his arm in mine and takes me to Oz. We find him several tables over, entertaining a group of well-decorated royals.

"Time for fireworks." Oz slips his fingers between mine, and he leads me to a raised clearing in the woods

The immediate family re-arranges several couches, so it's like our usual living room formation. This—this is what I've waited my whole life for.

CHAPTER TWENTY-NINE

I lean into Oz's hold, trembling from nerves. Gideon turned Dad the day we left for our honeymoon three months ago, and while he kept us updated, this will be my first time seeing him since.

My gaze fixes on the wooden path to our right. Everyone thought it best we meet in the open, considering I'm mortal—no use tempting dad in an enclosed space when the nature and the wind can help diffuse the scent of my blood.

The first face I see is Gideon's; he wears an easy smile and has deep affection in his eyes. My heart soars. I never thought I'd miss him so much. I rush to throw my arms around him, and he picks me up and spins.

"It's good to see you, Gideon. Thanks again for what you've done for us."

"I'd do anything for you, Lana." He sets me down and I take a sheepish step back.

Gideon and Oz do one of those manly hugs you see between best friends. It starts as a grasp of palms before turning into a tight embrace. Movement in my peripheral vision grabs my attention.

Auguste.

His handsome, megawatt smile lights up when he sees me before he dashes to my side. I wrap my arms around him and squeeze tight.

"You're positively radiant, Lana. We're so glad you're back. Your dad will be here in just a second."

"Thank you," I look between Gideon and Auguste, "the both of you. I'm so pleased to hear he's thriving under your care."

While Oz greets Auguste, I bounce on the balls of my heels next to Gideon.

"You'll want to keep your distance. No hugs. Over the coming days, we'll slowly bring you two closer to each other. We've had him around some of the human staff and he's done fine, but he hasn't been in close proximity to anyone."

I grab onto his arm when my legs nearly buckle at the sight in front of me.

Dad.

Gone is the frail man I left. He has so much vitality in him, he nearly glows, and his gait is fluid and steady now. A faint line of red circles his irises, and I know over time it'll disappear as he grows more accustomed to being a vampire. There's still the twinkle in his eyes I've come to love, and the lazy side smile crinkles the corner of one.

"Hi, pumpkin."

I try to blink away my tears, to no avail. I knew he was okay, but until seeing him for myself, I went about our honeymoon in bated breath. "Dad ... you look amazing."

He has grown in both height and width; strong shoulders hold up corded muscles, and while he still has some wrinkles, he looks much younger than he used to. Still old, but strong and healthy.

"Thanks, honey. I'm going to sit right here, and I want to hear all about your trip."

We sit on the path; me, between Oz's thighs, and Auguste and Gideon within easy reach. Dad is a good twenty feet away.

"I'll tell you all about it, but I want to first know how your transition went? These two," I tilt my head towards Auguste and Gideon, "only said everything was fine, but I suspect they wouldn't have told me otherwise."

They both scowl at me, and Dad grins. "I was damn near feral the first month, and poor Auguste spent so much time repairing things I broke. By month two, I was starting to get the hang of my strength and could also manage magic, so I made those repairs myself."

I chuckle. "And you feel okay?"

"I feel like a million bucks, kiddo. Like I drank an Olympian's blood."

Emotion rolls through me, and it's as though an enormous weight is no longer on my shoulders. *He's more than okay.* All feels right in the world.

We sit for hours, talking about the time we've missed. Oz and I share about the massive snowstorm we encountered high in the mountains, and how we had to use magic to melt snow to build us a better shelter for our tent so it wouldn't get pummeled by wind. We regale him with everything we saw in Antarctica, and how I convinced Oz to do a polar plunge with me; the cold didn't impact him a bit, but he was reluctant to let me do it.

When I ask Dad what his favorite part about becoming a vampire is—aside from curing himself of cancer—he tells me he can eat however much he wants without getting full. He's staying on the other side of the island with Pippa and Elliot, while the boys will come back to the main house. Our new vampire chef and dad have formed a close friendship, thanks to his voracious appetite and unending praise for Pierre's cooking.

While the men converse, I get lost in my head. I don't know what I've done to deserve a life so full of love, but I'm looking forward to spending eternity making myself worthy of it.

CHAPTER THIRTY

Oz and I got into an explosive fight tonight. I've never seen him so angry, and we both said things we don't mean. What hurts the most isn't what we were fighting over, but instead, the dig he made at me. This is so unlike him. With my leaving for Bedlam so soon, I'm afraid. What if he's not here when I get back? Or what if he falls in love with someone else while I'm gone?

It might be twenty years. Longer, even. The idea makes me ill. Oz isn't in the house now. He took the boat somewhere, and I'm alone in this big, empty house. The rest of the family is across the island.

I am abandoned yet again. He just got up and walked away, like I mean nothing to him. I put on the bathrobe Oz bought me in Montreal and sit with a cup of my birth control tea on the balcony. My feet rest on the railing, and I am too distraught to even drink anything. Stars twinkle above me, but there's no joy when I look at them.

Where did he go? Maybe he's looking at the sky now, too. Will he come back tonight? Ever?

The thought of not seeing him before Bedlam makes me sob even harder. A few twigs snap on the trail in front of the house, and I try to wipe the tears from my eyes. Someone must be back already.

Gideon emerges from the woods and spots me on the balcony. "Are you alright?" he calls up to me.

"Yes." I try to choke back my tears.

He scales the tree to the side of the balcony and leaps upon the landing.

"You're a terrible liar. I saw the boat speed away, and I didn't see you on it." He settles into the chair next to mine and puts his feet up on the railing, too. "What happened?"

"We just had a huge fight." I try to wipe more of my tears with the back of my hand. "I don't ... I don't think he's going to come back tonight. Maybe never." Grief consumes me, and Gideon puts his feet on the ground and turns his chair towards me.

"Hey, hey now," he takes my hand in his. "I don't know what the fight was about, but he'd be a fool to leave, especially just before you go to Bedlam."

I've never known Oz to be someone to pull a move like that, but if he were mad enough ... He's been acting differently ever since we got back from Antarctica. Nothing happened on our honeymoon to upset him. His sudden change in attitude started our fight. And now, I don't know if we can recover from it. Not with so little time left. My window of opportunity is closing fast.

"Gideon, you once told me you would turn me into a vampire, so I didn't have to go to Bedlam." My voice is just above a whisper. "Will you do that now?"

I know this is an enormous ask of me. I just can't bear leaving things unfinished between Oz and me.

"I don't think you understand what you're asking of me." He adjusts in his seat. Cinnamon invades my senses, and ice dances across the tops of my exposed thighs. I glance at him, and his eyes dart to mine. He leans forward on his forearms and searches my face.

"I know I ask a lot of you." He'd have to be the one to show me what it means to be a vampire, at least until I am strong enough to be around other vampires. It sure beats spending decades in Bedlam and coming back to Oz having moved on.

Gideon shakes his head. "You're mated, Lana." Regret hangs on his thick accent. "Not only that, but you're queen. I'd be committing trea-son." He's right. I can't ask that of him.

"Besides, it wouldn't be like me turning your dad. Because you're mated to my sire, I'd have to take you."

Take me ... as in mate me? Heat stirs to life low in my stomach at the prospect, and shame builds in me for having this reaction. The primal parts of Gideon recognize mine, and a low growl escapes from him. It startles me, and my eyes meet his again.

There it is, deep in gunmetal blue. I see desire. I know this because I desire him, too. My mind flashes back to the brief reel Oz played for me in my head when I first met Gideon. In his mind, he had me pinned against the door, with his teeth sunk into my breast. My heart races at the idea of it, and warmth spreads between my thighs like a wildfire.

This is dangerous.

"Lana ..."

I leap to my feet and cross into my bedroom to escape the situa-tion we find ourselves in. We can't do this. Pacing the floor, I sense Gideon leaning on the door frame and my gaze falls to him. It is hard to look away—he's beautiful. So, so, beautiful; sharp jaw, cut muscles, impeccable style, and that smile ...gods, his megawatt smile. Bedroom eyes dancing with mischief.

As though he knows my indecent thoughts, he runs his hand through his dark hair before his tentative walk towards me. My breathing shallows when he raises his hand to my cheek, but I do not move; I cannot move.

Ice tingles under my skin at his touch, and the buzzing sensation takes over me when he leans in close.

"I've loved you since the moment I laid my eyes on you." His words are but a sigh in my ear. His lips graze my neck, and his weight presses into my body before sliding a hand behind my head to draw me in for a kiss.

Time slows, and I'm keenly aware of the sensation of his breath on my lips; hovering so close, all I need to do is move in.

Instead of pulling away, I close my eyes and lean into him.

His touch is gentle, and my warm breath bounces back cool just as our mouths meet. Heat unfurls inside of me. It's like a blaze, and I am desperate for more.

The reel of him having his way with me and sinking his teeth into my breasts plays in my head as Gideon wraps an arm around my waist so I'm even closer. His impressive length weighs heavy against my stomach and his free hand slides between the fabric covering my chest. He cups my breast, and his fingers caress my pert nipple.

I snake my arms up to pull him closer, and he groans his approval. I know this is wrong; we shouldn't be doing this. But my flesh is on fire for him. Gods, it burns.

"Please don't stop, Gideon." My voice is heavy with desire, and it is all he needs before his mouth claims mine again.

My feet leave the ground when he lifts and spins me around to push me into the wall, his lips never leaving mine. His mouth trails along my jaw in slow, agonizing movements. Gideon's breath dances on my neck when he draws in a shaky breath before kissing behind my ear. "Gods, Lana." His voice is but a sigh, so close to me his lips move against my skin.

His hand slides down my stomach, and I suck in a breath. Electricity tingles along my skin; his cool touch leaves a trail of fire in its wake.

"Gideon." My voice comes out as a plea, and he draws back to look at me. Gods, those eyes. They're almost black now. "I want you to touch me."

My hands work with a certain ferocity to unbutton his shirt, and Gideon tears it off in hunger. His hands find their way to me again. This time, he hooks a finger through the bow on my robe. This sends the robe falling open, and a purr comes from deep in his chest when he sees I have nothing underneath.

Gideon takes a step back and drinks me in with his hungry eyes before sliding the robe off one shoulder, then two. It falls to the floor in an unceremonious heap. My chest heaves: anticipation makes it hard to breathe.

He meets my eyes, and my heart skips a beat when he reaches up for the buckle on his jeans. It comes undone at once, and he never breaks contact with my gaze when he pushes them down his thick thighs. His solid length springs free, drawing my attention, and it stands proud with a glistening bead at its tip.

Big, so big.

Gideon drops to his knees and raises my foot to his mouth for him to kiss. He trails his lips up the inside of my leg, starting at the ankle, and then making his way up to my inner thighs. Each kiss is a prayer. A benediction. He rests my leg over his shoulder and his mouth finds my mound. A soft moan escapes me before muscular arms loop under me, so now both of my thighs press into his shoulders, and I support myself against the wall.

His tongue moves in slow, languid strokes before sliding between my folds. With no effort at all, he stands and carries me to the edge of the bed without breaking contact. I lay on my back and give in to the line we've crossed.

He devours my core, and I wriggle under the pleasure. Just when I think I'm going to get my release, he doesn't let me come. Gideon sits back, in all his glistening glory, and hesitates before taking my cue to continue. He drags his steel length up and down my folds before pausing at my entrance, and his hooded eyes meet mine.

I buck my hips, drawing him into me with my legs wrapped around him. We both let out a moan of pleasure, having finally given into our desire for each other after all this time. The stretch of my channel is a pleasurable pain; Gideon's movements are slow, letting me adjust to his size. I am lost somewhere between wanting to stop us and begging him to take me. My heart is so conflicted. I know now I am in love with this man.

"Gideon, I ..." He pauses and pulls back, with confusion written all over his face. "I love you. I'm in love with you."

He is quiet, and his eyes search mine as he helps sit me up and kneels between my legs. Because he's so tall, we're face-to-face now.

This achingly beautiful vampire before me takes my hands in his and presses his lips to my knuckles. Love radiates off him, and I'm not surprised that when he speaks, he professes his own for me.

"Lana, I am in love with you. I told you I'd storm the gates of hell to roll around in bed with you, but I want more than that; I need more than that. It kills me to listen to you night after night, loving another man, knowing you and I are destined to be together. Say what you want about the prophecy being wrong—I believe it. I have to, because that's the only thing that might explain why I'd risk everything to be with you."

I pull Gideon in to embrace him. My bare chest presses against his, and desire for him overwhelms me.

"Take me." I see something flash behind his eyes—his darkness recognizing my own. We know this is wrong, but there isn't a thing in this realm or the next that can stop us. In one swift move, he hoists me back on the bed and sheathes himself in me and my breath catches in my throat.

Gideon drives into me, slowly at first, and then picks up steam. A ripple of love and passion envelops me now. He is marking me, and I let him.

"Take me." I don't even care I'm asking again. A growl reverberates from deep inside of him just before he sinks his teeth into my breast. The pleasure is sudden, and it's acutely sharp—the pain but a blip before giving way to ecstasy.

Memories from his life and mine pass between us, and nothing compares to the pleasure deep in the heart of me.

Pressure builds low in my belly, begging for release. His hips buck and drive into me hard, but slow. "More."

Gideon's pace picks up until I find my release. "I'm coming." My voice is taut. He pulls deeper and faster, and his hips grind hard against me.

Somewhere amongst the haze of my orgasm, his warmth fills me. After pulsing several times, he collapses on me, supporting his weight with his thigh and forearm on the bed.

"I love you." I am breathless, and the edges of my lips curl.

"I love you, too." There's a deep, carnivorous satisfaction to his voice. My heart has split in two. Oz owns half, and his best friend, the other. Who does this? I don't even know how to navigate this situation.

"What are we going to do?" I tilt my head towards him and his cool hand cups my face. I don't want to leave Oz, nor do I want to leave Gideon.

"I told you once it isn't uncommon for vampires to share mates." His fingers wind a curl of my hair. "All you have to do is ask him. What I know is this, Lana Finlandian Ankida: I don't want this to stop. I am madly in love with you."

The idea of having both Gideon and Oz is alluring. Although, on that same note—I could never share Oz. Or Gideon. What selfish monster does that make me?

He plants a kiss on my lips that leaves me wanting more. My core is still warm with his seed, but I want him again.

JUST WHEN WE'RE about to try for round two, the house quakes. Windows shatter, floors buckle, and the walls wobble. Gideon hunches over my body to protect me. The buzzing sensation roars now. Does Patagonia get earthquakes? They get earthquakes, I decide.

The bedroom door flies open, and Oz tears across the room in a blind rage and rips Gideon from our bed. Oz's eyes are pure onyx, and his fangs protrude from the snarl of his mouth.

Gideon sails through the air and disintegrates into a cloud of ash when he hits the wall. A blood-curdling scream escapes from my mouth and I scramble towards the far side of the room.

"No, no, no, no, no."

Gideon.

Gods, this can't be. Not my sweet, forever happy Gideon. My entire body shudders with sobs. I wail and clamber for some way to bring him back to me.

A torrent of tears soaks my cheeks, and I can't bear to look at Oz. Rage, torment, and shame consume me.

"I'm so sorry." I'm sobbing both for my marriage, and for Gideon, while clawing at the ash on the floor in front of me. "You didn't have to kill him!" I bellow in pure agony. What we did was wrong, yes. But Gideon is a good person, despite our indiscretion.

An enormous fissure has opened in my chest, and I am hollow inside. Raw and gutted. Never again will I be okay. This is all my fault.

Oz tries to hug me, but I fight him and scream instead. He has every right to be upset with me and Gideon, but I don't want him hugging me.

Not now. Never.

He killed him.

Oz folds me into his arms anyway, and I continue to wail and beat and claw against his chest.

"Lana, I need you to wake up." His voice is gentle. "You've been asleep for four days now, and I haven't been able to reach you. Something's happened."

I blink and rub the tears out of my eyes. "I'm dreaming?" Too afraid to cling to this brief glimmer of hope, I hold my breath.

He nods. I look around the room at my surroundings. The windows are intact; the floorboards are in place. I hold out my arms and see I'm wearing clothes now, and I finally exhale.

A dream.

It was just a dream.

No, a nightmare.

Even though I am in this dream state, I have immense guilt about what I've done. Was this actual desire? I can't imagine what's going on in Oz's heart and mind about witnessing this. And why can't I wake up?

"It wasn't easy seeing this, Sahira." There is great sorrow in his voice, and it kills me to hear him. "I can't fault you for any of it. First, you're dreaming. Second, even if you do desire Gideon—who am I to blame you? He has my blood; it is a biological fact you crave it. Mating bonds and sires is a complicated mess, and I can't vilify you for it."

Why is he so understanding? If I were in his shoes, I'd be livid enough to kill. I suppose he did kill Gideon in my dream. He was probably acting on his emotions then—but he also knew it was just a dream. None of this is real. Right?

My head is so jumbled. Will I still have feelings for Gideon when I wake up? For the sake of my marriage, I hope I don't, but now? I'm in love with both men.

"Why can't I wake up?" It would be a lot easier to have this conversation during a time and place where I know what my genuine feelings are, and it's not part of some figment of my imagination.

Oz helps me up, and I see my knees are no longer bloody. The ashes no longer scatter the floor, either. He takes me to our balcony to sit in the rattan chairs.

"I don't know, Lana. You've been dreaming for four days, and this is the first time I've been able to intercept one."

A breeze blows through my hair, sending a shiver through me. Oz goes to the bedroom and drags out our duvet to cover me.

"What's the last thing that happened before I went to sleep?" Maybe by retracing what happened, I can figure out why I'm still asleep.

"You took a bath before bed."

That doesn't sound all that unusual. I love baths, and so does he.

"You took it alone because we'd gotten into an argument."

We may have argued in my dream, but Oz and I don't argue often in real life. "What about?" He is hesitant to respond.

"You asked me again to turn you so you don't have to go to Bedlam." Ah, that sounds about right. This is one of the few things he and I disagree on. "So, you asked Gideon."

Crap. That'll cause a fight, alright. I know for a fact Gideon would turn me if I asked him. He's said so many times. This still doesn't explain why I can't wake from my slumber, though.

"What happened before my bath? Like between our fight and the bath?"

"Well, we'd been opening presents from our wedding during the fight, and you stormed off to the bedroom with a bath bomb someone had given us."

Opening presents with him would've caused me to have strong feelings about not wanting to leave him. Spending our honeymoon together made that even stronger. Can I survive without Oz for years? Hannah? Or my dad? Gideon? Auguste? Maeve or Pippa?

The idea of having both Oz and Gideon gnaws at me again. Would Oz even be okay with this? How would that even work out? I can't imagine us all sharing a bed.

"If you truly desire to have us both when you wake up, Sahira, then I won't stop you. You are the love of my life, and if it means I have to share you to keep you, then I will." The muscles in his jaw flex.

I saw the way his face contorted when he burst through the door. It was pure rage. A lot like the day the vampire almost killed me. At that moment, he was more beast than man. What would I do if Oz came to me with the same proposition? That he is in love with another woman and wants me to share him with her. I couldn't do it. I would throw myself off a cliff at the mere mention of it. These feelings inside have me so conflicted.

Oz takes my hand in his, and I meet his gaze. His eyes are tender now, and he is gentle when he speaks.

"There is no other woman but you. There can be no one else because you are my mate. For eternity."

This both reassures me and makes me feel like a terrible person. The sooner I can wake up, the sooner I can sort out my feelings about this.

"I've got to wake up." Panic is clear in my voice. Even in dreamland, my anxiety takes over.

"Pippa is running blood work to see what's going on. She will have the results any time now. I'm afraid to leave your dream though, for fear I won't be able to get back in."

If he tried for four days to get in, what made things different now? He said he could see my dreams, but just couldn't interact with me. What if Gideon taking me is what made the resolve to reach me that much stronger, and it's why he could get through?

Oz shrugs his shoulders at my train of thought. If there is one thing that will cause powerful emotions, it's that.

"So, what, should you go check on my blood test and I manifest Gideon back here so you can show up again?"

He doesn't look very enthusiastic about it. "I guess."

This must be difficult for him. "I'm sorry." My free hand rests lightly on his cheek. He closes his eyes and turns away; the tension between us is notable. He is wounded, yet again, thanks to me.

"I'm going to see if Pippa has any news." He stands. "We'll figure this out when I get back."

"I love you, Oz." I long for affection back, knowing I don't deserve it, but craving it anyway. The covers fall to my feet when I stand to face him. My eyes search his, and his are glossy. They soften before he folds me into his arms.

"I love you, too, Sahira." He disappears from my arms. He's gone back to reality.

I drag the comforter back inside and heave it onto the bed. It knocks a bath bomb off the nightstand, and it rolls before stopping at my feet. "Huh." I stoop to pick it up. Magical wisps encircle the entire thing, and I can make out black fruits and yellow and pink flowers embedded in it.

"What's that?"

I spin around in surprise. It wasn't too long ago I witnessed him die, and now he's standing in my bedroom again. At the sight of him, perfectly whole, fissures in my heart heal.

"Gideon!" I throw my arms around his neck. The bath bomb drops from my hand, but I don't even care. I grab his face and give him a bruising kiss, and after hesitating, he leans into it.

"Well, hello to you, too." There is a distinctive purr to his voice as he pulls back. He tests my forehead for a fever with the back of his hand. "I'm not sure what you've done with the Lana who denied her feelings about me, but I'm digging her replacement."

Crap. I'm not sure how this whole dream thing works, so perhaps Gideon and I are strictly platonic again. I take his hand and drag him to sit down on the bed next to me.

"We need to talk." After taking a deep breath, I tell him everything.

His face goes through a whole range of emotions while listening to me.

Gideon sits with this for a moment. "I have questions. I understand we're in a dream now, but you mean to tell me you're in love with me?" The vision of hope on his face is adorable, and I'm not sure how to articulate what's going on in my head.

"Dream me is, yes. I don't know if awake me is." I shrug my shoulders. That's the truth.

I feel awkward, laying everything bare for him. With Oz, he can just read my mind and know how I feel even if I can't vocalize it. This takes a lot more effort and is weirdly more revealing than him reading my mind.

"... and you let me take you." There is a hint of carnivorous satisfaction to his voice.

I squirm under his gaze and can't speak.

"Well, I'll be." Cinnamon takes over the space between us. He's more surprised at the fact I'm in love with him and let him mark me than he is Oz killed him.

Gideon turns to face me on the bed. "I have more questions; Now you've slept with me, do you want to make love again? Who is a better lover? Oz said he will share you with me when you wake. Will you ask him to?" He is so pointed; I have to take a deep breath before I answer his barrage of inquiries.

"Yes, I very much want to sleep with you again." Warmth spreads between my legs at the thought of this. "I will *never* answer your second question. However, I will say you are great in bed. As far as your third question goes, I don't know if I'm going to remember any of this dream."

My answers are fair. Gideon asking if he or Oz is better in the sack is like asking me to choose what I like better—breathing, or my lungs. Both are related and necessary components to my actual living. How can I possibly choose?

"May I kiss you?"

"Please do." My heart races. Why am I so nervous? None of this is real, I think.

Gideon's hand cups the back of my head when he leans in. His lips press to mine, and I melt into his arms. He is tender with his touch, like I'll disappear into thin air if he moves too fast. I'm surprised at his restraint when he pulls back to look at me.

"I love you, Striga." He doesn't speak with his usual Australian accent; I can't place the one he uses now. His fingers slip into mine and he squeezes.

"I love you, too. What does Striga mean?"

"Striga means witch in Latin." Gideon tells me about his life before becoming a vampire and where Oz turned him. I take a while to realize everything he's telling me is a figment of my imagination, as this is my dream, and not his.

I know for a fact he's around five thousand years old and is from where you can now find the Italian Dolomites; he's twice as old as the Roman empire. The things he's seen and lived through? I'm in awe. By the time he finishes telling me about his life back then, I am laying on his chest, and we're in bed.

Occasionally, I sit up to stare at him in wonder at some things he says. Like how he describes the way the sun peeks through the Dolomites and makes the grass look almost bright green. "Your home sounds beautiful."

"I can take you there, if you'd like?" Gideon rises on one elbow to look at me. "This is a dream, so I can show you when and where I lived."

I've never tried to travel so far back in time before, nor with another person. But what better place to travel than in a dream? Eagerly, I agree, and he tells me when and where to go. The picture he paints in my head of his small valley hut next to a lake facing the mountains. The water is crystal blue, and wildflowers have colored the landscape.

At our feet, a gap opens in the floor, and I lead Gideon through the rift. The picture he's painted is so vivid, my hair stirs from the cool breeze sweeping down the mountain and across the lake as we navigate through the darkness to the opening on the other side. Although the slit is a dark gray, this is nothing compared to the inky expanse we have to traverse across.

~

WHEN WE EMERGE, the moon hangs near the horizon as it gets ready to say good morning to the sun. Gideon hurries me towards a grassy spot near the bank of the water. I manifest a fur blanket for us to lie on because I don't know who, if anyone, we'll run into here.

I lay on Gideon's chest, and he is warm. The heat startles me because I'm so used to him and Oz being cold. He laughs, and I realize I can no longer sense his emotions.

"I'm human during this time." Seeing and feeling his chest move up and down draws my attention. He doesn't look any different; he's still his painfully handsome self with muscles and miles of jawline and breadth to his shoulders.

"It is good to be home after all this time. Thank you." He draws me nearer to him and before I can respond, the sun peaks over the Alps, and I grip his shoulder. The sun lights up the entire valley and radiant shades of orange and red streak the sky. The lake is so blue it almost glows, the grass; like a fresh-picked lime.

"Breathtaking."

A chill runs through Gideon, and I register it's been five thousand years since he's had to worry about the cold. "Do you want to head inside to warm up?" I nuzzle in closer to him.

"No, I have other things in mind to warm up." He is coy with his words. I don't see anyone; his is the only hut in the valley. He grabs the corner of the fur blanket and rolls, so he is on top of me and we are both wrapped up in fur.

"Ah, Lana? My stamina and strength aren't quite what they are when I'm a vampire. So, Dream Lana, if you would be ever-so-kind to give me that, I'd appreciate the courtesy."

I giggle at his very male human anxiety and give him a brief nod.

With one little thought, I've removed both of our clothes.

"Good god you're perfect." Gideon looks down at our nakedness. I forget that to him, this is our first time together, and now I get to witness his perfect face enjoying what I offer.

"Look who's talking! You're a living god. Now shut up and kiss me."

I don't have to ask him twice before we are entangled with one another. His mouth gives my core attention until I come. Satisfied he's gotten me off, he enters me in one swift move. I love how I get to witness his "first time" with me again.

Soon, we are too warm under the blanket and it is just us—bare skin, hot breath, wild hair, and sweat. Lots and lots of sweat. After coming again, I flip Gideon on his back so I can be on top. My hands cling to his chest to steady me, and he holds my hips to help me thrust deeper.

In the outdoors, we don't hold back. We are loud, and I am here for it. I can tell the noise riles Gideon up, too. I catch him watching my breasts bounce, so I grind even harder and place his hands on my chest. His grunts grow shallower, and I know he's close. His warm release fills me, and he pumps his hips under me several more times before he stills.

"Fuck, Lana." He's breathless as I fall to his side. We both lay on our backs, chests heaving, hearts racing.

I giggle, and we turn towards each other, both propping our heads up with our hands.

"I don't want this to end. I love you so much, Lana."

"I love you, too." My lips linger after a kiss.

I drift towards the water after getting up from the blanket. When I turn to look at Gideon behind me, he eyes me suspiciously.

"Come on in." I give him my best sultry look, and I'm now waist-deep in the freezing lake. It is not quite summer here, but the sun is warm on my back, and despite the cold, the water soothes my aching muscles.

"Don't think I haven't forgotten what cold water does to human males." He narrows his eyes at me.

"Lucky for you, I'm a witch and this is my dream." With a simple flick of my wrist under the water, a ball of water shoots at him where he lays. When the shock on his face wears off, he chases after me.

We splash around before ending up in each other's arms again. We're both still naked when I wrap my hands around the back of Gideon's neck. He is so tall I have to propel myself up in the water to reach his lips. He chuckles at my attempts before hoisting me up so my legs wrap around his waist.

"Much better."

"COME TO SPOIL OUR FUN?"

I follow Gideon's gaze to look behind me, and I hop down from his arms and hold my hands over my chest. While he's my husband, I don't want him watching me hang all over another man. I can sense his jealousy from here, never mind the firm press of his lips and tight muscles when he clenches his jaw. I manifest ourselves into clothes and we join Oz on the shore.

I'm sorry you had to see that.

"What did you find out?" Gideon doesn't want this dream to end, and a part of me doesn't want it to, either. For in the real world, I probably am not in love with Gideon. I don't want to hurt the other man I love, but now, my heart can't choose.

"Pippa and Auguste found remnants of mandragora officinarum, nerium oleander, atropa belladonna, hyoscyamus niger, and Polonium-210 in your system."

Oz's eyes gloss with unshed tears.

"Do you mean to tell me someone has poisoned me?"

He shakes his head. "If you were a mere mortal, yes. They use these ingredients in a curse called *Somno Consopiri Sempiterno*. This means eternal slumber."

The Lapis Templar, I suspect. "How did that happen?" My witch abilities can suss out what foods I'm consuming, so I can't imagine I would've ingested anything suspect. Besides, I figure any of the vampires in the house would have been able to sniff out anything questionable.

"We found traces of the ingredients in the tub."

I throw my hand up to my mouth. "The bath bomb! Who could've done this?"

"We documented who gave us presents, but the bag of bath bombs didn't have a sender's name or address on them. Maeve is working to track them down, but Gideon and Auguste are pretty sure it is the Lapis Templar."

When will they ever stop? Will it be enough when I'm dead? If I ever meet Dolphina Darling, she'll never survive my wrath.

"How do we fix this?" Gideon glances at Oz, who looks annoyed with the question; probably because Dream Gideon is but an extension of my subconscious—an unwelcome one at that. It isn't the real Gideon, just my interpretation of how he might act in dreamland. Oz entertains him anyway.

"I'm giving her my blood to counteract any of the poison in her body. The curse is a bit more difficult to undo."

I have zero experience with curses, which is all the more reason for me to get to Bedlam to have a crash course in everything I need to know as a witch. Oz is a powerful witch, but he never made it there. What I learn in the fae realm can keep us safe.

"Do you know how to break the curse?"

"It just takes some time to gather what we need. The antidote uses the same ingredients to undo the spell. Everything we need is on the island."

Everything?

"This seems too convenient," Gideon is quick to offer. "What are they distracting us from?"

The Lapis Templar curses me using a wedding present they knew I'd use right away. Then, I fall into a sleep I can't wake up from. But wait, we've got everything we need right on the island; it just takes time to get everything we need.

It is too perfect. "Oz, how well do you know the staff who work in our home?" I wince. In fact, I hate to ask. I'm not one to accuse anyone of anything without evidence, but it could only be someone within proximity to us who also knows where everything on the island is.

"Every single person working on our island has done so for years and years. Often, their entire families work for us over many generations. But you're right, we need to explore every angle once you're awake. I can call an all-staff meeting and read their minds. They won't get away with it; I need to know if any of them are members of the Lapis Templar."

The staff have all been very good to us, and it kills me to think any of them wish ill of me. After the events in my dream, and my killing Oz when I was awake, I can hardly blame them; I'm a terrible wife.

Oz wraps me in his arms to comfort me. *No, Sahira, you are my treasure.*

Yeah, maybe treasure, as in it is rare to find somebody as stupid as I am to not only kill her husband having sex, but to have sex with his best friend. An unnerving silence settles between us before he tilts my head to look at him.

Can you ever forgive me? I breathe in his scent of warm vanilla and sugar.

You know I already have. You're my reason for being. Oz has talked to me at length about the many lives he's lived. He was coming to a point where he wasn't sure what else there was for him on Earth, and seriously considered riding off into the figurative sunset. Until I came along. Now, he wants eternity with me. I've given him a renewed sense of purpose in life, far beyond what he's accomplished. But do I deserve the credit?

I look over at Gideon, and study his face. A lone whistle of the wind stirs the hair resting on his forehead. I know the look; he's wounded watching our interaction. Truth be told, Oz is my husband and who I've loved the longest. Together, we've shared so many firsts. I am in love with Gideon, and I'm mated to both of them, at least in this dream world, but no one can comfort me like my King can.

Oz can read what's in my head and knows what I'm feeling before I even recognize it. When I can't find the words, he understands. Our bodies, hearts, and minds are one. Nothing can take that from us. I don't know what reality has in store for my thoughts and feelings, but the way I feel now? I don't *want* to be in love with Gideon. Dream me doesn't want this to stop, though, and that's what scares me.

No matter what happens, Sahira, we'll get through it. Even if that means I have to share you.

I bask in his love.

"I'm going to go now. I'm keeping a lookout while everyone gathers supplies. The next time you see me, you'll be awake."

He gives me one last kiss before disappearing. There's a void inside me now that he's gone.

～

Warm arms envelop me from behind. "Are you okay?" Gideon's voice is but a whisper in my ear.

"Yeah." My words turn to ash on my tongue. I turn around to bury myself in his chest. Things aren't okay.

"I might not be a vampire now, but I can still tell when you're upset."

I take a deep breath and inhale what he smells like as a human. Forcing the tears back, I school my features and my thoughts hang around like a fog.

"I'm just scared because I don't want to lose you, but I also know if I am still in love with you when I wake up, this will forever change things between Oz and me, no matter how much he insists it won't. I'm also sad about this being our last day together as mates."

It was easy to explain my initial attraction to Gideon when he was a vampire—it's because he has Oz's blood. Since we've traveled back in time, the attraction is as strong as ever; I am still in love with him. Does this mean when I wake, I will be, too?

"It doesn't have to be." Gideon leads me to our blanket in the grass. I let his statement settle in my heart and my mind, but don't respond to it.

"Are you hungry?"

Before he can answer, I manifest a full picnic lunch for us. We feast on fruit, croissant sandwiches, and lots of sweet wine.

"I forgot what it was like to feel drunk and full." He lies on his back, and I clear away our food and lay next to him. We spend the rest of the afternoon and evening talking and making love.

Gideon holds me while we watch the sun disappear behind the mountains. Fireflies dance just above the grass, and we see the occasional fish jump out of the water to catch a bug.

"I'm going to miss this."

Whether he's talking about this time and place or my being in love with him, I can't be sure. Probably both.

In my dreams, we don't have to worry about what my love for him means. We've only got here and now. I know we're on borrowed time; Oz and Pippa will wake me soon. The idea of saying goodbye causes me to panic inside. I don't want to leave anything unspoken.

"I will miss you."

Sure, Italy is fun, and so is traveling back in time. None of this matters, though.

It makes me nauseous to think I may wake and forget all this; my love for Gideon, what we've shared, and the way his touch makes me feel. Or the face he makes when he orgasms, and the way his breathing shallows as he nears climax.

"Lana, do you hope you're in love with me when you wake?"

"A large part of me never wants to let go of this. Another part of me knows how dangerous loving you is." I bury my head in his chest. "It'd be a lie if I told you I love being in love with you. I don't like that I am because I don't want to hurt Oz."

Gideon caresses my arm that's draped across him. "In case you remember this when you wake, know that I hope you're in love with me then, because I love you, Striga."

Oz said he will share me if I request it. Will I?

"I love you, too, Gideon. More than you'll ever know." I fall asleep to the rise and fall of his chest.

When I wake, I am no longer in Italy, and the first face I see is Oz's.

CHAPTER THIRTY-ONE

When I try to sit up in bed, my entire body aches as though it's been hit by a freight train. My muscles strain and my mind clouds with haze.

"Uh, uh." It is Pippa who's scolding me. "Your body has been through a lot. Give it a few minutes to adjust before you go off to save the world."

I turn my head towards Oz.

"Hey, babe." He kisses my hand. It's tender and I have a slight bruise where I imagine they had me hooked up to an IV.

"Welcome home, Sahira. You're good to do a healing spell now."

I run my hands over my body, kneading and massaging slowly. Magic gossamer thread together the micro-tears in my cells, and it isn't long before I am feeling close to normal. Pippa's gaze flicks to mine.

"Call me if you need anything. I'm going to work on adding these notes to my medical journal. We'll need them should this ever happen again."

I thank her before she disappears through the doorway.

"I'm thrilled to be awake." Relief expands my chest.

"So am I. Sorry to tell you this, but you had a catheter again." He winces, and I groan.

Hey love, glad you're awake. I'm tired of emptying your bag of pee, I think to myself.

Oz shakes his head. "No, not that at all. I just know you hate it. You probably want to bathe, though. You've been out a while and it will make you feel better. Don't worry, we had the entire tub replaced while you were out."

I liked our tub. Oz had it installed for me just before we arrived before our wedding. He carries me to the bathroom and I'm happy to see they replaced it with a replica of the one we had installed. "Will you join me?"

He hesitates before agreeing. I sluice my body with the warm water. It revitalizes me.

I'm nestled between Oz's legs, and I could stay here forever provided we could keep the water warm. He washes my hair for me, paying careful attention not to get soap in my eyes. When he finishes, he soaps up my entire body before his fingers dance along the curves of my breast. He wants to please only me, but I shake my head no.

"I've missed this." I gesture to him. This—referring to *all* of him. I want him inside of me. My body craves his. He's happy to oblige now I'm feeling a hundred percent again. We make love in the tub before taking it to the bed. It's as though we've been apart for thousands of years, and in a way, we have.

The night turns to morning while we make love all over the bedroom. I don't think I've ever had this much energy, but Oz certainly isn't complaining.

We change into clothes so we can face the rest of our day. Before we leave the room, Oz stops me, and I still my hand on the doorknob.

"I think we need to talk."

My stomach lurches. I knew this was coming, but I just didn't want to face it.

"How much do you remember from your dream?" He leads me to the couch.

"Everything. I'm sorry, Oz. It must've been hard for you to watch that."

He shifts uncomfortably. I've never seen this man this uncomfortable before. Osgood Finlandian is a man with a stone face capable of bluffing his way through anything and lots of laughter, but never discomfort. He's far too confident in himself for it.

"Yes ... yes it was." He is tense, and his jaw works overtime from being clenched. This probably isn't the first time I've ever dreamt of something I'd rather him not watch or had thoughts dance across my mind he didn't like, but nothing can compare to what he had to endure. It was relentless dreaming—*about sleeping with another man.*

Guilt consumes me, and I take Oz's hand in mine and look into his soul. "I see the light in you, seeing the light in me. I meant what I said when I told you there is no other man for me. Not Auguste. Not Gideon. No one else. You are my far better half, and I am in love with no one but you." I will these words with every beat of my heart and breath in my lungs.

"Lana, I can learn to live with you being in love with another man. I may even like to watch. Although, it is important we discuss it first before you act on it. What I can't do is live without you."

The family are relieved when they see me up and about.

"Hi, Daddy." Dad wraps me up in a bear hug. I'm still getting used to the fact my dad is no longer wheelchair-bound, and instead he's a strong vampire capable of snapping me in two.

"Sorry, honey." Dad sets me down. "I forget about my strength and get carried away."

Oz places his hand on my shoulder. "Dad and I are going to gather the staff. Are you alright here for a bit?"

"Yes, I'm going to eat. I'm starving." He gives me a kiss before leading Dad across the island. I locate the cutting board and begin slicing vegetables. A poke bowl sounds pretty good, so I throw some rice in the cooker before returning to cut vegetables.

I CATCH movement out of the corner of my eye and a vampire stare dances across my chest. My head snaps in its direction and I freeze like a deer caught in headlights. I stand here, frozen, watching danger race towards me but doing nothing to get out of the way.

"You look like you've seen a ghost. You alright there?"

When I don't answer, Gideon prowls towards me and takes the knife out of my hand to place on the cutting board. My heart races like I've been caught by a hungry predator in the woods.

"Hey, Lana?" Gideon moves his hand in front of my face. How much does he know? My mind flashes back to us, splashing around in the water, and the feel of his touch on my skin. "You've cycled through just about six different emotions since I've walked into the room. Why don't you have a seat?"

He ushers me to sit down on my favorite couch, being careful not to touch me because my fight-or-flight response is in full force now. What do I even say to him? Do I say anything at all?

"Should I grab Pippa?" He rises from the couch to fetch her, and I grab his wrist to prevent him from leaving. Memories from my dream come flooding back to me; tender caresses on my skin, whispers in the dark, feeling his chest rise and fall under me, the sound he makes when he comes. The feeling of being in love.

He sinks to the couch and stares at me; confused.

"What's going on?" Gideon furrows his brows. I shake my head as though I am clearing it of unwanted cobwebs.

"Sorry." I take a deep breath. "I've just been sleeping for a while and had some pretty crazy dreams."

He's only wearing white board shorts, so when he leans back on the couch, I get a full view of his chiseled abs. Anxiety surges in my chest. *I don't want this. I don't want this. I don't want this.* A smirk crawls across his lips. "I know you were sleeping for a while, but ... what kind of crazy are we talking about?" There is mischief in his eyes.

Heat rises in my cheeks, and I close my eyes to work to build a safe in the house inside my mind.

"Uh uh," Gideon whispers into my ear, and my eyes fly open. "I overheard Oz tell Pippa you were dreaming of the Dolomites. What possibly could you be doing there?"

"If you're wondering whether you were there, you were." How can I position this so I don't lie to him, but I don't reveal the truth? "You showed me around a little lake nestled in a valley."

He asks me to describe the scene for him, so I tell him about the way the sun peeks over the mountains and lights up the entire valley. How the water is as blue as Oz's eyes, and how the grass is lime green.

"That sounds like home." He has a far off look on his face. "My hut was the sole building in the valley because I was the only one strong enough to tolerate the harsh winters up there. Sure, it got cold, but those views were worth it. Wildflowers dotted the land, and my sheep loved to graze on dandelions. If the grass was green, you probably didn't see any white crocus."

I shake my head. Then again, my mind made me witness whatever it wanted. It was scarily accurate, though.

"Come visit me any time in history and I'll show you around."

Before I can respond, the rice cooker beeps.

"What are you cooking? Can I help?"

It is a little early for lunch, but I've never known a vampire to turn down a meal.

"Poke bowls."

He follows me to the kitchen and asks how he can help. I toss him a knife, knowing full well he'll catch it unscathed, and even if he didn't, he'd heal. His eyes widen, and then a grin forms on his face.

I take both salmon and poke out of the fridge. "Which one?"

"Both."

Of course he'd say both.

When we finish making the food, we take our bowls outside so we can sit in the warming sun. Before taking a bite, I carefully watch Gideon maneuver his chopsticks. I'm surprised he's a master at using them.

"You forget I've been around for a long time." He quirks an eyebrow at me. "This isn't the only thing I'm good at." His open flirting makes my heart race, and I avoid his eyes. Instead, I stab a piece of poke and place it in my mouth.

Gideon inhales his bowl, and I'm not far behind him.

"So, what else did we do in Italy?" You were asleep for five days."

Heat rises in my cheeks, which is punctuated with his icy stare.

"You smell different, too."

Suddenly, I'm very self-conscious. He can sense my discomfort with that remark. "Not in a bad way, Lana. I can't place it, but it's pleasant."

I suppose that's a relief. Although, I'm surprised Oz said nothing. Maybe the curse changed me physiologically. The sun heats my skin, so I remove the cardigan I have on until I'm just in shorts and my tank top.

"We swam for a bit and ate until we were uncomfortable."

"I can't even remember what that feels like." Gideon sighs. "I'd love to go back someday. Just for a day."

Part of me wants to sneak away with him in time and be back before anyone knows we've left. But being there, where we spent our day and night making love to each other, isn't a boundary I want to tempt myself with.

"Maybe someday you'll get a chance to."

"Yeah, maybe. Wonder why you ended up there?"

I fight the urge to tell him everything. That wouldn't be fair to him, nor Oz.

"You asked me to show it to you." I speak plainly, trying not to raise any suspicion.

He sits up in his lounge chair and turns towards me. "Would you?" He looks hopeful.

Crap. I'm backing myself into a corner here.

"Sure, happy to take you if Oz is alright with coming along. I don't want him thinking anything is going on between us." I regret my words as soon as they leave my mouth.

"Now why would he think that?" Heat stirs at my core, and I fight it by trying to build my safe in my mind's house to stuff the memories. "Lana ... what aren't you telling me?"

He just won't give this up, and I've given him far too much already. The house in my head crumbles under the pressure, and I give up on building it.

"You died," I blurt out.

"You killed me?" His question is innocent, and if I weren't panicking, I'd find the humor in it. If I hadn't killed Oz, I'd swat Gideon's arm now. Of course, he'd think I could kill him.

"No, Oz killed you." I pick up both of our dishes and take them into the house. He sits in shock for a few moments before registering I've gotten up.

In a split-second, he's at my side. I can see his mind churning, and I'm afraid of what's coming next.

"You and I both know there is only one reason Oz would kill me, so I don't think your brain would've concocted anything else, even dreaming." He doesn't even need to continue based on the way my heart rate has sped up, but he does anyway.

He takes the dishes from my hands and places them in the sink behind me, invading my space rather than simply going around me. "Did Dream Lana want to root with me? Is that why you took me back in time?" He has that bedroom purr again.

I turn and roll off his arms so he's no longer cornering me against the counter.

Distance.

I need to put some space between us.

"Or maybe we *did*." He's toying with me now. "Here's how I envision that played out: We have a naughty, Oz walks in and loses his mind. Kills me in a pure, blind rage. Only, it is a dream, so you regenerate me after he's left. You feel guilt, but you don't want to stop because you know you and I belong together. Once you've given in to fate, you decide to take me home so you can get to know me. I wow you with my sheep-herding abilities, or perhaps it is my superior love-making skills, and you fall head-over-heels for me."

I'm speechless. Oz wasn't kidding; Gideon *is* the best detective in the world. He could discern most of it without me even giving much away.

"My only question is this." He puts his hands behind his head to stretch and I avert my eyes to avoid staring at the deep V of his abs. "What did Oz have to say about it?"

I plop on the couch, tucking one of my legs under me while I rest my head on my hand.

The cat is already out of the bag.

"He said he'd share if I asked him to." I can smell the cinnamon pour off him.

His eyes drill into me, but I don't feel uncomfortable under his stare. We feel close, despite our only intimate interactions being in my dreams.

"And will you?" He plunks down next to me. While he tries to project a calm and collected demeanor, I see right through it. Love and hope shine bright in his eyes.

Despite my body's reaction to him, I give one word: "No."

He leans forward on his elbows now, and I'm drawn to his long jawline and the striations on his shoulders. My gaze trails down his rib cage, over his obliques, and to the little trail of hair just above his shorts. They lower a little further, and I dart them somewhere else.

Holy hell. His erection is even bigger than in my dreams. I got a brief glimpse of him when I'd tested out my ability to control people, but never was it so obvious how ... blessed he truly is.

"The thing about me is I always wear my heart on my sleeve." His voice is indifferent, but I don't buy it. "And you—you simply pretend you don't wear any. I don't need to read minds to know what's on yours. I'm just wondering why you continue to feel the need to deny your feelings, especially knowing Oz is fine with it."

Is that what I'm doing? Can you love someone *and* want to sleep with them without being *in* love with them? Does the distinction even matter? When I woke, I was so sure of how I felt; Oz was the only man for me. But now it is just Gideon and me, alone, all my memories resurface.

"It is possible to want to bed someone without attachment." I stare at him defiantly. Am I trying to convince him, or me?

"You want to ...'bed' me?" He has an amused look on his face.

In this moment, yes, yes, I do, but I will not tell him that.

"You've established you love me, and now you want to ... fuck." He smirks. I suppose I made it sound like that, for anything more intimate would suggest a much deeper connection between the two of us than I will admit.

Both my body and my heart betray me. If I were unattached, there's no doubt I'd have Gideon take me right here and now. My breath hitches in my throat as I imagine it, like we'd done so many times in my dreams.

"Look, I will not pressure you into anything. Just know there is an open invitation when you're ready to act on those desires—strings, or no strings attached."

"That isn't the way it works. Do you think if we crossed that line, we'd ever be able to stop?" Heat rises in my face, and the atmosphere in the room shifts.

"No, you're right. It's taking everything I have in me not to throw you over my shoulder and ride off into the sunset with you. I am in love with you, Lana."

I feel an ache at my core when I turn my face to stare at the wall. I'm not sure what to say. Do I tell him how I feel?

My heart decides it should.

I turn my head back towards him. "I love you, too, Gideon." My voice is barely audible. Never did I imagine things would get so complicated being mated to the King of Vampires. Why don't I feel this way towards Maeve or Pippa? They're all more than desirable and achingly beautiful, but I am not *in love* with any of them. I have feelings for Auguste, too, though.

It has to be the prophecy. Right? Or is my behavior *causing* the prophecy?

"I'd better go clean the dishes." I try to escape my feelings.

Gideon stands when I do, and he follows me to the kitchen.

"Here, let me," he takes over the sink. He rinses off the dishes and hands them to me to put into the dishwasher. It is dangerous being in close proximity to him.

"Thanks." He tosses me a detergent pod and I start the dishwasher.

"What are you afraid of?"

I freeze. Oz has told me he'd allow it. Am I afraid I'll love Gideon more than my husband and mate? I don't think it's possible, but maybe it is what's holding me back.

"I don't want to lose what Oz and I have. He is my world. I feel guilty for even entertaining the idea."

He reaches into the fridge and hands me a bottle of water before taking one of his own. "Yeah, I can see how you might feel that way. I just don't know if you fully understand how different it is for vampires and their sires. If we were all human, you're absolutely right —this would be wrong on so many levels. But it isn't, which is why Oz even said he'd agree to it."

Gideon wraps me in his arms and gives me a kiss on my cheek when we're done. "Let's go track down the rest of the fam bam."

I'm glad we've had this talk. If Oz shares me with Gideon, it will only be with his consent I'd do it. Obviously, with the full under-standing Oz is my husband—we sleep together, decide together, and everything else is secondary. Having been alive so long, I'm not even sure what these vampires' ideas of threesomes are. Have either of them ever been with a man before?

"Put a shirt on," I scan his naked torso. I don't want staff getting the wrong impression or starting any rumors. He and I have been together in the house alone for a while now. Sure, we wanted to romp, but we didn't.

Gideon grabs a t-shirt from the stack of folded clothes sitting on top of the dryer in the hallway closet. "Is that even yours?"

"Nope." He grins. When he puts it on, I recognize it as Auguste's.

"Okay, that might arouse some suspicion," I laugh. Already, I can tell Gideon steps a little lighter. "Maybe just try not to think about what you and I discussed." We make our way towards the restaurant in the middle of the island. "I don't want Oz finding out that way. It is a conversation he and I need to have."

Normally, he can hear any thoughts that are loud or panicky anywhere on the island, but for transient thoughts, he has to be a little closer.

He pauses and I turn around to look at him. "How the hell am I going to manage that?" He asks in a near whisper. "I'm this close to being able to make love to you, and it hasn't left my mind since."

Too late. Oz is walking this way now. But where is everyone else?

"Hey, babe." Oz gives me a kiss when he reaches me.

"Hey, I was just coming to get you two. I'm certain we've figured out who's part of the Lapis Templar, but we don't plan on confronting them until tomorrow. Auguste is keeping them occupied for now."

It makes me nauseous to think about there being someone on the island who wants to hurt me. Not only that, but why haven't they made a bigger move until now?

"Good. Do you have a few minutes? We should all talk." I glance between Oz and Gideon.

"The rest of the afternoon actually. Everyone else is watching the game at the restaurant."

We find a long bench to sit on under the canopy of trees. Oz puts his arm around me and waits in anticipation for me to speak, and Gideon fidgets with the hem of his borrowed shirt.

"I know I told you I'm not interested in pursuing anything with Gideon," I ramble nervously. "But I think I'd like to try it. This changes nothing between you and me. I am still your wife, and you are my husband, my king, my mate, and my forever. He and I have done nothing—I swear it. I'd never do it without your blessing and you being present if you prefer."

When I finish speaking, I hold my breath. My nerves gnaw at my stomach, and I look up at Oz. I was afraid he'd be angry, or beside himself, but he isn't.

Will you say something? I beg him in my head. Without removing his arm from my shoulder, he takes my hand in his.

"I expected this eventually, even before the dream. They prophesied it long before you were ever born. Hell, even before Gideon was born. If it had to be someone, I'd want it to be my second in command. I trust him with my life, and yours. What you ask isn't unusual, and I'm sorry if I've made you feel that way. Vampires operate a little differently based on our physiological makeup."

Okay, I like where this is going. He hasn't said no, nor has he killed Gideon as he did in my dream.

"What I'm saying is ... yes. Thank you for asking first."

I let out the breath I was holding. That wasn't nearly as painful as I thought it was going to be. I can see why he reacted the way he did in my dream. It felt like a betrayal because it just happened, and I didn't ask first. But now, there is consent.

My mind drifts to Gideon. Is this fair to him? I can never be his wife, and how would I feel if he met someone? These are things I haven't considered yet, but it is something we all need to discuss before we ever cross that line.

We've got time. Let's talk now.

I turn to Gideon seated next to me. "Now that Oz has given the green light, it makes me wonder if this is even fair to you. I mean, talk about a third wheel. I can't ever be your wife, and I can't promise not to lose it when you meet someone else. It just doesn't seem fair to you." Jealousy isn't something I'm proud of. Because I recognize it, though, means I have to lay it all on the table now. What if he hooked up with someone I know? Or even another witch?

"In vampire families, they often share mates amongst members of a clan, if you will." Gideon speaks. "For example, Oz could share you with me, Auguste, Maeve, and many other immediate vampires—if you both wanted. Pippa is mated to Elliot now, so you couldn't mate with her because vampires can only be mated to one person while the mate is alive, but every other immediate vampire is fair game."

My eyes grow wide at this. It is so unusual for me. I was raised in monogamous households. Any time a third wheel entered the picture in any of my relationships, it was unwanted because they cheated on me; it doesn't feel good. But how would it feel to give myself to Oz's vampires? And how does Oz feel?

"I've never had a mate, nor has Gideon." Oz squeezes my hand. "So, I can't say how I'd feel in the moment. What I know from other vampires is usually, it enhances the relationship. By nature, vampires are jealous creatures. Possessive, even. But watching their mate with one of their own vampires can bring them even closer together, and it is far less dangerous for sires to share their mates than it would be for distant vampires to do it. That's why it's so commonplace among our kind. Together, our court can only grow stronger."

His explanation makes sense, and it also explains why Oz hadn't shut Gideon down when he was flirting with me. Having been cheated on though, I know for a fact I dislike the idea of someone flirting with my partner, let alone sleeping with them in front of me.

This is about you, Sahira. My only desire is for you. That's a biological fact. We're mates.

"So let me get this straight. Oz shares me with Gideon, and even other vampires of his." I fidget with the hem of my tank top. "To what end? I mean, we don't all live together 24/7, and what if Gideon wants to date someone? And why can I, as your mate, be with your vampires, but you can't? It makes little sense." I can feel the stress hormone in me releasing, and I know both of them can sense my body's reaction.

Jealousy. *I hate it.*

"If we do this, I will take you." Gideon grabs my other hand. "Think of it like a hierarchy. Oz is your mate. It isn't like human polyamory. We're not equals. You two are king and queen. Then, I take you, but that doesn't change the fact Oz is your primary partner. I'd be secondary, along with any other immediate vampires you choose to sleep with. It also means we couldn't take love interests of our own, nor can Oz. If any of us tried, the mating bond would sever and kill the offending party. Over the years, this has evolved so vampires who are mated never have a desire for anyone other than their mate."

"And, as far as living arrangements go, there's a reason our houses are so big." Oz smirks.

"Thanks for clearing that up for me. So, you two could never ... cross swords?"

Both men chuckle at this. "Nope. Sorry."

Damn. It might've been hot. Are we going to do this?

Oz meets my eyes. If this is what you want, then it is what I want, too.

"Come play." I grab both men by their hands and lead the way back to the house.

Suddenly, I'm nervous. Will Gideon like what he sees under my clothes?

He will love what he sees.

"Now you won't have to spend so much time on your balcony."

Gideon's steps falter and he looks at me. "You know I was just messing with you, right? I only knew about the pictures because I could hear you two. I'd never invade your privacy like that. Can't help overhearing, though. Vampire hearing and all." He shrugs.

I figured there was no way Oz would've let him get away with that. "Why didn't you tell me?" I cock my head and raise a brow at Oz. "I've spent this entire time thinking your best friend is a peeping Tom." They laugh, and Oz apologizes.

Once we're alone in our bedroom, things get real. "Remember, I support this, and you're not hurting my feelings, okay?" Oz nuzzles into my neck.

The only hesitation I have about this was not wanting to hurt him, aside from hoping I'm adequate for Gideon.

"Are you okay if I sit and watch from here?" He points to the chair Gideon placed in front of the bed. "I think it is important you and Gideon get to know each other ... intimately before I join in."

This is happening, and not only is Oz okay with it, but he's going to watch. I steel my nerves.

Yes, I tell him in my head. He takes a seat while Gideon saunters over to me. My heart thunders in my chest. I've made love to him so many times in my dreams, but now it's actually going to happen. The look on his face is like one I've seen so often before.

Desire.

Gideon is close to me now and traces his finger along my bare arm. Goosebumps dot my body in stark contrast to the warm room.

"May I kiss you?"

I nod, and my breath catches in my throat when his hand cups the back of my head and draws me in. My thighs squeeze in anticipation, and then our lips meet. His are soft, much softer than I imagined, and I can feel his erection press against my stomach through his shorts.

With one finger, he slides the strap of my tank top over my shoulder so it falls and reveals my breast. His hand kneads me while his other effortlessly unbuttons my jean shorts. They land at our feet, and I step out of them, kicking them behind me while he removes the shirt he stole from the folded laundry pile. After I slide out of my panties, I work to pull off his board shorts.

His erection springs forward, and I can't help but stare at it while he steps back to get a good look at me.

"You are perfection." He pulls me towards him. I wrap my hands around his steel length and stroke it. He lets out a soft moan, and before I can get on my knees, he picks me up instead and carries me over his shoulder to the bed. I make eye contact with Oz in his chair, and he smirks at me with hooded eyes.

Gideon places me on the bed before he kisses my thighs in benediction. I squirm and let out an involuntary shriek.

"Now, how are we going to get anywhere if you're ticklish everywhere?"

That's when I grab his hand and place it firmly on my mound. "Here."

"Oh, you want me to kiss you there?" Hunger drips from his voice. Under my hand, his fingers inch their way down until they are at my slick opening.

His mouth works in tandem with his hand. My hips buck and grind against him as he devours me. It doesn't take long for me to come, and he purrs in satisfaction. "God, you taste like vanilla ... and peaches."

It has to be a witch thing.

"Let me taste." I sit up and pull him to me. His kiss is slow and gentle while our tongues explore each other.

He moves to my neck—sucking and kissing it—while I stroke him.

Oz's heavy gaze meets mine, and it turns me on knowing he enjoys what he sees. He strokes his own cock, biding his time until he's ready to join.

My attention turns back to Gideon, whose hands caress my skin, and becomes more earnest with each movement. "I'd like you to take me now."

He pauses to search my eyes.

"I love you, Lana."

"I love you, too, Gideon." His arms wrap around my waist and lay me down again.

I grip his shaft and guide it between my thighs. My legs hug his hips, driving him forward and into me. We both let out moans as he fills my expanse. His movements are languid, bringing every ounce of pleasure to the surface.

Warmth and love pour over me. We are nothing but love, ice, and heat. At this cue, Gideon sinks his teeth into my breast, and fire sears my chest before he lets out a low growl that rolls through me for a moment before complete and total bliss.

Joy and light swirls through my body, like butterflies taking flight —so different than the passionate mating bond I share with Oz. Gideon's started out dark before blazing to an airy, weightless leash between us; like astronauts tethered to a shuttle. Wild and fun, but safe.

Thousands of lifetimes of his memories flood to me with every draw at my vein. When he is satiated, I hook my leg, so it swings me on top of him. I let my hair down and this riles him. I want to watch him fall apart beneath me.

"You are so fucking beautiful."

I give a feral grin while I grind my hips into him. I'm so caught up in pleasure I don't notice Oz get up from his seat until I feel his lips on my neck.

I was wondering when you were going to join us.

Do you mind if I use the backdoor?

I lower myself so I'm close to Gideon's face, chest against chest. This position will give easier access, and Gideon takes the opportunity to pull me in for a kiss.

Ready.

Oz massages my ass with a lubed finger before inching his thumb in. It doesn't hurt at all. Instead, it is pleasurable.

I've never done double penetration, but I'm eager to try it with the men I love. He slides his thumb back out, and the bulbous head of his shaft sits just at my back door. It is well-lubed, and I feel pressure but no pain.

Breathe, Oz coaxes in my head.

I take several deep breaths and that relaxes me enough for him to enter me completely.

A forceful moan escapes from my mouth, and I can't help but shudder with pleasure between them. I am stuffed in the most delicious way. Each of us moves together in a rhythm so coordinated it is like we've been practicing for this moment our entire lives.

"I want to hear you," I beg my men.

Both of them breathe for me now, and the sound of their grunts of effort sends me over the edge.

"I'm about to come." Several more bucks of my hips, and Gideon's warm seed fills me, and a loud groan comes with his release. He and I stop moving our hips, and I firmly root myself to him so Oz can pound me. It isn't long before he comes, too.

When Oz finishes, he helps me off Gideon.

"Fuck," Gideon grins. "If I lived to be a million years old, and that was the only time we ever made love, I'd still die a happy man."

A satisfied smile crosses my lips. My heart is still racing, and although I'm a mess, Oz holds me in his arms while we sit on the bed.

"I loved it. I am wet, though. Care to join me in the shower?"

When we shower, it is all business. I'm pretty spent. The water soothes my sore muscles, and it puts me in an almost meditative state of bliss. "You alright there, Lana?" Gideon eyes me while soaping himself up.

"Just happy and exhausted." It was interesting seeing some of his secrets when he took me as his mate. I suppose now I'm his mate, Oz knows all Gideon's secrets, if he didn't know them already. The download would've been playing in his head, too.

I knew most of them, but there were a few surprises.

"How are you both feeling?"

Are they okay with what just transpired? Is it something they want to continue?

Gideon, the far louder of the two, speaks first. "I wasn't kidding when I said I'd storm the gates of hell to be with you."

"It was hot, watching you get taken, Sahira." Oz whispers in my ear. Goosebumps pebble my skin when he does.

"Careful, vampire, I just got all clean. You don't want me dirty again."

"There you go again, threatening us with a good time," Gideon purrs.

I walk into the bedroom while toweling off. "What do you think Auguste is going to say?"

"Oh, I'm pretty sure he already knows. He came back to the house thirty minutes ago; I heard him on his phone." Oz tosses his towel in the hamper.

The blood drains out of my cheeks. I hoped he wouldn't stumble upon us, but then again, I'm not sure how I'd tell him. Oz told me Auguste is in love with me, too.

How is he going to feel knowing I let Gideon take me and he hasn't?

On that same note, how would I feel about Auguste taking me, too? I know he was mated once before, so I'm not sure how that works. Also, we couldn't all share a bed. That would be far too many people.

"We told you vampires can only be mated to one person while the mate is alive." Oz catches an errant drop of water on my arm with his finger. "When their mate dies, eventually some vampires find a new one. Not all, though." It has been a century since Auguste's mate died during the Spanish flu.

LAST NIGHT, Gideon and Oz helped Auguste put together an accelerated training schedule to help me learn how to fight without my magic to prepare for going to Bedlam. The fae are tricky creatures with the power to disable my magic, so I need to know both offensive and defensive strategies that don't use my power.

For the next month, he and I will work together from 5 am until 10 pm, with a two-hour break in-between—plus meals. Mortals would struggle with this rigorous training program, but because of my healing abilities, recovery takes mere minutes for any minor injuries.

After a quick breakfast, Auguste and I head to the woods to begin our combat lessons. It's still dark out, and I'm glad he told me to dress in layers; there's a slight nip in the air. By the time we reach a small clearing, a tiny sliver of light on the horizon makes it easier to see him. While he has great night sight, I don't.

Auguste leads me through a series of stretches to help limber me up. I'm eager to get started on training and want to skip the stretches, but I keep my mouth shut. He's gone out of his way to help, and I don't want to complain. I don't even groan about the sprints he makes me do across the grass, even though my legs burn, and I taste blood in the back of my throat from the effort. Despite hiking for the last three months, my chest still heaves, and I feel like passing out.

My hour of warming up earns me a ten-minute break, which I spend most of lying flat on my back, drenched in sweat, and cursing the gods internally. If his warm up routine is this vigorous, I'm nervous about the actual work we'll do. When Auguste reminds me I have two minutes left, I heal the ache in my legs and the pressure in my lungs.

For the next several hours, we cover drills; blocking, rear bear hugs, kicks, and uppercuts. Sweat plasters my face, and I'm down to my sports bra and shorts from the heat. I'm certain if I had a mirror, I'd find my hair wild and frizzy—which is a stark contrast to Auguste's sleek, barely tousled hair.

"You ready for some groundwork techniques?"

"Ready as I'll ever be!"

He smirks. "Lie on your back, knees up."

I quirk an eyebrow but lower myself to the ground and lay on the bed of grass and leaves. He kneels next to me, careful to keep a respectful distance from my body, but his pale blue gaze and scent of cloves betrays his thoughts. There's a slight hesitation before he swings his leg over to straddle me and places his palms on my shoulders. I involuntarily squeeze my thighs for friction, and the look on Auguste's face tells me he notices, but he doesn't comment on it.

"What are you thinking right now?" The words spill out of my mouth without my permission.

He leans in closer until my ragged breath stirs the hair hanging in his eyes. His tongue darts out to wet his lips, drawing my attention to his mouth. Anticipation makes my pulse thump wildly in my chest.

"How much I want to touch you," he whispers in my ear.

The intensity of his words makes my body flush with heat, and I forget how to breathe. I'm caught in the moment until he pulls away, obviously waiting for me to give him permission, but I won't grant him what he wants; not until I've discussed it more with my mates.

"You are touching me."

He grins. "That I am."

His head whips up and his smirk turns more devious. I follow his gaze and spot my mates casually leaning against trees at the perimeter of the clearing. I use this opportunity to catch Auguste off guard by bringing my arms up and out, so his arms fold and his grip weakens enough for me to roll on top of him.

With a Cheshire grin plastering my face, I give him a little pat-pat on the cheek. A soft, husky laugh comes out of his mouth and sends a shiver through my body, despite the Chilean heat.

"Snack time, lover boy."

I pop up from his chest and turn to face my mates, who now stalk towards us. It's hard not to laugh at how flustered Auguste looks, so I offer him my hand to help him up.

Oz reaches me first and slides his arms around my waist for a hug. I cringe inwardly because I'm so sticky and sweaty, but my thoughts don't dissuade him. He presses his mouth to mine and gives a little nip to my bottom lip, eliciting a small moan from me before I deepen the kiss, begging for more.

"Gonna admit, that was really hot." Gideon's purr sounds in my ear and I pull back from Oz and roll my eyes before looking my other mate's way.

"What's hot?"

"Watching you own Auguste like that."

"Is that so?" I throw my arms around his neck. "Then I suppose I'm glad you didn't see the first four hours he kicked my ass."

He chuckles before picking me up and wrapping my legs around his waist. After a quick peck, he sets me down and motions to the snacks and drinks they brought from the house.

Over the next several weeks, our routine continues; I train so hard I puke, and have my ass handed to me daily. And most days, Oz or Gideon will hop in on training for an hour or two. I grow to look forward to our training sessions, despite the strain on my body, because of the camaraderie, the playful banter, and the occasional touch that makes my heart race.

"ARE you thinking about bringing him into the fold?" Gideon plops on the bed.

"That's up to you guys. I don't know him as well as I know you, but we've grown close during training. I don't want him feeling inadequate or left out." Auguste is very attractive, kind of cross between Chris Pine and a *Top Gun* Tom Cruise, if they were vikings. He's also very kind—quite the gentleman.

"Are you crazy? Everyone at your wedding wanted to take you as a mate. You should've heard them talk." Gideon laughs. "I'm cool with it if Oz is."

People were talking about wanting to sleep with me at my *wedding*? I sure have a lot to learn about vampire culture. It's hard to fathom why people find me so desirable. Or maybe it's my title.

"It isn't your title, Lana," Oz responds to my thoughts out loud. "After that little speech Gideon made, people had questions and eventually, everyone knew you risked everything you had to save their lives. No one knows about the time travel, though. It is important to keep it that way—for your safety and theirs. Oh, and they're calling you the Oriflamme Queen."

"Oriflamme? Latin roots aurum ... and flamma ... gold flame?" I piece together my limited Latin out loud. What the heck does that mean?

"It's an old French word used to describe the banner the King of France used in the Middle Ages. He'd fly it to scare enemy troops, because his men would take no prisoners as long as it was raised," Gideon says.

I'm still not sure if this is a good thing. Am I that scary of a queen?

"The one carrying the flag was expected to die rather than give it up—it was a tremendous honor to serve in that role. They call you the Oriflamme Queen because *you* are their rallying point. They are devoted and will die for you if it comes to it."

I am speechless and fixated on the floor in a daze. A chill runs through me, breaking my trance.

"I am fine with Auguste." Oz kisses me on the cheek. "Do you want me to call him in here?"

My heart races at the idea of three men fawning over me. I'm just a regular ol' Peggy Guggenheim. Oz chuckles at my thoughts about the late sex-addict.

"As long as you know you're my King. Sure."

I crawl into the bed naked and pull the duvet up to my waist. Gideon gives me a kiss before walking bare-assed to his room next door to get on new clothes. "Be back in a jiffy."

Oz sends a text and throws on some shorts. There's a knock on the door after Gideon enters the room.

"Come in," Oz calls out.

Auguste crosses the room to the couch. His eyes dart to my bare breasts, and he looks away to not disrespect me.

"You wanted to talk?"

"I wanted to. I've called you in here because I'm wondering if you'd like to have me, too."

The look on his face is priceless. I will forever ingrain the memory of this dumbfounded, wide-eyed look.

"I ... I didn't think you were interested in me. The answer is yes, though."

I figured he might have thought this, and I feel bad about it. During our training sessions, he and I have grown close, but apparently, the lack of a mating bond weighs heavily on his mind.

"It isn't because I'm not interested in you, Auguste. Gideon is far more forward and outgoing, so I've gotten to know him better, faster. That doesn't mean you aren't worthy of being my mate."

The fact he answered yes so fast confirms to me this is such a common practice—it's not even a question. Being the queen of vampires has changed my predilection of feminism and sexual empowerment; I've spent most of my life thinking monogamy is the only way a relationship can work.

It reassures me, though, my mates can't physically or emotionally desire others. Does that make me a terrible person? Rules for thee and not for me?

No, Sahira. It is just the way things work with vampires. It helps establish powerful clans; Oz reminds me in my head.

Auguste is nervous. I can tell by the way he keeps tinkering with the ring he wears on his right hand. I suppose I'd be nervous, too; both Gideon and Oz have very dominant personalities. Auguste is more of a strong, silent type, no doubt his zest for life marred by having loved and lost his mate.

Do you think we should give you and Auguste some time alone?

Given his unique situation, having previously had a mate, it is for the best if we mate for the first time by ourselves. If my King is okay with it, I am too.

"Gideon, let's leave them to it. I have some trade reports I need you to look over, anyway."

Gideon looks my way with reluctance. He doesn't want to go anywhere, but he comes over to give me a kiss before leaving the room. Oz cups a hand under my chin and presses his lips to mine.

I throw the covers off me and strut towards Auguste. He doesn't take his eyes off my very naked body before I sit next to him on the couch.

"You are so beautiful." His pale blue eyes and scent of cloves reveal his arousal.

"Thank you." I take his hand in mine. "You are breathtakingly handsome, and an even kinder soul. I feel terrible you've thought this entire time I don't want you. I'm new to this, so I've spent a lot of time denying my feelings for fear of hurting the people I love."

"I imagine it's been an enormous change for you."

"Yes, it has, but I think I'm catching on now. It feels good to be loved ... and desired." The atmosphere between us shifts suddenly, and Auguste stares at my lips.

"I'd like to kiss you now, if I may?"

"I thought you'd never ask."

He grins and closes in. There's no hesitation from my strong and silent vampire; I'm like a doe caught in his sights. When his lips meet mine, they're soft, despite the bruising kiss he's giving me. It is a feverish lover's kiss.

Auguste draws me into his lap. His hand reaches behind my head for a light, but firm grasp of a fistful of my hair to deepen our kiss before pulling back.

"I've loved you since the moment I saw you." His voice rumbles in my ear like a hungry tiger's purr. "All those nights lying alone in bed imagining what your skin might feel like against my lips; I was self-torturing. Night after night, I fucked my fist to the sounds of you making love, and imagined it was me, instead."

"Oh Auguste, I never knew ..." His words send a blaze straight to my loins. Where has this dominant man been hiding?

He kisses me hungrily, almost violently.

"I can't get enough of you ... tell me to stop if you want me to." He trails his lips down my neck and nibbles my skin.

"Don't stop. I want this ... I want you."

He obeys my request to be kissed, and his lips reach mine again. His tongue slips inside my mouth and dances slowly; searching, probing.

He makes to lay me down, but the couch is not comfortable, so I teleport us to the bed. It momentarily startles Auguste.

"That's so cool."

I give him a feline grin.

I help him out of his clothes and my finger traces an intricate Nordic tattoo starting at his shoulder and down one side of his chest. "I have to have Oz enchant it once a year for me so it doesn't heal itself."

Auguste is hung like Oz and Gideon, and I can't help but feel like I've hit the jackpot; they're all well-endowed, handsome, and in love with me. He cups my breast with one hand and makes to eat me out before I stop him.

"You don't want to do that. I've showered, but no doubt their seed is still in me."

He looks at me sheepishly before deciding it's not a good idea.

Instead, I grip his shaft and put its rotund end into my mouth. He throws his head back and moans before tilting back up and caressing my hair, alternating between tender massages and a firm grip. My hands and mouth work together to bring him near the edge before I kiss the curve of his obliques until I know he's come back down.

He tucks a stray curl behind my ear, and our eyes meet. In one swift move, he pulls me in for a kiss and then flips me on my back. That's something I'll never tire of—my vampires being able to toss me around as though I were light as a feather. I love when they take charge in the bedroom, and I have a sneaky suspicion he is far more forward in the bedroom than he is in conversation.

"You may take me now."

I reach for his erection, but he pins my hands above my head instead. This is a dynamic I think I'm going to love. He takes his shaft in his hand and rubs it against my folds until I'm begging for him to enter me.

"You're so wet for me." His grin is feral just before he plunges into me.

I arch my back and let out a moan at the intrusion. The fit is snug, and borders along the sweet edges of both pleasure and pain. His thrusts aren't fast, but they're hard, which causes small whimpers to escape from me with every one of them.

He sits me up so I'm sitting in his lap now, and I've determined this is my favorite position. It's intimate. My nails claw at his back, but I'm careful about the fire within me. I can hear Auguste's breath in my ear now. He must've overheard me talking about wanting to hear it during sex because it turns me on.

"Don't hold back." I give him permission to be loud, to be rough. To take what he wants from me. His grunts pick up now, and I wrap my arms around his shoulders to drive him in even deeper to me. I brush my hair to one side, exposing my breast, and his teeth sink into it. Pain gives way to pleasure, sending me to high peaks before I receive his onslaught of memories. Secrets full of pain, loss, love and grief overwhelm me.

Our bond snaps in place, like a bulldozer mowing down any of its obstacles. My back arches from the force. Where Oz and Gideon's bonds felt like markings so certain, they drifted in slow and sure, Auguste's mark strikes with power so fierce, it settles over us like a thick shroud. It races over every crack and crevice, taking residence with such potency, I shudder in rapture.

When he's had his fill, I lay him on his back and ride him slow before fast and heavy. I come so hard I collapse on him.

He flips me over to my stomach and I raise my hips in the air by pulling my knees under me.

"I want you to pound me."

Auguste drives into me, hooking an arm over my neck and holds my shoulder. It doesn't choke me, but it allows him to pull me in firmly against him. I meet each delicious thrust with a soft moan.

Every buck drills into me hard until he stills, and his release fills me. His hips press several times, and I draw out every drop. We both fall to the mattress, tangled in each other. My chest heaves, but I have a huge grin on my face.

"Auguste Grey, you have completely surprised me today." This sweet, quiet vampire has a much darker and dirtier side than I could have imagined; I love it.

He chuckles and pulls me into him, so I rest my head on his chest and kiss his tattoo in front of me.

"How do you feel?"

I want to explain to him how thoroughly, blissfully fucked I am, in all the best ways.

"Like the luckiest woman to have ever lived." They've dropped me into the middle of an X-rated fairytale full of vampires.

"That may be true, but you're the best thing that's ever happened to us. I hope we can convince Oz to turn you so you don't have to go to Bedlam. If not him, then Gideon or me."

We're on the same page, although I'm still curious about what I can learn in the fae realm. Not just about how to live forever, but how to be a better witch and where, in time, I can find my mom. I'd give anything to bring her to the present. If not for me, then for Dad.

I'll be leaving for Bedlam soon, and it saddens me I could be gone for an indefinite amount of time.

Auguste senses my sadness and hooks a finger under my chin so I can look at him. "We'll get through it, no matter what happens."

A knock sounds at the bedroom door.

"Come in." I know it'll be Oz.

"Hey, babe. Get everything sorted with the reports?" He sits down at the foot of our bed.

"Yep, we've got it all taken care of. How are you feeling?"

"Happy, but exhausted. I'm thinking about taking a nap if you want to join me?"

Oz tells me he'd love to, and my newest mate climbs out of bed. Auguste dresses, but not before Oz catches the bright red marks streaking down Auguste's back. Both have an amused expression on their faces and Auguste gives me a kiss before leaving the room.

Oz hops under the covers and I nuzzle up against him, allowing the coolness of his body to chill me.

"You feel like home. I love you, Osgood Finlandian."

He takes my hand in his and rubs his thumb against my hand. "I love you, too, Lana Finlandian."

It is not long before I pass out, safe in the arms of my love. I wake when I feel Oz stir below me.

"You're hungry, Sahira. Let's get you supper."

I get dressed and think about how much the rest of the house knows by now. Will it be obvious? Oh my god, what will my dad think?!

Oz laughs at my thoughts. *Your dad is a vampire now, Sahira. He knows our ways. I promise you; it will only be awkward if you let it.*

That's not very reassuring. Has he met me? I am the queen of awkward and unusual encounters; has he forgotten our first night together?

He folds me into his arms and gives me a peck on the nose. "You'll be fine. The guys and I had a quick little chat, too, and think that in our bedroom and when it comes to decisions as a family, there's no hierarchy. You, Auguste, Gideon, and I are a unit. I'm no better than them just because I'm your husband and king. Hannah might have some questions, though," he offers.

I agree. While she and Maeve are still dating, I'm not sure she knows how clans work ... because I'm still figuring it out for myself.

CHAPTER THIRTY-TWO

"You're certain these people are members of the Lapis Templar?"

"One hundred percent, which means they have allies here, even though those allies aren't members." I hold a large clipboard bearing names and photos of the accused. Out of one hundred and forty staff, there are sixteen faces, most of them I recognize.

They call me Oriflamme Queen, but does that mean everyone does? The employees here aren't vampires, so it's doubtful. It makes me nauseous to think we may need to fire everyone on the island, considering many have worked here for years.

"What will happen to them?"

Oz folds me into his arms and rests his chin on my head. "After they attacked you in Mont-Tremblant, we classified the Lapis Templar a terrorist organization. I gave any members an opportunity for amnesty—anyone still taking part is a direct enemy of the crown; treason is punishable by death."

"No!" A scream burst from the deepest part of me and I push him away. "They are only trying to protect you. You can't." I am seething with red fiery rage. This is because of *my* curse.

Oz tries to console me, but I don't let him touch me. I am too upset, and afraid I'll lose control. It is rare I get upset with him, but now I'm beside myself. I storm out of the house and run. I'm not a runner and I don't know where my legs will take me; what I know is I need to let off steam before I hurt someone I love, whether through words or actions. It is smart of Oz to let me go.

⁓

I FIND myself in the middle of the woods and crumple to the ground, sobbing with anger. The scrapes on my knees and palms sting. The heaving of my breath drowns out the noise of the trees above, even though I'm in the best physical shape of my life after hiking Patagonia and Antarctica for months with Oz. I haven't been feeling well since I was cursed, and we suspect it is just the residual effects of the poisons and my rigorous training schedule.

The wind picks up, which is peculiar because I'm in the middle of the woods. It howls through the trees, and the creatures have gone silent. It is suddenly dark here. I stand and dust myself off, the pain non-existent now adrenaline courses through me. Something isn't right here. Am I causing this? I look around, but it is too dark to see anything.

I close my eyes and take a deep breath to activate my third eye. They fly open again when I see a tall, white figure between two trees in front of me. It moves fast, and I brace myself for impact, but it stops ten feet away from me.

Dolphina Darling.

I'd recognize her in a crowd of five million people. She may look like an angel with her billowy white aura, but the feeling of something sinister pours off her. I promised if I ever met this woman, I'd kill her myself. She's the leader of the Lapis Templar, and why thousands around the world want me dead.

And she poisoned Dad.

Energy draws from nature around me and it collects at my feet before traveling up to my core.

My hands tingle, but I am not afraid. It is not Dolphina that's doing this; it's me. I hold my hands out and watch out of my peripheral vision as fire and water gather and swirl at my fingertips. Power thrums through my body and I'm about to release it before she speaks.

"I wouldn't do that if I were you." The smirk on her face is evil incarnate. "Not if you care about your children."

With one flick of her wrist, she lassos a red magical cord around my wrists, and the fire and water disappear. I look at her, bewildered. "Children?" Maybe she's talking about my proverbial children: Oz's vampires.

"Why, the ones growing inside your womb." She speaks with a lover's purr that sends a chill right to my bones.

I shake my head. I'm not pregnant ... Am I? I've been drinking my tea ...

Oh gods. Panic races through me, and I try to wriggle free of her grip. I was asleep for five days.

"Let me go! Why are you doing this? I have done nothing to you!" To think someone could tell these prophecies thousands of years ago and create an entire religion set to destroy me is ridiculous.

"Oh, my dear. Oz didn't tell you? So typical of him." She tsks and is like a cat playing with a mouse.

Oz, please. Help me, I beg inside my head, praying he's able to hear my thoughts from the house.

"My mother was a powerful witch who could see the future, too. She prophesied Oz would have a love like no other in history; one that would span eternity and rival even the greatest love stories of all time. I had another vampire turn me so I could be with him forever. He turned down my father's offer for us to wed and said he didn't know me, but I've known him for as long as I can remember, so I forgave him for his silly little snub. He told me he didn't love me. It was you he loved."

"He didn't know me then." I don't believe a word out of her perfect mouth.

"Oh, but his heart and soul did. If it weren't for my mother telling Oz about you, he and I would be mated. So, I killed her. And now, I will take great pleasure in seeing his face when you have to leave him.

If you don't get to the fae realm on the next Bedlam Moon, you'll be dead." She cackles but stops abruptly when she senses people approaching rapidly.

I'm coming.

Oz, thank the gods, he heard me.

Dolphina puts us in a large sphere of protection. Heat and electricity bubble around the perimeter.

Be careful, don't come close. She has a protective ward up.

"Oz may have woken you and removed the poison from your body, but the curse is very well alive; you and your children will die if you are not in Bedlam by the time the sun rises after the Bedlam Moon."

Dolphina Darling thinks she's won. I don't know her long game, but I planned on going to Bedlam, anyway. My mate and his friend, Bonnie, said the fae have ways of finding out where my mom is in time—provided I can find a strong enough one in Bedlam.

Outside the orb, I see Oz, Auguste, Gideon, Dad, Maeve, and Pippa.

"That's fine." I struggle against the lasso burning into my skin. "But I find it peculiar how when Oz and I mated for the first time, and every time after that, I never once saw you in his secrets or memories. You must've been insignificant to him."

This infuriates her. She whips the magic cords around her arms to draw me in close to her. I'm just inches from her face now, and despite her physical beauty, there is nothing but ugly, jealous rage. She bares her teeth at me and rips my head back by my hair to display my throat. I hear my vampires roar and attack the bubble; it shakes and spits sparks but stays intact. Her teeth rip into my throat. It is violent and searing hot—far worse than the vampire in Mont-Tremblant.

For a moment, I am suspended in time, but then I remember what Dolphina told me. I'm pregnant.

In a split-second, I've built the forest inside my head, and I slip through the crack in the earth. It doesn't take long to come out the other side of the bubble.

Dolphina screams as she searches around it for me, tearing up the ground at her feet, but I am safe in Oz's arms. Together, we use our magic to build a shield around us she cannot penetrate, though she tries.

She disappears just as suddenly as she came. The wind stops, and the sky clears, although I see stars in my vision. My knees buckle and I can't feel my fingers or toes anymore.

"Lana!" Although I'm in Oz's arms now, he feels so far away. Auguste and Gideon, they're here, too. I smile because I am so loved. The trees spin above, and I've forgotten she bit me until Auguste applies pressure to my throat.

It doesn't hurt anymore. I try to say I'm sorry, but my mouth gurgles with blood.

Gideon and Maeve act fast; they both take Dad by the arms and haul him far away from the bloody mess I've made. I touch my hand to my throat and meet Auguste's eyes and I grin; my sweet, naughty vampire.

I can't hear anyone over the roaring in my head.

"Bb's," I choke out before the darkness closes in on me.

SWEET, metallic nectar drips down my throat. *Oz.* My eyes spring open, but they're blurry at first. I feel his wrist at my mouth, so I drink more, and it clears my vision. I mumble something incoherent.

"Shhh, don't talk." We are still in the woods. My body convulses from the cold, but his blood warms me up.

When I can be moved, Auguste scoops me into his arms to carry me back to the house while Oz keeps his wrist to my mouth. Both of my men fight back tears. Neither leave my bed when we reach the house, so Pippa tends to my neck over them. I sleep through the afternoon and am much better by the evening.

Gideon is at the foot of the bed when I wake.

"Where's dad?" My throat is scratchy, making my voice hoarse.

"Maeve took him to the mainland 'til morning. Best if he stays away from blood he can't take for a while."

It didn't occur to me how dangerous the situation had been, even if it weren't for Dolphina; Dad is a new vampire.

Tears trail to my chest when I speak. "I'm sorry. I shouldn't have taken off." It was stupid to do this on an island I know there are people out to get me on.

"Shh, you're okay," Oz strokes my hair. "What happened? I couldn't hear either of your thoughts or words in her protective sphere."

I wince at the poke Pippa makes on the inside of my elbow. At least it isn't a urinary catheter, I guess. This thought causes Oz to grin. I take in a deep breath and prepare to tell Oz about what happened. But, as the sequence of events plays in my mind, he looks at me like he's seen a ghost.

"Is it true?" His voice is incredulous, and I can't discern how he feels about the news. We've discussed having children, but now that I am potentially pregnant, has his mind changed?

"I don't know!" I'm afraid of what he might say if it is.

"Is what true?" Gideon crawls on the bed at my feet.

"I'm pregnant." My voice is barely above a whisper. Everyone in the room freezes as though to check and make sure I'm not pulling on their legs. Oz lays his head down on my belly and shoots a look around the room daring anyone to make a noise.

He erupts in a triumphant cheer that startles me, and I laugh.

Oh, my gods; I am pregnant. *We're* pregnant! Everyone in the room celebrates. If I weren't in a fragile state now, Oz would pick me up and spin me around the room. His entire face is beaming. Tears of joy dot my eyes before turning into a rush of grief.

"What, what's wrong?" Auguste takes my hand. "I thought you wanted to have kids?"

"If I don't go to Bedlam by the next Bedlam Moon, the children and I will be dead." Dying is an eventuality I figured I'd meet someday. But now I'm a mother, my maternal need to protect them outweighs anything else in this world.

Sorrow washes over the faces of the vampires I love. Oz roars in anger and grief and hurls a lamp that crashes against the wall. Pippa tries to calm him down while he paces the room, crying out in despair.

"I will rip out her throat and watch her burn at the stake! That murdering, traitorous bitch!" Oz howls.

"We will kill every last one of them, starting with Dolphina." Auguste approaches Oz carefully. "Lana needs mates who are level-headed. We've got to prepare her to leave."

Oz sits back down next to me and holds his hand on my stomach. "I love you, Sahira." Tears stream down his face, and it breaks my heart.

"I love you, too." I try everything I can to hold it together.

"Wait, did you say children, as in *plural*?" Gideon moves in closer.

I look at Oz. "I heard three heartbeats."

Twins. This should be the happiest moment of our lives. And now, I have to go to Bedlam, or we die. Every staff member who conspired for this moment deserves to be put to death for their crimes; I understand this now. No one threatens my children and gets away with it.

"I'll run some tests," Pippa offers. "Yours isn't the first vampire-witch offspring but they are definitely the first multiple vampire-witch offspring. It is best to keep a watchful eye until it is time for you to go." Vampires can't have children, but Oz can because he's also a witch.

Grief seizes in my chest. I knew this was coming, but to have it sprung on me so suddenly makes me reel in anguish. I blink back tears and agree to testing. Pippa has to order OB/GYN equipment from the mainland, so she'll have Dad and Maeve bring it on their way back. If I can heal my neck with a spell, we can have them back tonight. While there is a small lab and medical clinic on our island, it isn't equipped for a high-risk pregnancy or birth—yet.

"Spell casting won't hurt the babies, will it?"

Pippa shakes her head.

While she makes phone calls, I place my hand to my throat. Magic weaves in and out of my cells, carefully, but quickly, knitting my tissue back together.

Gideon and Auguste look on in amazement. "It is almost as fast as vampire blood," Auguste marvels. The two combined—blood and a spell—are the perfect pairing for fast healing. A wave of exhaustion hits me when I finish.

"If I take another nap, do you care?" My pregnancy must be why I've been so exhausted and hungry. Oz helps adjust my pillows and puts one under my knees. It makes me chuckle inside, knowing I've been pregnant for exactly three seconds, and he's already treating me like I'm nine months along.

He shoots me a grin. *Let me enjoy it.*

I WAKE to see dad in the room. "Hiya pumpkin, how are you feeling?"

"Tired. I've got something to tell you." He sits at the foot of the bed in anticipation of news.

"You're going to be a grandpa."

Pure, unbridled joy pours down his cheeks, but then he's startled to see blood. Gideon recognizes the alarm immediately and reassures him it is just tears and he has nothing to worry about.

"Oh, Lana. This is the best gift you two could ever give me."

I let him revel in this moment. He deserves it, after all he's lost. "It's a good thing you've got unlimited energy now, too. They're twins."

He about falls off the bed in shock, and instead jumps and pumps his fist in the air.

"How far along are you?"

"I'm not sure, but I can't be very far along at all. Pippa is going to run some tests, so I imagine we'll know more then."

As if we'd called her for dinner, she wheels in a large cart full of medical equipment and supplies.

"Alright you guys, I need some space to work." They clear out to the foot of the bed, awaiting to hear news. I lift my shirt to reveal my belly, and my eyes grow wide at the bump where my recent acquisition of abs used to be.

"I forgot to mention these pregnancies speed up thanks to vampire blood."

So long abs; it was nice to have you.

Oz snickers at the thoughts in my head and muffles it when everyone looks at him.

Pippa tucks what looks like a giant cloth into the waistband of my shorts and squirts a clear jelly on the end of a Doppler wand. The warmth is pleasant, and she presses on my belly while sliding it around.

She motions for the vampires to get behind her for a view of the monitor. There isn't a dry eye in the room while they witness two small babies on the screen, tiny and squirming. Oz takes the mouse and clicks around on the screen for measurements.

"Eighteen weeks." He cannot blink back his tears.

"You're almost half-way." Pippa confirms it with a measuring tape pressed against my belly. She also explains how because Oz fed me so much of his blood, from here out the babies will grow even faster, and will probably need blood when born.

"I'll be," Dad says in wonder.

Pippa asks Maeve to take Dad across the island so she can run some blood work on me and the babies. If this were a normal human pregnancy, I'd opt out of fetal blood sampling, but given the circumstances, we find it necessary. It is important to make sure they're both healthy. Besides, the risk is zero and they won't feel any pain thanks to Oz's blood.

Dad and Maeve leave the room after Dad kisses me on the head.

I lay on my side, and Auguste and Gideon each take one of my hands. Oz has to help Pippa with the procedure, considering he used to deliver babies. It's not pleasant for me because they collect the blood samples by going through my vagina. Oz does a great job of narrating what's happening, and the men help me breathe through the pain.

Before I know it, it's over, and Pippa uses a warm washcloth to clean me up.

"You're going to want to spend the rest of the evening and night in bed. And absolutely no intercourse for the next twenty-four hours. Understood?" She looks at all three men in the room, and now I know she is aware of the recent additions to my love nest—if you will.

Oz can't hold back his chuckle at my thoughts, and they ask what's so funny.

"Lana was just thinking about what you might call her group of lovers; A love nest."

The room erupts in laughter. It may as well be a nest of lovers, for they're always ready to go for me. Although, I'm not sure people love the members of their little group; I certainly do. They mean so much more to me than that and I'd die for any of them.

Auguste kisses me and says he'll bring up supper. "Thank you."

Pippa tells me she'll take the results to the lab across the island now and will have the results before I turn in for the night. I let her know how grateful I am for her, and she gives me a peck on each cheek.

"Think nothing of it."

Oz and Gideon settle in on either side of me. It's wild to think I'm almost halfway through my pregnancy. When did I conceive? I was diligent about drinking my tea, except I couldn't when I was asleep for five days. That probably ruined the effectiveness. Did it happen before, or after that? I suppose it doesn't even matter when it happened, especially given how rapidly our timeline is sped up compared to a human birth.

Auguste wheels in a giant cart with food. A smile spreads across my face when I notice the family-sized jar of whole pickles on the second shelf. Gideon picks up the jar with amusement and loosens the lid. He crawls into bed with it and holds it out to me.

"I'll have that for dessert."

He shrugs his shoulders and plops one in his mouth.

There's enough food to feed an army. Oz grabs my favorites from the cart. Macarons, bagels with cream cheese, and teriyaki salmon. The fat in the salmon is great for the babies, and the macarons will satisfy my sweet tooth; the carbs keep me happy.

Sticking true to my word, I save just enough room for a pickle. "I think we should look into one of those wall-to-wall beds." I chomp down on my sour dessert.

"For your love nest?" Gideon asks with a wicked gleam in his eyes, and I swat at him again.

"Bingo." I give him a vinegary kiss.

When we've had enough, the men clear the dishes and take them to the kitchen while Oz brings me my toothpaste-covered toothbrush and a cup of water. He gives me another cup to spit in. "You know, I can get up to take care of my hygiene. I'll be damned if I'm going to let you put another catheter in me."

He helps me out of bed. Instead of letting me walk, he picks me up and carries me to the bathroom. While I wash my face, he sits on the edge of the tub, watching me.

"I can't believe we're having twins," I say with the toothbrush in my mouth. It's probably best I get two in one shot, considering I will not get any younger.

Although, I'm concerned about not being with him for the birth of our children. I don't have a clue what Bedlam is like, but I imagine the obstetric care will be far better with a bunch of witches and fae than it would be in a regular human hospital.

"Have you thought about any names?"

I've just found out I'm pregnant, and while I had names picked out when I was a kid, they're not any I'd want to go with now. I had a bit of a boy band obsession back then.

Oz smiles at me and crosses his legs at the ankles.

"I'm not sure about first names, but I'd like to honor your first wife and son with their middle names. And maybe Auguste's wife, too, if that's okay with you? We'll have to see if we're having boys, girls, or one of each."

He crosses over to me and hugs me from behind, resting his chin on my head. "This is why you're my mate."

Setting my toothbrush in its holder, I turn around in his arms so we face each other. "I thought it was for my good looks and love-making abilities?"

He lingers on a kiss. "That, too."

Scooping me in his arms, he carries me back to the bed. It's been a while since I've worn his clothes, so he grabs a pair of gray sweats and one of his fitted t-shirts from the drawer for me to wear. They fit me better now my stomach is filling out.

"I didn't think you could ever get more beautiful than you already are." Oz ogles me. "Pregnancy looks good on you."

"You have to say that." I quirk an eyebrow at him.

As long as I don't get cankles, I think I enjoy being pregnant. Fortunately for me, a fast pregnancy also means less time to stuff my face, so I carry out front rather than growing wider. I've had such a complex about my weight and size after a college boyfriend verbally abused me about it; it messed with my feelings of self-worth.

Oz scowls before he answers the knock at our door, and it's Auguste and Gideon, back from the kitchen.

"I ordered your love nest." Gideon waggles his eyebrows. "Figured you might enjoy the extra room. And don't worry—I matched the aesthetics. It will be the coolest room on the entire island."

"Thank you, Gideon," I say warmly as they plop down on the bed.

Pippa strides in with a clipboard, presumably with the test results.

She doesn't look sad, so that's a bit of a relief. "The great news is they're both super healthy." She taps her pencil to her chin. "Have you decided if you want to know the sexes?"

I look at Oz. "Ah, well, mind reading and all ... I already know." He shrugs his shoulders.

"Then I want to know, too." It never made sense to me how some couples wait until the birth to find out. It's a surprise either way, right?

Pippa hands me an envelope and I open it. Inside, a small card reads:

Baby A: Boy

Baby B: Girl

I throw my arms around Oz's neck and give him a big kiss; he's on top of the moon. I pass the card to Auguste, who then passes it to Gideon. Both are pleased.

"There is something peculiar, though." she sits in the bedside chair. "Each of the babies carries a unique set of DNA."

Science wasn't my forte in school, but I'm pretty sure that isn't possible ... is it?

The men in the room look at me warily and I can feel the heat rise in my cheeks.

"Hetero paternal superfecundation," Oz says with a haunted look on his face. "It's when twins have the same mother, but different fathers."

Different fathers? Oh gods, no. I hope Oz doesn't think I've cheated on him. I don't see how this could even happen.

"Did you run the DNA across the database?" Auguste pipes up. "Maybe one of the Lapis Templar snuck in one night. I wouldn't put it past them." I appreciate he's trying to find an explanation for this and doesn't automatically jump to the conclusion I'd cheat on them.

Pippa worries her lip. "Six times, because I couldn't believe what I saw ... Gideon, you're the father of Baby B."

Confusion crosses everyone's faces. There is no way Gideon can be the father; he's a vampire. There is no witch in him at all, so he can't have kids.

"The prophecy ..." Gideon paces the room, running his hand through his hair. "It said a witch would travel back in time and fall in love with me. She'd carry my child. It was you—just as Dolphina predicted. Somehow, even though you were dreaming when you traveled back in time with me when I was human, we conceived our child."

I stare at him in disbelief, and guilt follows. I look at Oz, trying to gauge a reaction or emotion from him. He's about as shocked as I am.

Are you ... okay?

While Oz will share me as a mate, I don't know how he feels about having to share what should be his and my children.

Before he can answer, nausea sweeps over me. I run to the bathroom and heave into the toilet. Oz holds my hair back for me.

I'm okay, Sahira. It's just unexpected.

"I'm sorry," I choke out while holding the toilet.

"Shh, you're alright. You have nothing to be sorry for."

I brush my teeth again, and he helps me back into bed. Gideon still looks like he's off in space, and Auguste isn't sure what to do with the news. I imagine there is a small part of him that feels left out. That's how I would feel in his shoes. There are so many layers to the dynamics of our family now.

"Are you two okay?"

For once, Gideon isn't the first to answer.

"I'm happy for you," Auguste says sincerely.

Now, more than ever, I know I want to honor his wife. I'll just have to get Gideon on board with it, considering he's the father of our daughter.

"I am speechless ..." Gideon pauses his pacing. "Perhaps for the first time in my life, I am at a loss for words. I'm going to be a dad!" He is beaming now, and I release the breath I held now I know he's thrilled.

DAD ACCOMPANIES me to the forest where we can find the rest of the family before he takes the boat to another island for the day. When we approach the clearing, I see sixteen people on their knees and handcuffed.

I take my place next to Oz and hold my head high. These are the traitors who want my children and me dead. Some of them appear afraid, while others have smug faces.

One-by-one, Maeve calls their names and Gideon helps them up when they're called and brings them to Oz. Auguste records their names in his database and their sentences. We charge each one of these people with espionage and high treason for their crimes.

You may not want to be here for this.

Under normal circumstances, he's right. But not today. I'd rip each one of their throats out myself if I could; they don't deserve a swift death, but we aren't monsters, so they'll get one.

The first execution isn't easy to watch. It is a man, perhaps in his forties, with dark brown curly hair and chestnut-colored eyes. He wets himself in fear—and rightfully so—when Oz approaches. He is all predator now and is quick to dispatch his prey.

I flinch when blood spatter lands on my cheek, but I never look away.

The second person claws and fights to get away from Gideon, but they are no match for his vampire strength. It continues like this until all sixteen are dead: They beg for their lives, then seethe with anger as they try to get away. Then Oz violently rips their throats out with his teeth, and they fall limp.

The stench of metallic death overwhelms the woods. I take a deep breath through my mouth, trying to avoid the scent, but it is of no use; I am covered in blood from spurting carotid arteries.

This morning, Oz had to let go of everyone on the island. While most were loyalists to the Ankida family, it was too big of a risk to keep them on staff after so many cult members infiltrated them. Gideon has given them all a full pension and benefits for their service, so none will go hungry.

Terrorists do not get mercy, though. There is nothing welcoming them to the afterlife. We pile their bodies high and light them on fire. I thought the stench of death was bad, but it's nothing compared to the smell of burning flesh. It permeates the air and my nose. I don't leave the site; I am stoic as I witness the destruction of these monsters who wished my children ill.

I can't help it when waves of nausea take over me until I retch repeatedly—so hard, my abs hurt and my neck strains. I am weak and dizzy.

Auguste, who doesn't have a drop of blood on him, carries me back to the house after I've collapsed from the purge.

He takes me into the bathroom and helps me undress. Maeve warned me to wear black, and I'm glad I listened, but I don't think I can put those clothes back on even if laundered. Blood cakes my hair and eyelashes, and the water in the tub turns red when I lower myself into it.

"Do you ever get used to it?"

"I rarely take pleasure in someone else's pain, but I have zero remorse about anyone who tries to hurt you or anyone else in my family."

I drain the water and refill it again, and it isn't red anymore until Auguste lathers and rinses my hair. It feels like I've run a marathon—no doubt from the combination of physical and emotional stress.

"I think I need a shower to get the rest of this out."

He agrees and places a small wooden bench in the shower for me to sit on. I carefully get out of the tub and ease myself on the bench.

"Will you join me?" I'm not in the condition to play now but I could use help to get the rest of this blood off me.

Auguste undresses and seats himself next to me on the bench. He's grabbed the hairbrush I keep in the drawer, and he works the conditioner through my hair with it. The care and attention he pays to my tresses makes me think he's cared for curly hair before.

"Will you tell me about your first mate? You don't have to if you don't want me to know about her."

He pauses brushing, and I turn towards him.

"Her name was Rose," he says with a longing in his voice. "She had hair just like yours and always wore red lipstick. She had a fire in her; a quick-witted temper of a banshee, but she loved even harder. You remind me a lot of her."

His hand moves my hair behind my shoulder, and he gives me a kiss. It isn't one that screams desire. Instead, it is a kiss that stirs a knowing inside of me—we will all be alright. If it weren't for Rose, I'd offer to take Auguste back in time and give him a child, but it would be cruel for me to offer him that now.

"I love you, Auguste," I say, with no expectation of hearing it back. I simply want him to know it.

"I love you, too, Lana." We finish washing my hair and body, and death no longer coats my skin.

Auguste wraps me in a towel and leads me to his room. He wants me to change into something comfortable, and he's got a sherpa-lined hoodie and sweatpants I'll swim in. Just what I like.

I pull the sweater over my head and ease into the sweats. Auguste gives me a sheepish curl of his lips before lighting the fireplace in the bedroom. We're nearing fall in the Southern hemisphere, so there is a chill in the air that isn't quite cold, but it is moist and wicks right to the bone.

He drags the couch closer to it, and we snuggle up.

CHAPTER THIRTY-THREE

"According to the fetal scan, you're approximately thirty-six weeks pregnant. I don't know if you'll even make it to Bedlam to deliver." Pippa scoots back with the Doppler in her hand and blows a puff of air to get her bangs out of her eyes.

Oz squeezes my hand while I fight the internal panic running through my mind. Both Auguste and Gideon are pacing back and forth in front of the bed, each stealing glances between Pippa and me.

"Didn't Dolphina say you and the babies have to be in Bedlam for the moon?"

I shake my head. "No, she specifically said the babies and I would die if I wasn't in Bedlam for the next Bedlam Moon. Which means ... they probably won't have an Ebbswick key that young, right? They'll be able to come with me, right?" I am near-hysterical now; I can't go to Bedlam without my babies. I'm their mother. They need to be nursed, and rocked, and loved.

Dad sits at the foot of my bed and puts his hand on my ankle to help soothe me.

"Witches don't get their keys until they're teenagers at the earliest." There is a distinct grief in his eyes. I know he'd take this pain from me if he could.

No amount of calming magic can soothe the fissure cracking wide open in my chest. No one can get into Bedlam without an Ebbswick key. The only other witches in our immediate family can't even go; Both Oz and Dad's keys remain as scars now they're vampires.

That means I have to go to the fae realm without my babies or anyone I know and love. The Bedlam Moon is mere days away.

～

MY HAND FLIES out to grab onto Auguste's shirt while my other clutches my belly. I let out a groan of agony and watch as liquid slides down my thighs and pools on the forest floor.

"Lana!" He yells and squats down to look me in the eye where I'm hunched over. "Did your ... did your water just break?"

I take a moment to respond while I breathe through the contraction. Low in my belly is where I feel the most cramping.

"I think so." I straighten when the worst of it subsides. "I don't think I wet myself."

Perhaps the movies have it wrong; water breaking isn't like a tidal wave.

"Let's get you back to the house so Pippa can examine you. Can you walk or do you want me to carry you?"

"I can walk." I hold my belly. "Do you think we should call the boys?"

He quirks an eyebrow at me. "I won't tell them you call them that." He smirks. "But yes, I'll call them."

We continue walking towards the house while Auguste dials for Oz. The men are on the mainland getting some supplies for the babies.

"Auguste," I hear Oz on the other line.

"I think you three had better head—"

I double over and let out a wail. This time, it is not clear liquid. Blood gushes down my exposed thighs and soaks my dress. Auguste drops his cell, scoops me up and races towards the house while I writhe and groan in misery.

He enters the open breezeway near the pool and bellows for Pippa, who immediately scans her eyes over my body before darting away to get equipment and her team.

Auguste carries me to the bedroom where we've planned for me to deliver. Gideon installed an enormous birthing pool in there just last night. As soon as he places me on the bed, another contraction seizes my breath before I let out a blood-curdling scream.

I want to die. It is too painful; I can't do this.

Black spots my vision, and the room spins.

"Is she supposed to be bleeding like that?" Auguste asks Pippa when she and the medical team come into the room.

THE WARM GLOW of his chest can be felt through his shirt. I can't see his face but nuzzle into him further. There is no terror, just refuge.

Safe.

Safe.

Safe.

He is safe.

I am safe.

"I need you to stay with me now." His voice is like silk, a stark contrast to his muscular arms and firm abs.

Who are you? I think but cannot speak.

My entire life, he's been in my dreams, saving me.

I drift off to sleep, and the first face I see when I open my eyes is him. His skin glows, which makes little sense.

Not human. Not human.

His chuckle is like a purr.

"Hello," he whispers. "I'm going to heal you now, okay?"

I nod, but I can't take my eyes off this creature. He makes to set me down, but I cling to his neck and shake my head.

No, no, no. Safe. Tears spring to my eyes, and I don't know whether it's from my grave injuries or because I don't want to leave his arms.

"I won't leave you," he whispers.

A COOL HAND cups my cheek, but my entire body aches. I don't want to open my eyes.

"Sahira."

I blink several times and see Oz. My eyes dart to the room we're in, and my other men stand around the bed with concerned faces.

"Why am I in the recovery room?" My voice is groggy. Must've been from sleeping; I dreamed of him again; the man who always saves me.

"Your uterus ruptured, and you lost a lot of blood. You had to have surgery." Auguste takes my hand.

"The babies?" I brace myself for bad news. I don't breathe. I can't, with the ache gripping my chest.

Oz and Gideon part, and my eyes follow their gaze behind them. Maeve and Pippa walk towards the bed, each with a bundle in their arms, and I finally let go of the sob I was holding back.

Auguste helps me sit up in bed and the ladies place my babies in my arms. One has a blue blanket, the other has a pink blanket.

Joy rips open my chest and falls down my cheeks as I lose myself in the eyes of my perfect, beautiful babies.

"Hello," I whisper through choked tears.

The men help me unbundle them and place one at each breast—skin to skin, just like we read. After they're situated and taking colostrum, I blink away my tears and look at all the love in the room.

Maeve and Pippa give me a kiss on the cheek and leave to let Dad know I'm awake. The twins suckle and slurp—I can tell Rose is a champion eater. Her brother, Bennett, takes his time and paws his fist at my breast. They both eventually fall asleep, so I cover my breasts and lay them on my chest.

Dad rushes into the room with a huge bouquet; I recognize many of the flowers from the island. He sets the vase on the nightstand.

"Hiya, pumpkin."

"Hi, Daddy."

"You sure make beautiful babies."

"It runs in the family."

He chuckles but keeps his distance. I still have healing wounds on my abdomen, and he's too new of a vampire to get too close. When his pupils flare, he excuses himself from the room.

"You'll be able to come up to the bedroom in a few hours." Oz puts a straw in my mouth.

The metallic drink is still warm and thick as it goes down my throat. I catch the men stealing glances at each other.

"What's that about?"

"Lana ..." Oz's voice is somber when he sits next to me on the bed, and I dart my eyes to my other boys. He takes my hand in his before he continues. "To save your life, we had to do a hysterectomy."

While we hadn't talked about having additional children, it was decided for us: no more babies.

My chest feels hollow at this news.

"We could always adopt if we decide on more," Auguste volunteers.

I nod my head, but I can't stop the tears from tracking down my cheeks. I kiss each of my babies on the head and inhale their scent. It is like honey-sweetened cream with lavender and vanilla.

It immediately soothes me.

CHAPTER THIRTY-FOUR

Two days. That's what I get with them. It isn't fair, and they're growing at an exponential rate. We've settled into a bit of a routine; I'm a milk machine, and we all take turns changing diapers and snuggling with the twins. Bath time is fun because it is when they coo the most.

I did not sleep a wink last night. Instead, I sobbed while cradled in the arms of my men, grieving over my upcoming departure. Together, they all helped me care for the twins.

My eyes are bloodshot, and I spend the entire morning in a zombie-like trance when I'm not sobbing. My hormones are a mess, and I don't know if I'll see my family in a week, or fifty years from now.

Will the twins remember me? No, they won't.

Will my mates move on? No, thank the gods, because of the mating bond.

I don't know how long I'll be in Bedlam, so I write the babies letters about how much they're loved, and how I'd never leave them if I had a choice. I hope I'll either find my mom there or find a fae with the ability to locate her in time. Bonnie mentioned there are a few with those powers, but she couldn't recall their names.

We know it will be at least six months before I see any of them again, because the portal is only open on a Bedlam Moon. When I finish their letters, I write one to each member of the family, telling them how much they mean to me and the dreams I have of our future together.

I leave these on our nightstand next to our love nest bed.

Nothing can come with me through the portal, so there is not a thing for me to pack for Bedlam. I said goodbye to Dad, Pippa, Hannah, and Maeve this morning before the rest of us travel to the portal in the mountains.

I have the twins strapped to my chest, Oz has a backpack full of their supplies, and Auguste and Gideon carry the grimoire, food, and drinks.

WE MAKE it to the portal just before nightfall. The sky is red and orange, and you can see the scarlet-colored moon almost in position. The entrance to the cave shimmers, and that's when reality sets in and I sob. I'm not the only one crying now; Oz, Auguste, and Gideon don't hide their tears while we hold each other.

"Please don't forget me," I choke.

"Never."

We stay embraced in each other's arms most of the night. The twins wake to nurse, but otherwise, they sleep. My men and I talk last-minute strategies for making it through Bedlam as quickly as possible so I can return to them.

When the moon starts to go down and the sun begins to rise, I know it's time. I kiss my babies' heads and inhale their scent—I don't want to forget it. My entire body trembles from the sobs wracking it while I hand the twins over to Gideon and Auguste. Grief consumes me.

Each one crushes me in a hug and a fierce kiss before letting me go. Their chins quiver while they clutch the children to their chests and cup the backs of their heads. When it's Oz's turn, sobs wreck him while he squeezes me to his body.

"Please don't forget us."

I rock my head against his chest. "Never," I say angrily through my wails.

It's as though my heart is cleaving in two when I back away from them towards the shimmering portal. "I love you," I bawl.

"We love you, too."

I turn around and put one foot through the portal. It is bitterly cold and it tingles with magic. My Ebbswick key is in my hand, and I clutch the grimoire in my other.

Stealing one last glance their way, I witness the utter grief and despair on their faces, and it matches mine.

"I love you." I call out again before stepping fully into the portal.

It's dark, biting, and there are gale-force winds. This isn't anything like slipping through time or teleporting across the room. My shoes are gone, and so are my grimoire and Ebbswick key. The blood-red moon guides me to where I need to go.

Bedlam.

WHAT DOES fate have in store for Lana? Does she ever find her way back to her mates? Read Tales of Bedlam to find out. And if you want to know which supernatural creature you'd be in Bedlam, take the quiz at kathyhaan.com/quiz. Share your result in our brand new Facebook group, The Bedlam Fae Society.

ACKNOWLEDGMENTS

Dearest Readers,

I modeled Alphie "Dad" Bennett after my late father. He'd been on hospice in my home for almost two years for heart failure, and we found out he had metastatic cancer the day before he died. He was my biggest cheerleader in life, and it's my hope you grow a fondness for the character who has my heart.

This book wouldn't have been possible without the help of my husband, Kirk, who helps run our tight pirate ship. He does the cleaning, laundry, yard work, and brings me snacks and drinks on-demand. I don't know how I got so lucky.

To my kids, you are my reason for being. Thanks for supporting me, and shooting down any lame ideas I come up with—you're the reason your friends think I'm the cool mom. You kids make it easy. And Leo, my sixteen-year-old, thank you for helping me create such an incredible cover.

Theresa, thanks for being my sounding board for ideas during this process.

Thanks for showing me how important an education is, even while raising a family, Mom.

I need to give a massive thanking to Jess. You helped me turn my hovel of a novel into something I'm proud of. You truly are the *best*. And readers, you have her to thank for not inundating you with em dashes. I like them … apparently *a lot*.

And finally, dear reader: THANK YOU. You are a small but mighty crowd right now. You're who I write for. Thank you for taking a chance on my debut novel, and I'm sorry for the cliffy. The great news is that Tales of Bedlam is live and ready to read now.

You can view all of my upcoming events and progress on other novels on my author site.

xoxo

Kathy Haan

P.S. Don't forget to subscribe to my newsletter for bonus content, giveaways, and sneak peeks!

TALES OF BEDLAM CHAPTER ONE

Pain and I are intimately acquainted, like two scorned lovers passing in the night. Though I try, I can't forget the press of its claws against my womb, or the echoes of my soul ripping in two at the loss of my mate.

My body has writhed from the agony of labor. I've been beaten and on the brink of death after violent attacks by vampires. But nothing—nothing—cuts as deep as leaving my family for Bedlam. These emotional wounds are so severe, they will haunt me for the rest of my days.

The portal to the fae realm is a sea of black and biting cold. Gail-force winds take my shoes almost immediately—I'm lucky to still have a dress. The only light guiding me is a faint scarlet glow far in the distance. My eyes are mere slits to keep my contacts from drying, and the force of the squalls are so intense, I take hours to traverse the inky expanse.

When my bare feet touch the other side, I breathe a sigh of relief, and shake the dust and dirt out of my dress. The chasm between the portal and Bedlam is jarring; while still biting cold, there is no wind on the other side. I rub my hands together to create friction before tucking them under my armpits as I take in my surroundings.

The soft red glow of the moon overhead gives the forest I've landed in an eerie atmosphere. A gooey, glowing substance drips from the leaves of the trees, and frost covers the bark like a crystalline blanket. With tentative movement, I pad around the chilly forest floor, the sensation of mud squishing between my bare toes an unpleasant reminder of how much trouble I'm in without proper attire.

I take my time exploring the forest before I attempt to make shelter. Thanks to the color of the moon, my eyes have transitioned well from the dark portal to this red forest.

As I scout the area, the tree's twisted roots bulge from the soil beneath me, forcing me to step carefully. Their tangled branches form a canopy over my head. I've spent a lot of time in forests, but none like this one. Like something straight out of a fairytale, magic has warped and manipulated the trees into something *other*.

I couldn't bring anything to Bedlam with me, and this light dress I have on provides little protection from the elements. Before leaving Earth, my family taught me several skills and incantations to help me on my journey. The bulk of it I spent on spells, because both my dad and my husband, Oz, are witches. Granted, they're also vampires, but they still have magic.

Using the spell Oz taught me in our bedroom one night, I attempt to turn a seed I find on the ground into a hollow tree to shelter in. My body shakes from the effort and my nose runs while I struggle to will the kernel into something useful.

Not a single change happens. I rub my hands to warm them before trying again—perhaps my magic doesn't work well in the cold. Once they've warmed, I make the motions for the enchantment.

Casting is no use; the spell isn't working.

Do incantations work differently in Bedlam? The research my family and I did suggests otherwise, so why isn't this working? I reach into the oversized pocket of my dress for my grimoire, but the book is gone. My hands scramble to the other pocket, feeling for any holes. My Ebbswick key is gone, too. I need both in order to come back to the Earth realm. I hope they'll reappear when I need to go back through the portal.

I can't stay here forever.

Pausing my frantic movements, I crouch low to the ground and spot materials to reinforce my outfit. My fingers are so numb, I have difficulty keeping hold of the natural provisions while I work to weave vines into rope to bind branches. I rub them together frantically, breathing damp, warm air into my cupped hands. The reprieve from the cold is temporary, and near futile, but I manage to stave off the stiffness long enough to come up with something useful.

I fashion a makeshift belt to hold my dress up and tie goop-free leafy vines underneath for warmth. With sturdier branches, I craft a rudimentary bow and arrow. The vines don't hold high tensile strength, but they'll do for now.

I set out to find something to fill the pit in my stomach. Using my bow and arrow in the dim moonlight, I aim for a small animal resembling a squirrel, but miss. Archery wasn't high on our list of skills to practice before I left. Stumbling deeper through the woods, I come across a few berry bushes, though I don't dare eat them, given the circumstances. My stomach growls and aches from hunger, but I refuse to give in to the pain. Not until I can find something I know for sure is safe.

I spot a giant tree with a thick trunk that can serve as my shelter for the night, which is the most important thing. I'll work on finding water in the morning.

Exhaustion slows my movements.

Must.

Keep.

Going.

My dress is still too thin and papery to keep me warm, even with the additional greenery. I need a fire to stay alive, but the only flammable materials I can collect on the ground are damp from frost. If only my magic worked, then I could be warm right now.

Why isn't it working?

My body usually thrums with power, but there isn't even a trickle. I attempt to start a fire several times by rubbing a stick between my palms against a piece of wood before fatigue sets in and I give up. After some sleep, I'll have more energy and can try again.

I lug massive rocks to the base of the tree that's as wide as a sedan and build a retaining wall on each side to block the wind. When finished, I place evergreen boughs over the top before crawling into my makeshift shelter for sleep. The forest quiets, and I no longer hear the quiet hum of insects, nor the whistling of the wind through the trees. This should comfort me, but it lends an ominous pause to the night.

The cold seeps into my bones, but does little to numb the grief haunting my heart. It sits on my chest like a lead weight, making it hard to breathe, and buries me in despair. Thoughts of my life on Earth sneak up on me and roll down my cheek.

I'd planned to come to Bedlam to gain immortality and find out what happened to my mom, who disappeared somewhere in time when I was eight years old. What I hadn't planned on was Dolphina Darling, the evil cult leader obsessed with my husband, speeding up my timeline so I had to leave my two-day-old twins and family behind. I can see their faces in my mind. The twins: Rose and Bennett, and my mates: Oz, Gideon, and Auguste. If I concentrate hard enough, I can even feel the press of their fingers against mine. The soft stirring of the twins' breath on my chest while they sleep. All I can do is cry until I'm too tired to do so anymore.

The snap of a branch startles me from sleep. I peer through the triangular opening in my sanctuary, eyes wide when I spot two red glowing circles straight from nightmares. The umber figure morphs into a hunched silhouette of evil. My heart races and my stomach plummets as the vile woman gets closer.

My options race through my head. If I flee, she'll catch up with me in no time. If I fight, I'll lose; this fae must be over seven feet tall and nearly as wide. Either way, with no magic, my fate will be the same.

Death.

Maybe she's harmless. Before the errant thought can take hold, a shout barrels from my lungs as her five-inch-long claws dig into my ankles and yank me from my shelter. Using the combat moves Auguste taught me, I work to get loose, to no avail. Her enormous weight makes my attempts to get away futile.

"Mm ... it has been a long time since I've fed on a witch. Your kind doesn't come here much, but I'll enjoy you, anyway." The deep timbre of her voice reverberates through the woods before cutting off in a cackle.

I thrash and kick, making small gouges in her thick skin and screaming until my voice gives out. She grips both of my wrists in one hand above my head while using the other to tear at my dress, exposing me to the frigid air.

"Please ... don't. I'm a mother." My hoarse voice cuts through the space between us.

My entire body trembles while she laughs. She's the size of an ox, and almost as heavy as one. The bones in my wrist threaten to snap under the weight.

"You think I give a fuck about your family? I know exactly who you are. You're the Queen of Vampires. They are filthy, fucking vermin. *Abominations*." Spittle from her fang-toothed mouth lands on my cheek. "I'll take what I want from you. It's your womb I'm after. Behave and you might live."

I buck my hips up in another attempt to lift her off of me, and she chuckles. "Keep that up — I love when they put up a fight."

"Stop!" My raw voice warbles through the space between us. "You won't find—"

Her clawed hand clamps around my mouth, cutting me off, but also leaving me an opening. Despite the slice of her nails against my cheek, I use this opportunity to pull my leg free and sideswipe her face with my muddy foot, but she just laughs and pins me back down.

I sob and cry out while this monster slices my abdomen open with one of her talons. All thoughts leave my head, save for the excruciating pain. She lays a heavy arm to pin my hips down, and shame invades my psyche far more than fear does.

She shrieks when she finds me barren. "I'll rip her from limb to limb! She said I could have your womb before I killed you!"

With every move, her clawed grip carves into my flesh, wrenching sobs from my throat. I don't know how long she violates me, but I feel the weight of every single moment. By the time her anger retreats, I am but a husk.

Broken.

Bloodied.

So many lacerations, even slight movement is torture.

The cruel monster towers over me with menace in her eyes. "Don't think I'm done with you." She grips my leg hard enough to pierce through the skin and down to the bone.

Her next words aren't any I recognize, but the force behind them echoes through me. Searing heat races up my thigh, across my chest, and to the base of my skull. The pain is so immediate and intense; I shriek with renewed misery. "We'll see how your mates feel about that," she smirks and releases me. "If you survive it."

Rivulets of blood pour from my wounds, and my limbs fail me when I try to scramble away.

I curl into a fetal position while sobs rack my body. The heavy steps of her departure match the slow cadence of my heartbeat; the loss of blood is significant. Visions of my family play in my mind, and the passing of time means nothing. I'm numb.

My mom chasing me through the house with a hairbrush before tackling me to the ground to brush my wild curls.

Oz's sure and steady presence while I learn to fly.

Gideon's easy smile while we lay in the grass nestled in the Dolomites.

Auguste's grin when he realizes I bested him on the field where he gave me combat lessons.

The twinkle in Dad's eye when he pats his belly after a good meal.

My best friend, Hannah, and her giddy excitement at teaching her son, CJ, how to ride a bike.

Maeve's welcoming arms in her lab in Salem where she helped me figure out who sent me my mother's Ebbswick key.

Pippa's calming aura during the birth of the twins.

I don't feel the bite of the cold on my extremities, though my body is like ice. Sticky blood coats my eyelashes. When I close them, frost gathers like glue, and I don't open my eyes again.

I consider never getting up.

Just let the woods take me.

What does fate have in store for Lana? Does she ever find her way back to her mates? Read Tales of Bedlam to find out. And if you want to know which supernatural creature you'd be in Bedlam, take the quiz at kathyhaan.com/quiz.

ABOUT THE AUTHOR

A blood descendant of Wild Bill Hickok and a long line of artists and creators, like Jane Austen and Emily Dickinson, **Kathy Haan believes the secret to telling a great story is living one.** The second youngest, in a massive horde of children between her parents, she did her best to gain attention and kept everyone entertained with jokes and wild stories.

She lives a life of adventure with her hunky husband, three children, and Great Pyrenees in the Midwest United States. While this is her debut novel, you might've seen her work in Forbes or Fortune, where she's a regular contributor.

ALSO BY KATHY HAAN

<u>Bedlam Moon Trilogy (Complete)</u>

Lana sets out to find the truth about her past, and when a hot vampire begins to unravel it for her, she's caught up in the web of an evil cult, prophecies, and curses. All while falling for the King of Vampires and his royal court. This is a why choose romance.

Bedlam Moon (Bedlam Moon Trilogy Book 1)

Tales of Bedlam (Bedlam Moon Trilogy Book 2)

Wicked Bedlam (Bedlam Moon Trilogy Book 3)

<u>Fae Academia Series (Incomplete, 9 planned)</u>

A spin-off of the Bedlam Moon Trilogy, we follow Lana's daughter, Rose, while she attends a magical university. The summer before college is perfect until the family begins to receive threats, and Rose ends up getting into a different college from her twin brother and her boyfriend. A male roommate, his hot friends, and a sexy professor all find themselves eager to win her affection. This is a why choose romance. Books 1-3 are Rose's story, books 4-6 are Nova's, and 7-9 will be Bee's story.

Bedlam Academy (Fae Academia, Book 1)

Arcane Scholar (Fae Academia, Book 2)

Forbidden Rose (Fae Academia, Book 3)

Moonfire Academy (Fae Academia, Book 4)

<u>Aggonid's Realm Series (Incomplete)</u>

A Realm of Fire and Ash (Aggonid's Realm, Book 1)

A Realm of Dreams and Shadows (Aggonid's Realm, Book 2)

A Realm of Grief and Sorrow (Aggonid's Realm, Book 3)

When the commander of an elite group of phoenixes ends up dead for real, she tries to convince the fae devil there's been a huge mistake. Can she convince him to let her go before he snags her heart? This is an enemies to lovers why choose romance.

~

Fae Gods (Incomplete)

Fae Gods (April 2023)

Fae Guardians (TBA)

They watched their charge her entire life, completely invisible to her and only intervening when necessary. When they get fed up with her miserable marriage, Jocelyn's fae god watchers decide to help. After all, no fae of royal lineage deserves to be left to wilt away on Earth. They devise a plan to reveal their true selves to her, calling themselves the Marriage Doctors. But what happens when, during the course of their live-in lessons, the infallible gods fall for their off-limits charge? This is a why choose romance.

~

Bedlam Penitentiary (Incomplete)

Bedlam Penitentiary (TBA)

At the most ruthless prison in the fae realm, you're either at the top of the magical food chain, or you've got to form alliances with those with the most power. Because at a prison where you must expend your magic or you'll die, it's a no man's land full of dangerous criminals. This is a why choose romance.